THE MAN WHO WATCHED WOMEN

Translated by Marlaine Delargy

Hjorth & Rosenfeldt

CENTURY

1 3 5 7 9 10 8 6 4 2

Century
20 Vauxhall Bridge Road
London SW1V 2SA

Century is part of the Penguin Random House group of companies
whose addresses can be found at global.penguinrandomhouse.com.

First published as *Lärjungen* by Norstedts, Sweden in 2012

English translation first published in Australia and New Zealand as
The Disciple by Pier 9, an imprint of Allen & Unwin, in 2013

This edition first published in the UK by Century in 2015

www.randomhouse.co.uk

A CIP catalogue record for this book is
available from the British Library.

Proof ISBN: 9781780894553

Printed and bound by Clays Ltd, St Ives Plc

Introducing the national police homicide unit, based in Stockholm – also known as Riksmord . . .

Torkel Höglund – Chief Inspector

Ursula Andersson – police forensics expert

Vanja Lithner – investigative police officer

Billy Rosén – investigative police officer

Sebastian Bergman – psychologist and leading criminal profiler

Trolle Hermansson – former Chief Inspector, sacked for using surveillance for personal matters and planting false evidence

Other police

Thomas Haraldsson – ex police, now governor of Lövhaga Prison

As the taxi turned into Tolléns väg just before seven thirty in the evening, Richard Granlund didn't think his day could get much worse. Four days in Munich and the surrounding area. A sales trip. The Germans worked more or less as usual throughout July. Client meetings from morning till night. Factories, conference rooms and countless cups of coffee. He was tired, but contented. Conveyor belt systems might not be the sexiest things in the world – his work seldom aroused curiosity and was never the most obvious topic of conversation around the dinner table or with friends – but they sold well. The conveyor belts. They sold really well.

The plane from Munich had been due to take off at 9.05 a.m. He would be in Stockholm at twenty past eleven. Call in at the office and let them know how he'd got on. Home around one. Lunch with Katharina, then they would spend the rest of the afternoon in the garden. That was the plan.

Until he'd found out that the flight to Arlanda had been cancelled. He'd joined the queue for Lufthansa customer services and was rebooked on the 13.05 flight instead. Another four hours at Munich International. He wasn't exactly thrilled at the prospect. With a resigned sigh he dug out his phone and texted Katharina. She would have to have lunch without him, but hopefully they would still be able to spend a few hours working in the garden. What was the weather like? Perhaps a cocktail on the patio this evening? He could pick up something in the airport now he had plenty of time.

Katharina answered right away. Shame about the delay. She was missing him. The weather in Stockholm was fantastic, so cocktails later sounded like a great idea. Surprise me. Love you.

Richard went to one of the shops that was still advertising duty-free, although he was convinced this was no longer relevant

1

to the vast majority of travellers. He found the shelf of ready-mixed cocktails and picked up a bottle he recognised from the TV ads – Mojito Classic.

On his way to the newsagent's kiosk he checked his flight on the departures board. Gate 26. He reckoned it would take him about ten minutes to get there.

Richard sat down with a cup of coffee and a sandwich as he leafed through his newly purchased issue of *Garden Illustrated*. The minutes crawled by. He did a little window shopping, bought another magazine, one about gadgets this time, then went to a different café and drank a bottle of mineral water. After a visit to the toilet, it was time to head for the gate at long last. There he was met by the next surprise. The 13.05 flight was delayed. New boarding time: 13.40. Estimated departure time: 14.00. Richard took out his phone again. Informed Katharina of the latest delay and expressed his frustration with air travel in general and Lufthansa in particular. He found an empty seat and sat down. He didn't get a reply to his text.

He rang her.

No one answered.

Perhaps she had found someone to have lunch with in town. He put his phone away and closed his eyes. There was no point in getting worked up about the situation; there wasn't much he could do about it anyway.

At quarter to two the young woman on the desk welcomed them on board and apologised for the delay. When they were settled on the plane and the cabin crew had gone through the routine safety procedures, which no one bothered to listen to, the captain spoke to them. One of the lights on the dashboard was showing a fault. There was probably something wrong with the light itself, but they couldn't take any chances. A technician was on the way to check it. The captain apologised and asked for their cooperation. The inside of the plane quickly grew warm. Richard could feel his willingness to cooperate and his still relatively good mood seeping away at exactly the same rate as his shirt grew wetter and wetter on his back and under his arms. The captain spoke again. Good news: the error had been rectified. Not such good news: they had now missed their slot, and there were currently nine planes due to

2

take off before them, but as soon as it was their turn, they would begin their flight to Stockholm. He apologised.

They landed at Arlanda at 17.20.

Two hours and ten minutes late.

Or six hours. Depending on your point of view.

On his way to the baggage claim area, Richard rang home again. No reply. He tried Katharina's mobile. Her voicemail kicked in after five rings. She was probably out in the garden, and couldn't hear the phone. Richard reached the huge hall containing the luggage carousels. According to the monitor above number 3, the bags from flight LH2416 would be delivered in eight minutes.

It took twelve minutes.

And it was another fifteen minutes before Richard realised that his suitcase wasn't there.

Another wait in another queue to report the missing case at Lufthansa's service desk. After handing over his luggage receipt, his address and as good a description as he could manage of his suitcase, Richard emerged into the arrivals hall and went to find a taxi. The heat struck him with a physical force as he walked out through the revolving doors. It really was summer. They would have a lovely evening. He could feel his good humour returning slightly at the thought of Mojitos on the patio in the evening sun. He joined the queue for Taxi Stockholm, Kurir or 020. As they pulled away, the driver informed him that as far as the traffic was concerned, it was hell in Stockholm today. Sheer hell. At that moment he slowed down to just below fifty kilometres per hour as they joined the seemingly endless queue of cars heading south on the E4.

So by the time the taxi finally turned into Tolléns väg, Richard Granlund didn't think his day could get much worse.

He paid with his credit card and walked up to the house through the fragrant, beautifully tended garden. He put down his briefcase and plastic bag just inside the door.

'Hello!'

No answer. Richard took off his shoes and went into the kitchen. He glanced out of the window to see if Katharina was in the garden, but there was no sign of her. The kitchen was empty too. No note where it would have been if she'd left him one. Richard took out his phone and checked it. No missed calls or text messages. The house was hot and stuffy; the sun was shining directly on the windows, and Katharina had not lowered the awnings. Richard unlocked the patio door and opened it wide. Then he went upstairs. He would shower and change. He felt dirty and sweaty, right down to his underpants. He pulled off his tie and started to unbutton his shirt as he walked up the stairs, but stopped in mid-movement when he reached the bedroom. Katharina was lying on the bed. That was the first thing he noticed. Then he realised three things in quick succession.

She was lying on her stomach.

She was tied up.

She was dead.

The subway train shuddered as it braked. The mother with the buggy in front of Sebastian Bergman clutched the steel pole a little more tightly and looked around nervously. She had been on tenterhooks ever since she'd got on at St Eriksplan, and in spite of the fact that her grizzling little boy had fallen asleep after only a couple of stops, she seemed unable to relax. It was evident that she didn't like being in such close proximity to so many strangers. Sebastian could see a number of signs. Constantly moving her feet in order to avoid physical contact with anyone. The slightly moist upper lip. The alert expression, the eyes moving all the time. Sebastian had tried a reassuring smile, but she quickly looked away and continued to scan her surroundings.

Sebastian glanced around the crowded carriage, which had once again stopped with a metallic hiss in the tunnel just beyond Hötorget. After a few moments standing motionless in the darkness, the train slowly began to move and crawled into T-Centralen, the main station in the middle of Stockholm. He didn't usually travel on the subway, and he never used it during the rush hour or the tourist season. It was too uncomfortable, too chaotic. He just couldn't get used to humanity en masse, with all its noises and odours. He preferred to walk or take a taxi. Keep his distance from people. Stay on the outside. That was his normal practice. But nothing was normal anymore.

Nothing.

Sebastian leaned against the door at the end of the carriage and peered into the one next door. He could see her through the little pane of glass. The blonde hair, the bent head, reading a newspaper. He realised that he was smiling to himself as he gazed at her.

As always she changed trains at T-Centralen, walking quickly down the stone staircase to the red line. It was easy for him to follow her. As long as he kept his distance, he was hidden by the stream of travellers and by the tourists studying their maps.

When the train pulled in at Gärdet station twelve minutes later, Sebastian waited a few moments before stepping out of the carriage. He had to be more careful here. There were fewer people moving around on the platform; the majority of the passengers had disembarked at the previous station. Sebastian had chosen the carriage in front of her so that she had her back to him when she got off. She was moving fast, and was already halfway to the escalators when he caught sight of her. Gärdet had clearly been the destination of the woman with the buggy, too, and Sebastian chose to remain behind her just in case the person he was following should turn around for any reason. The woman pushed her buggy along at a steady pace behind the people hurrying towards the escalators, presumably in the hope of avoiding a crush up ahead.

As he walked along behind her, Sebastian realised how alike they were. Two people who always found it necessary to keep their distance.

6

A woman.

Dead.

In her own home.

Under normal circumstances there would be no need to call in the National CID murder squad, known as Riksmord, and Torkel Höglund's team.

In most cases it was the tragic result of a family quarrel, a custody dispute, a jealous rage, a boozy evening in what turned out to be the wrong company.

Anyone who worked within the police service knew that when a woman was murdered in her own home, the perpetrator was usually to be found among those closest to her, so it was hardly surprising that when she took the emergency call just after seven thirty Stina Kaupin toyed with the idea that she was speaking to the murderer.

'Emergency, how can I help?'

'My wife is dead.'

It was difficult to make out the rest of what the man said. His voice was thick with grief and shock. For long periods the silence was so intense that Stina thought he had hung up. Then she heard him trying to get his breathing under control. It was a struggle to get an address out of him; the man just kept repeating that his wife was dead, and that there was a lot of blood. Blood everywhere. Could they come? Please? In her mind's eye Stina could see a middle-aged man with his hands covered in blood, slowly but surely realising what he had done. Eventually she managed to get an address in Tumba. She asked the caller – and probably murderer – to stay where he was, and not to touch anything in the house. She would send the police and an ambulance to the scene of the crime. She rang off and passed on the message to the Södertörn police in Huddinge, who in turn dispatched a patrol car.

★ ★ ★

Erik Lindman and Fabian Holst were just finishing off a rather late fast-food dinner when they got the call telling them to head over to Tolléns väg 19.

Ten minutes later they were there. They got out of the patrol car and looked over at the house. Neither of the officers was particularly interested in gardening, but they both realised that someone had spent a considerable amount of time and money creating the idyllic splendour surrounding the yellow wooden house.

When they were halfway up the path, the front door opened. Both men reached instinctively for the holster on their right hip. A man was standing in the doorway, his shirt open, gazing at the uniformed officers with an almost blank expression in his eyes.

'There's no need for an ambulance.'

Lindman and Holst exchanged a quick glance. The man in the doorway was obviously in shock. Those in shock acted according to their own rules. They were unpredictable. Illogical. Lindman carried on up the path, while Holst slowed down and kept his hand close to his gun.

'Richard Granlund?' Lindman asked as he took the last few steps towards the man, whose gaze was fixed on a point somewhere beyond him.

'There's no need for an ambulance,' the man repeated. 'The woman I spoke to said she was going to send an ambulance. There's no need. I forgot to tell her . . .'

Lindman had reached the man. He took him gently by the arm. The physical contact made the man in the doorway give a start and turn to face him. He looked at Lindman with surprise, as if he were seeing the police officer for the first time and wondered how he could have got so close.

No blood on his hands or his clothes, Lindman noticed.

'Richard Granlund?'

The man nodded. 'I got home and she was lying there . . .'

'Home from where?'

'What?'

8

'Home from where? Where had you been?' Perhaps this wasn't the best time to question a man who was so obviously in a state of shock, but information obtained during initial contact could be compared with what was said during an interview at a later stage.

'Germany. A business trip. My plane was delayed. Or rather, it was cancelled first of all, then it was delayed, and then I was even later because my luggage . . .'

The man fell silent. A thought or a realisation seemed to have struck him. He looked at Lindman with a clarity in his eyes that hadn't been there before.

'Could I have saved her? If I'd been on time, would she still have been alive then?'

All those 'what-ifs' were natural when someone died; Lindman had heard them many times. In several cases in which he had been involved, people had died because they were in the wrong place at the wrong time. They were crossing the road at the exact moment when a drunken driver came careering along. They were sleeping in the caravan on the very night when the bottled gas started leaking. They were walking over the railway line just as a train came by. Falling power lines, violent men who were high on something or other, cars on the wrong side of the road. Chance, coincidence. Forgotten keys could delay a person for precisely those few seconds that meant he or she wasn't going to make it across an unmanned level crossing. A cancelled flight could leave a man's wife alone for long enough to give a murderer the opportunity to strike. All those 'what-ifs'.

Perfectly normal when someone died.

Impossible to answer.

'Where is your wife, Richard?' Lindman asked instead, keeping his voice calm and steady.

The man in the doorway seemed to ponder the question. He was forced to switch from the experiences of his journey home and the possible guilt he had suddenly become aware of to the present moment. To the terrible thing that had happened.

The thing he had been unable to prevent.

Eventually he found his way.

'Upstairs.' Richard gestured towards the interior of the house and began to cry. Lindman nodded to his colleague to go upstairs, while he followed the weeping man inside. You could never be

9

sure, you could never make that judgement, but Lindman had the distinct feeling that he wasn't escorting a murderer into the kitchen, his arm around Granlund's shoulders.

At the bottom of the stairs Holst drew his service weapon and held it against his leg. If the crushed man his colleague was taking care of was not the murderer, then there was just a chance that he or she might still be in the house. At the top of the stairs he came to a small area equipped with a two-seater sofa, TV and Blu-ray. Dormer window. Shelves along the walls, containing books and films. Four doors. Two open, two closed. From the top of the stairs Holst could see the dead woman's legs in the bedroom. On the bed. Which meant that Riksmord would have to be informed, he thought as he quickly went into the second room with an open door: a study. Empty. The two closed doors led to a bathroom and a dressing room. Both empty. Holst put away his gun and approached the bedroom. He stopped in the doorway.

A directive from Riksmord had been circulated a week or so earlier. They were to be informed in cases of death which fulfilled certain criteria.

If the victim was found in the bedroom.

If the victim was tied up.

If the victim's throat had been cut.

The sound of Torkel's mobile interrupted the last line of 'Happy Birthday to You', and he answered as he withdrew into the kitchen, leaving the sound of cheering behind him.

It was Vilma's birthday party.

Thirteen.

A teenager.

Her birthday was actually the previous Friday, but she had wanted to go out for a meal with her girlfriends and to see a film. Her older, more boring relatives, such as her father, could come on a weekday evening. Torkel and Yvonne had bought their daughter a mobile phone for her birthday. A new one – not her older sister's cast-off, or an old one of his or Yvonne's when they got a new one through work. Now she had a brand-new model – with Android, Billy had said when Torkel asked him for help in choosing it. According to Yvonne, Vilma had more or less been sleeping with it since last Friday.

The kitchen table was covered in presents this evening. Vilma's older sister had bought her mascara, eye shadow, lip gloss and foundation. Vilma had been given her gifts on Friday, but had laid everything out again to show off the total haul. Torkel picked up the mascara, which promised lashes up to ten times longer, as he listened to the information being fed into his ear.

A murder. In Tumba. A woman whose throat had been cut, tied up in the bedroom.

Torkel thought Vilma was far too young to be wearing make-up, but it had been made very clear to him that she was the only one in her year group who didn't wear make-up, and that the idea of turning up at school next year without it was out of the question. Torkel didn't put up a great deal of resistance. Times were changing, and he knew he should be grateful that he hadn't had to engage in this discussion with Vilma two years ago. Some of her friends' parents had been in that position, and had clearly lost the battle.

All the indications pointed to the fact that this was the third victim.

Torkel ended the call, put down the mascara and went back to the living room.

Vilma was talking to her maternal grandparents. He called her over, and she didn't look too unhappy at having to break off the conversation with the oldies. She came towards Torkel with an expectant look on her face, as if she thought he'd been out in the kitchen organising some kind of surprise.

'I have to go, sweetheart.'

'Is it because of Kristoffer?'

It took Torkel a few seconds even to understand the question. Kristoffer was Yvonne's new partner. They had got together a few months ago, but Torkel had met him for the first time this evening. He was a high school teacher. Aged about fifty. Divorced with kids. Seemed like a nice bloke. It had never occurred to Torkel that their meeting might be seen as difficult, uncomfortable or in any way a problem. Vilma obviously interpreted the delay in his response as confirmation that she was right.

'I told her not to invite him,' she went on, a sullen expression on her face.

Torkel was filled with tenderness for his daughter. She wanted to protect him. Thirteen years old, and she wanted to shield him from heartache. In her world it was obviously an extremely awkward situation. No doubt she wouldn't have wanted to see her ex-boyfriend together with someone else. If she'd ever had a boyfriend. Torkel wasn't sure. He gently stroked her cheek.

'I have to work. It's got nothing to do with Kristoffer.'

'Promise?'

'Absolutely. I would have to leave even if there were just the two of us here. You know how it is.'

Vilma nodded. She had lived with him for long enough.

'Has someone died?'

'Yes.'

Torkel had no intention of telling her any more. He had decided long ago that he wasn't going to try to gain his children's attention

12

by passing on exciting and grotesque details relating to his work. Vilma knew that. So she didn't ask any more questions, she simply nodded. Torkel looked at her, his expression serious.

'I think it's really good that Mum has met someone.'

'Why?'

'Why not? Just because she's not with me anymore, it doesn't mean she has to be alone.'

'Have you met someone?'

Torkel hesitated for a second. Had he? For a long time he had been involved in some kind of relationship with Ursula, his married colleague, but they had never really defined what it actually was. They slept with one another when they were working away. Never in Stockholm. They never had dinner together, they never had those ordinary conversations about their private lives. Sex and talk about work. That was all. And not even that much at the moment. A few months ago, Torkel had brought his former colleague Sebastian Bergman into an investigation, and since then his and Ursula's relationship had been restricted to nothing more than work. This bothered Torkel, more than he was willing to admit. It wasn't the fact that everything was so obviously conducted on Ursula's own terms – he could live with that – but he missed her. More than he would have thought. It annoyed him. And on top of everything else, it seemed as if she had grown closer to her husband Mikael recently. They had even been to Paris for the weekend not long ago.

So had he met someone?

Probably not, and he certainly wasn't about to explain the complexities of his dealings with Ursula to Vilma, who had only just become a teenager.

'No,' he said, 'I haven't met anyone. And now I really do have to go.'

He gave her a hug. A big one.

'Happy birthday,' he whispered. 'Love you.'

'Love you too,' she replied. 'And my mobile.' She pressed her freshly glossed lips gently to his cheek.

Torkel still had a smile on his face as he got in the car and set off for Tumba. He called Ursula. She was already on her way.

★ ★ ★

13

As he drove, Torkel had caught himself hoping that this would turn out to be something else. Someone else. That there wouldn't be a link to the other dead women. But as soon as he looked into the bedroom he could see his hopes had been futile.

The nylon stockings. The nightdress. The arrangement.

This was the third victim.

'From ear to ear' was an inadequate description of the gaping neck wound. It was, rather, from one side of the spinal column to the other. Like opening a tin and leaving a little bit so that you can bend back the lid. The woman's head had almost been severed from her body. A considerable amount of strength would have been required to inflict such an injury. There was blood everywhere, high up the walls and all over the floor.

Ursula was already busy taking pictures. She moved around the room carefully, making sure she didn't step in the blood. She was always first on the scene if possible. She looked up, nodded a greeting and carried on with her photographs. Torkel asked the question, even though he already knew the answer.

'Same?'

'Definitely.'

'I spoke to Lövhaga again on my way over. He's still in there, exactly where he's supposed to be.'

'But we knew that, didn't we?'

Torkel nodded.

He didn't like this case, he thought as he stood by the bedroom door looking at the dead woman. He had stood in other doorways looking into other bedrooms, he had seen other women in night-dresses, their hands and feet bound with nylon stockings, raped and with their throats cut. They had found the first one in 1995. Then there had been three more before they managed to catch the murderer in the late spring of '96.

Hinde was sentenced to life imprisonment in Lövhaga.

He didn't even appeal.

And he was still in there.

But these new victims were identical copies of Hinde's. Hands and feet bound in the same way. Excessive violence used to cut the throat. Even the blue tinge in the white nightdresses was the same. This meant that the person they were looking for wasn't just a serial killer, but also a copycat. Someone who was copying

14

murders from fifteen years ago, for some reason. Torkel looked down at his notebook and turned to Ursula again. She had been involved in the original case in the nineties. Ursula, Sebastian and Trolle Hermansson, who had reluctantly retired since then.

'The husband said he got a reply to a text message at around nine o'clock this morning, but no reply to a message at one o'clock.'

'She's been dead for more than five hours, less than fifteen.'

Torkel knew that Ursula was right. If he had asked she would have pointed out that rigor mortis had not yet reached the legs, that there was no indication of autolysis, that the initial signs of tache noire had begun to appear, and other technical terms relating to forensics which he still hadn't bothered to learn in spite of all the years he had spent in the police service. If you asked, someone would always explain in plain language.

Ursula wiped the sweat from her forehead with the back of her hand. It was several degrees warmer up here than downstairs. The July sun had been shining in all day. Flies were buzzing around the room, attracted by the blood and the process of decay, as yet invisible to the human eye.

'The nightdress?' Torkel wondered after surveying the bed one last time.

'What about it?' Ursula lowered the camera and gazed at the old-fashioned item of clothing.

'It's been pulled down.'

'Could have been the husband. Wanting to cover her up.'

'I'll ask him whether he touched her.'

Torkel left his place by the door and returned to the inconsolable husband in the kitchen. He really didn't like this case at all.

The tall man had slept for a few hours. He had come home and gone straight to bed. That was what he always did. Rituals. The adrenaline had been surging through his body. He didn't really know what happened, but afterwards it always felt as if he had used up a week's reserves of energy during the short period of activity. But now he was awake. The alarm clock had gone off. It was time to get to work. Again. He got out of bed. So much still to do. And it was vital that everything was done in the right way. At the right time. In the right order.

Rituals.

Without them there would be nothing but chaos and fear. Rituals created control. Rituals made the bad stuff less bad. The pain less painful. Rituals kept the darkness at bay.

The man linked his Nikon camera to the computer and quickly uploaded the thirty-six pictures.

The first one showed the woman weeping, her arms crossed protectively over her breasts as she stood waiting for him to give her the nightdress to put on. Blood was trickling from one nostril, down to her lower lip. Two drops had splashed her right breast on their way to the floor, leaving red marks like rain on a window pane. She had refused to get undressed at first. Thought her clothes might somehow protect her. Save her.

In the thirty-sixth and final picture she was staring blankly straight into the camera. He had squatted down by the bed and leaned in close, so close that he had felt the warmth of the blood seeping from the gaping wound in her throat. By that time most of the blood had left her body, and had been largely absorbed by the bedclothes and the mattress.

He quickly checked the pictures in between. Nightdress on.

16

The nylon stockings. The knots. Knickers off. Before the act. After the act. The knife and its work.

The fear.

The realisation.

The result.

Everything looked good. He would be able to use all thirty-six. That was the best outcome. In spite of the almost unlimited capacity of the digital camera, he wanted to stick to the confines of an old-fashioned roll of film. Thirty-six pictures. No more. No less.

The ritual.

Billy was kneeling by the front door examining the lock as Torkel walked down the stairs. He turned to his boss.

'No sign of forced entry as far as I can see. The indications are that he was let in.'

'The patio door was open when we got here,' Torkel informed him.

'The husband opened it when he got home,' Billy said. 'According to him, it was locked.'

'Is he sure about that? He seemed pretty much out of it with shock . . .'

'He sounded sure.'

'I'll ask him again. Where's Vanja?'

'Outside. She just got here.'

'There's a computer in the study upstairs. Take it with you and see if you can find anything. Preferably something that links her to the others.'

'So she's the third?'

'Looks like it.'

'Are we bringing anyone in, or . . .'

Billy left the question hanging in the air. Torkel knew that what he really meant was: Are we bringing in Sebastian Bergman? The same thought had occurred to Torkel, but he had immediately dismissed it. The drawbacks were obvious and significantly outweighed the advantages – but that was before tonight.

Before the third victim.

'We'll see.'

'I mean, bearing in mind who he's copying . . .'

'As I said, we'll see.'

The tone of voice told Billy it was time to stop asking questions. He nodded and got to his feet. Billy understood Torkel's frustration.

They had no evidence – or, to be more accurate, they had plenty. Footprints, fingerprints, semen and hairs, but in spite of all this they were no closer to making an arrest than twenty-nine days ago when they had found the first woman bound and murdered in the same way. The almost nonchalant way the perpetrator left behind forensic evidence indicated that the person in question knew he wasn't on any police register. He was far too organised for this to be mere carelessness. Therefore, he had no previous convictions, at least not for any serious crime. But he was willing to take risks. Or forced to do so. Both possibilities were alarming; in all probability, he would strike again.

'Take Vanja back with you and go through everything again.'

If they could just find a connection between the victims, it would be a great help. They would be able to learn something about the perpetrator and start to close in on him. The worst-case scenario was that the killer was choosing women at random, that he saw someone in town, followed her, noted where she lived, made plans and waited for the right opportunity. If that was how he was selecting his victims, they wouldn't catch him until he made a mistake. And so far he hadn't put a foot wrong.

Billy took the stairs in a few rapid strides, glanced into the bedroom where Ursula was still working, and went into the study. Quite small, perhaps six square metres. A desk in one corner, with an office chair. A sheet of Perspex under the chair so that the wheels wouldn't damage the parquet flooring. A low bench housing a printer, modem, router, papers, files and office supplies. On the wall above the desk there was a long picture frame with space for eight photographs. The victim – Katharina – was alone in one picture, smiling into the camera beneath an apple tree; dark hair, straw hat, white summer dress. Like an advertisement for the Swedish summer. Österlen, perhaps. The husband – Richard – also appeared alone in another photograph, in the prow of a sailboat. Sunglasses, tanned, focused. All the other pictures showed both of them. Close together, arms around each other, smiling. It seemed as if they did a lot of travelling. There was a white sandy beach with palm trees in the background, and Billy was able to identify New York and Kuala Lumpur. No children, evidently.

So at least no one had lost their mother this time.

He stood there for a while, staring at the pictures. Gazing at the couple's loving smiles. They had their arms around each other in every photograph. Perhaps they always posed for the camera like that. Perhaps it was just a pretence, to show the world how happy they were. But it didn't look that way; it looked as if they were genuinely in love, standing there wrapped around each other. Somehow Billy couldn't tear himself away from the images of the man and the woman. There was something about their happiness that affected him intensely. They looked so full of joy. So in love. So alive. Things didn't usually touch Billy like this. He had no difficulty in maintaining a professional distance between himself and the victims. Obviously he was always affected to a certain extent; he suffered with the relatives, but the sorrow didn't usually pierce so deeply. He knew exactly why it was different this time. He had just met someone whose happy expression and inviting smile reminded him of the woman in the pictures. It made the tragedy real. He thought about Maya, pulling up the covers and hugging him sleepily this morning. She had tried to get him to stay for just a little bit longer and a little bit longer and a little bit longer, until the whole morning had gone. The image of a smiling Maya fitted perfectly with the romantic photographs in front of him, but not with the grotesquely contorted, bound and raped woman in the room next door. And yet for a second he had seen Maya lying there face down in a huge pool of blood. He turned his head away and closed his eyes. He had never felt this fear before. Never.

And he must never let it happen again. He knew that. He must never let in the violence and the terror and allow it to poison him. It would destroy love. Make him fearful and constantly anxious. The importance of keeping his private life and his work completely separate was crystal clear to him; without that distance he could lose everything. He could hug Maya, hold her tight, but he could never share that feeling. It was too dark and bottomless to be brought into their relationship. He would hold her for a long time when he got home. She would ask him why. He would lie. He didn't want to reveal the truth to her. Billy turned around, picked up the laptop from the desk and went downstairs to find Vanja.

The tall man gave the computer the order to print out all the pictures, and the printer responded immediately with an efficient hum of activity. As the images emerged on high-gloss paper, he created a new folder for the photographs on screen, copied it, went into the password-protected web page, identified himself as the administrator and uploaded the folder. The web page had the nondescript address fygorh.se, which was actually a random combination of letters that would not appear high up on any list found through a search engine. If a casual browser should somehow end up on the page, they would see only badly laid out text, barely legible against the colourful, moving background. The text, which sporadically changed both colour and font, consisted of extracts from books, government investigations, dissertations, other websites and completely meaningless passages, with no separation or spaces between them. The text was interrupted here and there by strange pictures and drawings, with no discernible purpose. It looked like a digital version of the nonsense sometimes seen on bus shelters or electricity boxes, created by someone who was unable to choose between all the possibilities on offer, and instead had decided to try everything in one place. No one was able to concentrate on the site for very long. He had requested the visitor statistics. Of the seventy-three people who had inexplicably found their way there, the person who had stayed the longest had managed only one minute and twenty-six seconds. Which was just what he wanted. Nobody had bothered to click through to the fifth page, or noticed the little red button right in the middle of a piece about listed buildings in Katrineholm. If you clicked on the button it opened a new page, which demanded your username and password. Beyond this security check was the folder containing the pictures he had just placed there. The folder had the less-than-informative title '3'.

The printer had finished its work. He picked up the pictures, leafed through them and counted. All thirty-six were there. He took out a large bulldog clip and attached it to the top of the pictures. He walked across to the other side of the room where a sheet of hardboard had been nailed to the wall, and hooked the bulldog clip onto a nail in the top right-hand corner. Above the nail was the number three, ringed in black ink. He glanced at the topmost pictures below numbers '1' and '2'. Women. In their bedrooms. Half-naked. Weeping. Terrified. The bulldog clip on the far left held only thirty-four pictures. He had failed with two of them. Before the act. He had been too eager. Deviated from the ritual. It would never happen again. The second bundle was complete. He picked up the camera again and took a photograph of the board with its macabre display. The first phase had been completed. He put the camera down on the desk, picked up the black sports bag from the floor just inside the door.

Into the kitchen.

The man placed the bag on the kitchen table, unzipped it and removed the packaging from the nylon stockings he had used. Philippe Matignon Noblesse 50 Cammello.

As usual.

As always.

He opened the cupboard under the sink and threw away the packaging. Went back, took out the knife in its plastic bag, removed it and placed it in the sink. He then opened the cupboard under the sink again and threw away the bloodstained plastic bag. He closed the cupboard door and turned on the tap. Warm water cascaded down over the broad blade. The congealed blood began to loosen from the metal, and disappeared down the sink with the water, swirling gently clockwise. He picked up the knife by the handle and turned it over. When no more blood was coming off by itself, he used washing-up liquid and a brush to clean off the rest. Afterwards he dried the weapon carefully before replacing it in the bag. He opened the third drawer from the top in the unit next to the oven and took out a roll of three-litre freezer bags. He tore off one bag, put the roll back, closed the drawer and placed the bag next to the knife. Then he left the kitchen.

Billy found Vanja on the lawn. She was standing with her back to the patio and the big windows. A beautifully mown lawn lay in front of her, ending in two flowerbeds full of colour. Billy didn't know the names of any plants, and assumed Vanja wasn't fascinated by the pretty flowers either.

'How's it going?'

Vanja gave a start. She hadn't heard him coming.

'He didn't leave a visitor's card, if that's what you mean.'

'Okay . . .' Billy took a step backwards.

Vanja realised she had sounded somewhat harsh. Billy's question might not even have been work-related. He knew her. Knew her well. Knew how much she hated this type of crime. Not because of the blood and the sexual violence. She had seen far worse. But it was a woman.

Dead.

In her own home.

Women shouldn't end up raped and murdered in their own homes. They were constantly vulnerable anyway, everywhere they went. They really ought to get changed before they walked home from a club or a bar. They should avoid subways, parks and lonely streets. They shouldn't be listening to their iPod. Their freedom of movement was restricted, their opportunities were limited. They should at least be able to feel at peace in their own homes.

Relaxed.

Safe.

'I found this,' Vanja said as she turned and walked back towards the patio. Billy followed her. They stepped up onto the decking and walked past the four wicker chairs and the table with a closed green sun umbrella in the middle, which made Billy think of a seating area outside a restaurant rather than ordinary garden furniture. They went over to two white wooden deck chairs, where they could just imagine the Granlunds enjoying the evening sun over a drink.

'There.' Vanja pointed at a window on the left. Billy looked. Inside he could see most of the ground floor; Torkel was sitting chatting to Richard Granlund while the crime-scene team went through the rest of the house, but that couldn't be what Vanja wanted to show him.

'What?' he asked.

'There,' she said again, pointing. She was more precise this time, and now he saw what she meant. It was more or less right in front of him: an impression on the window pane. There was an almost rectangular mark measuring a few square centimetres, with a smaller dot below it, flanked by two half-moon shapes. The one on the left curved slightly to the right, the one on the right slightly to the left, like a pair of brackets enclosing the other marks. Billy immediately knew what they were. Someone – probably the murderer – had looked in through the window, with his forehead and nose resting on the glass as he cupped his hands to shut out the light, leaving secretions from his sebaceous glands on the window pane.

'He's tall,' Billy stated, leaning forward. 'Taller than me.'

'If he's the one who did this,' Vanja nodded towards the marks, 'then that means he was visible from those houses over there.' She pointed to the neighbouring houses beyond the flowerbeds. 'Somebody might have seen him.'

Billy was doubtful. The middle of a weekday in July. The nearby houses looked as if the occupants might be away on holiday. Very few curious souls had gathered on the street or discovered they had important things to do in the garden when the police turned up. This was the kind of area that more or less emptied in the summer. The residents had the time and money to go off to their summer cottages, to go sailing, or even abroad. Had the perpetrator been aware of this? Counted on it?

Probably.

They would knock on doors, of course. Lots of doors. If the murderer had been let in, as Billy believed, it was likely that he had approached the house from the front. Knocking on the patio door was peculiar and frightening, and his chances of getting in would be considerably reduced. In which case he must have walked up the garden path. He would have been in full view there, too. But the same thing had applied in the two previous cases, and it hadn't helped them at all. No one had seen anything or anyone. No car, no one behaving oddly in the area, no one who had asked the way, been creeping around, cycled past, turned up with a message.

Nothing and no one.

Everything had been perfectly normal in the neighbourhood, with the minor exception that a woman had been brutally murdered.

'Torkel wants us to head back,' Billy said. 'If we're lucky we'll find a common denominator this time.'

'It feels as if we need some luck. He's picking up the pace.'

Billy nodded. Three weeks had elapsed between the first and second murders, but only eight days between the second and third. Together they set off across the lawn, which almost resembled the green on a golf course; in spite of a long spell of hot, dry weather, there was not a single patch of yellow to be seen. Vanja glanced at her colleague as he loped along beside her in his dark blue hoodie, carrying the laptop in one hand.

'Sorry if I sounded a bit pissed off before.'

'It's cool – I expect you were pissed off.'

Vanja smiled to herself. It was so easy to work with Billy.

The bedroom.

With the bag in his hand the tall man went straight over to the chest of drawers by the window. He placed the bag on the piece of furniture and opened the top drawer. From the right-hand side he picked up a neatly folded nightdress and put it in the bag. From the left-hand side he picked up a pack of Philippe Matignon Noblesse 50 Cammello Light Brown nylon stockings, and put it in the black sports bag. He zipped the bag shut and put it in the drawer between the remaining clothes. It fitted perfectly.

Of course.

He closed the drawer.

Back to the kitchen.

He took a carefully folded paper bag from the cleaning cupboard and opened it as he walked over to the fridge. On the shelf inside the door of the fridge was a soft drink in a glass bottle and a packet of Marie biscuits. The drawer at the bottom of the fridge contained bananas. He took out two and placed them in the paper bag along with the fizzy drink, the biscuits and a bar of chocolate from the top shelf. For the third time he opened the door of the cupboard under the sink and took out a plastic bottle which had once contained chlorine. He was aware of the faint smell of disinfectant as he slipped the bottle into the paper bag, then took it into the hallway and put it down on the floor to the right of the front door.

He turned around and looked back at the apartment. All quiet. For the first time in several hours. The ritual had been carried out. He had finished. But he was also ready.

For the next one.

For number four.

All he had to do now was to wait.

It was a few minutes past midnight when Vanja walked into the room that was never referred to as anything other than 'the Room'. Six chairs arranged around an oval conference table on a pale green carpet. A control panel for group discussions, video conferencing and the projector on the ceiling above the table, which was bare apart from four glasses and several bottles of mineral water. No glass walls facing the rest of the department, which meant that nobody could see into the Room. On one long wall hung the whiteboard, where Billy made sure that all the information relating to the case they were currently working on was displayed. He was just putting up a picture of Katharina Granlund when Vanja came in, sat down and placed three folders in front of her on the table.

'What would you have been doing tonight?'

Billy was a little surprised by the question; he had expected her to ask about the case. Whether he had found a connection between the three dead women. Whether any progress had been made. It wasn't that Vanja had no interest in her colleagues, but she was the most focused police officer Billy knew, and rarely bothered with small talk or brought up personal matters when she was working.

'I was at the open-air theatre,' Billy replied, sitting down. 'I had to leave straight after the interval.'

Vanja looked at him with a mixture of surprise and disbelief. 'But you don't go to the theatre!'

It was true. On a number of occasions when they weren't talking about work, Billy had referred to the theatre as a 'dead art form', expressing the view that just as we had abandoned the horse and cart when the motor car came along, the theatre should have been allowed to die a quiet and dignified death when film was born.

'I've met a girl – she wanted to go.'

Vanja smiled; of course it was a girl.

27

'So what did she say when you had to sneak off?'

'I'm not sure if she believed me. She'd already had to wake me up once during the first act . . . So what were you doing?'

'Nothing really; I was at home reading about Hinde.'

Which led them to the reason why they were sitting in the virtually empty building at Kungsholmen when the new day was no more than a few minutes old.

★ ★ ★

Three-quarters of an hour later they were forced to acknowledge that they had made no progress whatsoever. There was no common denominator between the three victims. Different ages, two married, one divorced, one had children; they hadn't grown up in the same place, hadn't attended the same schools, hadn't worked in the same field; they weren't members of the same clubs or organisations, had no mutual hobbies; their husbands and ex-husband had no obvious links; they didn't appear to be friends on Facebook or other social networks.

They didn't know each other.

They had nothing in common.

At least nothing Billy and Vanja could come up with. Billy closed his computer and leaned back wearily in his chair. Vanja got up and went over to the whiteboard. She gazed at the photographs of the three women. One picture of each of them alive, several of them dead. On the far right a number of photographs had been arranged in a vertical line. Photographs from the nineties. Terrifyingly similar to the new pictures.

'He's copying them exactly.'

'Yes, I've been wondering about that. How can he?' Billy stood up and went to join her. 'Do you think they know one another?'

'Not necessarily; the old pictures have been published.'

'Where?' Billy asked in surprise. He found it difficult to imagine any newspaper printing the gruesome photographs, and in 1996 the internet was far from the inexhaustible well of information it was today.

'In Sebastian's two books, among other places.' Vanja turned to face him. 'Have you read them?'

'No.'

'You should. They're actually pretty good.'

28

Billy merely nodded without saying anything. Given Vanja's opinion of Sebastian, that was probably the only positive comment she was likely to make about him. Billy hesitated; it was very late and Vanja had already shown signs of irritation, but he heard himself saying: 'Do you think we'll be bringing him in?'

'Sebastian?'

'Yes.'

'I certainly hope not.'

Vanja went back to the table, gathered up her folders and headed for the door. 'However, we do need to visit Hinde in Lövhaga. I thought you and I could go.' She opened the door. 'See you tomorrow. Can you ring Torkel and tell him how little we've found?'

Without waiting for a reply she turned away, leaving Billy alone. So it was his job to call Torkel and pass on the bad news. As usual. He glanced at the clock. Just before one. With a sigh he picked up his mobile.

Sebastian was woken by someone touching his face. He opened his eyes, quickly orientated himself in the unfamiliar bedroom and turned his head to the left as he ran through the evening that had led him here. He had followed Vanja home. Watched her go inside. He had been on the point of moving to his usual vantage point when she suddenly came out again. Seconds later a patrol car pulled up and she jumped in. Something had happened.

Vanja was needed at the scene of a crime.

He wasn't needed anywhere.

Wearily he had headed back to his apartment, which was far too big, but had felt restless almost at once. There was only one way to get rid of the sense of unease and dissatisfaction. He had scanned the morning paper and settled on a lecture at ABF-huset: 'An Evening with Jussi Björling'. The subject didn't interest him in the slightest, but as usual at cultural events, the majority of the audience was made up of women, and after a brief assessment of the possibilities he had sat down next to a woman in her forties in the third row. She wasn't wearing a wedding ring. He had started a conversation during the interval. Had an alcohol-free drink with her afterwards. They decided to go for something to eat. Walked the short distance to her apartment in Vasastan. Had sex. And now she had woken him up. Ellinor Bergkvist. Shop assistant at Åhléns department store. Household goods. What time was it, anyway? It was light outside, but that meant nothing. It was high summer, after all. Ellinor was lying on her side facing him, her elbow on the pillow, head resting on her hand as she traced the contours of his face with the index finger of the other hand. A pose she might have seen in some romantic comedy. Charming in a film, incredibly irritating in reality. A lock of strawberry-blonde hair had fallen down over one eye, and she was wearing a smile which

Sebastian assumed was meant to be 'mischievous' as her finger stopped on the tip of his nose and gave a little extra push.

'Good morning, sleepyhead.'

Sebastian sighed. He couldn't decide which was worse: being spoken to as if he was a baby or the aura of romantic togetherness emanating from her. It was probably the latter. He had already sensed that things might turn out this way during the short walk back to her apartment last night.

She had taken his hand.

Held his hand.

All the way. Like a clichéd image of a couple in love, strolling through the Stockholm summer night. Five hours after they had met. It was appalling. Sebastian had considered putting an end to the whole thing there and then, making his excuses and leaving, but he had invested far too much time and energy to give up before he got what he came for. What he needed.

The sex had been boring and detached on his part, but at least it had enabled him to sleep for a few hours, which was something.

Sebastian cleared his throat. 'What time is it?'

'Half past six. Almost. What would you like to do today?'

Sebastian sighed again. 'I have to work, unfortunately.'

A lie. He didn't work. He hadn't worked for many years, unless you counted his brief stint with Riksmord in Västerås a few months ago. These days he did nothing, and he intended to carry on doing nothing. There wasn't actually anything he wanted to do, and he certainly didn't want to do anything with Ellinor Bergkvist.

'How long do you think you would have slept if I hadn't woken you?'

What kind of a fucking question was that? How was he supposed to know? Presumably the dream would have woken him – there were very few nights when it allowed him to escape – but it was impossible to say when. Not that he had any intention of telling her about that. He was going to leave. Leave the apartment and Vasastan as quickly as possible.

'I've no idea – until nine maybe. Why?'

'Two and a half hours.' The index finger was back, moving across his forehead, down his nose, over his lips. A gesture that was somehow far more intimate than anything they had done a few hours earlier. 'So if you don't want to go back to sleep,'

31

Ellinor went on, 'that means we have two hours to do something else without encroaching on your important work.' The finger continued down his chin, his throat, his chest, and underneath the duvet.

Sebastian met her gaze. Her green eyes. There was a brown patch on the iris of the left eye, he noticed. The hand continued its downward progress.

It turned out there was something Sebastian might consider doing with Ellinor after all.

★ ★ ★

Breakfast.

How had she managed to get him to agree to that?

An unconsidered, throwaway post-coital promise?

The kitchen window overlooking the courtyard was open, but the apartment was still warm. The sound of a motorbike roaring past came from outside, but otherwise it was quiet. The stillness of a summer morning. Sebastian wondered what day it was as his eyes took in the breakfast table. Yoghurt, two kinds of cereal, muesli, freshly squeezed juice, cheese, ham, German sausage, gherkins, tomatoes, peppers, slices of watermelon. Wednesday, could that be right? Tuesday? The aroma of fresh bread filled the kitchen as Ellinor removed the baking tray from the oven and placed the mini-baguettes in a tea towel. She laid the tea towel in a woven bread basket and put it on the table with a smile, before turning back to the island in the middle of the spacious kitchen. Sebastian wasn't hungry. The kettle clicked off; Ellinor came over and poured the boiling water into the cup in front of him. Sebastian gazed down into the cup, watching the water turn dark brown as soon as it came into contact with the freeze-dried granules at the bottom. A look which Ellinor clearly interpreted as a criticism.

'I'm sorry I've only got instant coffee; I always drink tea myself.'

'It's okay . . .'

She poured water into her own cup and took the kettle over to the island. Halfway back to the table she stopped.

'Do you take milk?'

'No.'

'I can heat it up if you want? Like a latte.'

'No, it's fine.'

'Sure?'

'Yes.'

'Okay.'

She smiled, sat down opposite him, picked up a tea bag – lemon and ginger – popped it in her cup and dunked it up and down a few times. Once again she caught Sebastian's eye and smiled. In return he managed something which with a certain amount of goodwill could be interpreted as a smile, then looked away. He didn't want to be here. He usually avoided situations like this. Now he remembered why. He couldn't bear the false sense of togetherness, the idea that they had something in common, in spite of the fact that they would never see each other again – not if he had anything to do with it. He fixed his gaze on one of the kitchen cupboards and allowed his mind to wander while Ellinor stirred a spoonful of honey into her tea. She took a mini-baguette out of the basket, split it in two, spread butter on it, then added cheese, ham and two rings of yellow pepper. She took a bite, gazing at Sebastian as she chewed. Sebastian, who was still staring out into the room beyond her.

'Sebastian?'

He gave a start and looked at her enquiringly.

'What are you thinking about?'

He really had disappeared. Again. To the place where he always ended up. To the thing that seemed to occupy his every waking hour these days. It was a virtually unknown feeling for Sebastian. The obsession. Even during the most successful phase of his career, when he had been totally committed, he had never had any difficulty in pushing aside unwelcome thoughts. If a case was threatening to take over his life in a way he didn't like, he simply stopped thinking about it for a few days. Did something else. Reclaimed the initiative.

Sebastian Bergman was a man who did not lose control. Not for anything, not to anyone. At least, that was how things used to be.

Now things had changed.

Life had shaken him up. Damaged him.

Not just once. Twice.

He'd been nowhere near finding his way back after the disaster in Thailand on Boxing Day 2004 when he went to Västerås three months ago. The purpose of the trip had been to sell his parents' house, and as he was clearing the place out he had found some letters. Letters sent to his mother in 1979. From a woman who said she was pregnant with his child. Letters he had not received at the time. Three months ago he had done all he could to trace the sender. Sebastian's former colleagues from Riksmord had been in Västerås to investigate the brutal murder of a young boy, and he had wormed his way into the case in order to make use of all the resources available to the police so that he could put a face to the sender of those letters. To find an address. Information.

He had found it all. A woman at Storskärsgatan 12 had opened the door to him. A face. Anna Eriksson's face. He had been given information. Yes, he had a daughter, but she would never know that Sebastian was her father. She already had a father. Valdemar Lithner. Valdemar, who knew that Vanja was not his.

So they would never meet, Sebastian and his daughter. It would destroy so much. Destroy everything. For everyone. Sebastian had to more or less promise that he would never seek her out.

The problem was that they had already met.

More than that.

They had worked together.

In Västerås. He and Vanja Lithner, an investigator with Riksmord. Smart, driven, efficient, strong.

His daughter.

He had a daughter.

Again.

Since then he had been more or less stalking her. He couldn't really explain why, not even to himself. He got to see her, but that was all. He never let her know he was there. What would he say? What could he say?

Now he looked at Ellinor, who had gently asked what he was thinking about, and responded with the word that would probably provoke the minimum amount of follow-up: 'Nothing.'

Ellinor nodded, apparently satisfied with the answer, or at least with the fact that she had got his attention once more. Sebastian reached for a slice of melon. He ought to be able to get that down, surely.

'What are you working on?'

'Why?'

An unpleasant response, positively rude, but it was just as well to put a stop to things straight away. Sebastian really didn't want this already unpleasant breakfast experience to develop into an opportunity to get to know one another. They knew enough. He knew more about her than she did about him. She knew that his name was Sebastian Bergman, and that he was a psychologist. He had managed to evade any further personal questions by pretending to be interested in her.

'You said you had to work,' Ellinor went on. 'It's the middle of July, most people are on holiday, so I just wondered what you were doing.'

'I'm working on a kind of . . . report.'

'What's it about?'

'It's a . . . follow-up. For the police academy.'

'I thought you said you were a psychologist?'

'I am, but I sometimes work with the police.'

She nodded. Took a sip of her tea and reached for her baguette. 'When does it have to be finished?'

What a fucking question.

'In about two weeks.'

Those green eyes. She knew he was lying. It didn't really matter to him. He couldn't care less what she thought of him, but he wasn't at all comfortable with this everyday breakfast situation when they both knew it was just a sham. A chimera. Enough. He pushed back his chair. 'I have to go.'

'I'll call you.'

'Sure . . .'

The door closed behind Sebastian. Ellinor listened to his footsteps as he walked down the stairs. She smiled to herself. When she couldn't hear him anymore, she got up and went back into the bedroom. Over to the window. If he crossed the street and turned left she would be able to see him. He didn't.

Ellinor sank down onto the unmade double bed. She lay down on his side. Pulled his sheet over her, buried her nose in his pillow and inhaled deeply. She held her breath, as if she were trying to keep the smell of him inside her.

Hold on to him.

Vanja lived in an apartment on the hill above the Free Port. Sebastian was fairly sure it was a three-room apartment. As sure as he could be from his observation point on a small hillock a hundred metres away. It was a modern, pale yellow building. Seven storeys. Vanja lived on the fourth floor. No one was moving around inside the apartment, as far as he could see. Perhaps she was still asleep. Or at work. It didn't really matter if he didn't see her right now. He had come here mostly because he didn't know where else to go.

A few weeks ago it had been different.

He had got it into his head that he had to see her. Needed to see her. See what she was doing. He had decided he had to get a better view than the hillock could provide, and to achieve this he had tried to climb one of the large leafy trees growing in the hollow below the hillock. The first metre had gone much better than expected. He managed to get a good grip on a couple of branches higher up, and kept going. Then he spotted a suitable branch even higher up, and after groping around for a while he was able to heave himself up a few more metres. The sun was shining through the leaves, which smelled wonderfully fresh. He suddenly felt like a little boy in the middle of an adventure. How long was it since he had climbed a tree? Many, many years. But he had been good at it.

Agile.

Fast.

His father hadn't encouraged him; he had always been of the opinion that Sebastian ought to be devoting his time to intellectual challenges, developing his musicality and his artistic and creative talents. His mother had been more worried about the state of his clothes. Neither of them had been happy about his tree-climbing,

36

so he had done it often. As often as possible. And now he was once again enjoying the feeling of doing something adventurous, something forbidden.

Then he looked at the ground and realised that even from this height he was going to have considerable difficulty getting back down, at least without injury. Agility and speed were no longer the first qualities that came to mind in connection with Sebastian. Just as this startling and terrifying insight hit home, his jacket caught on a sharp protruding branch behind him, and he lost his balance. Suddenly the young boy on his way to an adventure was replaced by an unfit middle-aged man, dangling several metres above the ground as the lactic acid built up in his arms. Sebastian was forced to sacrifice both the illusion of youthful daring and his jacket; he edged his way laboriously over to the trunk, then shuffled, or rather slithered unceremoniously, down to the lower branches, where he managed to put a rather painful stop to his rapid descent. He clambered to the ground; his legs were shaking, his jacket was ripped and he had long, painful grazes on the inside of his thighs.

After that he made do with standing on the now familiar hillock to observe Vanja's apartment.

That was enough.

It was certainly crazy enough.

He didn't even dare to think about what would have happened if Vanja had looked out and seen him dangling from a tree outside her apartment.

The place where she lived looked so lovely. Modern curtains. Red and white flowers in the windows. Small lamps with dimmer switches on the windowsills. A north-east-facing balcony where on fine days she drank her coffee between seven twenty and seven forty-five in the morning. This meant that Sebastian had to crouch down behind some juniper bushes; he had never imagined he would become quite so familiar with them. She was obviously a woman who stuck to routines, his daughter. Up at seven on weekdays, around nine at weekends. On Tuesdays and Thursdays she went jogging before work. Six kilometres. On Sundays she doubled the distance. She often worked late, and rarely got home before eight. She didn't go out much; she went for a drink maybe once or twice a month. With the girls. No boyfriend, as far as

Sebastian could tell. On Thursdays she had dinner with her parents on Storskärsgatan. She went there alone, but Valdemar Lithner usually walked her home.

Her father.

They were close, that was perfectly obvious as they strolled along together. Very close. They were often laughing, they always parted with a tender, loving hug, and Valdemar would kiss Vanja on the forehead before he left. Always. The signature of their relationship. It would have been a beautiful picture, but for one thing. Her real father was standing a short distance away, watching them. Those moments caused Sebastian the most pain. It was a strange pain.

Worse than envy.

Greater than jealousy.

Harder than anything else.

It was the pain he felt for a life that had never been lived.

Two weeks ago, when Sebastian had seen Vanja and Valdemar having lunch together at an Italian restaurant not far from police headquarters, he had had an idea. It wasn't the most sympathetic idea he'd ever come up with. Quite the opposite, in fact. But it felt good. At the time, anyway.

As the weeks went by, the envy he felt towards Valdemar had slowly morphed into anger, then into something that could only be described as hatred. Hatred towards the tall, slender, elegant man who was able to stroll along beside Sebastian's daughter. His daughter! He was the one who should be getting those hugs, that tenderness. He was the one who should be getting the love.

Sebastian!

No one else!

Several times he had considered telling her everything, but he always changed his mind at the last minute. He was nurturing the idea of getting close to Vanja in some way and then, when they had built up a relationship, telling her the truth. At least that would enable him to spend time with her. Get to know her. Perhaps she would think he had deceived her, but that wasn't what was stopping Sebastian. The big problem was that irrespective of when or under what circumstances he told Vanja the truth, it would destroy her relationship with Valdemar. She would hate Sebastian for that. She already disliked him intensely.

Nothing was simple when it came to Vanja.

Unless of course she began to have her own doubts about her counterfeit father. That might be one way forward, if Sebastian could just get Vanja herself to bring Valdemar down from the pedestal on which he had dared to place himself. It shouldn't be impossible. What if she started to find out a few things about Valdemar, dirty little truths, secrets that blackened his name and made his halo slip. There was nothing more likely to get someone to change their views than personal experience and discoveries. Sebastian knew that. Often it was only personal experience of a situation that made you see the reality of it all. Therefore, action was always more valuable than words, and personal action was the most valuable of all.

If Vanja should make such a discovery herself, then this might cause her to question Valdemar's character. To think that he might not be the perfect father. That he might be something else. Something much worse.

If Sebastian could help Vanja to reach this insight, it would lead to despair and confusion. She would feel alone and let down, and she would be open to other influences, open to the truth; perhaps deep down she might even welcome it. Welcome a father figure who was waiting for her, who had secretly been close by. At that precise moment she might even throw her arms around him, need him. When she was hurt and had lost her footing. She would be ready for him.

It seemed like a really good plan. Complicated, difficult to carry through, but life-changing if it succeeded.

The research was vital. Nobody's perfect. Everyone has something to hide. It was simply a matter of finding it. Then exposing it in the best way possible.

The plan was so malicious that even Sebastian had hesitated briefly.

If it ever emerged that he had been involved in some way in blackening Valdemar's name, any chance of a relationship with Vanja would be gone for good. But if his plan succeeded, it would be the turning point he had been seeking. Lurking in the doorway opposite the Italian restaurant, he had decided that she was worth it. That she was worth fighting for.

He had no life anyway.

He had pushed his doubts to one side and gone straight home to look up a phone number. A number he hadn't used for a very long time. The number of the former chief inspector who was everything Torkel Höglund was not.

Impulsive, unscrupulous, perfectly prepared to walk over dead bodies if necessary.

He had been kicked out of Riksmord when it turned out that he had been carrying out private surveillance on his ex-wife, and had planted evidence to try to get her new husband convicted of drug-related offences, all so that he could gain sole custody of his children. He was exactly the person Sebastian needed right now.

Trolle Hermansson.

He answered after the phone had rung nine times. At first he wanted to talk about the old days, but Sebastian made it clear that he wasn't interested, and briefly outlined what he wanted. He finished his explanation with the promise of several thousand kronor in payment, but Trolle waved away his offer. He seemed genuinely pleased at the thought of having something to do. He just needed a few days.

That was two weeks ago.

Trolle had called him several times since then, but Sebastian had ignored him every single time. Sat motionless in the apartment, listening to the telephone as it rang and rang and rang. Only Trolle would let the phone ring so many times before giving up. Sebastian was no longer sure that he wanted to know. If he pursued this, would there be any boundaries left for him to cross?

But now he could feel the exhaustion taking hold. The hours on the hillock outside Vanja's apartment. The sex. Last night it had been Ellinor, the night before and tomorrow someone else. The empty apartment. The empty life. He had to do something. Anything. Change things. He took out his mobile and keyed in the number.

Trolle answered almost right away.

'I was just wondering when you were going to call,' a hoarse, sleepy voice said.

'I've had things to do,' Sebastian replied as he started to walk away from Vanja's building with the phone pressed to his ear. 'I've been away.'

'Don't lie to me. You've been following her. The daughter.'

Sebastian stiffened for a second before he realised that Trolle was referring to Valdemar's daughter. Of course.

'How do you know that?'

'Because I'm better than you.' It seemed to Sebastian that he could hear his former colleague smiling smugly on the other end of the line.

'I didn't ask you to check her out,' Sebastian said crossly.

'I know, but I'm thorough. An old-school cop.'

'Did you find out anything?'

'This and that. But no dirt. The old man seems to be a paragon of virtue.' Trolle paused, and Sebastian could hear him riffling through papers which in all probability were in a heap in front of him.

'His name is Ernst Valdemar Lithner. Born in Gothenburg in 1953. Started off at Chalmers, then changed to economics. Married Anna Eriksson in 1981; she didn't take his surname, by the way. No ex-wives or other children. No police record. Worked as an accountant for some years, then had a change of heart in '97 and did a few different things – everything from bookkeeping to tax advice. He must have made good money, because he paid the deposit on Vanja's apartment and bought a big summer place in Vaxholm the following year. No lovers that I can discover, male or female, but I've got someone hacking into his computer, so we'll see. He got sick last year.'

'What do you mean, sick?'

'Some kind of cell mutation in the lungs. Cancer, the thing that gets us all in the end. What did your mother die of?'

Sebastian didn't even respond to the implication that Trolle had clearly spent some time checking out him as well as Lithner over the last couple of weeks. He shivered in spite of the heat. Valdemar had cancer? That couldn't be right. The man who had stolen his daughter seemed to be full of life. Perhaps it was just a mask he assumed when he was with Vanja, making an effort for her sake.

'He's been in remission since the spring,' Trolle went on. 'Whatever that's worth. My contact hasn't managed to get hold of his notes, but he's only booked in for normal follow-up appointments, so he must be out of danger.'

Sebastian grunted with disappointment.

'Okay . . . anything else?'

'Not really. But I've only just started. I can dig much deeper if you want me to.'

Sebastian thought about it. This was worse than he had imagined. Not only was Valdemar loved by his daughter, he had just survived cancer. A saint who had returned to his family from death's waiting room.

Sebastian didn't have a chance. It was over.

'No, there's no need. Thanks anyway.'

He ended the call.

So much for that particular plan.

His third day in the job. He had finally got hold of one of those machines that allowed you to print out labels and self-adhesive strips, and he was now standing in the corridor in front of the metal plate which indicated that this room was the domain of the governor. He removed the protective strip from the back of the printed label and stuck it on the door. It was a bit crooked, but it didn't matter. It was perfectly legible. Governor Thomas Haraldsson.

He stepped back and looked at the sign with a contented little smile.

A new job.

A new life.

He had applied for the post several months ago, but hadn't really expected to get it. Not that he wasn't well qualified, but it had been a period in his life when nothing was going his way. Things were bad at work; he didn't get on with his new boss, Kerstin Hanser, and professional success had been eluding him, to be honest. This was largely down to the fact that Hanser refused to acknowledge what an asset he was, and actively worked against him, but even so. It had started to get him down. The situation at home was also rather strained. It wasn't down to a lack of love, or the fact that they'd got into a rut, it was just that things were very . . . focused. His wife Jenny had embarked on a series of fertility tests, and their entire lives centred on her attempts to get pregnant. Her every waking thought was fixed on conception, while he was obsessed with Hanser, the job, and a growing sense of bitterness. Nothing felt right, and Haraldsson hadn't dared to hope that he might get the job he had applied for towards the end of the winter, purely on the off chance. The advert had stated that the position would not be filled until the summer, so he had carried on working with the Västerås police and had more or less forgotten his application. Then that boy had been murdered, Riksmord had been brought in, and Haraldsson had ended up having surgery following a bullet wound. To the chest, if he was describing the incident. To the lower part of the shoulder, according to his notes. At any rate, he wasn't yet fully recovered. It still pulled a little; he could feel it as he smoothed down his new name label one more time.

Somehow the bullet wound had been a turning point. When he came round after the operation, Jenny had been there. Anxious, but also thankful that he had survived. That he was still there. They were told that he had been lucky. The bullet had created a split in the parietal pleura, the membrane lining the chest cavity that contains the lungs. This had caused a bleed into the pleural cavity itself, and consequently in the upper lobe of the right lung. Haraldsson just knew that getting shot was extremely painful. He had been off work for three weeks. While he was at home he had time to think about what things would be like when he got back to the station. No doubt the chief superintendent would give some kind of welcome-back speech, highlighting his heroic contribution; perhaps there was even a minor medal for just such an occasion: injured in the course of duty. There would be coffee and cake, of course, gentle pats on the back to avoid causing any discomfort to his injured chest, and a desire on the part of his colleagues to know how he was feeling and what he thought.

It hadn't quite turned out that way.

No chief superintendent, no speech, no medal, but the girls on reception had organised a cake. There hadn't been all that much curiosity or too many pats on the back either, but he still felt that a change had taken place. There was something about the way his colleagues received him, how they treated him. He wanted to believe there was a certain measure of respect. Respect, and perhaps subconsciously a sense of relief. Not many police officers were shot in the line of duty, and from a purely statistical point of view it was highly unlikely that it would happen again in Västerås in the foreseeable future. He had taken a bullet for the entire team, so to speak. For the first time in ages he had felt happy going to work. In spite of Hanser.

Something had happened at home, too. They were more relaxed, closer to one another, as if the life they had together right

44

now was more important than the life they were trying to create. They still had sex – a lot of sex – but there was more tenderness in their lovemaking now; it was warmer, less mechanical. Perhaps that was why it worked.

Suddenly everything seemed to be working.

Five weeks to the day after he had been shot, he was called for an initial interview. The same day Jenny's pregnancy test proved positive.

That was the turning point.

He got the job. Hanser had given him a glowing reference, he was informed. Perhaps he had misjudged her. True, they had had their differences during the time she had been his boss, but when it really mattered, when she had been forced to judge his work objectively, to assess his chances of doing a good job at Lövhaga, she had been professional enough to put her personal views to one side, and had spoken truthfully about his excellent leadership qualities, and what a good administrator he was.

He had heard some spiteful talk at the station, people saying that she just wanted to get rid of him, that she had even tipped Lövhaga the wink about him, but they were just jealous. Of him.

Of Thomas Haraldsson, governor of Lövhaga.

He went into his office; it might not be very big, but it was his. No more workstation in an open-plan office. Haraldsson sat down in the comfortable chair behind the desk, which was still comparatively clear. He switched on the computer. His third day; he hadn't really got to grips with the job yet. Which was perfectly natural. The only thing he had done so far was to ask for all the available material on one of the residents in the secure wing, since Riksmord had shown an interest in him. Evidently they had phoned again last night. Haraldsson placed a hand on the folder on his desk, but wondered whether he ought to ring Jenny instead. Not because he wanted anything; just to check how she was. They didn't see each other quite so much now. Lövhaga was a good sixty kilometres from Västerås. Almost an hour by car in each direction. His working day was likely to be quite long. So far it hadn't been a problem. Jenny was positively glowing with happiness. Right now her world was full of nothing but opportunities. The very thought of her made Haraldsson smile, and he had just decided to call her when there was a knock on the door.

45

'Come in.' Haraldsson replaced the receiver. The door opened and a woman of about forty-five came in: Annika Norling, his PA. 'You have visitors.'

'What?' Haraldsson glanced quickly at the open diary on his desk. His first meeting was pencilled in for one o'clock. Had he missed something? Or, to put it more accurately, had Annika missed something?

'Riksmord,' Annika replied. 'They don't have an appointment,' she went on, as if she could read Haraldsson's mind.

Haraldsson swore silently to himself. He had hoped that Riksmord's interest in Lövhaga would be restricted to telephone calls. They hadn't treated him well during their time in Västerås. Not well at all. Quite the reverse. They had done everything in their power to exclude him from the investigation, in spite of the fact that over and over again he had proved himself to be an asset.

'Who's here?'

Annika looked down at the post-it note in her hand. 'Vanja Lithner and Billy Rosén.'

At least it wasn't Torkel Höglund. When they first met, Torkel had told Haraldsson he was to be an important part of their investigation, only to kick him out a day or so later without any kind of explanation whatsoever. Not a person to be trusted. Admittedly, Haraldsson had no desire to see Vanja or Billy either, but what could he do? He looked over at the door, where his PA was waiting. He could ask Annika to tell them he was busy, get them to come back at some other time. Later. In a few days perhaps, when he had had time to familiarise himself with the job a little more. When he would be better prepared. Could one ask one's PA to lie? Haraldsson had never had a PA before, but assumed that it was somehow part of her job. After all, she was there to make things easier for him. Putting off a visit from Riksmord would definitely make his day easier to cope with.

'Tell them I'm busy.'

'With what?'

Haraldsson looked at her with a quizzical expression. Surely there weren't that many things a person could be busy with in their office?

'With work, of course. Ask them to come back.'

Annika gave him a look which could only be interpreted as disapproving, and closed the door. Haraldsson keyed his password into the computer, then spun his chair around and looked out of the window as he waited for his personal settings to be loaded. It was going to be another beautiful summer's day.

There was another knock on the door. This time he didn't even manage a 'Come in' before the door opened and Vanja marched in purposefully. She stopped so suddenly when she caught sight of Haraldsson that Billy almost bumped into her.

'What are you doing here?'

'I work here now.' Haraldsson straightened up a fraction in the comfortable office chair. 'I'm the governor. I've been in the post for a few days now.'

'Is it just a temporary thing?' Vanja couldn't get her head around it.

'No, it's my new job. It's a permanent position.'

'Right . . .'

Billy quickly jumped in with the reason for their visit. 'We're here because of Edward Hinde.'

'I realise that.'

'And you still weren't prepared to see us?' Vanja again. She sat down in one of the armchairs provided for visitors, a challenging look on her face.

'There's a lot to do when you're new in a post.' Haraldsson waved his hands over the desk, which he quickly realised was rather too empty to make much of an impact when it came to visualising his workload. 'But I can spare you a few minutes,' he went on. 'What would you like to know?'

'Has anything happened with Hinde over the last month or so?'

'Like what?'

'I don't know . . . Unusual behaviour, any deviations from his normal routine, changes of mood. Anything outside the norm.'

'Not that I've heard. There's nothing in his notes. I haven't met him personally. Yet.'

Vanja nodded, apparently satisfied with his response. Billy took over.

'What opportunities does he have to communicate with the outside world?'

Haraldsson pulled the folder on the desk towards him and opened it, thanking his lucky stars that he had brought it back from home this morning. Having all the available information on Hinde to hand the day after Riksmord had made enquiries about him was a sign of initiative.

'It says here that he has access to newspapers, magazines and books in the library, as well as limited access to the internet.'

'How limited?' Billy asked quickly.

Haraldsson didn't know. However, he did know who to call: Victor Bäckman, security chief at Lövhaga. Victor answered immediately and said he would come straight up. The three of them waited in silence in the bare, impersonal office.

'How's the shoulder?' Billy asked after a minute or so.

'Chest,' Haraldsson corrected him automatically. 'It's good. I'm not completely recovered, but it's . . . good.'

'Great.'

'Yes.'

Silence once more. Haraldsson was just wondering whether he ought to offer them coffee when Victor arrived. He was a tall man in a checked shirt and chinos, with brown eyes, a crew cut, and a handlebar moustache that made Billy think of the Village People as they shook hands.

'No porn, of course,' Victor replied when Billy repeated his question about Hinde's access to the net. 'Very, very restricted when it comes to violence. It's the strictest form of adult lock you can imagine. We programmed it ourselves.'

'Social media?'

'Nothing. Completely off limits to him. He has no way of communicating with the outside world via the computer.'

'Can you check his history?' Vanja asked.

Victor nodded. 'We save all web traffic for three months. Would you like a copy?'

'Yes please.'

'He also has a computer in his cell, doesn't he?' Haraldsson chipped in, not wanting to feel totally excluded from the conversation.

Victor nodded again. 'But it has no internet connection, of course.'

'So what does he use it for?' Billy turned to Haraldsson, who turned to Victor.

48

'Crosswords, Sudoku, that kind of thing. He does some writing, too. Keeps his brain active, so to speak.'

'And what about phone calls, letters and so on?' Vanja asked.

'He's not allowed phone calls, and he hardly gets any letters these days. But the ones that do arrive are all the same.' Victor gave Billy and Vanja a meaningful look. 'From women who can "cure" him with their love.'

Vanja nodded. Yet another of life's little mysteries: the way certain women were attracted to the most disturbed and brutal men in the country.

'Do you still have them?'

'Copies. Hinde gets the originals. I'll pass them on to you.'

They thanked him for his help and Victor went off to gather up the material they were going to take with them. Haraldsson leaned forward over the desk when the door had closed behind the security chief.

'May I ask why you're so interested in Hinde?'

Vanja ignored the question. So far they had managed to keep the fact that they were hunting a copycat killer away from the press. No one had even linked the latest three murders to the same perpetrator. Temporary staff working on the newspapers over the summer, presumably. Riksmord would prefer press interest in the investigation to remain minimal, and the fewer people who knew what they were actually dealing with, the greater the chance of maintaining that state of affairs.

'We'll need to speak to him,' she said instead, getting to her feet.

'Hinde?'

'Yes.'

'That's not possible.'

For the second time since her arrival Vanja stopped dead. She turned to face Haraldsson. 'Why not?'

'He's one of three prisoners on the secure wing who are not allowed visits unless they are pre-booked and approved. Unfortunately.' Haraldsson spread his arms wide in a gesture intended to further underline how sorry he was that he was unable to help them.

'But you know who we are.'

'Those are the rules. There's nothing I can do, but Annika can give you a form so that you can apply for a visiting order. She's my PA . . .'

Vanja couldn't help feeling that Haraldsson was enjoying his position of power. Perhaps that wasn't so strange – he had been well down the pecking order the last time they met – but even if it was understandable and perhaps human, it was still extremely frustrating.

'How long does it take for one of these applications to be processed?' she asked, struggling to keep the irritation out of her voice.

'Three to five working days, but I'm sure we can speed things up for you; you are from Riksmord after all. I'll see what I can do.'

'Thank you.'

'You're welcome.'

Vanja marched out without saying goodbye. Billy nodded before he left the room.

Haraldsson gazed at the closed door. That had gone well. Now he was going to get himself a cup of coffee and call Jenny.

This was going to be a good day.

His third day.

'So you're still stalking her?' Stefan was looking at Sebastian with an expression he recognised. The expression that said: 'I know more about you than you know yourself, so don't lie to me.'

The expression Sebastian hated.

'That's not the way I see it.'

'You stand outside her apartment block every day. You follow her around town, you follow her to work and to her parents' place. What else would you call it?'

'I'm interested in her. That's all.'

Stefan sighed and leaned back against the soft, pale upholstery of his armchair.

'She's my daughter,' Sebastian ventured by way of an excuse. 'I have to do it. I can't let her go.' He knew how lame that sounded. He was glad he hadn't mentioned anything about Trolle.

Stefan shook his head and gazed out of the window for a moment. They always ended up at this point. Vanja. The daughter Sebastian had suddenly discovered. The daughter who knew nothing, and could never be allowed to find out. Or could she? Was there a way? That was the hope. That was the question Sebastian always came back to, sooner or later. The point he was unable to get past. The issue he was constantly fighting with.

Stefan could certainly understand the problem. It was like the meeting of two opposite poles. The desire, the longing and the need on one side cannoning into the reality on the other, apparently irreconcilable. This was where the most difficult questions arose. Stefan came across them all the time in his work. That was when his patients came to him – when they suddenly found themselves unable to come up with the answers. It was human. Nothing strange about it. The strange thing about this situation was that the person sitting in front of him was Sebastian Bergman. A man

51

who had always had all the answers. A man Stefan had never expected to seek his help.

Sebastian had been Stefan's tutor at university. Everyone in the group had felt a certain reluctance to attend his lectures. They were always memorable, but on the very first day Sebastian had immediately made it clear to everyone that he was the star, and that he had no intention of sharing the limelight. Any student who questioned Sebastian's arguments or attempted a critical discussion of his theses and theories was humiliated and mocked. Not just for the remainder of that particular lecture, but for the rest of the academic year, the rest of his or her university career. This was why Sebastian's 'Any questions?' was always followed by complete silence.

The exception was Stefan Larson. He came well equipped to meet Sebastian. As the youngest son in a family of academics, dinner at home in Lund had prepared Stefan for verbal sparring, and he had often sought discussions with the sharp, impossible man who was feared by so many others. Sebastian also reminded Stefan of his older brother Ernst, who had the same powerful need to make his point, and always went that bit too far in the battle to be proved right. That was the most important thing to both Ernst and Sebastian: to be proved right. It made them formidable intellectual opponents, which suited Stefan perfectly. He provided the opposition they required, but he never gave them the final victory. He came back with the next question, and the next, and the next. They were looking for the final killer blow, but instead they were faced with a long war of attrition. It was the only way to stand up to them.

To wear them down.

One morning almost two years ago, Sebastian had been waiting for Stefan outside the door of his practice. From the exhausted expression and the crumpled clothes, it looked as if Sebastian had been waiting all night. He was already a shadow of his former self by then. He had lost his wife and daughter in the tsunami in 2004, and since then he had been caught in an increasingly frightening downward spiral. Gone were the lectures and the book tours, replaced by tormented thoughts, apathy and a growing problem with sex. There was no one else he could turn to, he had said. No one. They had started to meet, always on Sebastian's terms. Sometimes months would go by between meetings, sometimes just a few days. But they never lost touch.

'How do you think Vanja would feel if she found out about this?' Stefan went on.

'She'd say I was crazy. She'd report me to the police and she would hate me.' Sebastian paused for a moment before carrying on. 'I know that, but . . . she's the only thing I think about, all the time, going round and round . . .' The end of the sentence was little more than a whisper. 'This is something completely new. I'm used to being in control.'

'Really? So you mean that until you found out she was your daughter, you were in control? It was your brilliant plan to fuck up your life one hundred per cent? In that case, congratulations; you certainly succeeded.' Stefan leaned forward. That was the best thing about having Sebastian as a patient. You could take off the gloves. Hit him hard. 'You don't want me to pander to you. All your life people have let you have your own way. I'm not doing that. You lost your family in the tsunami, and now you've lost your grip. Completely.'

'That's why I need her.'

'But does Vanja need you?'

'No.'

'She's already got a father, hasn't she?'

'Yes.'

'So who do you think would gain if you told her the truth, given the current situation?'

Sebastian sat there in silence. He knew the answer. He just didn't want to say it out loud. But Stefan was still leaning forward, waiting. He said it instead.

'No one. Not you, not Vanja, not anyone.'

Stefan leaned back. His expression grew kinder. Warmer.

'Don't tell her, Sebastian.' His voice was warmer too. More intimate. 'You have to have a life of your own before you can be a part of someone else's. Stop following her, and spend some time getting back on your feet. When you've done that, we can talk about the next step.'

Sebastian nodded. Stefan was right. Of course.

Get a life before you can share a life.

Sensible, boring Stefan in his soft, boring room was right. This annoyed Sebastian. Thinking Trolle was the solution might

53

be wrong, but it was easy. Easier than getting a life. More fun to think about, anyway.

'I run a counselling group,' Stefan continued. 'We meet twice a week, this evening and tomorrow. I think you should come.'

For the first time Sebastian stared at Stefan in surprise. 'Me? In a group?'

'They're people who don't seem able to move on, for one reason or another. Does that sound familiar?'

Deep down Sebastian was glad Stefan had come up with something as banal as group therapy. It moved him a few steps away from the black thoughts, and filled him with a simple, liberating irritation.

'It sounds incredibly familiar and incredibly tedious.'

'I'd like you to come.'

'No.'

Sebastian got to his feet, making it clear that the session was over and that he had no intention of discussing the matter any further.

'I insist that you come.'

'Insist all you like, but the answer is still no.'

Sebastian headed for the door. This feeling of irritation was terrific. It provided him with fuel. Did Stefan really think he was going to see Sebastian Bergman in some snivelling, sobbing self-help group?

Not a chance.

Sebastian closed the door behind him. The energy gave him a lift, cheered him up. He might get something done today after all.

★ ★ ★

Sebastian had managed to get all the way to the university buildings at Frescati before the energising irritation dissipated. He wanted to show Stefan that he could get himself a life, but the weariness was starting to take over.

The whole thing had started at home in his apartment on Grev Magnigatan earlier in the week, when he had found the old manuscript of a three-hour lecture entitled 'An Introduction to Offender Profiling'. It had been at the bottom of a pile of newspapers and other documents in his study, a room he never used; in a moment of boredom he had suddenly decided to have a good clear-out. He couldn't remember when he had written

54

the text, but it was obvious that it was before the disaster, since it was largely free of the suffocating cynicism that now dogged his every thought. Sebastian had read it straight through twice, and was actually quite impressed with himself. He really had been able to write once upon a time.

The lecture was sharp, well-informed and riveting.

Sebastian had sat at the desk for a while with the document in his hand. Discovering a better version of himself had been a strange, almost surreal feeling. After a while he had looked around the room, and suddenly found signs of the better Sebastian everywhere. The diplomas on the walls, the books, the press cuttings, the notes he had once made, the words he had once written. His study was full of the flotsam and jetsam of another life. To escape the memories, he had gone over to the window, looked at the street below, but the remains of his old life were everywhere, and he remembered how he used to park his car just there, opposite the antique shop. Back when he had a car and somewhere to go.

After the conversation with Stefan he had felt uplifted, almost inspired. He had gone straight home and into his study, where he started searching through the piles of papers, hunting for the contract, looking for a name. Someone must have ordered a three-hour lecture from him. After a while he had found two copies of a draft contract from the university's department of criminology. Dated 7 March 2001, and relating to a total of three lectures providing an introduction to offender profiling. He tried to remember why he had never actually delivered the lecture. In 2001 he had been at the top of his game. Sabine had been born, and he was living with Lily in Cologne, so presumably he had simply thought he had better things to do. The contracts hadn't been signed, but the other party was a university lecturer called Veronika Fors. He didn't recognise the name. Head of Faculty. He had called the department. It was many years since she had sent the contract, but she was still there. The switchboard had put him straight through, but his courage had failed and he had hung up before she had time to answer. He had sat down again with his manuscript in his hand. At least she was still there.

★ ★ ★

He stopped a few hundred metres from the building which housed the department of criminology; some visionary had named it Block C, presumably because it was the third building along. Sebastian looked at the tall, corpse-blue buildings; they looked more like part of some building programme from the 1960s than the capital city's temple of knowledge, and suddenly the doubts came pouring in. Did he really think this was going to make a scrap of difference? He cursed his hesitation. Tried to fight it. He would go and see Veronika Fors. Start there.

His idea was a simple one. A few quick guest lectures to begin with. A little spur, a distraction from everyday life to send him in a different direction, away from the women at night and, above all, away from Vanja during the day. Away from the feeling of being an outsider. Away from the mindset that had made him call Trolle.

But the first doubts had set in as soon as the taxi turned into the eastern car park. He was struck most forcibly by the feeling that nothing had changed. The place was the same. He was the one who was different. Could it work? He tried to push the thought aside by heading as purposefully as possible for Block C, as if he could overcome his hesitancy through sheer muscle power.

A group of girls was coming towards him; students, judging by their age and the books they were carrying. One of them reminded him of Vanja, with her blonde hair; she was probably a little younger, but not much. He looked at the girl. It was for Vanja's sake that he was standing here outside Block C. Stefan was right. He needed a life of his own if he was ever going to be able to face her properly, to reveal who he was. Perhaps be accepted. Probably not loved. But possibly accepted.

He needed a life. That was why he was here.

He felt the energy coming back.

He walked into Block C.

Into a world he had not visited for many, many years.

He was in luck. Veronika Fors was free, and could see Sebastian straight away. The woman on reception led him down a long corridor to a small, well-ordered office with a desk and two chairs.

The woman behind the desk looked surprised when he walked in. He smiled and shook hands before sitting down uninvited in the chair opposite her.

'Hi, my name is Sebastian Bergman.'

'I'm well aware of that.' She wasn't smiling back at him. She closed the file she had been working on and stared at him. He couldn't work out whether she was just surprised to see him, or annoyed as well. There was definitely something.

'You're Veronika Fors?'

'Yes.' Still terse.

'Well, it's about this lecture we planned a while ago.' Sebastian took the contract out of his inside pocket and put it down in front of her. 'It's a detailed introduction to offender profiling.'

Veronika picked up the contract and glanced at it.

'But this must have been ten years ago.'

'Something like that,' Sebastian answered. 'I thought you might still be interested. The material is still relevant.' He smiled again, as sweetly as he could manage.

'Are you joking?' Veronika Fors removed her reading glasses and looked at him.

'No, when I'm joking I'm much funnier. I can be positively witty.' He smiled again. She didn't. There was something about her eyes. Something he recognised.

'Give me one good reason why I should be having this conversation with you. Are you still involved in research? You simply disappeared from the surface of the earth, and now you turn up here wanting us to honour a contract from ten years ago.'

Sebastian quickly decided to stop smiling. That particular tactic had proved totally ineffective with the woman who was now glaring at him. He was starting to get annoyed with her. After all, she was the one who had once requested his services. Had wanted his expertise and his depth of knowledge. Which he still had. A little respect wouldn't go astray.

'I am still the best profiler in Sweden. I can promise you that you won't be disappointed, even if I perhaps haven't been all that active in the academic world of late.'

'And where have you been active? Have you actually published anything at all since the nineties? Are you working? Are you doing anything?'

'Look, if you have doubts about my abilities I can offer a guest lecture. So that you can see what I'm capable of. Just as a one-off, so to speak.'

'Oh yes, you're used to that kind of thing, aren't you? One-offs.'

The tone of her voice startled Sebastian. This sounded personal. Furious. Possibly hurt. He looked at her, but still didn't recognise her. Even the eyes which he had thought seemed familiar a second ago provided no clues. Had she put on weight? Or lost it? Cut her hair? He had no idea. His brain was working at top speed. There was something about her. About that angry, slightly high voice. Suddenly a vague memory came into his mind. Too unclear to grasp fully, but he became convinced that in spite of the fact that he didn't really remember her, he had seen her naked. In a stairwell in Bandhagen. The faint frozen image of a moment long ago. A naked woman screaming furiously at him in a stairwell. Surely he hadn't told her to go to hell? Or had she said it to him?

Could the situation really be that bad?

Veronika Fors tore up the contract in front of him and gave him the finger.

The situation probably was that bad.

Unfortunately.

'Guess who's the new governor of Lövhaga?'

Vanja settled comfortably in her chair and allowed her gaze to sweep over her three colleagues around the table in the Room. Billy smiled to himself. She really couldn't let it go. In the car on the way back to Stockholm she had made several references to the fact that they had come across Thomas Haraldsson again. As a prison governor. How was that possible? What were they thinking of? Bribes, total brain freeze or someone who was determined to finish off Lövhaga were the only explanations she could come up with to explain his appointment.

Billy had listened quietly. Haraldsson didn't particularly bother him, and he had been quite pleased to see him again. He might not be the sharpest knife in the drawer, but there was something appealing and slightly pitiful about the man from Västerås who struggled so hard. There was nothing wrong with his ambition, and with the right support he might make a good job of his new post. Billy hoped so. Quietly, to himself. He was fairly sure he was the only person in the room who felt that way. He looked at Ursula and Torkel, who were both shaking their heads in response to Vanja's question.

'I didn't even know they had someone new,' said Torkel, taking a sip of his fourth cup of coffee from the machine.

'Thomas Haraldsson.' Vanja looked expectantly at her colleagues as she waited for the reaction. It came.

'Thomas Haraldsson from Västerås?' Ursula's expression was quizzical, as if she thought she must have misunderstood. Vanja nodded. 'How the hell did he end up there?' Ursula went on.

'I have no idea – it's a mystery.'

'How is he?' Torkel asked quietly. He looked neither surprised nor annoyed, Vanja noticed. More concerned, in fact.

'He looked very much at home.'

'I meant his shoulder.'

'He said he could still feel it a little bit, but otherwise everything seemed fine,' said Billy.

'Good.' After all, Thomas Haraldsson had been shot while he was under Torkel's command, and Torkel felt slightly guilty because he hadn't been in touch with Kerstin Hanser and the Västerås police to find out how he was. He had intended to follow up several times, but had never quite got around to it.

'So what did he say about Hinde?' Torkel went on, reminding the team of the real reason for their meeting.

'He's where he's supposed to be and he's behaving just as he always does, if we're to believe the staff at Lövhaga.'

'Did you see him?'

'We put in an application for a visiting order. Apparently nobody is allowed to see him without first being approved.'

'And how long does that take?'

'Three to five days.'

'I'll see if I can speed things up.'

Vanja nodded her thanks. Someone was copying Edward Hinde, which meant he became a part of their investigation. She wanted to see him, if only so that she could eliminate him. Until then he was a loose end, and Vanja hated loose ends. Dismissing something because a connection seemed improbable – she just couldn't do it. It would have made her feel as if she wasn't doing her job, as if she wasn't doing her best. And that was something she had learned at home, from when she was a child. Something her father had said to her when she was worried about how she would cope with her first day at school. You didn't have to be the best, but you should always do your best. You couldn't do any more than that, but it would be foolish to do less. Twenty-five years later, those were still words she lived by.

'Anything else from Lövhaga?' Torkel wanted to know. Vanja turned to Billy, who produced four sets of stapled A4 sheets from the folder in front of him and handed them out.

'I've gone through the websites Hinde has visited over the last three months. Nothing worth mentioning. Lots of newspapers, both Swedish and foreign, and he follows a number of blogs; you can see them listed there. And he quite often joins various forums, mostly those discussing philosophy, psychology, other humanities.'

Ursula looked up from her print-out. 'Can he join in the discussions?'

'No, he's only allowed to read. His sole communication with the outside world is through letters. He has received three in the past six months. Two were from women who want to meet him, asking how they could visit him and inviting him to come and see them when, or if, he gets out.'

'Sick,' Vanja interjected. Both Torkel and Ursula nodded in agreement.

'The third letter might possibly be of some interest.' Billy turned to a new page in the print-out, and the others did the same. 'It's from a Carl Wahlström here in Stockholm. He writes that he has followed Hinde's activities with great interest, and would very much like to meet him personally in order to, and I quote, "gain a deeper insight into the decision process which led to four women losing their lives". He's writing a dissertation on practical philosophy, but he seems pretty impressed by Hinde, if you ask me.'

'Have they met?' Ursula asked.

'No. According to Lövhaga, Hinde didn't even reply to the letter.'

'Check him out after the meeting anyway,' Torkel said. 'At least it's something.' He put down the papers and pushed his glasses up onto his forehead. 'The door-to-door enquiries in Tumba didn't turn up a thing. The Granlunds' friends and parents knew nothing about the couple feeling as if they were being watched, or threatened. The husband is completely out of the picture. He was in Germany, or in the air on his way home.'

A heavy silence descended on the group. With a few minor variations, this was the third time they had heard Torkel report that no one had seen anything at the scene of the crime, and that no one close to the victim was able to come up with even the slightest hint of a motive.

'So that leaves forensics.' Torkel turned to Ursula.

'Sperm and pubic hair. Again. I've sent samples to Linköping for analysis, but I think we can assume it's the same perpetrator. The preliminary autopsy report states that the carotid artery and the trachea were severed, which means that she choked before

61

she could bleed to death. Again.' Ursula fell silent and spread her hands. There wasn't any more.

Torkel took over: 'As you are all aware, we haven't managed to find a link between the three women, so we have no idea who his next victim will be.'

Torkel's closing remark was received in painful silence. Nobody could dispute what he had said. It seemed highly improbable that the perpetrator would not strike again. Another woman would lose her life, and there was nothing they could do to prevent it. Vanja pushed back her chair and stood up.

'We'll go and see Wahlström.'

Vanja and Billy had gone to look for Carl Wahlström in the philosophy department, but had been informed that he wasn't there. The university was virtually deserted at this time of year. Had they tried calling him? No, they hadn't, nor did they have any intention of doing so. Had they been to his apartment? Carl was working on his dissertation over the summer. They were given an address which they already had. Forskarbacken. Second floor. Student accommodation.

They could hear music coming from the apartment. Vanja took out her ID as she rang the bell, keeping her finger on the button for a long time. She couldn't decide if her hearing was particularly sensitive, or if the music was really loud.

Carl Wahlström opened the door with a cup of tea in his hand and looked enquiringly at his visitors. The music was really loud, Vanja decided as she and Billy showed their police IDs.

'Police – Vanja Lithner and Billy Rosén. Could we have a word, please?'

'What's this about?'

'Could we come in?'

Carl stepped aside and let them in. The apartment was warm, and there was the aroma of freshly baked bread.

'Could you please take off your shoes? I've just finished vac-uuming.' Carl edged past them in the narrow hallway and went into the bedroom; he walked over to the computer, which was standing on the desk along with a printer, and turned off the music.

DAUNT BOOKS

INDEPENDENT
BOOKSELLERS

Also at:

83-84 Marylebone High Street
London W1U 4QW
020 7224 2295

112-114 Holland Park Avenue
London W11 4UA
Tel: 020 7727 7022

158 -164 Fulham Road
London SW10 9PR
020 7373 4997

61 Cheapside,
London EC2V 6AX
020 7248 1117

and

www.dauntbooks.co.uk

Vanja and Billy stepped out of their shoes and into the apartment. There was a small kitchen in one corner of the living room, which was equipped with a sofa, a wall-mounted television, and in the other corner a desk with a neat pile of textbooks, and an office chair. A perfectly ordinary student apartment, had it not been for the large pictures, almost like display cases, hanging on one wall above the sofa. Behind the glass each one contained a number of butterflies and moths; six or eight if they were large specimens, perhaps fifteen or twenty if they were smaller, their brightly coloured wings spread in a wing beat frozen for all eternity. Vanja recognised a handful, and she knew the names of two: peacock and brimstone yellow. She didn't even know if the rest were native to Sweden.

'What was it you wanted?'

Carl had emerged from the bedroom and closed the door behind him. He folded his arms and looked at the two police officers. Vanja glanced at Billy and noticed that he too was fascinated by the display of insects.

'We're here as a result of a letter you sent to Edward Hinde some weeks ago,' Vanja explained, sitting down on the sofa. Billy leaned against the kitchen wall.

'Oh?' Carl spun the office chair around and sat down, an enquiring expression on his face.

'Why did you write to him?' Vanja went on.

'I wanted to get in touch with him.'

'Why?'

'I hoped he might be willing to help me with my studies.'

'In practical philosophy?'

'Yes. Why is that of any interest to the police?'

Vanja didn't reply. The less Carl knew about the reason for the visit, the less likely he would be to adapt his answers accordingly. Billy was thinking the same way, and changed the subject completely.

'What does a practical philosopher do? I mean, what kind of job would you end up with?'

Carl spun around a quarter turn and looked at Billy with the hint of a smile at the corners of his mouth.

'Why? Are you tired of being a cop?'

'Isn't philosophy purely theoretical?' Billy went on as if he hadn't heard the question. 'What does a practical philosopher do? Go out preaching? Run evening classes?'

'Just because you don't understand it, there's no need to have a go at me.'

'Sorry, I was just curious.'

The look of displeasure on Carl's face made it clear that the apology had not been accepted. Vanja broke in to get the conversation back on track before Carl decided he wasn't prepared to speak to them at all.

'We read your letter to Hinde.'

Carl kept his gaze fixed on Billy for a second or two longer before turning to Vanja.

'I realise that.'

'It sounds as if you look up to him.'

'No, I wouldn't say that. He fascinates me.'

'He murdered four women. Does that fascinate you?'

Carl leaned forward in his chair, clearly more interested in the conversation now.

'Not his actions in themselves, but I do find his journey to that point incredibly interesting. The decisions he took, the deliberations he went through. I'm trying to understand him.'

'Why?'

Carl fell silent for a moment, obviously pondering his answer as if he were explaining to his professor rather than speaking to the police.

'The murders he committed were deliberate acts. Planned and considered. He had a desire to kill, and he fulfilled that desire. I want to know where the desire came from.'

'I can tell you that – his sick brain.'

Carl smiled almost superciliously at Vanja. 'That's not quite enough for a dissertation. Besides which, your assertion demands an acceptance that certain desires can be classified as "sick", while other more socially acceptable desires, such as wanting a puppy, are "healthy".'

'Are you saying it's healthy to kill four women?'

'For very good reasons, the act itself is not accepted in our society, but I find it very difficult to talk about the desire to carry out that act in terms such as healthy or sick. We have established

64

rules on how to behave, and of course we do not accept the killing of another human being. But can we really not accept the desire to do so?'

Vanja sighed to herself. Was it necessary to analyse everything, to turn everything inside out, to understand and explain? To her it was perfectly simple. If you wanted to kill another person, you were sick. If you actually did it, you were even more sick. Or evil.

'Did you get a reply from him?' Billy broke in, partly because he couldn't stand listening to the philosophical lecture any longer – if it was philosophy – and partly because he could see that Vanja was running out of patience.

'No, unfortunately.'

'Do you contribute to any of these forums?'

Billy handed over a print-out of the websites Hinde had visited over the past three months. Carl took the paper and studied it carefully. A bell pinged on the kitchen bench; Carl put down the print-out and stood up. 'My bread is ready.'

He went into the kitchen, turned off the oven and opened the door. He picked up two pot holders and lifted the baking tray out of the hot oven. When Vanja saw the two golden-brown loaves in their rectangular tins, she realised she was hungry. They waited while Carl prodded the bread to check that it was ready, then tipped one of the loaves out and placed it upside down on a cooling rack on the draining board. As he repeated the procedure with the second loaf, he turned briefly to Vanja. 'Which department are you with?'

'Riksmord.'

Carl's attention was diverted from his baking. 'Has he escaped?'

'No.'

'But someone has died, and you're interested in Hinde?'

Vanja glanced at Billy. Either Carl Wahlström was very bright and had put together what little information he had with unusual speed, or he knew that someone was copying Hinde's murders. Without giving away what she was thinking, Vanja went on: 'Where were you yesterday between ten a.m. and three p.m.?'

'I was here. I was studying.'

Carl placed a clean tea towel over the loaves, closed the oven door and came back to the little living room.

'Were you alone?'

'Yes.'

'So nobody saw you all day?'

'No.'

Silence. Vanja didn't need any more; she had already decided to run a thorough check on Carl Wahlström. She got to her feet.

'Would you be prepared to provide a voluntary DNA sample?'

Carl Wahlström didn't even bother to answer. He tipped his head back and opened his mouth wide. Vanja dug a sterile cotton bud out of her bag and quickly drew it over his tongue and the inside of his cheeks.

'So what about that list I gave you?' Billy asked as Vanja placed the cotton bud in a small plastic container and closed the lid.

Carl turned around, picked up the list and handed it back to Billy.

'One. That one.' He pointed and Billy looked at the name. It didn't help much. It didn't help at all, in fact. Even if Hinde knew that Carl was contributing to that particular forum, he couldn't communicate with him. But at least it was a point of contact, which was something. And something was more than nothing, which was what they had had so far.

On the way out into the hallway, Vanja turned around. 'Your insects?'

'What about them?'

'Where does the desire to stick pins in butterflies and moths come from?'

Carl smiled at her again, as if to show that he was prepared to indulge her ignorance. As if she was a little girl who didn't know any better. It was a smile that Vanja already hated, after only ten minutes in Wahlström's company. It reminded her far too much of Sebastian Bergman's superior smirk.

'It's not a desire, it's an interest. I'm a lepidopterist.'

'I presume that means you're a butterfly collector.'

'Expert. A butterfly expert.'

'How does it work? Are they still alive when you stick a pin in them?'

'No, I kill them first with ethyl acetate.'

'So you're interested in killing things?'

Carl tilted his head to one side as if Vanja had just said something enchanting and sweet.

'Aren't you going to ask if I used to wet the bed and enjoyed setting fire to things as well?'

Vanja didn't reply. She bent down next to Billy to put on her shoes, avoiding that supercilious look.

Carl went on: 'You do know it's a gross simplification to believe that when serial killers are young, they wet the bed, start fires and kill animals?'

Billy straightened up. 'You seem to know a great deal about serial killers.'

'I'm writing a dissertation about them. Among other things.'

'And what's it about? This dissertation?'

'When the desires of the individual collide with the rules of a civilised society.'

Billy met Carl's gaze and suddenly had the feeling that the topic was very definitely based on personal experience. In spite of the warmth in the apartment, he shivered.

★ ★ ★

'He was creepy.'

Vanja and Billy had stepped out onto Forskarbacken and were walking along the pavement to the car when Billy put into words what they were both thinking. Vanja nodded, put on her sunglasses and unbuttoned her thin jacket.

'Creepy, and taller than you.'

'Yes, I noticed that too,' said Billy, unlocking the car even though they were still twenty metres away. 'Shall we put him under surveillance?'

'He seemed a bit too relaxed. If it is him, he knows we've got forensic evidence.'

'Perhaps he wants to be caught?'

'Why would he want that?'

'The media haven't linked the murders yet. He's getting no publicity, no attention. If the kick he gets from killing is becoming weaker and weaker, he might need something else. An arrest and trial would not only show what he's done, but would provide him with acknowledgement. Make him someone.'

Vanja stopped dead and stared at Billy in surprise. Not only because that was probably the most she had ever heard him say without interruption, but mainly because she couldn't remember him speaking with such authority and insight. He was an expert when it came to technology and new gadgets, of course . . . but serial killers? When Billy noticed that Vanja had stopped, he turned back; even though he couldn't see her eyes behind the sunglasses, he could tell that she was surprised.

'What?' he said.

'You've been reading up on this.'

'Yes, and?'

'Nothing.' There was something in Billy's voice that told Vanja she shouldn't go any further, and that she definitely shouldn't joke about this. Not right now, anyway.

'We'll keep an eye on him until we get the results of his DNA sample,' she went on. They got in the car and closed the doors. Vanja fastened her seatbelt as Billy started the engine.

'So who's the girl, by the way?'

'What girl?'

'The girl you went to the theatre with.'

'Nobody.'

Which meant it was definitely somebody. Vanja smiled to herself. She would get the details out of him during the short trip home.

Polhemsgatan. Again. Sebastian was sitting in the café where he could call himself a regular customer by now. At his favourite table, the one with the best view of his former workplace. Riksmord. Which was now her workplace. He was on his third cup of coffee, and he looked once more at the white plastic clock on the wall. He cursed himself. He cursed Stefan, who had got him to go all the way to Frescati to see a woman who hated him, as it turned out. He should have stayed in the café instead. Waited for her. It would have cost less.

He needed to see her.

Here in the café on Polhemsgatan he felt almost comfortable. The closer he was to his former workplace, the safer he felt. Here he didn't need to hide himself quite so carefully. There were several reasons why he should be here. If Vanja or anyone else saw him, he could always say that he was visiting. That he was waiting for a former colleague. That he had a meeting which had been cancelled. If they didn't buy that, he could always change tactics and claim that he was there because he wanted them to take him back. They would believe that.

Not that Torkel would ever do it. Not after Västerås.

But it would be logical. They would understand why he was sitting here with his cup of coffee, staring over at the concrete-grey building. It would be considerably more difficult to explain his presence if Vanja spotted him on the hill outside her apartment.

The big hand on the plastic clock had moved half a circuit, and was now showing five twenty-five. There were no other customers left in the café; the young couple who seemed to have relationship problems had disappeared without Sebastian noticing, and the older lady who he suspected was probably the owner had removed the ready-made sandwiches from the chilled counter.

Sebastian looked out of the window again. At the concrete-grey facade. Failed to find what he was looking for. Suspected it might be time to make a move. The question was what to do now? He didn't want to go back to his apartment and the debris of his other life, and he didn't know if he had the nerve to go back to the familiar spot outside her building. It was too dangerous. From a statistical point of view, the danger of discovery increased each time he went there. But he had to do something. Something to ease the impatience and the irritation. He had no intention of seeing the woman from yesterday again, otherwise she would have been the simplest alternative. Ellinor Bergkvist. There was something about the way she had tried to keep him there in the morning, constantly wanting to know more and more, that had annoyed him. That and the fact that she had held his hand. There were limits when it came to intimacy.

Sebastian took out his frustration on the woman on the till.

'The coffee's crap,' he said, staring at her.

'I can make a fresh pot,' she suggested.

'Go to hell,' he said, and stormed out.

That was probably the end of his stint as a regular customer, he thought as he walked out into the warm summer's evening. But he could always find somewhere else.

If there was one thing there was no shortage of in Stockholm, it was cafés.

And women.

★ ★ ★

After a few brief but failed attempts in hotel bars, trying to find someone with whom to finish off a bad day, Sebastian was on the verge of giving up. By this time even the Royal Library was closed. The ostentatious building in Humlegården was one of his favourite places when it came to fishing for female company. His technique was simple. Find a central seat in the big reading room. Borrow some books; it was important to take along a few copies of his own work and to make sure they were clearly visible. Then he would sit down and begin to struggle with a new text, battling to find the right words, and at the appropriate moment he would turn to a woman who happened to be passing: 'Excuse me, but I'm working on a new book, and I wondered if you might just have a look at this sentence.' If he played his cards right, they were soon partaking of a glass of wine in the Hotel Anglais next door.

Sebastian was beginning to get annoyed with himself as he ambled aimlessly through the heat of the city; nothing he did seemed to work these days. He was getting crosser with every step. Positively furious.

Why the fuck did everything have to be this way?

Why the fuck did nothing ever turn out the way he wanted?

He ought to hit back at everything and everyone. Ring Trolle and ask him to dig as deep as he could. Drill right down into the lives of those perfect people until he finally reached the shit. Anna Eriksson and Valdemar Lithner were to blame for all of it. He ought to check out Anna too. Perhaps she was the weak link, the fissure that could make their perfect middle-class facade crack open. Surely he would be able to find some dirt on her. She wasn't exactly a stranger to secrets and lies. Vanja didn't even know the truth about her own father. No doubt Anna justified this to herself by claiming it was in Vanja's best interests. But who had given her the right to decide? Who said she could play God? He wanted to be close to his daughter, but right now that seemed to mean at least a couple of hundred metres away. As if he'd been issued with some kind of restraining order. He stopped. He would ask Trolle to widen the search. Take a look at Anna Eriksson. Sebastian took out his mobile, then put it away again. Why call? He turned around and headed for the nearest taxi rank. After all, he had nothing better to do. Trolle lived in Skärholmen.

Trolle was a person you could trust.

He would understand.

He had lost his own family.

Billy was sitting on the sofa with his iPad, surfing the net. Maya was in the shower. Billy was hoping they could go out and eat when she'd finished.

They had been together since midsummer. An old school friend of Billy's had a place on Djurö out in the archipelago, and it was the third year Billy had been invited to celebrate with them. This year another friend was there, along with his sister. Maya Reding-Hedberg. They ended up sitting next to one another at the traditional pickled herring lunch, and they stayed there all evening and most of the night. They had been together ever since, and saw each other nearly every day.

In spite of this he hadn't said anything about Maya on the way home from Forskarbacken when Vanja tried to pump him for details. He usually told Vanja everything. Or most things. Sometimes he felt as if they were more like brother and sister than colleagues, but this time he held back, for the simple reason that he was fairly sure Vanja wouldn't like Maya.

She was a life coach.

Vanja had many good points, but she was such a high achiever that she found it difficult to cope with people who didn't make the most of their lives. On their own. It was one thing to improve your education, to go on courses, attend lectures, set goals, but she regarded it as a sign of inherent weakness and spinelessness if someone needed help to find their motivation and achieve results. If you didn't know what you wanted, then you didn't want it enough – that was her mantra. If you had real problems you went to a qualified psychologist, not some half-baked New Age character with a diploma who provided encouragement at a thousand kronor an hour.

No, Vanja wouldn't like Maya.

Not that he needed Vanja's approval, but it was simpler if she didn't know anything. That meant he could avoid the gibes, the ironic little comments. This was particularly important now, when he had actually started making a serious attempt to change his situation within the team.

It had begun with Maya asking him if he was happy in his work. A simple question, a simple answer. Yes, he was. He couldn't imagine a better place to work or better colleagues. As time went by, they had talked more. She was interested in what he did, what his role was. A lot of people just wanted to hear the gory details of an exciting murder enquiry, but Maya wasn't like that. No, she was interested in the job itself. In him. That was something he liked about her, the fact that she could make him talk. So he started to tell her about his work. About what he did each day. He kept it practical and concrete. Afterwards she had looked at him with a slight furrow in her brow.

'It sounds to me as if you're more of an IT technician than a detective.'

That had hit home. He became more conscious of the tasks he was given. Checking police records. Downloads. Searches.

The more he became aware of it, the more he realised that his role within the investigations was increasingly that of a kind of advanced secretary rather than an investigative police officer. He talked to Maya about it, and she suggested that he should take some time to think about where he was going. And have the courage to listen to the answer. The answer was that he didn't know. He'd never even thought about it.

He went to work.

He enjoyed it.

He went home.

He was able to make use of his ability to create structure by building timelines, and by gathering and collating information from every imaginable source, but was he using his full potential? No, he couldn't say that he was. It was difficult to assert himself within the team. Torkel Höglund was one of the most highly qualified police officers in Sweden, and both Vanja and Ursula were in the top three — if not number one — in their respective fields. But he didn't need to reach that level. He hadn't said so to Maya, but if he were to be perfectly honest he didn't really think

73

he had what it took; however, he could certainly become a more equal member of the team. He had already started working on it.

Maya emerged from the bathroom wearing his dressing gown, with a towel wound around her hair. She sat down beside him on the sofa.

'Have you decided what we're going to do?' she asked, giving him a kiss and nestling into his shoulder.

'I'm hungry.'

'Me too. Then there's a concert in Vitaberg Park tonight. Eight o'clock.'

Vitaberg Park. Concert. Summer's evening. Some folksy troubadour, if he wasn't very much mistaken. Very nice if you were over seventy-five. Billy decided to pretend he hadn't heard her.

'We could go and see a film,' he suggested instead.

'It's summer.'

'That's not an answer.'

'It's nicer to be outdoors.'

'It's cooler indoors.'

For a second Maya seemed to be weighing cooler against nicer; eventually she nodded. 'Okay, but in that case I want to choose the film.'

'You choose such boring films.'

'I choose good films.'

'You choose films that get good reviews. It's not the same thing.'

She raised her head and looked at him. He had given in last week when Cinematek started its summer season of French new wave films. So this time it had better be spaceships or robots or whatever it was he wanted to see.

She shrugged. 'Okay, you can choose the film, but in that case I'm picking the restaurant.'

'Deal.'

'Go on then, book the ticket with your new little toy.' She tapped the iPad on his knee.

'It's not new and it's not a toy.'

'If you say so . . .'

She got up, bent down and kissed him on the mouth before going into his bedroom to get dressed. Billy watched her go with a smile on his face.

She was good for him.

That would do for today.

Thomas Haraldsson switched off the computer. A while ago one of the electricity companies had run an advertising campaign claiming that if everyone switched off their electrical appliances instead of merely leaving them on standby, it would be possible to heat the three largest cities in Sweden with the energy saved. Or maybe it was to do with providing lighting. And it might have been three houses. Three houses in the three largest cities, maybe that was it. No, that sounded a bit complicated. He couldn't really remember, to tell the truth, but anyway it would save electricity, save resources. That was important; the earth's resources were not inexhaustible. He had a child on the way. There had to be something left for him. Or her. So he switched off the computer.

He got up, pushed in his chair and was just getting ready to leave when he noticed the file on Edward Hinde, which was still lying on his desk. He stopped. Riksmord were interested, and they would be back. It wouldn't do any harm to read up on Hinde, but he probably wouldn't have time tonight. He glanced at the clock. Jenny would have dinner ready at eight. Rigatoni with minced lamb. Some celebrity chef had cooked it on TV, and it had been a regular feature at home ever since. The first time Jenny made it Haraldsson had said he liked it, and he didn't have the heart to tell the truth now. Jenny had done the necessary shopping after work, but after she got home she had developed a craving for liquorice ice cream, and had asked Haraldsson to call in at Statoil on the way home. Perhaps he would rent a DVD; they would have time to watch a film before it got too late. But in that case he definitely wouldn't have time to read up on Hinde.

Decisions, decisions.

He looked at the clock again. Forty-five minutes to get home. Fifty-five if he stopped to pick up the ice cream and a film. That gave him half an hour before he needed to set off. It certainly wouldn't do any harm to have some personal knowledge of Hinde by the next time Riksmord turned up. Reports and psychological assessments were all very well, but after all he did know quite a lot about criminals, and would be able to make a valid contribution. Perhaps he could get Hinde to reveal something in a confidential, private conversation that he wouldn't be prepared to give away in a standard interview with Riksmord. After all, Haraldsson wouldn't be there as a police officer, but more as a fellow human being. After one more glance at the clock he decided to make a quick unscheduled visit to the secure wing.

Edward Hinde had been surprised when the guards came to fetch him from his cell just before half past six. As a general rule nothing happened after six, when dinner was served. He had twenty minutes to eat, then the tray was collected, and after that he was alone until the wake-up call at six thirty the following morning. Twelve hours with his books and his thoughts. Every day. Weekdays and weekends. Uneventful hours which over the years had become half his life.

To be fair, not much happened during the other half of the day either. After breakfast he was allowed twenty minutes in the washroom, then an hour in the exercise yard. Alone. Back to his cell for lunch, followed by an hour in the library, then another hour in the yard. This second hour was optional, and if he preferred to do so, he could stay in the library. He usually chose to stay. The washroom again, then back to his cell to wait for dinner.

Every other week he had an appointment with a psychologist. An hour each time. Edward had met many over the years, and the one thing they all had in common was that they bored him. At the beginning of his stay in Lövhaga he had said what they wanted to hear, but now he didn't even bother doing that. None of them really seemed to care anyway. Fourteen years without any discernible progress dampened the enthusiasm of the most persistent soul. The latest incarnation didn't even appear to have read his predecessor's notes. And yet the visits continued. He must not only be punished. He must be rehabilitated.

Become a better person.

Routines and pointless activities. These made up his days. His life. With few deviations. But this evening something had happened. He was collected from his cell by two guards and taken to one of the visiting rooms. It was a long time since he had been there. How many years? Three? Four? More? He couldn't remember. At any rate, the room looked exactly the same as it had done then. Bare walls. A fine-meshed grille covering windows made of shatter-proof glass. Two chairs on either side of a table that was fixed to the floor. Two metal loops screwed to the surface of the table. The guards sat him down on one of the uncomfortable chairs, then attached his hands to the metal loops with handcuffs. Then they left the room, leaving Edward sitting there. He would soon find out who wanted to talk to him, so there was no point in speculating. Instead he tried to think of who he had met the last time he was shackled to this particular table.

He hadn't come up with the answer by the time he heard the door open and someone walk in. Edward resisted the impulse to turn around. He sat there motionless, staring straight ahead. There was no reason to give the guest the impression that he was eagerly awaited. The footsteps behind him fell silent. The person who had come in had stopped and was looking at him, presumably. Edward knew what the visitor could see. A skinny little man, no more than a hundred and seventy centimetres tall. Thin hair to just below his collar, too thin to be as long as it was, at least if you had any interest in wanting to look good. He was wearing the same clothes as all the inmates on the secure wing: soft cotton trousers and a plain, long-sleeved cotton sweater. When the visitor moved around the table he would see watery blue eyes behind rimless spectacles. Pale, slightly sunken cheeks with a few days' stubble. A man who looked older than his fifty-five years.

The man who had come in was moving again. Edward was sure it was a man. The footsteps and the lack of any kind of perfume were strong indicators. He was proved right when a small, very ordinary man sat down opposite him.

'Good evening. My name is Thomas Haraldsson, and I am the new governor here.'

Edward's gaze travelled slowly down from the window to the man opposite, and he looked him in the eye for the first time.

'Edward Hinde. Pleased to meet you. You're my third.'

'I'm sorry?'

'Governor. You're my third.'

'Right . . .'

The bare room fell silent. The only sound was the faint hum of the air-conditioning system. Nothing from the corridor, nothing from outside. Edward kept his eyes fixed on the new governor, convinced that he wouldn't have to be the one to break the silence.

'I just thought I'd drop by and say hello,' Haraldsson said with a nervous smile.

Hinde smiled back politely. 'That was nice of you.'

Silence once more. Haraldsson shuffled on his chair. Edward sat motionless and stared at his visitor. No one ever just dropped by to say hello. The man opposite him wanted something. Hinde didn't know what it was yet, but if he sat still and didn't speak, he would soon find out.

'Are you happy here?' Haraldsson asked, in a tone of voice which might have been appropriate if Hinde had just left home and moved into his first apartment. Edward had to suppress a laugh. He looked at the patently insecure man in front of him. The first governor had been a hard bastard, two years from retirement when Hinde arrived. He made it perfectly clear to Edward from the start that he had no intention of putting up with any nonsense. By nonsense he meant anything that didn't involve Hinde going exactly where he was told to go, speaking when he was permitted to speak, and giving up any attempt at independent thought. Hinde had spent a great deal of time in solitary confinement. He had barely glimpsed the second governor, who had stayed for twelve years. They had never spoken, as far as he could recall. But this one, this Thomas Haraldsson, could well be worth getting to know better. He unleashed a disarming smile.

'Yes, thank you. And how are you getting on?'

'Well, it's only my third day, but so far so . . .'

Silence again. But the nervous man opposite seemed to like meaningless small talk, so Edward deviated from his strategy of allowing the other person to lead the conversation, and smiled at Haraldsson once more. 'What's your wife's name?'

'What?'

Edward nodded at Haraldsson's left hand, which was lying on top of the right on the table. 'The ring. I noticed you were married. But perhaps you're one of those modern men who have a male partner?'

'No, no, not at all.' Haraldsson waved his hands defensively. 'I'm not . . .' He stopped. What made Hinde think that? Where had that come from? Haraldsson had never heard anyone say he looked gay. Never.

'Jenny, my wife's name is Jenny. Jenny Haraldsson.'

Edward smiled to himself. There was no better way of finding out about someone's wife than to suggest that the person in question might not be straight.

'Children?'

'First one on the way.'

'How lovely. Boy or girl?'

'We don't know.'

'So it's going to be a surprise.'

'Yes.'

'I've never killed a pregnant woman.'

Haraldsson suddenly felt a little unsure of himself. So far things had gone well. An initial contact, a chat about this and that, getting Hinde to lower his guard before gradually leading the conversation to Riksmord. But Hinde's last comment had confused Haraldsson, and frightened him a little. Was Hinde saying that he couldn't imagine killing a pregnant woman, that this would be a step too far even for him, or was he saying that he'd just never had the opportunity? Haraldsson felt himself shudder. He really didn't want to know. Time to steer things in the direction he wanted.

'Riksmord want to talk to you,' he said, keeping his tone of voice as normal and noncommittal as possible.

There.

The real point of this visit.

For the first time Edward looked genuinely interested. He straightened up in his chair, and his gaze was alert. Penetrating.

'Are they here now?'

'No, but they'll be here in a day or two.'

'What do they want?'

'They didn't say. Any ideas?'

Hinde ignored the question. 'They want to talk to me.'

'Yes. Why do you think that might be?'

'Who's coming?'

'Their names are Vanja Lithner and Billy Rosén.'

'And they're happy for me to know all this?'

Haraldsson was taken aback; he hesitated, thought about it. Maybe not . . . His plan had been to tell Hinde that Riksmord were on their way in the hope that Hinde would reveal why they were interested in him. If he knew. So that Haraldsson could be of some help to Riksmord. Once a cop, always a cop. But now he had the feeling that things hadn't quite gone according to plan. Still, there was no need for Riksmord to find out about that.

'I'm not actually sure,' he replied, looking serious. 'I thought you had the right to know, but perhaps you don't need to mention it to them when they turn up. I mean, it's not necessary to tell them you knew they were coming. That I told you. After all, you know what cops can be like.' He ended with a broad smile, an us–against–them smile, as if they faced a common enemy.

Edward smiled back. He'd smiled more in the last few minutes than in the past fourteen years. 'Yes, I know exactly what cops can be like. Don't worry, I won't say a word.'

'Thanks.'

'But you owe me a favour.'

Haraldsson couldn't work out whether the shackled man was joking or not. He was still smiling, but something in his eyes suggested that he was deadly serious. Haraldsson shuddered again, unable to hide it this time, and got to his feet.

'I must go . . . Nice to meet you.'

'And you.'

Haraldsson walked over to the door and knocked. He glanced back at Hinde, who was once again gazing at the window. After a few seconds the door was opened from the outside, and Haraldsson left the impersonal visiting room with the feeling that Hinde had got more out of the conversation than he had. Not a good thing, perhaps. But not a disaster either, he persuaded himself. Riksmord would never know that they had spoken.

He would go and buy some ice cream and rent a DVD.

Hinde wouldn't be a problem.

At first Trolle refused to open the door. Sebastian could hear him moving around inside the apartment, but he had to ring the doorbell for more than five minutes before his former colleague eventually opened the door a crack. A bloodshot eye stared out through the narrow gap. The apartment behind the face was dark, and it was difficult to make out any details. A stuffy, dusty smell combined with old rubbish drifted past Trolle and out into the stairwell.

'What do you want?'

'Were you asleep?'

'No. What do you want?'

'I want to talk to you.'

'I'm busy.'

Trolle made a big show of trying to close the door, but Sebastian managed to insert the toe of his shoe in the gap just in time. It occurred to him that he had never done this before, tried to stop a door from shutting by using his foot. He had seen it in films hundreds of times, but had never done it himself. Oh well, there was a first time for everything.

'You're going to like what I have to say.' Sebastian paused briefly before deciding to sweeten the bait a little more. 'I've got money.'

The gap widened a fraction, and the light from the stairwell illuminated Trolle's face. He really had aged. He had to be just under sixty, but he looked ten years older. His hair was uncombed and peppered with grey, he was unshaven, skinny, and gave off an acrid stench of tobacco and alcohol. Trolle had always drunk, even when he was working, and now, fifteen years later, with neither a job nor a family, alcohol seemed to be his only companion. He was dressed in a scruffy white T-shirt and a pair of boxer shorts. His feet were bare, his toenails yellow, gnarled and too long. He hadn't just aged. He had fallen into a decline.

82

'I don't care about money.'

'Maybe not, but it does no harm to have a little bit.'

'So how much have you got, then?'

Sebastian dug out his wallet and showed Trolle all the money he had: a few hundred-kronor notes and a twenty.

'I don't do it for the money,' Trolle proclaimed as soon as the notes were in his hand.

'I know that.' Sebastian nodded. Unless Trolle had changed completely over the past few years, this was true. He didn't do anything for the money. Admittedly he had never said no to a bit of extra cash on the side, not even when he was a police officer, but the remuneration had never been his driving force.

That had been the pleasure of messing with people's lives.

Ruining things for them.

Planning, waiting, gathering information, directing the course of the action and then finally making their lives hell.

That was Trolle's real driving force. The money was just a bonus.

'Can I come in?' Sebastian asked, putting his wallet away.

'So you've changed your mind?' Trolle cackled, his laughter echoing in the stairwell, but he still didn't open the door. Instead he pressed his face against the gap so that it filled the space. 'You need old Trolle after all . . .'

Sebastian nodded and leaned forward so that the conversation could be conducted with a little more discretion.

'Yes, but I don't want to discuss it here.'

'You never used to be shy. You can stay right where you are.' Trolle fired off a broad, almost challenging wolfish grin. Sebastian looked at him wearily. Trolle had always been difficult, but the years and the alcohol appeared to have made him even worse. For a brief, terrifying second Sebastian saw himself standing there in the doorway. If he had carried on drinking. If he had chosen the mind-numbing drugs, the ones he had tried the year after the tsunami. If he hadn't had Stefan. If he hadn't found Vanja. Suddenly everything became much more important. He was only four 'ifs' away from being Trolle Hermansson. A man who had nothing left to lose.

'I want you to go all the way. Find out whatever you can. About the whole family, including the mother. Her name is Anna Eriksson . . .'

'I know what her name is,' Trolle interrupted. He took a deep and slightly rattling breath and ran his hand over the stubble on his chin as he appeared to consider Sebastian's offer. 'Okay. But in that case you have to tell me why.'

'Why what?' Sebastian suspected that he knew the answer, but hoped he was wrong.

'What's so special about this family? Why are you following the daughter? She's a bit young, isn't she – even for you?'

'You wouldn't believe me.'

'Try me.'

'No!'

Trolle met Sebastian's determined gaze and realised this was non-negotiable. Oh well, with a bit of luck he would be able to work it out along the way.

'I used to like you, Sebastian. I was probably the only one who did. When you rang I said yes because I used to like you.' Trolle fixed his bloodshot eyes on Sebastian with what could be interpreted as a hurt, pleading look. 'Friends tell each other things.'

'You didn't say yes because it was me. You said yes because you thought you might be able to fuck things up for somebody. Because you get a kick out of doing that. I know you, Trolle, so don't even try. Are you going to do it, or not?'

Trolle laughed out loud, more naturally this time.

'You don't like me. You're here because you haven't got anyone else.'

'Same applies to you.'

The two men looked at one another in silence. Then Trolle held out his hand to Sebastian, who took it after a moment's hesitation. It was damp. Cold. But the grip was firm. Strong.

'Even if I don't do it for the money, I don't work for free.'

'How much do you want?'

'A thousand. You can have a discount because you're such a loser.'

With that Trolle slammed the door shut. His voice came from inside the apartment: 'Call me in a few days.'

Sebastian turned and slowly walked down the two flights of stairs.

Annette Willén loved these evenings. She began to prepare herself mentally as early as three o'clock. Always the same routine. First a long hot shower; she washed her hair, and scrubbed her body with that apricot-scented exfoliating soap she had bought from The Body Shop. Then she allowed herself to dry naturally for a little while in the warm bathroom before applying body lotion to her slightly damp skin. She had read somewhere that this locked in the moisture and had a deeper softening effect. Then she put on her dressing gown and wandered barefoot into the combined living room and bedroom. She could have moved into the apartment's only real bedroom, but it was her son's, and even though he had moved out, she didn't want to make it hers. The room was her last hope that he might come back one day.

Need it again.

Need her again.

Moving his things would make his departure all too definitive and real.

Annette opened the wardrobe and began carefully removing blouses, skirts, dresses and trousers. Once she had even taken out the suit she had bought for that interview she didn't attend. But it stood out like an overdressed and under-confident dinner guest, and after its brief guest appearance long ago, it was always left hanging there alone. She placed the various items of clothing on the bed, and when there was no more room she used the three-seater sofa or the coffee table. Then she positioned herself in the middle of the room and drank in the different colours, styles and fabrics spread out all around her. She was in control. She might be insignificant out there, beyond the confines of the apartment, but here and now she was the one in charge. It was her life that lay in front of her, the life she would soon begin to taste hungrily, to try out.

When she felt ready she went into the hallway, lifted down the mirror, carried it into the living room and propped it up against the wall. Took a couple of steps backwards and looked at herself as she stood there, freshly showered, wearing the pink, slightly too short dressing gown her son had given her on her fortieth birthday. Every time, she was struck by how old she had become. It wasn't just her hair that had grown thinner and duller, it was her entire self. She had given up standing naked in front of the mirror a long time ago. It was too depressing to see herself as time's depredations became too obvious. She wasn't ashamed of her body. She had always had womanly curves, and she had never had a problem with her weight. No, she was still petite; she had good legs, and her breasts were still firm and rounded, but there was something about the way her skin grew paler and less elastic with each passing year. As if it were slowly shrinking, like a peach that has been left in the sun for a little too long, regardless of how many exfoliating, anti-ageing and anti-wrinkle products she used. It frightened her, particularly as she knew that time had barely begun its journey with her. It had much left to do, and one day she would stand there unable to recognise herself. And just when she was about to start living.

Properly. For real.

She started trying on clothes in order to escape from her thoughts. Who did she want to be today?

She could be the carefree girl in jeans with an oversized top, or the artistic type in the short black dress made of slightly too daring lace. Annette loved being that girl, particularly when she was brave enough to wear the darker lipstick. She thought the woman in black would be fantastic if only she had the courage to dye her hair black, but she couldn't do it. And the outfit kind of demanded it. So off it came as usual, to be replaced by the more sedate, businesslike white blouse with the dark skirt. She too was a woman Annette felt comfortable with. Timeless in a way she longed to achieve. But she also demanded too much. Too much hair. A better figure. Better posture. Better everything. In a while, perhaps. Soon. Clothes came off and went on. Annette loved meeting the different identities that had been waiting for her inside the dark recesses of the wardrobe. Women stepped forward in the mirror. New women, better women, exciting women. Never

Annette. Always someone else. That was the problem. However much she loved meeting those women standing in front of her, she never dared allow them to take that step out of the mirror. The certainty and the game were gradually replaced by fear and second thoughts. Her choices became more limited, more cowardly. The routine took up half the day, and as usual she went from being overdressed and colourful to diminishing herself and her clothing.

In the end she finished up with the three choices that always remained.

The black blouse. The white blouse. Or the polo-neck sweater.

Always with jeans.

Stefan knew exactly where to look for Sebastian. Outside the police station or Vanja's apartment were the two locations that constantly recurred in their discussion, so he decided to start there. It was after eight, so the police station seemed less likely. A quick call to directory enquiries gave Vanja Lithner's address as Sandhamnsgatan 44, and Stefan allowed the car's sat nav to guide him there. He was running out of time. The group session was due to start at nine, and he was actually going against his own principles at this point. The whole thing was supposed to be based on free will. The person in question should choose to participate. That was important. But Sebastian was different. It was as if the knowledge almost stood in his way. As if he deliberately made the wrong decisions. Stefan had come across this kind of patient before. Usually he had been forced to give up. Let them go. But Sebastian was his friend, in some way. However complex their relationship might be. And if Stefan let him go, who else would try to catch Sebastian when he was in freefall?

Stefan parked his car a short distance from number 44 and set off on foot. He looked around the pleasant residential area. The buildings were arranged in rows, not too close together, but with due deference to the countryside on their doorstep. In front of the entrance to number 44 a cycle rack housed several adults' and children's bicycles. Stefan stopped and looked around, trying to work out where he would position himself if he wanted to spy on an apartment a couple of floors up without anyone spotting him. As far from the road and as well hidden as possible, he decided. Behind the block he saw a hill covered in deciduous trees. Leafy bushes provided plenty of cover, and the fact that he had made the right choice became clear when Sebastian Bergman suddenly peered out from behind the biggest tree with a horrified expression on his face.

'What the fuck are you doing here?' he barked. Stefan almost burst out laughing at the sight of the man staring at him through the trees, looking absolutely furious. He reminded Stefan of a teenager who had just been caught having a cigarette on the sly.

'I wanted to see you in your new home environment.'

'Very funny. Fuck off before someone sees you.'

Stefan shook his head and made himself even more noticeable by planting himself a short distance away from Sebastian on the open, grassy area.

'Not unless you come with me. Your group therapy starts in half an hour.'

Sebastian stared at him, his expression livid. 'Aren't you supposed to stick to certain rules and regulations? What happened to people doing things on a voluntary basis?'

'That doesn't apply to middle-aged men lurking around behind trees, spying on young women they claim are their daughters. Coming?'

Sebastian shook his head. Inside he was ice-cold. His world was beginning to seem more and more fragile. He felt naked and embarrassed, and would have liked nothing more than to go on the offensive. At the same time there was something about the man standing in front of him that suddenly enabled Sebastian to see himself through someone else's eyes, and however he manipulated the truth, the answer was always the same.

He had been to see Trolle.

He had come here.

He was lost.

'Please, Stefan. Just go. Leave me in peace.'

Stefan stepped into the leafy little world where Sebastian was hiding and took his hand.

'I'm not here to stress you out. I'm not here to make you feel bad. I'm here for your sake. If you really want me to go, I will. But deep down you know I'm right. You have to stop this.'

Sebastian looked at his therapist and quietly withdrew his hand.

'I'm not joining a group. I do have some pride left.'

'Really?' Stefan gazed at him gravely. 'Look around you, Sebastian. Look where we are.'

Sebastian didn't try to come up with an answer.

Even he couldn't find a way out of this one.

'I mean, I said last week I was going to try to clear out the garage so I could get the car in there. Chuck out a load of stuff. Do you think I actually did it?' The man opposite Sebastian whom the others called Stig had been talking for more than ten minutes. However, it seemed as if he was nowhere near finished. He just went on and on, as if his huge body contained an infinite number of words.

'I haven't got the energy. I can't do anything. Just washing up after a meal or taking out the rubbish is a major undertaking. And you know how it is when you get into that state. You get nowhere. Nowhere . . .'

Sebastian nodded. Not because he agreed – he had written off the man as uninteresting and stopped listening after thirty seconds – but because somewhere in the back of his mind he thought that if he nodded in agreement, perhaps the fat lump would realise he'd made his point, and that he didn't need to come up with more examples in order to prove his total lack of initiative to the group. This motley collection of damaged individuals who, according to Stefan, might be able to save him. Four women and two men, not counting Stefan and himself. Stig took a deep breath and was about to continue his lengthy diatribe when Stefan jumped in. Sebastian felt a great wave of gratitude, even if he was still annoyed with him.

'But you've been diagnosed with mild depression, Stig. Have you been to the doctor for your medication?'

Stig shook his head, and for a second it seemed as if he might leave it there. But then he took one of those deep breaths that Sebastian had already learned to loathe after only fifteen minutes.

The breath became a sound.

The sound became words.

Too many words.

'The thing is, I don't want to take a whole load of tablets. I did try once, and I had this reaction . . .'

Sebastian shut out Stig's babble with a yawn. How could they stand it, the other people sitting in silence around him? Did they share Sebastian's frustration, or were they just waiting for their opportunity to take a deep breath and then talk about their own uninteresting lives for far too long? Surely they couldn't seriously care about each other's banal problems? Sebastian tried to reach Stefan with an angry, pleading look, but Stefan seemed fully occupied in listening to Stig. What saved him was the slim, almost invisible woman opposite him, dressed in a white blouse and jeans. She leaned forward and, in what was little more than a whisper, interrupted Stig's monotonous drone.

'But if it helps you to start doing things, then perhaps you should give the medication a try. There's no shame in getting help that way.'

The rest of the group nodded and made noises of agreement; Sebastian couldn't decide whether it was because they were pleased that someone else had stepped into the limelight, or because they actually agreed with what she said. Sebastian looked at her. She was probably somewhere in her forties, slender, with fine, dark hair and discreet make-up. Simply dressed, constantly fiddling nervously with a necklace that was far too big. She looked at each of the others in turn before continuing. Sebastian got the feeling that she wanted to be seen, but wasn't quite brave enough to step forward. Oppressed too many times? Used to being silenced? He gave her an encouraging smile, trying to catch her eye, but suddenly she was looking everywhere but at him.

'I recognise myself in your situation,' she said. 'You feel as if everything is just piling up, that you can't get anything done.'

Sebastian continued to smile at her, having realised all at once that he might get more than he had thought out of this evening.

'Exactly, Annette,' Stefan agreed. 'If you're stuck, then you have to find the courage to try something new. That's certainly what you did.'

Annette nodded and carried on talking. Sebastian watched her grow with the praise, daring to take up more space, to share her experiences. They know each other well, she and Stefan, he thought as he listened to her. She was a stayer. A patient who had been in therapy for so long that she had started to sound like the therapist. Stefan's encouraging nods confirmed his theory. Invisible little Annette had been seeing Stefan for a long time. Sebastian smiled to himself. Stefan cared about his patients. He too had experienced Stefan's weakness a couple of hours ago, when he had come looking for Sebastian under a tree outside Sandhamnsgatan 44.

He cared just a little too much to be a true professional.

A little too much to be really effective.

Invisible Annette was definitely one of the patients he cared about. Sebastian could see that from the interplay between them. He smiled at the dark-haired woman again. Perfect. He knew exactly how he would show Stefan that it was not possible to put Sebastian Bergman into group therapy and go unpunished.

★ ★ ★

The group had been sitting in a circle for seventy-five minutes when it was finally time for the obligatory coffee before they broke up. Stefan had summarised the evening with a few well-chosen clichés about being there for each other and the beneficial effects of social interaction, trying to convey to Sebastian with a meaningful look that he had made no contribution on any level. Sebastian had responded with a yawn. When they got up he quickly moved over to the coffee table and the woman. Stefan became bogged down in a discussion with Stig and a younger man who insisted on referring to alcohol as 'booze' and his wife as 'the missus' or 'she who must be obeyed'. Perfect company for Stefan, Sebastian thought as he looked over at Annette; she had walked straight past the coffee table without taking anything, and seemed to be on her way out. Sebastian hurried after her.

Annette was heading for the exit, unsure whether or not to stay for coffee. She normally did; she usually thought it was the perfect end to the evening. She was the one who had been coming to these meetings the longest. She was important. Stefan had once called her a real professional when it came to group therapy, and even though the words had been spoken in jest, she had carried them with her for several weeks.

A real professional. Annette.

No one else had ever said anything like that. This was her place, she knew it. When she was sitting in the circle she was brave enough to step forward, to be seen, to play her part, and during coffee afterwards she loved to fish for comments from the other participants and to give positive feedback on their contributions that evening. But tonight was different. Because of the new man, the one who had sat opposite her. The way he looked at her. It was as if he could see right through her; she couldn't describe it any other way. When she began to speak he listened, really looked at her. Not in a condescending way; it was more of an erotic experience, as if he were undressing her, although intellectually rather than sexually. She couldn't put the feeling into words. She'd never experienced anything like it.

He could see her. Properly.

It was both exciting and frightening, and when Stefan had brought the evening to a close, Annette had decided to go straight home. But she knew that she wasn't moving towards the exit quite as quickly as she should be. In her peripheral vision she could see the man coming towards her. Confident. Purposeful. She realised that he wanted to meet her. She had to be ready. She would regret it if she didn't at least try to say a few words. He hadn't said anything all evening. But now he was speaking.

'Aren't you staying for coffee?'

She liked his voice.

'I don't know. I . . .' Annette thought quickly. She didn't want to sound dismissive, but nor did she wish to seem weak and indecisive. She did want to stay for a coffee, but how could she say so? She was practically halfway out of the door when he stopped her.

'Come on, surely you've got time for one cup and a cake beautifully encased in plastic?'

He saved her. Realised she was on her way. Persuaded her to stay. It would almost have been rude to say no. She smiled at him gratefully.

'Well, yes, I suppose so.'

They walked back to the coffee table together.

'Sebastian Bergman,' said the man by her side, holding out his hand. She took it, clumsily she thought, but his hand was warm and his smile even warmer, if that were possible.

'Annette Willén. Nice to meet you.' It felt as if all her gaucheness disappeared when he held her hand for just a little too long. He looked at her, and she felt something beyond simply being seen by another person. Far beyond. He saw her as the woman she really wanted to be.

'You didn't say much this evening,' she said as he poured her a coffee.

'Did I say anything at all?' he replied, still smiling.

Annette shook her head. 'I don't think so.'

'I'm better at listening.'

'That's unusual. Coming here to listen, I mean. Most people want to talk about themselves,' Annette said, moving away from the coffee table. She didn't want to be disturbed by any of the others.

Sebastian followed. 'How long have you been part of the group?'

Annette wondered whether to tell the truth: that she couldn't really remember anymore. No, that would sound pathetic. Weak. He would get the wrong idea about her. Be quick to judge. She decided to lie.

'About six months. I got divorced, lost my job, and then my son fell in love and moved to Canada. I ended up in a kind of . . . vacuum.'

Too much too soon. He hadn't asked why she was here, just how long she'd been coming. Annette shrugged her shoulders as if to play down her problems.

'I needed to talk about things. But I'm in the process of reducing my attendance,' she said quickly. 'You have to move on, don't you?' She smiled at him. For a second Sebastian glanced over at Stefan, who was still deep in conversation with the two men. Annette suddenly got the feeling that Sebastian was already tired of her, that he was looking for a reason to make his apologies and leave, that their encounter would soon be over. She was breathing more heavily. A slight feeling of panic, the panic that came from her deepest fear: that whatever she did, however hard she tried, she was doomed to be alone forever.

But then he turned to her once more, the charming smile firmly in place.

'So why are you here?' she went on, in a tone of voice that she felt was very natural and unforced.

'Stefan thought I might get something out of it.'

'What made him think that? What's happened to you?'

Sebastian looked around before replying.

'I don't think we're quite there yet. In our relationship.'

'No?'

'No. But maybe we can get there.'

The directness of his answer surprised her. 'You mean here, in the group?'

'No, I mean somewhere else, just you and me.'

His self-confidence fascinated her. She couldn't suppress a smile as she bravely looked him in the eye. 'Are you coming on to me?'

'Maybe a little. Does it bother you?'

'Most people don't come here to meet someone.'

'Good, that means there's less competition,' he replied, taking a small but definite step towards her. She could smell his aftershave. He lowered his voice. 'But I can leave if you think I'm overstepping the boundaries of respectability.'

Annette took the risk. She touched his shoulder and realised how long it had been since she touched another person.

'No need. Just so you know, I'm a good listener too.'

'I don't doubt it. But I'm not interested in talking.'

She didn't look away this time either. His boldness gave her courage.

Sebastian nodded to Stefan as he and Annette left together.

It had been a little too easy.

But he would take it.

★ ★ ★

They started kissing after only a few minutes in the taxi. Annette's kisses were tentative. She refused to meet him with her tongue. She knew she wasn't a good kisser. And she couldn't quite bring herself to believe that the man who was caressing the back of her neck really did want her. Perhaps he would suddenly break off and look at her not with warmth and desire, but with coldness and contempt. Smile at her again, but nastily this time. Ask what she thought she could possibly give him, and supply the obvious answer: nothing. If she didn't let herself go, then she could convince herself that it was of no importance to her either. It wouldn't hurt so much when he left her. It had worked before.

95

Sebastian felt Annette stiffen as his hand moved over her body. But she didn't push him away. A sexual neurotic, he thought wearily, wondering whether he ought to make his excuses and get out of the cab. But there was something tempting about Annette. Her vulnerability turned him on; it made him forget his own weakness and fed his ego. It didn't really matter to him if she was incapable of relaxing and enjoying herself. He wasn't there for her sake. She was a distraction.

An acceptable end to a crap day.

Part of a revenge strategy.

He kissed her again.

★ ★ ★

Annette's apartment was in Liljeholmen, five minutes from the recently built shopping mall with a view over Essingeleden. Once they were home she seemed able to relax a little. The living room was a mess, with clothes strewn around everywhere. Annette apologised; she quickly cleared the bed and ran out of the room with her arms full of clothes.

'No need to tidy up on my account,' Sebastian said, sitting down on the bed and taking off his shoes.

'I wasn't expecting company,' he heard her say. He looked around the room. A perfectly ordinary living room, but with details that told him something about the occupant. First of all a fairly large single bed by the wall under the window. Sebastian had noticed another room when he walked into the apartment. Why didn't she sleep in there? She had said that she lived alone, and there was only one name on the letterbox.

The second thing was a collection of cuddly toys on the shelves. Animals of every size and colour. Teddy bears, tigers, dolphins, cats. Toys and rather too many cushions, soft blankets and throws. The whole room signalled a longing for security, a desire for a warm, kind, protective cocoon to stop cold, hard reality getting in. Sebastian saw himself in the mirror that was propped up against the wall. She had invited that cold, hard reality into her life. She just didn't know it yet.

Sebastian wondered what had happened in her life to cause such poor self-esteem and this exaggerated longing for security. Some trauma, a bad relationship, the wrong life choice, or was there something worse, an attack or an abusive relationship with a parent? He didn't know, nor did he have the energy to find out. He wanted sex and a few hours' sleep.

'Is it okay if I move the mirror?' he asked, picking it up. The thought of seeing himself having sex with her in this room almost frightened him. He would prefer it if they could slide under the covers and turn off the light before they did anything else.

'Put it in the hallway,' she said from what he suspected must be the bathroom. 'I usually move it into the living room when I'm trying on clothes.'

Sebastian carried it out and quickly found the hook on which it usually hung.

'Do you like clothes?'

Sebastian turned as he heard her voice. Different. She had put on a sexy black lace dress, with dark lipstick. She looked like a different woman. A woman you would notice.

'I love clothes,' she went on.

Sebastian nodded. 'You look good in that dress. Really good.' He meant it.

'Do you think so? It's my favourite.' She stepped forward and kissed him. With her tongue. Sebastian returned the kiss, but now she was the one seducing him. He let it happen. She took what she wanted from him. He tried to take off the dress so that he could feel her body against his, but she wanted to keep it on. He got the feeling that it was important to her to make love wearing that dress.

Ursula had reached the last few pages in her third reading of the preliminary autopsy report on Katharina Granlund when there was a knock and Robert Abrahamsson stuck his well-groomed head around the door. He was the surveillance team leader she had the least time for.

'Time you fuckers dealt with your own crap.'

Ursula looked up with an enquiring expression.

'The papers have started ringing me,' Abrahamsson went on. 'They're saying you lot aren't even answering the phone up here.'

Ursula looked crossly at Abrahamsson: his tan a fraction too perfect, his jacket a fraction too tight. She hated being interrupted, particularly by a self-satisfied peacock like Abrahamsson. Even if it was justified. She answered as curtly as she could: 'Take it up with Torkel. He deals with the press. You know that.'

'So where is he then?'

'No idea.'

Ursula went back to the report, but instead of leaving, Abrahamsson strode purposefully towards her.

'I'm sure you have a great deal to do, Ursula, but when they start ringing *me* about *your* cases, it means one of two things. Either you're not communicating with them sufficiently, or they've found an angle they want to push. In this case I suspect it's both.'

Ursula sighed wearily. She was the team member who always ignored what the newspapers wrote; she wanted to keep to a minimum any information that could influence her ability to interpret evidence rationally. And yet she understood that this wasn't great. Riksmord were very keen to avoid the murders of the three women being linked, leading to the inevitable Serial-Killer-on-the-loose-in-Stockholm headlines. Minimising the possibility of journalistic speculation was one of Torkel's strategic cornerstones. When the press started desperately searching for sensational stories, anything could happen. Particularly within the police service itself. Everything suddenly became political, and politics could be catastrophic for an investigation. That was when 'decisive' action was needed in order to 'bring home results', which could lead to officers thinking less about the quantity of evidence and more about satisfying their superiors.

'Who is it?' she asked. 'If you give me their numbers I'll make sure Torkel rings them.'

'There's only one. So far. Axel Weber from *Expressen*.'

Ursula took in the name and leaned back in her chair with an excessively happy smile on her face. 'Weber! So there's probably a third reason why he chose to ring you, wouldn't you say?'

Robert went bright red. He wagged his index finger threateningly at Ursula in a gesture that made him look like a schoolmaster from some 1950s film. 'That was a misunderstanding, as you know perfectly well. The commissioner accepted my explanation.'

'In that case, he was the only one.' Ursula leaned forward again, suddenly serious. 'You leaked information to Weber. In a murder enquiry.'

Robert looked at her defiantly. 'Think what you like. This is the twenty-first century, and we have to learn to work with the press. Particularly in complex cases.'

'Particularly if you get your picture on page seven with a story that makes you look like something of a hero for your trouble.' Ursula paused; she realised that she was on the point of being petty and cheap, but she couldn't help herself. 'I recognise the jacket, but you must have been slimmer then. You need to think about what you're shoving in your mouth these days. You know the camera adds five kilos.'

Robert unbuttoned his jacket, but she saw his eyes darken with anger. He seemed to be gathering himself for a counter-attack, but he managed to suppress the worst of his indignation and headed for the door instead.

'I just thought you ought to know.'

Ursula wasn't done yet. 'That was very kind of you, Robert. And if Weber writes anything unusually intuitive about this case, we'll know where it came from.'

'I don't know anything about your case.'

'You're here. You've seen the board.'

Robert turned and marched away. Ursula could hear his angry footsteps as he stomped down the corridor and through the glass door at the end. She got up, went over to the door and looked out to make sure he really had gone before she left the Room and took a walk through the virtually empty open-plan office. It might be nothing, but she wanted to give Torkel the opportunity to act quickly. His room was empty. His jacket was gone and his computer had been shut down. What time was it anyway? She checked her mobile: eleven twenty-five p.m. She ought to call him, but she couldn't quite bring herself to do it. It was idiotic and pathetic and ridiculous.

But she still couldn't quite bring herself to do it.

Seeing him at the station every day was one thing; working side by side was perfectly okay. But ringing him late at night . . . If she rang him at night, it was hardly ever to do with work, unless it involved a new murder or a technical breakthrough in an ongoing investigation. This wasn't on that level. She could speak to Torkel about Weber tomorrow. When she rang him at night it was because she wanted him. Wanted him to come to her hotel room, or to let her come to his. She rang when she needed him. That was why she was hesitating now. Did she need him? Recently she had begun to ask herself that question. It had been easier to withdraw from their clandestine relationship than she had thought. And at first it had actually felt quite liberating. Simpler. She focused on Mikael and cut away the other part of her life. Torkel was a professional, so it made no difference as far as the job was concerned; they still worked well together. In the beginning she could feel Torkel's eyes on her, but when she didn't respond it happened more and more infrequently, which confirmed her belief that she had made the right decision.

But she still thought about him.

More and more.

★ ★ ★

Ursula went back to the Room, gathered up the autopsy report and her things, and took the lift down to the car park. She had lost the desire to carry on working tonight. She needed to sort out this business with Weber, pass it on to Torkel so that it became his headache rather than hers. They had a clear communications strategy. One person spoke to the press. Always Torkel. Other departments had designated press officers, but Torkel had declined the offer. He wanted full control.

The fluorescent lights in the underground car park came on automatically as she opened the heavy metal door and set off towards her car, which was parked virtually on its own at this hour.

In the middle of the night, in the middle of summer.

She unlocked the car, got in, inserted the key in the ignition and turned it. The car started immediately.

She didn't want to ring Torkel. Not tonight. It was too reminiscent of the past. Of hotels in other towns. He would misinterpret it. Think she was ringing about something else. She switched off the engine. Did it really matter what he thought? He could think whatever he liked. This was work, she needed to tell him about Weber. Nothing else. She decided to text him instead. She got out her mobile and quickly keyed in a message: *Weber from Expressen trying to get hold of us. Has evidently rung several times acc. R Abrahamsson.* She pressed send and put the phone down on the passenger seat. She thought about what Mikael had said to her the other day.

It's always on your terms, Ursula. Always.

This was both true and not true. She really had tried to change. She had even broken things off with her lover.

Admittedly it hadn't been because of Mikael to begin with, but because she was angry and felt let down. But then it had become for his sake. Because he deserved it. Was that really true? She leaned back in her seat and gazed blankly at the nondescript car park. After a while the lights went out; they worked on motion sensors to save energy. Ursula sat there in the darkness; the only light came from the green emergency exit signs and the display screen on the mobile beside her, faintly illuminating the interior of the car with its pale blue glow. After a while it too went off, and she was left in darkness. Mikael's words were still with her.

On your terms.

Always on your terms.

But she really had tried to find a kind of harmony with her husband. A point where they were both dictating the terms.

Weekends away. Dinners. Bubble baths. But the truth was that those things, while superficially pleasant, romantic and relaxing, were just too shallow for her. It had been particularly striking during the last trip to Paris. They had strolled along hand in hand, talking. Gone for long walks down romantic boulevards, ambled around the charming tourist attractions and sought out romantic bistros with an out-of-date restaurant guide in their hands. All the things you were supposed to do in Paris. All the things you were supposed to do as a couple. But that wasn't her.

She was an angular creature in a soft world. A shape that didn't really fit into this thing that was called a relationship. She needed distance. She needed control. Sometimes she needed intimacy. But only sometimes. When it suited her. But then she needed it. Really needed it. And that was exactly what Mikael meant. He knew her so well.

The lights came on and shook her out of her reverie. Robert Abrahamsson entered the car park carrying his briefcase. Even the way he walked annoyed her; he moved with a conscious suppleness, as if he were modelling the latest summer collection rather than heading towards his car just before midnight in a grubby underground car park. He got into a black Saab a short distance away and drove off. Ursula waited until he had disappeared, then started her car and set off for home.

For a while Torkel wondered what to do with the text Ursula had sent him. Axel Weber was a good journalist, and if he was involved it was only a matter of time before he spotted the link between the murders. Perhaps he already had. Torkel sat down at the computer and checked to see whether there was anything on *Expressen*'s home page, but the big news was still the heat wave. He had to scroll down to the fourth article to find a report on the latest murder.

Nothing so far, then. But Weber had been trying to get hold of him. Torkel picked up his mobile. It would have been more normal to call Weber back during the day, but it was better to find out what he knew before it went to print. The journalist's number was in his directory, and he answered right away.

'Weber.'

'Hi, Torkel Höglund from Riksmord. I believe you've been trying to get hold of me.'

'That's right – good of you to call. I've just come back from a little break and . . . I see three women have been murdered.'

No small talk. Straight down to business. Torkel didn't say anything. *A little break*. That explained why Weber hadn't made the connection before.

'Within a month,' Weber went on when Torkel didn't respond.

'Yes . . .'

'In the Stockholm area, I mean. I've asked around and it seems as if it's the same perpetrator, and since Riksmord are involved, I was just wondering whether you had any comment?'

Torkel thought fast. He had two choices: to confirm Weber's suspicions, or refuse to comment. Torkel tried to avoid lying to the press unless the case demanded such a course of action. This one didn't. The fact was that he had already been toying with

103

the idea of a press conference, giving out a limited amount of information in the hope of picking up new leads. But he wanted to be better prepared, to have thought through what details they were actually going to release. He really didn't want to say too much, so he replied: 'I can't comment at this stage.'

'You don't want to confirm that you're dealing with a serial killer?'

'No.'

'Do you wish to deny it?'

'I don't want to comment at this stage.'

Torkel knew and Weber knew that his refusal to deny or comment was the same as confirmation, but no one was ever going to be able to say that Torkel had leaked information to the press. Nor did he need to. There were plenty of other police officers who were happy to do so. Not in his team, but elsewhere in the station. So many that it had become a problem when it came to interviews and dealing with witnesses. Too many people knew too much too soon.

'I will be calling a press conference first thing tomorrow morning.'

'Why?'

'Well, if you come along you'll find out.'

'I'll be there. And I'll be making use of the information I have.'

'I know.'

'Thanks for calling.'

Torkel rang off. A press conference. Tomorrow. Just as well. With Weber snapping at their heels they needed to go public in order to retain some kind of control over the flow of information. It was always a balancing act. If they waited too long to share what they knew, there could be a real backlash leading to a difficult debate on public safety, and why the police had kept quiet about the fact that a serial killer was on the loose. And yes, they needed information. He would have preferred to have a few more leads to work on before the case became public property, perhaps even highlighted a few suspects so that the attention would move the investigation forward rather than simply expand it. But that wasn't the case. They had nothing. They had got nowhere. With a bit of luck the attention might lead to something positive. Because one thing Torkel knew for sure: the day the headlines began to appear, one person would read every article, notice every comment, follow every debate: the serial killer himself. Their copycat. It might push him. Make him overconfident. And then he might make a mistake.

Wishful thinking.

Torkel closed the internet browser and stretched. It had been a hard day.

Too many questions, too few answers.

His mind wandered. To his daughters, to the summer cottage and what he should do with it now the girls were getting to an age when they soon wouldn't want to go there anymore. It was mainly Elin who protested at having to spend the final weeks of the summer holiday at the cottage, but no doubt Vilma would soon be singing from the same hymn sheet. She was a teenager now. Torkel had dreaded this moment. The moment when they started to grow up. For real. When they wanted to be with their friends and live their own lives, far away from their old dad in a summer cottage in Östergötland that was far too small. It was only natural. After all, that was the aim when you were bringing up children: to make them into independent individuals. He knew he had succeeded. But that didn't make it any easier.

Although it wasn't just that. There was no one who would want to go with him to the cottage. Or anywhere else, for that matter. Yvonne had Kristoffer. Not that he would think of asking her to spend two weeks by Lake Boren, but it made him realise with even greater clarity that he was alone. Totally alone.

Torkel got up stiffly from his desk and took a walk around his apartment. He didn't like what he saw. It was messier than usual, and in spite of the late hour he decided to tidy up. He was basically a very orderly person, but these brutal murders had taken up all his time. That was usually the way of things. When a really complicated case landed on his desk, his home went into a rapid decline. There had been some improvement when he joined Riksmord, for one very simple reason. The team worked wherever they were needed, all over Sweden. The whole point was for the national CID to have a special unit to help with complex murder investigations for which the local police didn't have the resources. This meant that Torkel was often away from Stockholm and staying in a hotel during the most intense periods, so his apartment managed to survive without descending into chaos. But not this time. This time Stockholm was at the centre of the storm, and in the worst possible way. There had been no question of tidying the apartment, but now he had a choice: clean up or try to sleep.

He decided to make a start on the kitchen. The remains of the dinner he had shared with his daughters the previous week were still on the draining board and in the sink, and there were newspapers and letters strewn all over the table. He quickly got into the swing of it, and after half an hour he was happy with the kitchen. He moved into the living room, cleared the rubbish from the coffee table and armchairs and was just about to go through the post he had gathered up when the doorbell rang. He looked at the clock. It was late, so he peered out through the little peephole before he opened the door.

It was her.

He was surprised, but managed to say hello as he let her in. She walked into the hallway, and the first thing that occurred to him was how glad he was that he had cleared up the worst of the mess. She probably wouldn't care, but even so. It made him feel better. She looked at him and carried on into the living room.

'Did you get my text?'

'Yes.'

'Weber's been trying to get hold of you.'

'I know. I've spoken to him.'

'Good.'

Torkel stood in the doorway of the living room staring at her. Was she really that interested in his dealings with Weber? 'I'm calling a press conference tomorrow. Weber has made the connection.'

'With Hinde?'

'No, between the three murders.'

'Okay . . .' She nodded and walked back into the hallway. 'I just wanted to check that you'd got my text. I'll be off home now.'

She was so beautiful.

'You could have phoned.'

'My battery's dead.'

A lie. She could see that he knew.

'I must go.'

He wondered what to say to make her stay.

She wondered what to say that would allow her to stay.

106

He was the one who broke the silence, trying to put things into words as best he could, but as usual his first question was far more banal than he would have wished. 'So how are you really, Ursula?'

She looked at him. Sat down on the white chair by the door, the chair hardly anyone used these days. She was more direct. 'What are we going to do?'

'What do you mean?'

'About you and me.'

'I don't know.' He cursed the fact that he couldn't say what he was feeling. He decided that his next response would be more honest. Completely honest. She was looking at him, but he couldn't interpret her expression.

'Maybe I should move to a different department?'

He felt a surge of anxiety. 'Hang on, what are you talking about? Why?'

This wasn't going the way he'd hoped. He reached for her hand. He might not be able to say what he wanted, but perhaps his hands could show her.

'I was in Paris a few weeks ago.'

'With Micke, I know.'

'It was really strange. We did everything you're supposed to do on a romantic weekend away. But the more we tried, the more I wanted to be at home.'

'But that's not you. You're not that kind of person.'

'What kind of person am I, then?'

Her bewilderment seemed genuine. Torkel smiled at her. Stroked her hand, which grew warm in his.

'You're more . . . complicated. Never entirely satisfied, never entirely at peace. You are Ursula.'

'Does everything happen on my terms?'

He might as well carry on being honest. 'Yes. It's always been that way.'

'But you don't have a problem with that?'

'No. I don't believe I can change you. I don't think I even want to.'

She looked at him and got to her feet.

But she had no intention of leaving.

★ ★ ★

When she got home, around three, she crept into Bella's room. Bella slept there sometimes when she was back from Uppsala and needed a place to stay. Ursula almost hoped that their daughter might have surprised them with an unannounced visit, but the room was empty. Bella hadn't been home for several weeks. She and her boyfriend Andreas had slept there for a few days at the beginning of June, before heading off to Norway to spend the summer working in a restaurant and getting some money together before the start of the new academic year. Ursula moved the pile of Bella's clothes to one side and sat down on the desk chair. She gazed at the neatly made bed. Bella's favourite top still lay on the shelf of the bedside cabinet – a black Green Day T-shirt from a concert she had been to when she was fifteen. Ursula had driven her there. There had been a lengthy discussion in the car about the purchase of the T-shirt, with Ursula maintaining that it was far too expensive and Bella making it clear that it was absolutely necessary, in fact essential, that she should have it.

Her daughter was so good, so conscientious. At university, at work, when she played volleyball, everywhere. She reminded Ursula of herself. A high achiever at school, always with a book in her hand, as if knowledge were the only thing necessary in order to understand life. Ursula felt that she really should try to get closer to Bella; they were so alike, with the same strengths, the same flaws. There was a lot she could teach her daughter. The fact that there were things you couldn't learn through reading, through discussion or logical reasoning. Closeness to other people was one of those things. That was the most difficult. Without it you chose distance, that position a little removed from the centre of life; a position Ursula knew well. But perhaps it was too late for her to approach Bella; her daughter demanded the same distance that Ursula needed. This had become clear to Ursula during Bella's last few years at home. Ursula picked up the neatly folded T-shirt and buried her nose in it. Freshly washed, but Ursula thought she could just detect the scent of her daughter. In her mind were the words she ought to say whenever she had the chance, but never did: 'I love you. I'm not very good at showing it, but I do love you.' She sniffed the T-shirt one last time, then put it back on the shelf and went into the bathroom.

She had another wash. Although she had already showered at Torkel's, it felt like the natural thing to do. Then she brushed her teeth before quietly slipping into bed next to Mikael. She lay on her side and gazed at the back of his head and his frizzy hair as he lay turned away from her. He seemed to be in a deep sleep. She relaxed; she didn't feel whole, but she did feel contented. She knew that she spent all of her time just taking bits and pieces from the people around her. Just bits and pieces, never the whole.

And she gave back only bits and pieces. She wasn't capable of anything else. It was like the business with the T-shirt in Bella's room just now.

She loved her daughter, but she said the words to her T-shirt.

Sabine came to him in the dream. He was holding her hand. As always.

The swirling water. The power. The noise. He let go and she was swept away by the wave.

As always.

He lost her.

Forever.

Sebastian woke up with a start, as usual unsure of where he was. Then he saw Annette. Still in her black dress. The dark lipstick was smudged and had left marks on the pillow. She was pretty. He hadn't really noticed yesterday. Like a flower that opens only at night, when no one can see. Imagine if she could be just half of that person when she stepped out of the door and faced the world. He pushed the thought away. It wasn't up to him to understand her or help her. He had enough to cope with – himself. He crept out of bed feeling stiff; the mattress was too soft and the bed was too narrow. In addition, the dream always left him tense, and his right hand was aching. Next to his clothes on the floor lay a brown teddy bear with a rosette and writing on its tummy: 'To the best mum in the world'. He wondered whether she had bought it for herself. He found it difficult to imagine that the sleeping woman was the best at anything. He picked up the bear and placed it beside her as a greeting. He looked at her one last time, then quickly and silently got dressed and left the apartment.

It was hot. Really hot. The heat enveloped him as soon as he stepped out into the street, even though it wasn't yet five o'clock in the morning. He had heard somewhere that Stockholm was in the middle of a tropical heat wave. He didn't know what was

110

required in order for the heat to qualify as tropical; he just thought it was too bloody hot. All the time. Night and day. The sweat was pouring down his back before he had gone a hundred metres from Annette's door. He didn't really know where he was or how to get to the centre of Liljeholmen, and ambled along at random until the streets began to look familiar.

There was a coffee shop and newsagent's next door to the subway station. He pushed open the door, went straight over to the coffee machine and filled a large cup with cappuccino.

'For another six kronor you can have a Danish pastry as well,' the young man behind the counter said when Sebastian put the cup down in front of him.

'I don't want a Danish pastry.'

The lad gave Sebastian a searching look then ventured an understanding smile. 'Hard night?'

'Mind your own fucking business.'

Sebastian took his coffee and walked out. Turned right. A fair distance to go. Across the Liljeholm Bridge, Hornsgatan, Slussen, Skeppsbron, Strömbron, Stallgatan, then Strandvägen and home. He would be drenched in sweat by the time he got there. But he didn't want to use the subway. If the heat got too much he could always hail a taxi.

On Hornsgatan his shoelace came undone. Sebastian put down his coffee on an electricity box, bent down and retied it. As he straightened up he caught sight of his reflection in the tinted window of a shop selling shirts. He could see that the question as to whether it had been a hard night had been justified. He looked older than his fifty years this morning. More worn out. His slightly too long hair was plastered to his forehead with sweat. Unshaven, exhausted, hollow-eyed. Alone with a paper cup of lukewarm coffee at five o'clock in the morning. On his way from yet another night with a woman. On his way to . . . ? Where was he actually on his way to? Home. But to what? The spare room in the flat on Grev Magnigatan; it was the only room he used in the elegant apartment, except for the kitchen and bathroom. Four rooms were unused, untouched and silent in permanent semi-darkness behind closed blinds. Where was he actually going? Where had he been going since Boxing Day 2004? The simple answer was: nowhere. He had convinced himself that this was perfectly okay. That this was how he wanted things, that he had made a conscious choice to let life pass him by.

He knew why. He was afraid he would have to give up Sabine in order to come back. And Lily. That the price of being able to live again was to forget his daughter and his wife. He didn't want that. He knew that plenty of people, the majority, found their way back to their lives after losing someone close. Life went on, with only a fragment missing. Not completely shattered, like his. He knew that. But he just hadn't been able to repair it. He hadn't even tried.

But Vanja had let a strip of light, of meaning, into his existence once more, and he had found the courage to take the first steps towards change. If Trolle just did what he was supposed to do, Sebastian would be able to drive a wedge between Valdemar and his daughter. The only question was how to proceed after that? If he managed to turn Vanja's world upside down, shouldn't he be there to catch her when she fell? It would be even better if he was a part of her everyday life before disaster struck. An unpopular part, perhaps, but still a person who was close enough to be able to approach her in a perfectly natural way when she needed it.

He might actually derive a double benefit from that particular strategy.

Become a part of her everyday life. Her everyday life was Riksmord. Riksmord was Sebastian's former workplace. The place where he had once experienced a feeling of belonging, where he had been able to make use of his expertise. Where he had made a contribution. Worked. Had a life.

Get a life before you can be part of a life.

He made a decision.

He would be close to Vanja and make a life for himself once more.

One last glance in the dark shop window, then he turned and went back the way he had come.

Torkel pulled into his space in the car park beneath police headquarters, switched off the engine and got out of the car. The Audi's air-conditioning system had kept the temperature at a pleasant seventeen degrees, and he felt rested and refreshed as he locked the car and walked towards the lift, in spite of the fact that he had had only a few hours' sleep. He was trying not to think too much about last night. Not to create false hopes. Lying in his bed afterwards, he realised how much he had missed her. For a while he thought about shuffling nearer and simply holding her, but he didn't dare. He knew that wasn't what she wanted. But she had been closer to him last night than ever before. They had been in his apartment. She had come back. Chosen him. Not completely, but still.

Ursula was probably incapable of choosing someone completely.

And he was mature enough to be able to live with that.

She had already gone when he woke up in the morning. He hadn't heard her leave. She hadn't woken him to say goodbye. But what had he expected? After all, this was Ursula.

Torkel walked into reception, nodded to the uniformed officer who handed him the morning papers, and fished out his key card for the internal door. However, before he had time to use it he heard: 'Good morning.'

Torkel's first impression when he turned around was that he had been hailed by a homeless person, but a fraction of a second later he recognised his visitor. Sebastian got up from one of the two sofas at the other end of the reception area and walked across the stone floor towards Torkel.

'Sebastian. What are you doing here?' Torkel suppressed an

113

impulse to hug the man and held out his hand instead. Sebastian shook it briefly.

'I've come to see you. I haven't made an appointment, but maybe you could spare five minutes anyway?'

That was absolutely typical of Sebastian, Torkel thought. Just turning up. When it was convenient for him, it had to be convenient for everybody else. After they had solved the case in Västerås together back in April, Sebastian had simply disappeared again. He had shown no desire whatsoever to resume the friendship that had lain fallow for so many years. God knows Torkel had given him the opportunity, but Sebastian was adept at evading every attempt at a deeper contact.

For a few seconds Torkel actually considered sending him away. Experience told him that Sebastian's sudden appearance couldn't possibly be good news. And yet Torkel found himself nodding, swiping his key card and letting Sebastian into Riksmord.

'You look tired,' Torkel said as they stood in the lift.

'That's because I am tired.'

'Were you waiting long?'

'An hour or so.'

Torkel glanced at his watch. Ten to seven. 'You're up early.'

'I haven't really been to bed.'

'Do I want to know where you've been?'

'Even I don't really want to know where I've been.'

They fell silent. An anonymous female voice informed them that they had reached the fourth floor, and the doors slid open. Sebastian stepped out first, and they walked down the corridor.

'So what are you up to these days?' Torkel asked in a neutral tone of voice as they headed towards his office. Sebastian was impressed; a polite reception in spite of everything.

'Oh, you know – the usual.'

'Nothing, in other words.'

Sebastian didn't reply. Torkel waved Sebastian into his office. He left the door open, shrugged off his jacket and hung it up. Sebastian sank down onto a two-seater sofa.

'Coffee?' Torkel asked as he sat down behind his desk and gave the mouse a little push to wake the computer from energy-saving mode.

'No, I want a job. In fact, I need a job. That's why I'm here.'

Torkel didn't really know what he'd been expecting. He'd realised that Sebastian's appearance at this early hour could mean only one thing: he wanted something. For himself. But this? Had he really heard Sebastian correctly?

'You want a job. Here. Just like that.'

'Yes.'

'No.'

'Why not?'

'I can't just take people on.'

'You can if you say you need them.'

'Exactly . . .'

For the first time Torkel found it difficult to look Sebastian in the eye. Perhaps they really did need Sebastian right now? So why hadn't Torkel picked up the phone? Was it his personal reluctance to bring Sebastian in again that had decided the matter? He felt let down by his former friend; had that clouded his professional judgement? He had convinced himself that even with a third victim, Sebastian's presence would do more harm than good.

Sebastian interpreted Torkel's silence as an indication that he was actually considering the suggestion. He leaned forward.

'Come on, Torkel, you know what I can do, you know how I can contribute. Didn't we have this discussion in Västerås?'

'No, we didn't. As I recall it, you joined us in Västerås, treated me and the rest of my team like shit, then disappeared.'

Sebastian nodded; that was probably more or less what had happened. 'But it worked.'

'For you, perhaps.'

There was a knock on the door frame and Vanja walked in. She glanced at the guest on the sofa, and there was no mistaking her opinion of the visitor.

'What the fuck is he doing here?'

Sebastian quickly got to his feet. He had no idea why. It just felt like the right thing to do. As if he were a suitor in some novel by Jane Austen. The fact that he had seen her less than twenty-four hours ago was irrelevant; it felt like far too long.

'Hello, Vanja.'

She didn't even look at him. Instead she kept her gaze fixed on Torkel, her expression challenging.

'He's just dropped in. He happened to be passing . . .'

'How are you?' Sebastian tried again.

Vanja carried on as if he wasn't even in the room. 'Everyone's here. We're waiting for you.'

'Fine,' said Torkel. 'I'll be there as soon as I can. We've got a press conference this morning as well.'

'A press conference?'

'Yes. We'll discuss it in the briefing. Two minutes.'

Vanja nodded and left the room. Still without so much as a glance in Sebastian's direction. Torkel noticed Sebastian's eyes following her as she walked away. She had been unusually harsh. Positively rude, in fact. Perhaps he should have said something to her, but at the same time it confirmed his feeling that he had made the right decision in refusing to let Sebastian rejoin the team. Torkel got to his feet and Sebastian turned his attention back to his former colleague.

'A press conference . . . What are you working on?'

Torkel knew better than to give Sebastian even a hint. He went over to him and placed a hand on his upper arm.

'I think a job would be very, very good for you.'

'That's exactly what I'm saying.'

'And I really wish I could help you.'

'You can.'

'No, I can't.'

Silence. Torkel thought he saw a light go out in Sebastian's eyes.

'Come on, don't make me beg . . .'

'I have to go. Give me a call if you want to meet up sometime. Outside work.' Torkel squeezed Sebastian's arm briefly, then he turned and left the office.

Sebastian stood there. The result of his visit was more or less what he'd expected, but he still felt disappointed. Empty. He stayed where he was for a little while, gathering his thoughts, before he left Torkel's office and set off for home.

Get a life before you can be part of a life.

How the hell was he supposed to do that when nobody was willing to give him a chance?

He really needs to clean these, Sebastian thought as he stared out of the filthy windows looking out onto Karlavägen. A white rented van from Statoil was double-parked just outside. Two men in their thirties were trying to lift out a piano that was far too big for them. Sebastian watched with interest; he had decided in seconds that it was an impossible task. The piano was too heavy. The men were too skinny, and there weren't enough of them. Simple maths.

Stefan had nipped down to the 7-Eleven to buy milk for the coffee he always insisted on offering, leaving Sebastian alone. Sebastian pushed aside the left-hand curtain to give himself a clear view, then settled comfortably in the big armchair and watched the two men's efforts with the piano for a little while. Then he leaned back and closed his eyes.

He felt almost expectant, probably because of what was going to happen very soon.

The return.

The moment when Sebastian took control once more and struck back. Hard. He opened his eyes and had a quick look at the piano fiasco outside. There was a break in the proceedings; the men seemed to be having a discussion on how best to move forward. Sebastian lost interest and picked up the daily newspaper from the table in front of him.

Something had happened abroad.

Something else had happened in Sweden.

He didn't really care; he just needed something to occupy him.

He noticed the vase of flowers on the table. The whole thing summed up Stefan perfectly, somehow. The current edition of *DN* and fresh flowers. Freshly brewed coffee with milk. Stefan lived in the moment. As if every day had significance.

After a few more minutes Sebastian heard the outside door open, and a second later Stefan appeared with a carton of semi-skimmed milk in his hand. Sebastian put down the newspaper, still virtually unread, and welcomed Stefan back with a nod.

'You will have a coffee, won't you?' Stefan asked as he headed towards the coffee machine.

'As you went out specially to buy milk, I suppose I can't really say no.'

'You never have any problem saying no.' Stefan smiled.

Sebastian smiled back. 'In that case, no.'

Stefan nodded and poured himself a cup; he opened the carton of milk and added a dash to his coffee.

'It's not long since you were last here,' he said, balancing the slightly overfilled cup carefully as he made his way to the other armchair.

'I know.'

'You look pleased. Has something happened?'

'No, what makes you say that?' Sebastian smiled his most disarming smile. He wanted to prolong the pleasure as much as possible.

'I don't know, it's just a feeling.' Stefan put his coffee on the table next to the flowers and sat down. There was silence for a few seconds. Sebastian decided it was time to begin.

'I met Vanja today.'

Stefan looked weary rather than surprised. 'I thought we'd agreed that you weren't going to contact her. What did she say?'

'She said: "What the fuck is he doing here?"'

Stefan shook his head. 'You promised.'

'It wasn't like that. I was trying to get a job.'

'Where?'

'With Riksmord.'

'Of all places . . .'

'Come on, you said I ought to sort something out, and I want to get back to work. I need . . . structure. You're right about that. But it has to be something interesting. Challenging.'

'Not like everything you had to sit through yesterday evening?'

Sebastian didn't reply. He glanced out of the window again. The men were sitting smoking. The piano remained in exactly the same place.

'Group therapy works much better if everyone participates,' Stefan went on. 'Makes a contribution.'

'It's not my thing, I told you that. For God's sake, they never stopped talking about their banal problems. How can you stand it?'

'You get used to it. I have patients who are considerably more trying,' Stefan said meaningfully. Sebastian allowed the irony to pass; he still had the heavy artillery in reserve.

'Anyway, I'm not coming tonight.'

'I think you should give it one more chance.'

'I don't think so. The thing is . . .' A deliberate pause. He knew from his experience of giving lectures that sudden changes of topic are usually more effective when they follow an introductory pause. He was going for the maximum effect now. Time for the bombshell: 'I slept with Annette after the meeting last night.'

Stefan's face lost its colour. 'Why the hell did you do that?'

Sebastian spread his arms wide in an apologetic gesture. 'It was a mistake. I didn't mean to do it.'

'You didn't mean to do it? What the fuck are you talking about, you didn't mean to do it?'

Stefan tried to calm himself by leaning back in the chair. It didn't seem to work all that well, Sebastian noted with satisfaction.

'It was . . . something to do. A distraction. You know me. That's the way I am.' He looked at Stefan with feigned interest. 'Do you know her well?'

'She's been my patient for a long time. She feels utterly abandoned by everyone. Her son, her ex-husband, everyone. She has issues with trust, and very low self-esteem.'

'Yes, that was obvious. She absorbed intimacy like a sponge. But she went like a train in bed.'

Stefan leapt up from the chair, splashing coffee all over the table. 'Do you realise what you've done? Do you have any idea how she must have felt when she woke up alone? I presume you didn't stay for breakfast.'

'No, I've had bad experiences when it comes to that kind of thing.'

'And now you're intending to avoid her?'

'That's the plan. It usually works.' Sebastian opted for another deliberate pause, gazing at Stefan with obviously insincere sympathy. 'I'm sorry, Stefan, but I did tell you I don't belong in group therapy.'

119

'The question is whether you actually belong anywhere. Get out.' Stefan pointed to the door. 'I can't fucking look at you anymore.'

Sebastian nodded and got to his feet, leaving Stefan with the current issue of the daily newspaper and his cut flowers.

Stefan was right.

Every day did have significance.

The tall man was as close to excited as he could be when he got home. He had seen the placards and the headlines in the evening papers. The police had held a press conference. About him. He wanted nothing more than to start reading, but simply rushing indoors and opening the newspapers he had bought was out of the question.

The ritual.

He had to follow the ritual.

Sticking to the routine, he quickly switched on the light in the hallway and locked the door behind him. Took off his shoes, placed them on the shoe rack, put on his slippers, took off the thin jacket and hung it on the only coat hanger on the hat shelf, which was empty but for a large torch. When he had taken off what he intended to take off – in winter his scarf, hat and gloves would also be placed on the shelf, always in that order – he opened the door to the toilet and switched on the light. As always he felt a pang of distaste the second he looked into the thick darkness of the windowless room, before the fluorescent tube flashed into life. He went in, checked that the torch within reach on the small shelf was working, then unzipped his fly and urinated. He took the torch over to the basin and washed his hands, returned the torch to its proper place, and left the toilet door open when he went into the apartment. He switched on the main light in the living room as he turned left into the kitchen, and switched on the lights over the cooker and on the ceiling. Two torches to check in the kitchen. Both working. Only the bedroom left. Ceiling light, bedside light, check the torch on the bedside table.

All the lights were on. Not that it was necessary. Sunlight was pouring in through every window of the apartment. There was nothing to stop it or to subdue its effect. No shutters on the outside,

121

no curtains on the inside. The first thing the tall man had done when he moved in was to remove all the blinds. No, the electric light wasn't needed today. But it was part of the ritual. If you did it even when it wasn't necessary, there was no need to worry about forgetting it when it was important.

Once, many years ago, there had been a power cut in the area where he was living. Everything had gone dark, not just in his apartment but everywhere. Pitch-dark. He had quickly found the nearest torch, but either the batteries were dead or the bulb had blown. He hadn't checked it for a long time. That was before the ritual. The panic, the paralysing fear that had gripped him, had caused him to vomit, then lie motionless on the floor for several hours, until the power was restored.

He loved the summer. Not necessarily the heat, but the light. The best time was around midsummer, but it was the light he loved, not the celebrations. He didn't like any celebrations. Particularly midsummer.

It was one midsummer's eve when he first noticed that something was wrong.

That she wasn't like everyone else.

He was three, perhaps four years old. They had all got in the car and driven down to the big meadow by the lake. The pole was already up when they arrived. There were lots of people, and they ended up quite a long way from the centre of the celebrations with their blankets and their picnic basket. From time to time fragments of folk music were carried over on the breeze as they sat with their sandwiches, a strawberry tart, and white wine for Mum and Dad. The dancing began at three o'clock. There were lots of people, and they ended up forming four or five circles. He loved dancing; some of the traditional dances were such fun. It might have started earlier, it probably had, but he had no memory of that. The first time was there. At midsummer. In the sun in the outermost circle. When she was dancing with him. His little hand in hers. He remembered feeling happy and looking up at her. She was staring straight ahead into the distance as she danced. She wasn't really there. She wasn't singing. Wasn't smiling. Her body carried out the movements of the dance as if she were asleep. Completely without emotion. Indifferent. He remembered feeling a little afraid, tugging at her hand. She looked down at him and smiled, but the smile never reached her eyes. It was mechanical, learned behaviour, there to assure him that everything was as it should be. But it wasn't. Not then, and definitely not since then.

'Mummy's not feeling very well at the moment.' That's what she would say to him when he wasn't allowed to climb up on her knee, or when she was lying down in the middle of the day with the bedroom curtains closed. When she was sitting on the floor with her knees drawn up to her chin just weeping, and his father had to collect him from nursery because she simply hadn't turned up. That's what she would say when she couldn't cope with preparing anything to eat on the days when he was at home with her, or just before she closed the door behind her, leaving him alone for several hours.

'Mummy's not feeling very well at the moment.' That's what his father would say to him as he tried to explain in a whisper why he must wear soft slippers indoors, why he mustn't show that he was upset or worried or cross. To explain why he had to sit still, almost invisible for several hours on the days when she did actually manage to get out of bed. To explain why they never did things together, why he had to be a good boy and look after Mummy while Daddy went out to earn money.

That's what he himself would say later on, when he was older and his classmates asked why he was away from school so often, why they couldn't come round to see him, why he never joined in with anything after school, why he never came to parties or took up any kind of sport.

'Mummy's not feeling very well at the moment.'

Sometimes, when she was a little better, she said it was a shame he'd had to grow up with such a bad mummy.

But more often she would tell him that it was his fault she was ill. If only he hadn't come along, everything would have been fine. He had destroyed her.

When he was ten years old it became impossible for her to remain at home. She disappeared. He didn't know where she had gone. Oddly enough, his father spent more time at home after that, which was ironic because by then he was perfectly capable of looking after himself, partly because he was older and partly because he no longer had to take care of his mother. It was only much later that he realised his father had used work as an escape all those years. Stayed away. His father couldn't handle her illness, and so passed the responsibility on to his son. He assumed he could have hated his father for that, but by the time the realisation came there was so much and so many others that he hated with far greater intensity.

His mother died six months after she left them. At the funeral, people spoke quietly of suicide, but he never knew for sure.

After another six months a woman he didn't know turned up on his birthday. Sofia, her name was. He didn't have a party. Who would come? After several years of virtually no social contact and a significant amount of absence from school, he had no friends. Sofia had brought him a present. A Super Nintendo. He had wanted one ever since it came out the previous year, but had always been told it was too expensive, they couldn't afford it. But Sofia hadn't seemed to think it was a particularly extravagant present. She gave him four games as well as the console! He realised immediately that she must have more money than them. More money than they had ever had.

She stayed the night.

Slept in the bedroom with his father.

They had met at the auctioneer's where he worked, his father told him later. Sofia was both knowledgeable and interested. She had brought in a number of items to sell, but had also bid for quite a lot of beautiful pieces. Expensive pieces. He liked Sofia. She made his father happier than he had been for a very long time.

He saw more of Sofia over the next few months. A lot more. One weekend his father and Sofia went away, and when they came back they were engaged. His father sat him down for a serious talk. He and Sofia were getting married, and they would be going to live with Sofia, who had a lovely place in the middle of the city. He never really doubted that his father was very fond of Sofia, but he realised that the money was not unimportant.

It was to be a fresh start.

A new life.

A better life.

He deserved it, after all that had happened. This time everything would be fine. Nothing and no one would destroy it.

A few weeks after the engagement he had been introduced to Sofia's family for the first time. Her mother and father, Lennart and Svea, who were in their sixties, and her brother Carl. Dinner at Villa Källhagen. Very pleasant. He had spilled his drink and crept away, afraid of the consequences, but no one had been cross. The longer the meal went on, the more he had felt able to relax. Sofia seemed to have a nice family, no idiots there. As they were leaving, Sofia's father had drawn him to one side.

'My name is Lennart, as you know, but you can call me Granddad if you like, now we're going to be related.'

He was happy to do so. He had liked the man with the greying hair and the kind brown eyes that always seemed full of laughter.

At the time. When they had just met.

Before the outings.

Before the games.

Then he wasn't afraid of the dark.

With the ritual completed, the tall man sat down in the kitchen and opened the newspapers with trembling fingers. They had finally realised. It had taken time, but now they had linked the first with the second with the third. They were writing about him. He was spreading fear, the first paper said. Pictures of the houses he had visited. An anxious neighbour clutching her daughter. He turned to the second newspaper. Much the same. There was nothing about his role model, in spite of the fact that the murders were exact copies. Either the journalists didn't know the details, or they were simply unaware of the Master's greatness. The police comments were brief. They merely wished to state that they were probably dealing with a serial killer. They wanted to warn the public, and particularly women on their own, against letting strange men into their homes. They said they had several leads, but that was all. They were not prepared to comment on any possible similarities between the three victims. They gave no details whatsoever. They were trying to diminish him, turn him into someone invisible, someone whose actions were unimportant. Again. They would not succeed. It wasn't over. They would be forced to acknowledge that he was a worthy opponent. As great and as capable of instilling fear as the Master.

The tall man stood up, opened the second drawer down and took out a pair of scissors. He sat down and meticulously cut out the articles that were about him. When he had finished he folded up the newspapers and placed them in a pile on the table. Then he sat motionless. This was new. He needed to create a ritual. There would be more articles to come, he was sure of it. This was just the beginning. His whole body was tingling, as if he had suddenly moved into the next phase. The phase where the whole world would begin to search high and low for him, the hidden one. The phase where he existed.

He got up and went over to the cleaning cupboard. Next to the vacuum cleaner was a paper sack for the recycling. He picked up the newspapers from the table and placed them in the sack. Then he closed the door, picked up the cuttings and walked to his desk in the other room. He opened the top drawer. He kept envelopes in the drawer. In three different sizes. He took out one of the largest and placed the cuttings inside it. The ones from *Expressen* on top of the ones from *Aftonbladet*. If any more newspapers wrote about him, they could go behind *Aftonbladet*, he decided. If he printed out anything from the internet, it would have a separate envelope. He went over to the chest of drawers, opened the top drawer and placed the envelope containing the cuttings underneath the black sports bag. That was what he would do. Cut out, gather together, recycling, into the envelope, into the chest of drawers. A ritual. He immediately felt calmer.

The tall man sat down at the computer, opened his web browser and went into fygorh.se. He had reported on his recent observations, and the information had been extremely well received. On page seven he clicked on the small blue button right in the middle of a long extract on runic script. A new page opened and he entered his password. He gasped when he saw the change on the page.

He had been given a new task.

He was ready for the next one.

Number four.

The lift had been out of order all week. Sebastian walked up the three flights of stairs to his apartment. It didn't matter; he couldn't get much sweatier. The sun had been beating down on him all the way home. This summer it didn't seem to make any difference which direction you were going in or at what time of day. From the moment the sun rose at around four in the morning, it seemed to be at its zenith. Shade was in short supply. The area of high pressure had lingered over the country for so long that the tabloids had been forced to invent new phrases. 'Record Temperatures' and 'What a Scorcher!' were no longer enough. 'Sizzling Sun Strikes Again' and 'The Inferno Summer' were a couple of examples from the last week's crop, both linked to articles detailing how several people had ended up in hospital with the symptoms of dehydration, and tales of dogs dying in parked cars.

There were flowers hanging on his door. A bouquet in grey paper with a note attached. Sebastian ripped it off as he unlocked the door and went inside. He read the note as he pulled off his shirt without unbuttoning it, but it merely told him things he already knew or had worked out for himself: that someone had sent him flowers, but he hadn't been at home to receive them, so they had been left on the door. Sebastian went into the kitchen and tore off the paper. Roses. A dozen, perhaps. Red. Definitely expensive. A card attached to the stems. Evidently he was being congratulated on something. That was all it said. 'Congratulations' in fancy writing. And a name: Ellinor.

The hand-holder.

He knew breakfast had been a mistake. He had known it at the time, and this was the confirmation. He threw the flowers in the sink and took a glass out of the cupboard. Filled it with water, drank it greedily and filled it again. Then he walked out of the kitchen. For a moment he wondered what the congratulations were for, but he decided not to worry about that.

The apartment was only marginally cooler than outside. It smelled stuffy. Dusty. He considered opening the window, but realised it wouldn't make any difference. He took off all his clothes and threw them on the unmade bed in the spare room. He needed to do a couple of loads of washing, but decided not to bother with that either.

It struck him that the building was unusually quiet. No pipes humming away, no flushing toilets, no children yelling in the apartment above, no footsteps on the stairs. The whole place felt empty. Which it probably was, more or less; most of his neighbours were away on holiday. Not that he missed them – he hardly knew the names of any of them. He deliberately avoided residents' meetings, communal clean-up days and neighbourhood parties. The children in the block had even stopped ringing his doorbell trying to sell Christmas magazines, May flowers and other crap. But it was quiet. Too quiet.

The encounter with Stefan hadn't had the desired effect. He had gone there as a victor. He had won. He was going to show Stefan once and for all who set the agenda for their contact with one another. He would make it clear that if Stefan was intending to take the initiative and force him into something like that bloody group therapy session, then Stefan would have to wear the consequences. Sebastian had been fully prepared for an invigorating fight. Instead Stefan had seemed almost resigned. Highly unsatisfactory.

Sebastian went into the spare room and switched on the television, which was mounted on the wall at the foot of the bed. He was about to lie down on the unmade bed when the telephone rang. He gave a start at the unfamiliar sound. His landline. Must be Trolle. For a moment he considered letting it ring, but curiosity got the better of him. Perhaps Trolle had found something. Something juicy. He went into the kitchen. This could be fun.

'Yes?'

'Did you get the flowers?'

Sebastian closed his eyes. Not Trolle. Most definitely not Trolle. A woman's voice. Not fun at all.

'Who's this?'

'Ellinor Bergkvist.'

128

'Who?' He managed to sound suitably puzzled. He had no intention of giving her any encouragement.

'Ellinor Bergkvist. We met at the talk on Jussi Björling, and you came back to my place.'

'Oh yes,' Sebastian said, as if he had just succeeded in putting a face to the name.

'You knew who I was when I said my name, didn't you?'

'What do you want?' Sebastian snapped, not even trying to hide his irritation.

'I just wanted to congratulate you on your name day. Jacob.'

Sebastian didn't reply. Presumably his full name was on some Wikipedia page. He could just imagine her surfing around to find a link, a reason to call him. Get in touch. Flowers to his address and a phone call to his landline. Wasn't his number ex-directory these days? It had been in the past, he knew that, but nowadays?

'Your name is Jacob Sebastian Bergman, isn't it.' No hint of uncertainty in her voice. A statement. Sebastian cursed himself. The second she'd slipped her hand into his he should have pushed her away. He would have to do it now instead.

'If you'll excuse me, I've just screwed some woman and I need a shower.'

He put the phone down. He stood there for a moment, almost expecting it to ring again, but it remained silent. He left the kitchen. It had been a half-truth, anyway. He hadn't had sex, but he definitely needed a shower. He was heading for the bathroom when a voice from the television caught his attention.

'. . . *but according to the police there are indications that the same perpetrator is involved . . .*'

Sebastian went into the room. Some news programme. A young man in front of a house, with a glorious garden in the background.

'. . . *would make this the third woman who has been murdered in her own home. The police are asking the public to be careful, particularly . . .*'

Sebastian stared at the television.

As Torkel pressed the button and opened the door leading to the foyer, he knew what was waiting for him. The call had come a minute ago when he was sitting in the Room with the team. Reception. He had a visitor. Sebastian Bergman.

Torkel had explained that he was busy, and that his visitor would have to wait. The receptionist had replied that Sebastian had said Torkel would say that, and if Torkel didn't come down immediately Sebastian was going to start telling anyone in the foyer who was interested everything he knew about Torkel. Everything. Every single detail. He would kick off with a wet evening at the Stadshotell in Umeå with twins, he said. Torkel said he was on his way.

It wasn't unexpected. As soon as the news was out and the press began to carry the story, Torkel knew he would hear from Sebastian.

He had barely managed to get the door open before Sebastian was there.

'Is it true? Have you got a serial killer?'

'Sebastian . . .'

'Have you? Has he killed three times? That's extremely unusual. I have to be involved.'

Torkel looked around. This was a conversation he really didn't want to have in the reception area, but nor did he want to let Sebastian any further into the building. 'Sebastian . . .' he tried again, as if the repetition of his former colleague's name would calm him down, and with a bit of luck make him forget the purpose of his visit.

'I don't have to be a part of the team if that will cause problems. Bring me in as a consultant. Like last time.'

Torkel saw a small escape route opening up. A tiny hole he might just be able to crawl through.

'I can't do that,' he said firmly. 'Do you know how much that would cost? I won't be given any additional resources to bring you in.'

Sebastian was lost for words. He simply stared at Torkel for a few seconds, trying to work out if he had heard him correctly.

'You're not seriously trying to use your useless organisation and your pissing finances as a reason to keep me away? For fuck's sake, Torkel, surely you can do better than that?'

Yes, he could, Torkel realised. Or he should have been able to. But now he had taken this route and he intended to follow it a little further, even if he was pretty sure it was a dead end.

'You can think what you like, but it's true.' His voice wasn't quite so firm this time. 'I can't afford you.'

The look Sebastian gave him was almost one of disappointment. 'I can afford me. I'll work for free. Like last time. Seriously, Torkel, if you don't want me you're going to have to come up with something better than the idea that I'd be buggering up your finances.'

'Sebastian . . .'

'At least let me have a look at the case. Surely that can't do any harm. It's what I do, for fuck's sake!'

Torkel stood there in silence. It didn't matter what he said. Sebastian had no intention of listening.

'Okay, so the team got a bit stressed by my presence last time, but it would be professional misconduct not to bring me in if you're dealing with a serial killer.'

Torkel turned around, took out his key card and swiped it. The door unlocked with a click. Torkel yanked it open. Sebastian obviously interpreted this as a sign that the conversation was over, and changed tactics.

'I'm trying to get a grip on my life, Torkel. I really am trying, but I need a job.'

Torkel thought for a second. He wasn't impressed by Sebastian's assertion that he was trying to get control of his life; he'd tried that line in Västerås as well. Joining the team on that occasion hadn't made a scrap of difference to him, as far as Torkel could see. However, his previous remark . . . Perhaps it would be a serious error of professional judgement if he didn't make use of Sebastian's expertise. Particularly in view of the person the murderer was copying. Three women were dead. The whole team was convinced there would be more. They were no closer to an arrest today than they had been a month ago. Wasn't he obliged to do everything he could to stop the murders? He turned to face Sebastian again.

'I'm going to let you in. Through this door. Not into the investigation.'

'And what am I supposed to do when I get through the door?'

'I need to speak to the team first.'

'About me?'

'Yes.'

'What are you going to do? Take a vote?'

'Yes.'

Sebastian met Torkel's serious gaze and realised the other man wasn't joking. He nodded. One step at a time. If he'd got this far it was going to take a hell of a lot to get rid of him.

Torkel walked back into the Room. The others were sitting where he had left them. The coffee cups had been topped up. Including his.

'I got you coffee as well; I wasn't sure if you wanted a top-up,' Ursula said as he pulled out his chair and sat down; it was as if she had read his mind.

'Thanks.' He smiled at her. She smiled back. A smile which Torkel chose to interpret as more than just an exchange between colleagues. Which made him wonder once again whether his reluctance to bring in Sebastian was actually based on pure selfishness.

'I was just saying that we've had a preliminary result on Wahlström's DNA sample,' Ursula went on. 'It's not him.'

Torkel nodded to himself. He had never had great hopes of Carl Wahlström. It might seem strange, but it had always seemed just a little too easy. When their killer was caught, it wouldn't be because he had sent a letter that gave him away. Torkel allowed his thoughts to stray from the case again. If there was something happening now between him and Ursula, he had no intention of ruining it by making the same mistake as last time. There were rules when it came to their relationship, and Ursula had established seventy-five per cent of those rules.

Only at work.

132

Never on home ground.

No plans for the future.

And Torkel had added one more rule of his own: he must show her unswerving loyalty.

The first two were really the same thing, but now she herself had taken the initiative and broken them. She had come to his apartment. Her idea. Not his. Perhaps she might even consider altering the third rule too . . .

'Who was on the phone?' Vanja wanted to know.

Torkel turned to face her. If he wanted a future with Ursula he was quite sure he must never break the fourth rule, the one he had added after Västerås. Always remain loyal. Therefore he cleared his throat and leaned forward as he spoke: 'It was Sebastian. I'm wondering whether to bring him into the investigation.'

The reaction was more or less as expected. Vanja and Ursula immediately exchanged a look which made it very clear what they thought about the suggestion, about Sebastian. Billy leaned back in his chair, a faint smile on his lips.

'I'm well aware of Ursula and Vanja's views on the matter,' Torkel went on, 'but I wouldn't suggest it if I didn't think Sebastian could help us.'

Vanja took a deep breath and seemed to be about to speak, but Torkel stopped her with a wave of his hand.

'I also know that anything we might gain by having him here we will lose in terms of increased irritation, an occasional loss of focus and the possibility of a reduction in efficiency. So I want us all to agree to bring him in this time.'

'And if we don't agree?' Vanja asked.

'Then we don't bring him in.'

The room fell silent. Vanja and Ursula exchanged glances once again, as if to determine which of them would be the one to stop Sebastian before he got through the door. Should one of them have that pleasure, or should they share it between them?

'I don't have any problem with the idea,' Billy said suddenly. 'I think he could be useful.'

Vanja looked at him crossly. What was he playing at?

Billy met Vanja's gaze. 'After all, he is an expert on serial killers, and we are looking for a serial killer.'

Vanja didn't speak; she pushed back her chair abruptly and went over to the whiteboard. She studied the pictures, even though she was already familiar with every detail. Torkel could see that she was chewing her lower lip, and assumed he wasn't the only one torn between personal opinion and a professional decision. Vanja turned to face him.

'Do you really believe we have a better chance of catching the person who's doing this if Sebastian is with us?'

She made a sweeping gesture towards the pictures of the murdered women behind her. It was a fair question. If Torkel put aside his own feelings and considered the matter objectively, there could be only one answer.

'Yes, I do.'

Vanja nodded to herself and went back to her seat. 'Then we'll have to agree to differ. Sorry.'

Torkel looked over at Ursula, who was leaning back in her chair, her arms folded across her chest, her gaze fixed on the surface of the table.

'With Wahlström out of the picture, we've got nothing. If we had something, however small, I would say no, not in a million years.' Ursula looked up and met Torkel's eyes. 'But we've got nothing.'

'So as far as you're concerned he's welcome?'

'No, but if you're asking whether I think he can make a valid contribution to the investigation, then the answer is yes.'

The room fell silent.

Vanja got to her feet again. 'He's a walking disaster.'

'If it doesn't work, we kick him out,' Billy said, looking at both Vanja and Ursula. 'He didn't get it completely wrong in Västerås, did he? And you've said yourself that you think his books are good.'

Vanja looked searchingly at Billy. Something had definitely happened to him. After a few seconds she gave in.

'If all three of you think that he really can improve our chances, then there's nothing to discuss, is there? Bring him in.'

'Is that what you want?'

She shook her head grimly. 'No, but I'm prepared to go along with it. I'm not going to be the one to tear this team apart. Sebastian is perfectly capable of doing that without my help.'

'If it doesn't work, we'll do as Billy says and kick him out,' Torkel promised, directing the comment at Vanja.

Ursula let out a brief, dry laugh which made it very clear that she didn't believe him for a moment.

Torkel chose not to react, and headed for the door. 'I'll go and get him.'

It had been easier than he thought. Much easier.

Which unfortunately was an indication of the panic they were all feeling.

★ ★ ★

Sebastian came into the Room and went straight over to the whiteboard without bothering to say hello. He seemed almost excited, Torkel thought. Like a child on Christmas Eve.

Sebastian stopped in front of the pictures and quickly glanced over them. He couldn't make any sense of it. Were they taking the piss?

'Are these new?'

'Yes.'

He turned back to the board and studied the photographs again, more intently this time. The murders had been copied down to the last detail as far as he could see, but now he could see the differences too.

Different rooms.

Different women.

A copycat.

He looked at Torkel, this time more angry than bewildered. 'Why the hell didn't you call me in when you found the first one?'

'It's not Hinde,' Vanja said.

'I know it's not Hinde, but this is someone who is trying to imitate his crimes as faithfully as possibly. They look virtually identical! You should have brought me in right away.'

'Why?' Vanja snapped defiantly.

She had been annoyed the second Sebastian walked through the door. Not a word about how pleased or grateful he was to be back. No polite remarks, no questions about how they all were. Nothing that a normal person might have done in his situation. He had just come marching in as if he had every right to be a member of the team. It infuriated her. And so did that crooked little smile he was wearing now, as if she was slightly stupid. The same smile Carl Wahlström had given her.

'Why do you think?' Sebastian said. 'I know more about Hinde than anyone else.'

'And what's that got to do with anything?' Vanja decided to stick to her guns. How long had Sebastian been here? Two minutes? And already he was taking over the meeting, the room, the entire investigation. Time to reclaim it. 'This is someone else with a completely different motive. Whatever you know about Hinde is of no help here.'

'Whatever I know is always of some help. Otherwise you wouldn't have brought me in. I'm not here because you think I'm charming. So can one of you tell me what you've got?'

Billy stood up. 'I can bring you up to date.' Without waiting for any kind of response, Billy went over to the board. Torkel looked at Vanja, who shrugged.

Sebastian pulled out a chair and sat down next to Ursula.

'Good to see you,' he whispered. Ursula gave him a look which suggested that the pleasure was far from mutual. 'Have you missed me?' She shook her head and turned her attention to Billy. He was pointing at a picture of one of the women, around forty years old, brown eyes under a full fringe, smiling straight into the camera.

'Twenty-fourth of June. Maria Lie in Bromma. Single. A friend became worried when she didn't get in touch and didn't come in to work after the midsummer weekend.' Billy moved his finger from the portrait to a photograph from the scene of the crime. 'Tied up with nylon stockings, lying on the bed on her stomach. Raped and killed with a powerful slash with a knife which severed both the trachea and carotid artery.'

Sebastian nodded to himself. Every detail was familiar. It was as if he had been transported back in time. In his mind he started to go through what he actually knew about copycat murderers. There were some, but very few who copied serial killers. It was more common in the case of school or college campus massacres, or when someone imitated individual, violent murders from films or games. The copycat had an unhealthy fascination with the original, of course, but what else? A psychological disorder, obviously, but of a different kind. Where the serial killer frequently managed to maintain a facade of normality, of being 'ordinary', the copycat was often a more unusual character. More withdrawn. Poor self-image. Low self-esteem. A product of his or her upbringing.

136

As always.

A person who, like the killer he was copying, was capable of crossing the line and using extreme violence, but who wasn't strong enough to take the initiative, or imaginative enough to come up with a method and select his victims on his own. He needed a role model. It was clear in everything he did. The man they were looking for kept a very low profile.

'No sign of forced entry,' Billy went on. 'It seems as if she, like the others, let the killer in. However, there are signs of a struggle inside the apartment. Sperm, pubic hair and fingerprints left at the scene.'

He placed his finger on a new picture. A blonde woman, forty-five to fifty years old. Blue eyes. A small scar on her upper lip, probably from an operation to correct a harelip when she was a child. No obvious similarities to the first victim. A germ of an idea flashed through Sebastian's mind as he looked at her, but it was too small and too fast for him to catch.

'Fifteenth of July. Jeanette Jansson Nyberg, Nynäshamn. Her husband and sons came home after a football trip and found her. She had written in her blog that she was going to be alone all weekend, "just chilling out". Perhaps the murderer knew when to strike.'

'Did the others write a blog? Maria Lie?' Sebastian asked.

Billy shook his head. 'No, but she was on Facebook of course, with her status posted as single.'

Sebastian nodded. He was amazed at the amount of information people were prepared to share with strangers. These days burglars didn't need to bother finding out when a property was empty; the owner cheerfully provided the information via their blog, writing about how wonderful the coming holiday or trip was going to be. The same thing applied when it came to personal information. Single equalled alone equalled vulnerable.

'We found a footprint in the flowerbed at the bottom of the steps,' Vanja chipped in. 'It didn't match the husband's or sons'. Sperm from the same person as with Maria Lie.'

'So he's deliberately leaving evidence?'

'It seems that way,' Torkel replied. 'Or else he's unusually inept. But if he's that useless he should have had dealings with us before, and he hasn't.'

137

'He should definitely have had dealings with the police,' Sebastian nodded, looking troubled. 'Copycats usually have some kind of criminal background. It's extremely unusual for them to start off by killing.'

'Does the fact that he leaves forensic evidence behind mean anything?' Billy asked.

Sebastian looked at him. There was something different about him, wasn't there? Last time Billy had been content to take on responsibility for those aspects of the investigation that were to do with technology – CCTV cameras, mobile phones, call records – and he was the one everyone turned to if they thought the answer to a question might be found in a computer somewhere. But this time he seemed more engaged in questions he wouldn't even have had an opinion on before. By and large he appeared to be much more switched on than the last time they had worked together.

'It's a demonstration of power: you can't find me even though I'm leaving clues behind . . . It makes him feel smarter than the police. It's also a cast-iron way of making sure all the crimes he commits are linked to him. No clever barrister is going to be able to rob him of his triumph in the future.'

'So he wants to be caught?' Vanja asked, sounding extremely doubtful.

'No, but if he does get caught he wants to be sure that it doesn't end there.'

'Anyway . . .' Billy went on with his interrupted summary. 'Same MO. Same nightdress.' He moved his finger to the third woman on the board. Dark hair again. 'The day before yesterday. Katharina Granlund. Same traces, same MO, same everything. And that's all we've got.' Billy sat down.

Sebastian leaned forward. 'He's stepping up the pace.'

'Is that important?'

'Hinde had a fairly consistent cooling-off period. It became only marginally shorter.'

'What's a cooling-off period?' Billy asked.

'The time between the murders.' Sebastian got up and started to walk around the room. Vanja watched him with obvious distaste. It struck him that he had barely given her a thought since he came into the room. The case had immediately grabbed him, pushing everything else aside for the moment. There were links to Hinde. There were links to the old Sebastian.

The better Sebastian.

The best.

'Serial killers lie low after a murder. Partly because they're actually afraid of being caught, and sometimes they feel guilt and regret at having lived out their fantasies, but mostly it's just a period of calm. Until the desire, the compulsion, returns. The cycle gets shorter, but not this short.' He stopped and gestured towards the pictures on the board. 'The man who's done this isn't reflecting afterwards. He isn't going through the various phases.'

'And what does that mean?' Billy again. Definitely more switched on.

'That the act of committing murder is not a compulsion for him. He regards it as a job. Something that has to be done.'

'How do we stop him?'

Sebastian shrugged. 'I don't know.' He turned to Torkel. 'I need to visit the scenes of the crimes. At least the latest one, from the day before yesterday.'

'We have gone over them, you know,' Ursula broke in before Torkel could speak. 'You only have to ask if there's anything you want to know.'

'You've missed something. If this is a real copycat.'

Ursula could feel the irritation bubbling up inside her. She missed nothing. During all the years she had worked, first of all at the national forensics laboratory in Linköping and then with Riksmord, she had never missed anything. Sebastian knew that, of course.

'What have we missed?' She almost managed to keep the rising anger out of her voice.

Sebastian didn't answer; he simply turned back to Torkel. 'Can I visit the scene or not?'

Torkel sighed. He knew Ursula pretty well by this stage. Calling into question her professional expertise was not something that would go unpunished. She might have other flaws and weaknesses, but she was the best at what she did, and God help anyone who claimed otherwise. Torkel got the feeling she was already regretting the fact that she hadn't opposed the idea of bringing in Sebastian.

'Vanja, take Sebastian over to Tumba.'

Vanja stiffened. Her expression, her entire body made it clear what she thought of the idea of spending time alone in a car with Sebastian Bergman.

'Do I have to?'

'Yes, you do.'

'Okay, let's go,' Sebastian said with a broad smile as he pushed open the door. He caught himself experiencing a feeling he hadn't known for many, many years as Vanja reluctantly got up from her chair.

Excitement.

He was working again, and on his very first day he would be spending time alone in a car with his daughter.

Get a life before you can be part of a life.

He had the feeling that this case really could be the road along which he would take his first steps back.

They sat in silence in the dark blue Volvo. Vanja drove out of the underground car park at Fridhemsplan, stopped briefly at the security barrier to show her ID, then turned onto Drottningholmsvägen. Sebastian looked at her closely. There was no mistaking the fact that she was sulking. Every movement was suffused with irritation – changing gear, aggressively switching lanes, the look she gave him when he opened the window, letting the warm, humid summer into the car.

'The air con doesn't work if the window's open.'

'Oh well, you can't have everything.'

He dangled his arm out of the open window. He liked her directness. It made her real. Alive. Strong.

He had watched her from a distance for such a long time that being so close to her now almost made him feel dizzy. He couldn't remember when he had last felt so contented, so calm. However furious she might be, he wished this time in the car with her could last forever. Even the Stockholm traffic seemed harmonious for a while. They continued south along the E4 in silence. By the time they reached the Essinge Islands she could no longer keep quiet.

'Are you a masochist?'

Sebastian was jerked out of his daydream. He turned to face her, not really understanding the question. 'What . . . ? No.'

'So why have you come back, then?' Her eyes flashed with anger. 'Why do you insist on being in a situation where nobody likes you?'

'Billy likes me.'

'Billy doesn't openly dislike you.'

'Same shit, different name.' Sebastian allowed himself a little smile. Did she really think his actions were dictated by what people thought of him?

'Are you so used to being hated that you're happy with people who tolerate you?'

'Probably.'

'If you weren't such a bastard I might almost feel sorry for you.'

'Thanks.' He gave her a grateful look. Noticed that this made her even crosser. It was a strange feeling, being so close to her and yet the only one who had the full, accurate picture of the situation.

There was so much he wanted to know about her. What did she dream about? What did she think about when she was sitting at the breakfast table in the mornings? What was it she laughed about with the man she thought was her father? Would he ever come close to getting to know her in that way?

'Stop it,' she said with sudden fury as he scrutinised her.

'Stop what?'

'Looking at me like that!'

'Like what?'

'Like that. Like you're doing now. I don't even want to know what you're thinking about.'

'You'd never guess . . .'

Vanja glared at him; she looked almost disgusted.

Sebastian turned to face the front. Without realising it she had come close to the truth, nudged it without knowing, without thinking. He wanted to carry on touching the impossible, somehow. The idea was difficult, the words even more so.

'If you and I had met in a different . . .' He broke off. Started again. 'At another time in our lives. What I mean is, there's a reason for everything, and . . .'

She interrupted him. 'Sebastian?'

'Yes?'

'Shut the fuck up.'

He shut up.

She put her foot down.

They didn't speak for the rest of the journey.

★ ★ ★

Number 19 Tolléns väg was one of many well-cared-for, charming houses in one of many residential areas near Stockholm. Hours of dedication and love had gone into the garden, Sebastian noticed, but otherwise there was nothing unusual about the place. Only the bright yellow sign on the front door gave away the fact that a tragedy had occurred here: CRIME SCENE. NO ENTRY. Vanja led the way up the steps and unlocked the door. Sebastian was in less of a hurry, and stopped on the neatly swept path to look at the house. Two storeys. Red-tiled roof. Yellow with white window frames. Clean and tidy, with curtains at the windows, plants in white pots. Until just a few days ago, a couple with dreams and aspirations had lived here. They might not have wanted to stand out. But they had wanted to live.

Vanja opened the door and looked back at him. 'Are you coming?'

'Absolutely.' Sebastian joined her and they went inside. It was oppressively warm, with a stuffy, almost sweet metallic smell. She must have bled a great deal, Sebastian thought, if the smell was still around.

'Where's the bedroom?'

'She was murdered upstairs. What is it we're looking for?'

'I want to see the bedroom first.'

Vanja nodded irritably and led the way. 'Up here.'

They made their way up the stairs, subdued. It was always like this. Death had a way of lowering voices, slowing things down. They reached the bedroom and stopped in the doorway. The room was decorated in beautiful yellow textured wallpaper with a restful pattern. The curtains were closed; the bedclothes had been removed, but the large dark stain that had spread across the double mattress said it all. Sebastian walked slowly into the room and looked around.

'So what is it we've missed?' Vanja sounded impatient.

'A little room, a cubby hole or a cupboard,' Sebastian replied, crouching down by the bed.

Vanja looked at him wearily and pointed to the white sliding door on the other side of the room. 'There are some wardrobes in here.'

Sebastian shook his head without even looking at them. 'It has to be lockable from the outside.' He stayed where he was and gazed around the room. On the bedside table a few paperback books lay in front of a black and white photograph of a smiling couple in a silver frame. Splashes of blood on the glass. Richard

143

and Katharina Granlund. He recognised her from the briefing back at the station. He picked up the photograph.

'Okay, so what's supposed to be in this cupboard?' he heard from the doorway.

Sebastian didn't reply, but went on staring at the picture in his hand. They were standing on a beach somewhere, and they looked happy and in love. The woman was hugging the man, who was gazing straight into the camera. It looked like Gotland, or maybe Öland. A shingle beach somewhere. One summer not so very long ago. Or a lifetime ago, if you were the grieving husband. He gently replaced the photograph. A thought.

Faint.

Fleeting.

Sebastian reached for the photograph again.

'I said, what's supposed to be in this cupboard?'

Vanja was starting to get annoyed. Sebastian decided to forget about the photograph; he straightened up and looked at her. 'Food.'

Vanja went back downstairs while Sebastian methodically checked the upper floor. There were three more rooms; one seemed to be the couple's shared study, with a printer and photocopier. He presumed Billy had taken the computer. Along one wall a bookcase contained everything from Tom Clancy thrillers to cookery books, all neatly arranged. Sebastian didn't find what he was looking for, and went back to the small living room.

In passing he glanced into the bathroom, which looked as if it had recently been renovated. White, clean, tiled from floor to ceiling, with both a shower and a spa bath. A decent size, the way modern couples like their bathrooms. But not what he was looking for. The dressing room would be better suited to the purpose, but it couldn't be locked from the outside.

He went downstairs. The kitchen was at the back of the house, leading out onto a large patio, with the beautifully laid out garden stretching beyond it. The kitchen was just as light and fresh as the bathroom, open and pleasant with white cupboard doors and black granite worktops. An island in the centre with two bar stools beside it. There were a few dishes on the draining board, but otherwise it was surprisingly clean and tidy. He was about to move into the dining room when Vanja called to him.

'Sebastian!' She sounded as if she were some way off.

She shouted again, 'Sebastian!'

'What is it?'

'The cellar!'

The cellar stairs were right by the front door, and it took him a little while to find them. Dark, narrow steps led down into semi-darkness. Even though the Granlunds had put up some modern art posters, it was clear that this part of the house hadn't been a priority. Gone were the bright colours and the perfect finish. It was faintly redolent of cellar, but that was almost preferable to the sweet smell in the rest of the house. At the bottom of the steps was what had evidently once been a hobby room, but it now seemed to be used mainly for storage. The ceiling was low, and Sebastian had to duck underneath hot water pipes. A window set high in one wall provided a limited amount of light, and there was a plain floor lamp in one corner of the room. Vanja was standing in front of a scruffy cupboard door, a challenging look on her face. The yellow light from the lamp behind her made her hair look like spun gold. She pointed at the door. There was an ordinary internal key in the lock.

'What about this? Could this be what you're looking for?'

'Have you opened it?'

'No, I thought you'd want to do it.' She moved to one side to let him pass. 'And I'm hoping you'll explain what we're doing here before too much longer.'

Sebastian looked at the door, then at Vanja. 'I really hope I'm wrong.'

'No you don't.'

He couldn't bring himself to answer; he reached out and tried the handle. The door was locked. With the other hand he turned the key. Pushed down the handle again, and the door opened. It was dark inside; the light from the lamp behind them didn't reach very far. But it was enough to make out the shape of the objects on the floor. Sebastian felt his entire body lock. His fingers groped for the light switch that he knew should be somewhere on the wall just inside the door. He found it, and the white light from the naked bulb turned his spiralling anxiety into fact.

Perfectly arranged.

A soft drink.
A packet of Marie biscuits.
Two bananas.
A bar of chocolate.
An empty chlorine bottle.
It was him. It *was* him.
Hinde.

They were back in the Room. Vanja was putting up the pictures they had taken in the Granlund house. Sebastian was walking around and around. Restless. Wound up. Of all the things that could come back to haunt him, he never thought Hinde would be one of them.

'Our man has information about Hinde's modus operandi, and there's only one way he can have acquired that information,' Sebastian said when the others were all sitting down.

'From your books?' Ursula asked. That had also been Vanja's first thought when he had discussed his theory with her in the car on the way back from Tumba.

Without stopping his pacing, Sebastian gave Ursula the same answer he had given Vanja. 'My books just said that he had a store of supplies. Not what. Not how.' Sebastian stopped by the board and tapped his knuckle on the picture of the neatly arranged food and drink from the Granlunds' cellar. 'The content and the way the items are placed is absolutely identical to Edward Hinde's supplies,' he went on. 'That hasn't been written about anywhere. Our man has had contact with him.'

'But how?'

That had also been Vanja's response to Sebastian's assertion. Sebastian sighed; he was no wiser now than he had been in the car twenty minutes ago. He didn't know how. He just knew that he was right.

'I don't know, but he can only have got this information from Edward.'

'Or a police officer who was part of the investigation at the time.'

All activity in the room stopped as everyone turned to look at Billy.

147

'Hinde can't communicate with the outside world, so I'm just trying to find another explanation.'

'Sebastian, Ursula, Trolle Hermansson and I made up the investigating team back then,' Torkel said matter-of-factly. 'Three of us are here in this room, and I think it's highly unlikely that Trolle has decided to relive his glory days by getting involved in murdering women. But we'll have a chat with him.'

Sebastian stiffened. Could Trolle have anything to do with this? He'd gone downhill, but this? He might possibly have said too much to the wrong person when he was drunk. Nobody in the team really thought he was involved, but what would happen if Vanja went to see him and started asking questions? Sebastian felt dizzy. He could just picture Vanja speaking to Trolle. Trolle telling her what Sebastian had asked him to do. Bloody hell, Vanja wouldn't even need to push him; Trolle was perfectly capable of dumping Sebastian in the shit just because it was fun. Sebastian swallowed and tried to concentrate on the discussion in the room.

'I didn't say it was one of you. There must have been any number of uniforms and forensics around at the scenes of the crimes,' Billy persisted. 'If you found the food, surely one of them could have seen it?'

'I found the food afterwards. Hinde told me about it. If we'd found it,' Sebastian gestured towards his colleagues, 'then Torkel and Ursula would have remembered it, wouldn't they?' Sebastian glared at Billy. 'Think, for God's sake.'

'I am thinking. I was just trying to think outside the box, that's all. So I was wrong.'

Vanja stared at her colleague, unable to conceal her surprise. It was Billy's voice, but someone else's words. Since when did Billy think outside the box? Or maybe he did, but since when did he call it that?

'You can bring it up with Hinde tomorrow morning,' Torkel broke in. 'Your visitors' permit has come through.'

'What's with the food?' Ursula asked. 'Why does he hide it away?'

'It's in my books,' Sebastian replied curtly.

'I haven't read your books.'

Sebastian turned to face her. She met his eyes with a contented smile. Was it possible? Had she deliberately not read the best books ever written in Swedish about serial killers, out of pure spite?

'Neither have I,' Billy chipped in.

Sebastian sighed. Was it really the case that half the country's leading murder investigation team hadn't read his books? He knew that Vanja had, but what about Torkel? He glanced at his former colleague, but Torkel's expression gave nothing away. He must have read them, surely. Sebastian sighed again. He had spoken about Edward Hinde in a number of lectures. He knew Hinde's story inside out. It looked as if he would have to go through it again now. A shortened version, at any rate.

'Edward grew up alone with his mother. She was bedridden. Ill. In more ways than one, unfortunately. He told me that he remembered the first time. A Wednesday. He remembered it well. He had come home from school, and he . . .'

★ ★ ★

. . . is standing in the kitchen preparing a meal. The fish fingers are sizzling in the pan. The potatoes are boiling away in a pot with the lid on, just as she taught him. He is looking forward to his dinner. He likes fish fingers, and for pudding they can share the cake that was left over from his birthday. He is humming to himself. The Beatles, 'A Hard Day's Night'. It's at the top of the charts. He has just started slicing tomatoes when she shouts to him. He puts down the knife and switches off the cooker to be on the safe side before he goes upstairs. Sometimes she wants him to read to her, and that can take time. He doesn't read very well. It's not that long since he learned to read. He works his way slowly through simple children's books, but she says she likes to hear his voice. And it's good practice. His mother is almost always in bed. She gets up for just a few hours each day. On good days for a little longer, on bad days a lot less. Today seems like a pretty good day. She looks bright in her nightdress as she pats the space on the bed beside her invitingly. He goes over and sits down. He is an obedient child. Obedient and well-behaved. Things are going well in school. The teachers like him. He likes learning new things, and finds it easy. Both his mother and his class teacher say he is intelligent. There is talk of him starting on next year's maths work as early as the spring. His mother says he has turned into such a big boy. She says he is such a good boy. She strokes his arm and takes his hand. He is her big boy, her good boy. There's something else she would like him to do for her today. She takes a firmer grip on his hand and guides it beneath the covers. Into the warmth. She places it on her thigh. Edward looks at her enquiringly. Why does she want his hand there? Sometimes he has warmed his own hands by tucking them between his thighs when he has felt really cold, but he isn't cold now.

★ ★ ★

'He'd just turned eight that first time. He didn't really understand what was happening. Of course. He was thirty-eight when it stopped. By then it had destroyed him.'

'It went on for thirty years?' Vanja looked sceptical.

'Yes.'

'Why didn't he just leave her? Or stop?'

Sebastian had been asked that question many times. Edward's mother was ill, she had no way of stopping him from leaving, and he became an adult. Why did he stay?

'At first he was too small. Then he was too scared. And then . . . it had gone too far.' Sebastian shook his head. 'I can't explain it more clearly without going into more detail about what makes us the people we become, and that wouldn't help in this case. You don't have the imagination to understand their relationship.'

Vanja simply nodded. Sebastian's dismissal might have been intended as an insult, but she could take it. She was glad she couldn't imagine everything the lonely eight-year-old had gone through.

'Didn't anybody find out? Didn't anybody suspect anything?' Billy was leaning forward, interested. 'I mean, it must have affected his schoolwork, among other things.'

'His mother threatened to kill herself if he told anyone. It was essential that he should behave in a perfectly normal way so that no one would suspect anything. If he did anything even remotely different, people might begin to wonder, might find out. Oddly enough, he became more and more "normal" the longer it went on. He became a master at dealing with any situation that might

150

arise. He had to. If he didn't do what he was supposed to do, she would die.'

★ ★ ★

His mother lies down on her stomach on the bed and pulls up her nightdress. He never sees her face. It is buried in the pillow. At first she explained how he must lie down on top of her, what he must do, how he should move. She has stopped doing that now. Now she is silent. To begin with, anyway. He knows exactly what will happen. There are no deviations. She shouts for him, asks him to sit down beside her, tells him what a big boy he is, what a good boy he is, how glad she is that she has him, how happy he makes her. Then she takes his hand and guides it beneath the covers. Everything happens in exactly the same way every time.

After a while the noises start. From deep down in the pillow. He hates the noises. He wishes they would go away. The noises mean that it will soon be over. He doesn't like what they do. He has realised by now that other mothers don't behave like this. He doesn't like it. But he likes what comes next even less. After the noises . . .

★ ★ ★

'Every time he was forced to have sex with her, he was punished afterwards. He was unclean. Dirty. He had done something ugly and disgusting, and his mother couldn't stand the sight of him.'

★ ★ ★

Her head is turned away as she opens the door of the windowless cupboard under the stairs. He goes in and sits down on the cold floor. There is no point in crying or begging to be let off. That will just make it worse. He will be in there for even longer. He wraps his arms around his knees. She closes the door without a word. She has not spoken since she made those noises into the pillow. And he isn't even sure if those were words. It is dark. He never knows how long he sits there. He can't tell the time. No one has taught him. They have just started learning in school. He knows the hour and half past and quarter past and quarter to. But it doesn't matter, because he has no watch to look at anyway.

151

Sometimes he thinks that's a good thing. If he had a watch, he would know how long he has been locked up for, and he might panic. Think she had forgotten about him. Or gone away. Left him. As it is, the time and the darkness flow into one. His teacher once told him that dogs have no concept of time. They don't know if they have been alone for an hour, or a whole day. In the darkness he is a dog. He loses all concept of time. Is it five hours or two days? He never really knows. He is just happy when the door opens. Like a dog.

He doesn't understand. He will never understand. He does everything she tells him to do, and yet he ends up here. In the darkness and the cold. It is never his suggestion that they should do what they do. Never his idea. She is the one who shouts for him. The one who pushes his hand down the bed. And yet she cannot look at him afterwards. She thinks he is dirty. Ugly. He gets hungry, but the hunger disappears. The thirst is worse. He pees on the floor. He would prefer not to. He knows he will have to clean it up afterwards. When she opens the door. When the punishment is over. Sometimes he defecates as well. If he's in there for a long time. He can't help it. When she doesn't open the door for a long time . . .

★ ★ ★

'Eventually he was let out. He was forgiven, but it wasn't over. He must be reminded of his sins, and so that he wouldn't repeat them she would attach one of those big bulldog clips to his foreskin. And there it would stay until she gave him permission to remove it.'

Everyone in the room grimaced, Billy and Torkel perhaps with a little more feeling.

'I don't buy it.' Billy again. 'How is it possible for someone to go through all this without anyone noticing? He must have had a fair amount of time off school.'

'She rang and said that he was ill. Asthma and migraine. Otherwise he was very successful in school. In spite of everything he got through junior school, high school and university. Top grades all the way. Afterwards he got a low-grade job, just to make enough to live on. He was obviously overqualified, but lied on his CV. He had superficial contacts. Colleagues. His IQ was somewhere in the region of a hundred and thirty, so he was certainly intelligent enough to play "normal", but he was completely incapable of forming deeper relationships which required empathy or any kind of genuine emotion. He might be found out if something like that happened.'

Sebastian paused and drank a glass of water.

'His mother died in 1994. Just over a year later, Edward began to seek out other women. His first victim was a colleague at the National Board of Health and Welfare, who was obviously interested in him and sometimes tried to chat to him.'

He is waiting. In one hand he holds the bag containing the nightdress and the stockings. He knows that she wants him. She is planning to take over. She wants to continue what his mother used to do. She wants to do the dirty thing. The bad thing. She wants to make him do things that will lead to the punishment. The pain. The darkness and the humiliation. They all do. But he does not intend to allow it. Not this time.

He rings the doorbell. She smiles. He knows why. He knows what she wants, but she is going to get a surprise. This time he is going to take control. She barely has time to invite him in when he hits her. Hard. Twice. He forces her to show him the bedroom. Off with her clothes. On with the nightdress. Down on her stomach. He ties her up with the stockings. When she cannot move, he leaves the bedroom. He takes the bag containing his supplies and the empty bottle into which he intends to urinate. He searches for the place. The place where she will lock him up. He finds it in the cellar. A lock on the outside. Dark on the inside. He arranges the things he has brought with him on the floor. Now he will be able to get through the punishment. Afterwards.

'But there is no afterwards. He cuts their throats, just to escape the punishment.'

Torkel's mobile rang. They all jumped as the sound broke the dense silence. Torkel turned away and took the call.

'But surely he must have known they weren't going to survive?' Vanja took up the thread once more. 'Why did he put the food there?'

'A safety measure. Just in case she did survive against all expectations, and he was punished. He didn't want to starve. But as we know, he never needed to make use of his supplies.'

Torkel ended the brief conversation and turned back to the team. The look on his face told them it wasn't good news.

'We have a fourth victim.'

Vanja's car was first on the scene. The uniformed patrol who had found the body had already cordoned off the area outside the grey apartment block, following procedure to the letter. Vanja jumped out of the car and hurried over to the officer standing behind the blue and white tape. Sebastian remained by the car, looking up at the building. Once again he had irritated her by taking it for granted that his place was by her side in the front seat, but Vanja had decided it would be inappropriate to get into an argument with him when they were out on a job. He could be childish. She wasn't going to be. She was working. But when all this had calmed down a little, she was going to make it very clear to Torkel that Sebastian Bergman could travel with someone else from now on. Torkel himself would be a suitable alternative. After all, he was the one who had insisted on dragging Sebastian back in. The officer by the door nodded to her in recognition. She recognised him too; Erik something-or-other. She remembered him as a good officer, well organised and always calm. After he had briefed her in just a few sentences, she saw no reason to revise her opinion. Following instructions, he and his colleague had immediately alerted Riksmord as soon as they entered the apartment on the third floor and found the woman bound and murdered. They had tried to avoid touching anything, and had immediately left the scene in order to cordon off both the apartment itself and the main entrance, with the aim of avoiding any contamination of the scene of the crime. Vanja thanked Erik and went over to meet Ursula, Billy and Torkel, who had just arrived.

'The scene has been secured. Third floor. Billy, can you take a detailed statement from Erik? He was the first to arrive.' She pointed to the uniformed officer by the cordon.

'Can't you do that?'

Vanja stared at him in astonishment. 'Why, what are you going to do?'

'I can go up to the apartment.'

'Have a word with Erik, then come up,' Torkel intervened.

Billy quickly swallowed a protest. It was one thing to remind Vanja that they were equals within the team, something she sometimes forgot, but another thing altogether to question the boss's orders.

'Okay.' He headed towards Erik while the other three went inside.

Sebastian was still standing by the car. He could see Billy waving to him, but couldn't decide what to do: stand there worrying, or find out if his whirling thoughts might be right. It didn't seem possible. This was a large building. Absolutely, totally and completely impossible. There were lots of buildings that looked exactly the same. And yet he couldn't shake off the feeling, couldn't make his legs work. Billy waved to him again. Annoyed.

'Come on!'

Sebastian couldn't put it off any longer. Although a part of him didn't want to do this, he needed to know for certain. He managed to get his legs moving and set off towards Billy. He would let him take the lead. Follow his energy.

They went into the apartment block and up the stone steps. Billy was moving quickly. Sebastian was moving more and more slowly. It was an ordinary grey stairwell. There were thousands, tens of thousands like this. Anonymous, identical, they all looked exactly the same. Why should this particular stairwell be anything special? Feverishly he searched for details that might suppress the feeling of rising panic.

He heard Billy reach the third floor. Heard him talking to someone up there. A uniformed officer, he saw as he rounded the corner of the stairs. They were standing in front of an open door. He could just see Torkel inside the apartment, in the hallway. Took a few more steps, then sank to his knees, breathing heavily.

He pulled himself together sufficiently to glance inside the apartment once more, in a final desperate hope that he was wrong.

He wasn't.

He could see it lying on the floor of the living room.

A brown teddy bear wearing a red rosette with writing on it. 'To the best mum in the world.'

Torkel had put on shoe protectors, but had avoided entering the living room where the bed was located. There was no doubt whatsoever that they were dealing with the same murderer. The nightdress, the bound arms and legs, the gaping wound in the throat – everything pointed to one conclusion. He felt both impotence and rage. Yet another victim they had been unable to protect. Ursula was standing in the middle of the room, methodically photographing the scene. No doubt it would be several hours before she had finished her preliminary investigation. He and the others could start talking to the neighbours. He was intending to begin with the woman who had called the police a few hours earlier. Suddenly he heard Sebastian's voice behind him.

'Torkel.' It sounded weaker than usual. He turned and saw an ashen-faced Sebastian standing just outside the door, leaning against the concrete wall of the stairwell. It looked as if the wall was the only thing holding him up.

'What?'

'I need to speak to you.' Sebastian was virtually whispering now.

Torkel went over to him, and Sebastian drew him a little way down the stairs. Torkel was annoyed; the last thing he needed right now was a game of Chinese whispers.

'What do you want, Sebastian?'

The look in Sebastian's eyes was almost pleading. 'I think I might know her. Annette Willén, is that her name?'

'We think so. She's the person who lives here, anyway.'

It looked as if Sebastian lost his balance for a second; he leaned heavily against the wall once more.

'How do you know her?' Torkel wondered, slightly less annoyed. Sebastian was obviously upset.

'We were in the same counselling group. Once. I only went there once . . . We had sex.'

Of course. Did Sebastian ever meet a woman he didn't have sex with? Torkel doubted it. It didn't usually mean anything to Sebastian, but he was clearly upset now, which gave Torkel a bad feeling.

'How long ago did this happen?'

'I left here just before five.'

'What? This morning?'

157

'Yes.'

Every sound receded.

'For fuck's sake, Sebastian!'

'I'm sorry, I don't know . . .' Sebastian was searching for the right words. He failed to find them. 'I mean . . . what the hell should I do?'

Torkel looked around. Saw the uniformed officer standing with Billy and Vanja as they discussed door-to-door enquiries. Saw Ursula fetching a black bag and a different lens for the close-ups. Then he looked back at Sebastian's colourless face. The man he had let into the investigation – which had just turned into a nightmare as far as the police were concerned.

'You will go back to the station. And you will stay there until I get back.'

Sebastian nodded almost imperceptibly, but made no attempt to move.

Torkel shook his head in frustration and turned to the uniformed officer. 'Someone needs to drive this man back to the station – can you get it sorted, please?'

Then he went back to join Ursula in the apartment. Back to the terrible crime which had previously seemed complex enough, but which now appeared to be the simpler of two problems.

Sebastian didn't recall much about the drive back to Riksmord. He remembered that he had chosen to sit in the back of the car. He remembered that the driver had been a female officer. He was fully occupied in trying to understand this day somehow. The paralysing feeling of panic began to subside around halfway to the station. His logical thought process returned. He welcomed it. He needed to be able to function. He needed his intellect. The situation was critical. Annette Willén was dead. Murdered. The big question which Sebastian hardly dared ask was whether he had been allocated a role in the course of events. He had slept with Annette Willén. She had been murdered shortly afterwards.

He wanted to believe in chance.

Coincidence.

A twist of fate.

His entire being wanted it to be a mistake. But how great was the probability that the murderer had just happened to choose Annette Willén? Almost non-existent.

So far they hadn't been able to find any kind of geographical pattern in the murderer's choice of victim. One in Tumba, one in Bromma, one in Nynäshamn. And now Liljeholmen. The other women had been murdered in their own houses – two detached, one terraced. Now he had struck in a large apartment block, which involved a greater risk of discovery, and suggested even more strongly that this was not a random attack. Unfortunately. However Sebastian turned things over in his mind, he always reached the same conclusion.

There was a connection of some kind.

Him and Annette.

Annette and the murderer.

159

★ ★ ★

Sebastian went up to Riksmord. He didn't really have a plan. He would wait for Torkel. He didn't even know if he would be allowed to stay around for much longer.

He found his way to the Room. At least he could close the door and be alone with his feverish thoughts. He went and stood in front of the board with the photographs and notes. Looked at Billy's timeline and the pictures of the previous victims. Soon Annette Willén would be joining them. None of them was exactly young. They were all over forty. Perhaps there was something in that. They all had history. More possible patterns in their past. He knew Billy had already gone through everything, but he had to wait for Torkel anyway, and it could be hours before he got back. He might as well do something. With a bit of luck, working would keep those other thoughts at bay.

On the table lay the three files about the victims, left behind by the team when they dashed off to Liljeholmen. Sebastian sat down and pulled the files towards him. They contained all the available information on each one, from official tax documents and details held on the electoral register to forensic evidence and interviews with everyone from the victims' nearest and dearest to work colleagues and neighbours. Could he find something that no one else had noticed? The chances were very small. This team was the best in Sweden. But he intended to try.

He needed to do this.

He needed to try to understand.

He began to read. The first victim. Maria Lie. Separated from her husband Karl relatively recently, but the divorce hadn't gone through yet. There was a lengthy interview with the ex-husband-to-be; it ran to ten A4 pages. Maria and Karl had been married for a long time, but the relationship had been childless, and they had drifted apart. Maria Lie worked as a finance officer with a recruitment company in the city. He worked for Tele 2, and the previous year he had met a younger woman and started an affair. Then came the discovery, the quarrels and the break-up in quick succession. Maria Lie had bought Karl out of the house; he needed the money, because his new partner was already pregnant.

160

Maria Lie had recently applied to go back to her maiden name, Kaufmann, and they had . . .

Sebastian stopped. Read the name again. It couldn't be.

KAUFMANN.

Ursula had finished taking photographs and wanted to wait for the crime scene investigation team to arrive before the body was moved and examined. The body wagon had been held up due to a serious road accident, and Ursula walked over to the living room windows to rest her eyes on something other than the pale, dirty grey body and the congealed blood on the bed.

Outside it was still a perfect summer's day, with a clear blue sky. The blazing sun had moved west and was no longer shining straight into the apartment with full force, but the heat was still stifling in the stuffy room. Ursula carefully opened the balcony door and stepped outside. At least it was slightly cooler out there. The balcony was small, but had been lovingly tended; a beautiful yellow climbing rose in an ornate terracotta pot covered the concrete wall. Two folding chairs stood by the French-style bistro table in white-painted metal. The only thing on the table was a pale blue sugar bowl with slender white flowers on the enamel surface. Before long no doubt someone would pick it up and wonder what he or she should do with it, and all the rest of the stuff in the apartment. The things we leave behind. Ursula went over to the railing and looked out over the Essinge intersection and the green forest beyond. She watched the cars speeding by on the multi-lane highway. Inside the apartment a life had ended, while outside life continued to race by. That was how it worked. Life was a river; you couldn't stop it however much you wanted to. However hard it seemed on the person who had been affected, just a short distance away life went on.

She took a deep breath, letting the oxygen fill her lungs. Closed her eyes and thought. There wasn't a shred of doubt that it was the same murderer. Everything fitted, from the nightdress, the nylon stockings, the gaping wound in the throat to the rape from behind. In order to be absolutely certain she had looked for the storeroom that could be locked from the outside. There was nowhere inside the apartment itself, but Ursula assumed that not much had changed since she herself had lived in an apartment, even if it was many years ago. There ought to be a storeroom. And there was. In the cellar.

On the other side of a steel door she found a long corridor with a concrete floor. Naked light bulbs every five metres illuminated small storage areas behind chicken wire attached to wooden battens. A rough wooden door with a bolt on the outside led into each separate storeroom. A faint but unmistakeable smell of mould.

Ursula had walked past the identical cages until she reached 19, the number of Annette's apartment. The padlock was broken. She had opened the door slowly and carefully, wearing gloves, and peered inside. This must now be regarded as part of the crime scene. There was comparatively little in Annette's storeroom. Most of the ones Ursula had passed along the corridor were more or less packed. Annette's housed only a few cardboard boxes, a floor lamp, a folding table, and four wooden chairs stacked on top of one another. In the middle of the floor the supplies were neatly arranged: the soft drink, the biscuits, the bananas, the bar of chocolate, the empty bottle for urine. They stood in a perfect line, each item precisely equidistant from the next. Exactly the same as at the other crime scenes. Ursula, the experienced crime scene technician, suddenly shuddered; it was something she would never admit to the others, but she found the precision with which the perpetrator re-created the same arrangement in every case terrifying. She crouched down, took out a small metal ruler and measured the distance between the items. As she suspected: 4.5 centimetres. He must measure it on every single occasion, she thought. That took time. But he allowed himself the time. That was how cold he was. How unstressed. That was how important it was to get it right.

To complete the ritual.

To do exactly the same as Hinde.

She had shuddered again.

Her thoughts were interrupted as she heard Torkel walk into the apartment. He seemed to be looking for her; he didn't notice her on the balcony and headed for the small kitchen.

'Torkel!' she called out, tapping on the window. He looked up and nodded to her. His expression was serious. He came out onto the balcony and started with the simple stuff. The stuff he could understand.

'We've been knocking on doors, but nothing so far. Annette was a quiet, respectable person. Didn't draw much attention to herself. Apparently her ex-husband was a bastard, but nobody's seen him for months.'

Ursula turned back to the view. 'What about the friend who found her?'

'Lena Högberg; she lives not far away. They were supposed to have lunch today, but Annette didn't turn up. Lena kept ringing her all afternoon, but there was no reply.'

Ursula nodded in confirmation. 'She's been dead for less than twelve hours.'

'Evidently things had been pretty tough for Annette over the last few years,' Torkel went on, 'so Lena got worried and decided to come over after work. She saw bloodstains on the floor through the letterbox . . .'

'In what way had things been tough?'

'The divorce, the son moved abroad, she lost her job. She was at a pretty low ebb, apparently.' Torkel looked over at the traffic before continuing, 'Vanja's checking out the ex-husband.'

'That's probably a good idea, but it's the same murderer. No one else.'

Torkel sighed heavily. Ursula looked at him. His expression was particularly grim, she thought.

'We just have to make sure we do everything by the book now,' he said, perhaps more to himself than to her. 'We mustn't miss anything.'

They fell silent for a moment, both gazing out across the motorway. Torkel took her hand and looked at her. She was surprised, but didn't pull away.

'We've got a problem. A big problem.'

'What?'

'Are you sure she's been dead for less than twelve hours?'

'It's difficult to say because of the heat, but somewhere between six and twelve hours. Why?'

Torkel squeezed her hand even harder. 'Sebastian had sex with her last night.'

'Sorry?'

'Sebastian Bergman had sex with her and left this apartment about twelve hours ago.'

Sebastian felt everything flow out of his body. Everything. The air. The power to act. The physical ability to orientate himself. He almost fell to the floor, and saved himself only by grabbing hold of the table. He clung onto the laminated surface as if it was the only thing keeping him from the abyss that had just opened up in front of him.

It was an impossibility.

It was a complete, utter impossibility.

And yet it was true.

This was what he had realised as he feverishly searched through the pictures, the interview transcripts, the witness statements, the personal details. Everywhere he discovered connections and memories he hadn't seen before. The truth rose up before him like a pale figure, obliterating doubt, hope and blurred uncertainty. It took over his soul like an alien force. He was shaking, he could hardly breathe. The brutal realisation reminded him of that time on a beach in Khao Lak, where his inner being had met that deathly-white, implacable figure once before. On that occasion as he sat half-naked, sore and bleeding among wreckage and palm leaves, the movement had been coloured by the blackness of grief, paralysing him. This time in an office at police headquarters the insight crystallised into pure terror. Destructive fear. He tried to concentrate, to push away the thoughts so that he could somehow deal with the panic that was threatening to overwhelm him. He banged on the table with his clenched fist. Forced out a strangled roar. Anything to find some kind of focus and direction. After a few minutes he managed to get to his feet with a gargantuan effort. He swayed, but regained his balance and staggered over to the window, desperate to look at something other than the images of the dead women spread all over the table and pinned up on the wall. Outside, the sun was still shining. It had been shining on the beach on that day too, he found himself thinking, and suddenly he was groping for Sabine's hand in his mind. He wanted to hold onto her. Not let go this time. Hide inside her child's hand, disappear into her sun-warmed skin, her soft fingers. For a brief second he could see her there in front of him, those rounded cheeks, the blue eyes full of life, the hair curling over the back of her neck. He held her tight. Wanted to protect her as well as seeking protection himself. Protection from the truth that was there in that impossible connection. Disappear with his daughter forever.

But suddenly she was gone. Torn from his grasp. Again. He was standing there all alone. In a conference room full of pictures of other dead people. With the devastating truth as his only companion.

He stretched.

Just as he had done on the beach that day, he straightened up.

And slowly walked away.

At first Ursula's reaction had surprised Torkel. He had expected fury, but her response was more like a pale silence. Then came a barrage of questions. How was this possible? Could it really be true? It wasn't unusual for Sebastian Bergman to mess things up, but to do so on this scale and in this particular way was unbelievable. Sebastian had slept with the woman in that room. The woman who had subsequently been murdered. Everything had happened within the course of half a day, give or take a few hours. Someone was copying Edward Hinde. Down to the very last detail. Sebastian was the person who had been responsible for putting Hinde away, the person who had put the final pieces of the puzzle together. It had been Sebastian's finest hour as a profiler, and it had made him the man he was. However Ursula turned things over in her mind, she kept coming back to the same impossible conclusion.

There was a connection.

But that just couldn't be true.

Together they had quickly decided that the rest of the team must be told. As they ran down the stairs a small part of Torkel was relieved that he had had the wisdom to involve everyone in the decision to bring Sebastian in. Otherwise this would have been exclusively his problem. He hated thinking that way; it felt petty when there was a woman lying murdered in an apartment upstairs. But the thought was there.

Billy had moved away from the police cars and the curious onlookers who had begun to gather. He was on the phone, walking up and down as he talked. Vanja came to meet them and nodded in Billy's direction.

'He's trying to locate the ex-husband so we can send a car. We've found Annette's son in Canada, and the local police out there are going to speak to him. If he doesn't get in touch with us, we'll call him later.'

Torkel nodded impatiently. That was all very well, but informing the next of kin was way down his list of priorities at the moment.

'Tell them you'll call back if you haven't got hold of him yet,' he said sharply to Billy.

'They've just gone to find him.'

'You'll have to ring back. We need to talk. Now.'

Billy ended the call. It was very rare for Torkel to use such a peremptory tone. Obviously whatever he had to say couldn't wait.

Those who had gathered behind the police tape looked at them curiously as they stood in an intimate circle.

'We have a situation,' Torkel began. 'Sebastian slept with the victim about twelve hours ago.'

Billy and Vanja stared at him in silence. Billy's phone rang. Presumably the ex-husband had been located. Billy didn't take the call.

★ ★ ★

Torkel and Billy sped back to the station in Vanja's car. They had decided that Ursula would head over to the lab to try to persuade them to establish a definite time of death for Annette as soon as possible.

Vanja was really gunning for Sebastian this time, but Torkel had asked her to calm down for once. For a while, anyway. They needed to know what had happened, they needed to gather facts and information, then act. They mustn't forget that four women were dead, and that had to be their main focus. Nothing else. They would need to deal with Sebastian professionally. They couldn't let their feelings gain the upper hand at this stage, however powerful those feelings might be. Vanja gritted her teeth and shut up, but Billy could see that she was seething.

They parked in the underground car park and took the lift up to the department in silence. They started by looking for Sebastian in the Room. It was empty, but the table was a mess; the files relating to the previous victims had been opened, and there were pictures, transcripts and A4 pages strewn all over the place. A chair had been overturned. Someone had been there. Sebastian, in all probability.

'Stay here and see if you can sort this lot out.' Torkel made a sweeping gesture across the table as he turned to Billy.

'Okay.' For a second Billy thought about asking why Vanja couldn't do it instead. But this was not the time.

'Check that nothing's missing. If it is, I want to know,' said Torkel, heading for the door.

Billy stopped him. 'You don't seriously think Sebastian is involved in all this?'

Torkel's expression was grave as he turned back to face Billy, his hand on the door handle. 'As far as we know, he was the last person to see Annette Willén alive. So yes, he is involved.'

Torkel and Vanja hurried down the corridor, calling in at the staffroom where a group of uniformed officers were helping themselves to coffee from the machine. One of them had seen Sebastian a while ago and said hello, but Sebastian hadn't replied. Torkel's office door was open. Sebastian was slumped on the brown sofa, his head bowed. As Torkel entered, Sebastian looked up slowly. His expression was resigned, yet somehow powerful. As if he had reached the end of the road and had nowhere to run, but intended to fight anyway. He got to his feet. Vanja appeared in the doorway and looked Sebastian straight in the eye, her gaze full of suppressed rage.

'Leave us alone, please.' Torkel felt instinctively that it would be best to speak to his old friend alone. He needed dialogue, not immediate confrontation. He glanced at Vanja. 'Close the door.'

Without a word she did as she was told. The hint of a slam, perhaps.

Torkel looked at Sebastian. 'We've got a few things to sort out, you and I.'

'More than you think.' Sebastian's voice was clear, and at least as forceful as Torkel's. This unexpected show of strength annoyed Torkel; Sebastian should be speaking in no more than a whisper, he thought before he went on.

'As far as you're concerned, it ends here. You will have nothing further to do with this investigation.'

'Yes, I will.'

'Sebastian, listen to me!' Torkel couldn't stop his anger flaring up. Did Sebastian really not see the problem? 'You had sex with one of the victims.'

170

'I've had sex with all four.'

Torkel's face drained of colour as he stared blankly into Sebastian's burning eyes.

'This is no ordinary copycat, Torkel. This is personal. And it's aimed at me.'

It took a while to gather the whole team. Ursula was called back from pathology, even though the autopsy was nowhere near complete. Billy had sorted out the files and tidied up by the time Sebastian and Torkel arrived in the Room; nothing was missing, as far as he could see. Although she found it frustrating, Vanja had willingly agreed to take over the task of trying to track down Annette's ex-husband. After what had happened she needed to feel that they were still effective as police officers, and were capable of acting correctly. She had managed to locate him and had sent a patrol to tell him what had happened. If he already knew they would question him briefly anyway, just to establish whether he had an alibi for the relevant time frame. Vanja was the last to arrive in the Room, and made a point of positioning herself near the door with her arms folded. As far away from Sebastian as possible.

'We're facing a critical situation here,' he began.

Vanja shook her head. '*You* are facing a critical situation. Not *we*. Don't drag us into this, if you don't mind.'

Torkel silenced her with a look. 'Let him finish.'

Sebastian nodded gratefully to Torkel and glanced apologetically at Vanja. He didn't want to fight with her now. Anything but that. It was a long time since he had felt so alone.

He turned and pointed to a picture of the first victim. 'I didn't recognise Maria Lie at first, but her name was Kaufmann when she was at university. According to the documentation, we were students there at the same time, and I remember I was seeing a Maria Kaufmann for a while.' He swallowed and moved on to the picture of Katharina Granlund.

'I should have recognised Katharina. She came to a book signing back in '97. At the book fair. She was already married at the time. We saw each other a few times. I realised it was her when I read

172

that she had a small tattoo of a green lizard in an . . . an intimate place . . .'

'You can't be serious?' Vanja said. 'You don't remember what the women you've shagged are called or what they look like, but you remember their tattoos down there?'

'A tattoo is easier to remember than a face,' Billy said.

Vanja turned to him like lightning. 'Are you sticking up for him?'

'I'm just saying that . . .'

'Stop it. Both of you!' Torkel interrupted the discussion as if he were separating two quarrelsome children. 'Sebastian, please go on.'

Sebastian couldn't look at Vanja as he turned to the last picture. The blonde woman in Nynäshamn. Victim number two.

'Jeanette Jansson . . . I don't recognise her, I don't remember her at all, but I read in one of the interviews that she was known as "JoJo", and I was . . . I went to bed with a JoJo a few years after I left university. In Växjö . . . She was blonde and she had a scar here.' Sebastian pointed to his upper lip. 'Jeanette Jansson comes from Växjö and had an operation to correct a harelip when she was a child.'

His words were met with total silence. Vanja was staring at him with pure disgust written all over her face. Sebastian suddenly looked immensely old and weary.

'So it's my fault that these particular women are dead. I'm the link you've been searching for. Me and Hinde.'

'But Edward Hinde is locked up in Lövhaga,' Billy pointed out. 'Can we really be sure he has something to do with this?'

'It's beyond unlikely that someone would be copying Edward's murders down to the last detail with all the victims linked to me without Edward having anything to do with it. Four murders, four women I've slept with – there has to be a connection!'

The room fell silent again. They knew Sebastian was right. It was impossible to disregard the pattern, however much they might want to.

Ursula got up and went over to the whiteboard. 'Why now? Why is this happening now? Hinde committed his murders more than fifteen years ago.'

'That's what we have to find out,' Torkel replied, suddenly realising that whichever way he looked at it, Sebastian was the key

173

to the solution. 'Sebastian, have you had any contact with Hinde since you interviewed him in the nineties?'

'No. None at all.'

Torkel looked at his team. It was a long time since he had seen such a mixture of surprise, shock and anger. In a moment of clarity he knew what he had to do. It was likely that no one else would understand. But he was absolutely certain. Torkel didn't know Edward Hinde as well as Sebastian did, but he knew him well enough to be aware that their opponent was a calculating, highly intelligent psychopath. Back in the nineties he had been one step ahead of them all the way along, until Sebastian Bergman joined the investigation.

Most of the team had been sceptical about the involvement of the egocentric psychologist, but Torkel at least had changed his mind very quickly. It was only with Sebastian on board that they had begun to find the patterns which eventually led to Hinde's arrest. That was the truth. He needed Sebastian. He tried to catch Vanja's and Ursula's eyes, and cleared his throat.

'You're not going to like this. But you have to trust me. I want Sebastian there when Hinde is questioned.'

'What do you mean?' Vanja appeared to have calmed down slightly but now she found a new burst of energy. Her cheeks acquired a faint red flush. An angry flush.

'If Hinde sees Sebastian as his opponent, if he's gone as far as he has in order to make that clear . . .' Torkel broke off and glanced at Sebastian, who seemed strangely indifferent. 'Then he shall have Sebastian as his opponent. For real.'

'Why?' Vanja again. Of course.

'Because until we show him that we've understood, the danger will continue.'

'So if Sebastian turns up, he'll stop?'

'Maybe. I don't know.'

Nobody else spoke. They didn't even know where to start. Torkel turned to Vanja again.

'You will accompany Sebastian to Lövhaga tomorrow.'

'No way! There are other people on this team.'

'But you're the one I'm asking to keep an eye on Sebastian. Somebody needs to kick the shit out of him if he doesn't behave. You'll do that better than anyone else.'

Vanja looked at Sebastian, then back at Torkel. Sebastian and Hinde seemed to be linked in a way she didn't understand, and now Torkel was proposing to give Hinde precisely what he wanted. That certainly wasn't doing things by the book. On the contrary, it could end very badly. She took a couple of steps towards him. 'Do you realise what you're doing?'

'Yes.'

Vanja looked around for support from the others, but none was forthcoming.

Billy leaned forward. 'I was just thinking: should we issue some kind of warning?'

The others stared at him uncomprehendingly.

Billy looked slightly embarrassed. 'I mean, there must be a lot of women who . . . who are at risk, if you know what I mean.'

Vanja shook her head. 'And what are we supposed to do? Issue a mug shot – "Have you slept with this man?" How many are there? A hundred? Two hundred? Five hundred?'

Sebastian looked at her, then at the pictures of the dead women. 'I have no idea, to tell the truth.'

Ursula got to her feet. 'I'm going to ring the lab; I need to have a conversation with someone sane.'

Torkel tried to catch her eye, but failed.

Before she reached the door Billy was on his feet too. He seemed to have thought of something, and was full of energy. 'Hang on, there's something else. How does he select them?'

He moved quickly across to the board and pointed to the photographs. 'Look. Let's say that it's possible to track down your past relationships if you do a bit of hunting around and plan for a long time, but what about Annette Willén? How did he know about her? You only met her yesterday, didn't you?'

The others took in what Billy had just said. It was as if the monster they were hunting was suddenly breathing down their necks. Billy looked at Sebastian, his expression serious. 'Have you had any kind of feeling that someone might be following you?'

The question took Sebastian by surprise. Why hadn't he thought of that possibility himself? Why hadn't he seen that the gap in time between himself and the dead women had suddenly shrunk? From decades to less than twenty-four hours. It must have been the stress of having to accept the impossible that had stopped him from seeing.

'I haven't thought about it.'

But he was thinking about it now.

Seriously.

The following morning they were standing in the lift together. Vanja kept her eyes firmly fixed on the numbers counting down just above the door. They were heading for P, the car park.

Sebastian suppressed a yawn and rubbed his eyes wearily. He hadn't slept much. He had found it difficult to stop his whirling thoughts. Hinde, the four dead women, the link. Everything was spinning around in his mind. He had dropped off at about four, only to be woken by the dream an hour or so later. By that time there was no chance of going back to sleep. He had got up, had a coffee, showered and driven to the police station to wait for Vanja. So that they could go and see Hinde.

'If this is true, four women have died because of you,' she said now, without looking at him.

Sebastian didn't respond. What could he say? Sex with him was the only thing the four victims had in common. Sex with Sebastian Bergman. A death sentence.

'You should have a warning sign around your neck. You're worse than HIV.'

'You might think I deserve this,' Sebastian said quietly, 'but would you be kind enough to keep quiet for a while?'

Vanja turned to him, her expression uncompromising. 'I'm sorry, is this difficult for you? Well, let me tell you something: you're not the victim here.'

Sebastian gritted his teeth and refrained from answering back. There was no point.

Perhaps he wasn't the victim in the true sense of the word, but nor was he to blame. He couldn't possibly have predicted that someone would track down some of his nocturnal adventures decades later and brutally murder them in order to demonstrate his power over Sebastian in a perverse way. Just as he could not have predicted or prevented the tsunami. He kept his mouth shut. She would never understand. He found it painful. More painful than Vanja could possibly imagine.

★ ★ ★

'Have you had any kind of feeling that someone might be following you?'

Sebastian couldn't get Billy's words out of his head. How could you tell if someone was following you? He had no idea. In the taxi on the way to Kungsholmen this morning he had glanced out of the rear window from time to time, but it was impossible to tell whether any of the cars behind them might be following him or not. Perhaps it was an instinct that police officers developed, and he wasn't a police officer. But no, that couldn't be true either. He had been following Vanja for several months, and she hadn't noticed anything. He was sure of that. If she had, he wouldn't be sitting in this dark blue Volvo with her.

Vanja negotiated her way adeptly out of the car park and drove up to the security barrier. As they drove out she indicated right.

'Hang on.'

As always her expression was irritated as she glanced at him. He wondered if she saved that particular look for him, but didn't pursue the thought.

'Turn left instead. Drive past the main entrance.'

'What for?'

'A long shot. If someone is following me, he or she might be waiting there. I always go in that way, and if I'm not on foot, that's where the taxi drops me off.'

Vanja flicked the indicator to signal a left turn and pulled out into the traffic. After another left turn they rounded the corner into Polhemsgatan.

'Stop.'

Vanja did as he asked. Sebastian scanned the street ahead. There weren't many pedestrians around, but Kronoberg Park lay opposite Riksmord. It was impossible to gain an overview of the park, at least from the car. Not like this, anyway.

Sebastian turned to Vanja. 'Have you got a pair of binoculars in the car?'

'No.'

Once again Sebastian's gaze swept over the street. He knew quite a lot about following someone. Keep out of sight, but at a reasonable distance so that you could follow the person quickly if your target moved. Everyone he could see appeared to be on their way somewhere. No one was just hanging around or ambling along aimlessly. So that left the park. And, it struck him, the café on the corner. Of course. A perfect view without arousing the least suspicion. That was why he had chosen the place himself.

'Drive up to the café on the next corner.' Sebastian pointed and Vanja started the car. As they drove slowly past the main entrance to Riksmord, Sebastian looked out of the side window at the cars parked on the right. Tried to remember if there had been any other regular customers. Someone who had been there as often as him. He couldn't think of anyone, but then he hadn't really been interested in the clientele. His focus had been elsewhere.

There was nowhere to park, so Vanja drove halfway up onto the pavement, far too close to the pedestrian crossing. They both got out and crossed the road. Vanja took the two small steps leading up to the café in one stride and pushed open the door. Sebastian heard the familiar tinkling sound of the little bell on the inside. He was just about to follow Vanja up the steps when he stiffened.

A memory.

Just before they'd passed the entrance to police headquarters. Parked on the right-hand side. A blue Ford Focus. Pale blue. The blue of a little boy's pyjamas. A man wearing sunglasses in the driver's seat.

His thoughts wandered back to the day he had decided to tidy his study. He had looked out of the window. Looked down at his old parking space outside the antique shop. There had been another car there at the time. A pale blue car.

'Are you coming?' Vanja was still waiting, holding the door open for him. Sebastian barely heard her. His mind was whirling. The visit to Stefan. When he had gone out to fetch milk. The men failing to unload the piano. Behind the van. A pale blue car. Possibly a Ford Focus.

'Sebastian?'

Without a word Sebastian turned, crossed the road and set off in the direction from which they had come. Towards the parked car.

'Where are you going?' Vanja shouted after him, but he didn't reply. He increased his speed. Far behind him he heard the little bell tinkle again as Vanja let go of the door and followed him. He broke into a run. The suspicion grew into certainty as he saw the person in the driver's seat of the pale blue Focus begin to move.

The driver leaned forward.

Started the car.

Sebastian lengthened his stride.

'Sebastian!'

The blue car pulled out. Sebastian ran between two parked cars and out into the street. Some idea in his head of blocking the road with whatever he had. His body. For a moment it looked as if the driver of the Ford was intending to do a U-turn, but Sebastian could see that he would never be able to swing around; the street was too narrow. Evidently the driver realised the same thing; he straightened up the car and put his foot down instead. Aiming for Sebastian.

'Sebastian!' Vanja again. Too far away. More urgency in her voice this time. She realised what was about to happen.

The car was only a dozen metres away from Sebastian, and showed no sign of slowing down. Quite the reverse. The sound of the revving engine grew louder and louder. The car was picking up speed. Realising that the driver had no intention of stopping, Sebastian hurled himself sideways, between two parked cars. It might have been his imagination, but he thought he felt the Ford catch the heel of his shoe as it raced past.

It continued at high speed. Vanja drew her gun, but knew she couldn't shoot at a fast-disappearing car in the centre of Stockholm, and slid it back into its holster. She ran to the spot where Sebastian had fallen. From where she was standing it had been difficult to see whether the car had hit him or not. She crouched down beside him.

'Are you okay?'

Sebastian turned towards her. Out of breath. Shaken. He was bleeding from a small cut on his temple, and the palms of his hands were grazed.

'The number. Get the number of the car.'

'Already done. Are you okay?'

Sebastian considered the question. Raised a hand to his head and stared at the blood. He must have hit one of the parked cars as he fell. Used his hands to break the fall. It could have been much worse. He let out a long breath.

'Yes. I'm okay.' He got to his feet with Vanja's help and dusted himself off as best he could, then they set off towards their illegally parked car.

'Did you manage to get a look at him?' Vanja wanted to know.

Sebastian shrugged his shoulders. It hurt a bit. He must have fallen more heavily than he had first thought. 'Sunglasses and a cap.'

They walked the rest of the way to the car in silence. Before Sebastian got in, he turned to Vanja. 'Billy was right. Someone was following me.' He realised he was stating the obvious, but he needed to say it. Put it into words. Someone had been following him. Everywhere. He hadn't had a clue. It was an almost unreal feeling. Unreal and unpleasant. He had been under surveillance.

'Yes.' Vanja gazed back at him across the roof of the car, and this time she didn't look annoyed. Even the least positive interpretation of her expression would reveal a certain sympathy. Sebastian decided there and then that whatever happened he would stop following her. Never stand outside her apartment block again. Never travel in the next carriage on the subway. He would ring Trolle and tell him to pack in the whole thing. Enough.

★ ★ ★

An hour or so later they parked and got out of the car. It was going to be another glorious summer's day, and the heat struck them as they opened the door. They had barely spoken during the drive, which had suited Sebastian very well. He needed to be left in peace with his thoughts.

Vanja's mobile rang. She took the call as she locked the car, and moved away slightly. Sebastian stayed where he was, looking over at the impersonal concrete building behind the high fence. Another greeting from his past. Another place that turned out to be more or less unchanged. This wasn't the plan at all. He was supposed to be picking up his life again. A new beginning. A fresh start. That was the idea of trying to get back into Riksmord.

To get a life before he could become part of a life.

But then the past had caught up with him. Hinde. The dead women. Everything about this case was dragging him back. Many years had passed since he was last here. He had completed his interviews with Edward Hinde in the summer of 1999 and left Lövhaga for what he thought would be the last time. And now here he was again. Behind those barred windows, the high fence topped with barbed wire and the reinforced doors was Sweden's most dangerous and most disturbed criminal. Sebastian realised he was a little nervous about the forthcoming encounter. Edward Hinde was extremely intelligent. Manipulative. Calculating. He had the ability to see through most things. You needed to be on top form for a meeting with Hinde, otherwise he quickly gained the upper hand. With everything that had happened, Sebastian wasn't sure he could manage to keep his guard up.

Vanja came over to him. 'We were already looking for the Focus. It was reported stolen from Södertälje. In February.'

Sebastian looked enquiringly at her as if to check that he had heard correctly. She nodded. That didn't necessarily mean that someone had been following him for six months, but it was a possibility. Sebastian took a deep breath. One thing at a time. He needed to concentrate on the interview with Hinde. Together he and Vanja set off towards the gate and the security guard who had been watching them in silence ever since they got out of the car.

'So what's Hinde like?' Vanja asked curiously, her voice free of the judgemental tone she usually used when speaking to him. It was as if she sensed that they were walking into the lion's den.

Sebastian shrugged. He was certain that Vanja had never met anyone like Edward Hinde. Few people had. Hinde wasn't the usual perpetrator: the jealous husband or the uneducated young thug from a broken home. Hinde was something completely different, which meant she had no reference points. She couldn't possibly imagine the depths of evil that lay within Hinde. Comparing him with any of the perpetrators Vanja had encountered over the years would be like comparing an eleven-year-old in a physics lab with a Nobel Prize winner.

'You need to read my books.'

'I have read your books.'

Vanja walked up to the security guard. 'Vanja Lithner and Sebastian Bergman, Riksmord.' They showed their IDs and visiting order. The guard took the documents and went into the small booth next to the gate; it looked as if he was making a call.

Vanja tried again with Sebastian. 'Come on, you've met him.'

'And soon you will have met him too.'

'Is there anything in particular I need to bear in mind?'

The gate buzzed and Sebastian pushed it open; he let Vanja pass, then followed her inside. The guard gave them back their papers.

'Be careful,' Sebastian warned.

Edward Hinde was sitting in the visitors' room once more. He had been brought down ten minutes ago. Two guards. Manacled hand and foot.

Into the room.

Onto the chair.

Shackled to the table.

Everything was the same, except for the fact that there were two chairs on the other side of the table this time. Riksmord were on their way in. Vanja Lithner and Billy Rosén, that was what Thomas Haraldsson had said they were called, the officers who were coming to talk to him. He wondered what they wanted to talk about. How far they had got.

The door behind him opened and once again he resisted the urge to turn around. Wait. Let them come to him. An immediate if minor advantage. They were approaching the table. From the corner of his eye he saw them pass on the same side. His right. He carried on looking out of the window, even when they were both standing in front of him. He didn't allow his eyes to move until the woman sat down opposite him. Blonde, attractive, around thirty, blue eyes, and fit, judging by her upper arms beneath the short-sleeved blouse. She placed an anonymous black folder in front of her on the table and met his searching gaze without blinking. Edward didn't say a word, but simply switched his attention to her colleague, who was still standing by the wall next to the table.

It wasn't Billy Rosén. It was someone very, very familiar. Edward had to exercise every scrap of self-control to avoid showing how surprised he was.

Sebastian Bergman.

They had got a long way.

Much further than he had dared hope.

Edward kept his eyes fixed on Sebastian until he was absolutely certain that his voice would hold. Then his face broke into a satisfied, almost welcoming smile. 'Sebastian Bergman. What a surprise.'

Sebastian did not return his greeting. Edward didn't take his eyes off him. Sebastian remembered that look. Searching. Observing. Penetrating. You sometimes got the feeling that Edward wasn't just looking you in the eye, but that he could see right through into your brain, where he picked out the information he wanted, information to which he wouldn't otherwise have access.

'And this is . . . ?' Edward continued, sounding relaxed as he turned to Vanja.

'Vanja,' she replied before Sebastian had the chance to introduce her.

'Vanja.' Edward seemed to be savouring the word. 'Vanja . . . Vanja what?'

'Vanja will do fine,' Sebastian broke in. There was no reason to give Hinde any more information than necessary.

Edward turned to Sebastian again, still wearing a disarming smile. 'And to what do I owe the honour of a visit after all these years? Are the royalties drying up? Are you considering making it a trilogy?' Once again Edward directed his attention to Vanja. 'He's written books about me. Two of them.'

'I'm aware of that.'

'I was his claim to fame . . . That's the correct phrase, I believe?'

Vanja sat motionless, her arms folded over her chest, apparently uninterested in Edward's comments.

'Anyway,' Edward went on, 'first he helped to get me arrested, then he revealed . . . the mechanisms behind the monster.' He smiled again. Not at Vanja this time, but more to himself, as if recalling a fond memory, a better time. Or as if he was just extremely happy with the way he had expressed himself.

'We topped the bestseller lists. Book signings. Lectures all over Europe. Perhaps the USA too – how did that go, Sebastian?'

Sebastian didn't respond either. He leaned indolently against the wall and folded his arms just like Vanja, while keeping his eyes fixed on Edward with an almost challenging expression.

Hinde met his gaze and tilted his head slightly to one side before addressing Vanja once more. 'He's not saying anything.

185

Good plan. We don't like uncomfortable silences in this country. So we fill them. Babble on. Give ourselves away.' Edward paused, as if to consider whether he had said too much, whether he had just provided an example of the very fault he had described. 'I'm a psychologist too,' he explained to Vanja. 'I was two years above Sebastian. Did he mention that?'

'No.'

Sebastian was watching Hinde carefully. Where was he going? Why had he mentioned that? Nothing Edward Hinde did was unplanned. Everything had a purpose. The only question was what that purpose might be.

'He doesn't want to admit how alike we are,' Hinde was saying. 'Middle-aged psychologists who have a complex relationship with women. That's what we are, isn't it, Sebastian?'

Hinde released Vanja from his gaze and looked up at Sebastian. Suddenly Vanja had a strong feeling that Sebastian was right. Hinde *was* mixed up in the four murders. Not only as the inspiration, but actually involved. For real. Somehow. She had no idea how, but he knew why they were here.

It was only a feeling, hard to get hold of – intuition. It came to her now and again. She was sometimes struck by it when she was sitting with a suspect or double-checking an alibi. A sudden deep conviction that there was a link. That there was some kind of involvement, perhaps guilt. Even when there was no physical proof, perhaps not even a chain of circumstantial evidence pointing in that direction. But the feeling was there. It could come from anywhere: body language, how the person in question looked her in the eye, or a tone of voice that struck a false note in an otherwise perfectly ordinary conversation. Vanja knew she was good at spotting that false tone, and there was something about the way Hinde had spoken to Sebastian. A tiny, almost imperceptible undertone of smugness and triumph. Easy to miss. But it was there, and that was enough for Vanja. Torkel had probably been right, even if it would be virtually impossible for her to come out and admit it: putting Sebastian in front of Hinde in this room had been the right decision.

'What do you know about my women?' Sebastian asked; nothing in his voice gave away the fact that they were getting close to the reason for their visit.

186

'There are a lot of them. Or there used to be, at any rate. I don't know what the situation is these days.'

Sebastian left his spot by the wall, pulled out the spare chair and sat down. Edward examined him carefully. He had grown older. Not only because of the years that had passed. Life had been hard on Sebastian. Edward thought he knew why. He wondered briefly whether to bring up the marriage to the German.

The daughter.

The tsunami.

The news which had brought such joy to his heart when he finally heard about it. It had taken quite some time. Sebastian's loss certainly hadn't featured heavily in the press. Edward had been forced to do a little detective work. Assemble the pieces of the jigsaw. Put two and two together.

It had begun when he had seen some names he thought he recognised in a list of those who were dead or missing. Swedes or those with Swedish connections. There, among the 543 names, were two that seemed somehow familiar: Lily Schwenk and Sabine Schwenk-Bergman. Then he had to go back through the newspaper archives. He found it when he reached 1998. A small notice stating that Sebastian Bergman, the world-famous profiler and author, had married Lily Schwenk. And a year or so after that, in a German newspaper, little Sabine. Sebastian's wife and daughter on a list of those dead or missing. At first he was pleased. Then, after a while, he began to feel disappointed. Cheated. Almost envious. As if he wished he could have been that great wave, the unstoppable force that took Sebastian's family away from him and left him broken. But it was still useful information, regardless of how he felt, and it would no doubt come in handy at some point, but not here and not now. Not at their first meeting. He wanted to find out what they knew. How far they had got. So Edward kept quiet. It was their turn to talk.

'Four women have been murdered.'

Vanja saw the flash in Edward's eyes as he leaned forward across the table, suddenly interested.

'Could I possibly ask for some details?'

Sebastian and Vanja exchanged a glance. Sebastian gave a brief nod, and Vanja opened the folder she had placed on the table. She took out a photograph of the first crime scene; it was a wide-angle shot that showed everything.

'The nightdress, nylon stockings, a hidden supply of food, the victim raped while lying on her stomach,' she said, pushing the picture across to Hinde. He gave it a cursory glance then looked up with an expression of genuine surprise.

'Someone is copying me.'

'Imagine that,' Sebastian said in a measured tone of voice.

'So that's why you wanted to talk to me. I was wondering.' The voice was filled with sudden insight, as if he had just been given the answer to a question he had pondered for a long time. A master class in total surprise. It would have fooled anybody. Even Vanja, if she hadn't been on her guard. But she was actively looking for signs that would confirm her intuition, and it was clear to her that Hinde hadn't been wondering any such thing. He knew. He had known all along. He was just playing games.

Hinde shook his head wearily. 'Can't people come up with their own ideas anymore? That's the problem nowadays. There's no originality out there. They just copy those who were first. And best.'

'This isn't an idea someone has come up with on their own. This is you.' Sebastian's voice had hardened.

An accusation.

Clear and unmistakeable.

Vanja wasn't sure if this was the right technique when it came to Hinde, but Sebastian knew him better than she did, so she swallowed her objections.

Edward looked up from the photograph on the table, total surprise in both his expression and his voice. 'Me? I never leave the secure unit. I don't have any privileges. My freedom of movement is extremely limited.' He extended his arms, stretching the chains attached to his handcuffs to demonstrate how fettered he was. 'I'm not even allowed to use the telephone.'

'Someone is helping you.'

'Really?' Edward leaned forward across the table, manifesting a clear and sincere interest. He had missed this, he realised. The discussion. The game. A statement from Sebastian which he could then counter. Choose to go along with his reasoning, question him, or try to divert his attention, go around in circles, challenge and be challenged. God, how he had missed it. Most people he met in the secure unit were sub-humans, free of any scrap of intelligence. In this room there was at least some intellectual fibre, something to chew on. It was wonderfully liberating.

He leaned back. 'And how exactly might that happen, do you think?'

'How do you choose them?' Sebastian opted to ignore the bait. He wasn't in the mood. Every time you answered a question, you lost control of the conversation. You were being led instead of leading. Sebastian couldn't allow that to happen. Not with Hinde.

'Who?'

'The women.'

Hinde sighed deeply and shook his head. Disappointed. The right thing for Sebastian would have been not to respond at all. To allow Hinde's 'Who?' to lie unanswered between them. Their eyes would have met. As in a duel. Who would pick up the thread first? And how? Giving the right answer to the question immediately killed the excitement for Hinde. Killed the conversation. Killed his interest.

'Sebastian, Sebastian, Sebastian . . . What's happened to you? Straight down to business. No finesse. No conversation. You ask, I am expected to answer. Whatever happened to a meeting of equals?'

'We are not equals.'

Hinde sighed a fraction too loudly. Sebastian didn't even pick up on that. He couldn't bring himself to embark on a dialogue when prompted, measure his strength against Hinde's. Edward leaned back in his chair. Disappointed again.

'You're boring me, Sebastian. You never used to do that. You were always more of a . . .' Hinde searched for the right words, found them after a while, '. . . stimulating challenge. What's happened to you?'

'I got tired of playing games with psychopaths.'

Edward decided to let Sebastian go. This was too boring, too pointless. He was obviously not the same formidable opponent he had once been. Hinde turned to Sebastian's attractive colleague. Perhaps she would give him a little something back. She was young enough; it should be possible to lure her into his labyrinth.

'Vanja, may I touch your hair?'

'Pack it in!' Sebastian's words sounded like a whiplash. Hinde was taken aback. A strong reaction. Raised voice. It sounded like genuine anger. Interesting. So far Sebastian had seemed calm and decisive. Determined not to be drawn into any kind of discussion, not to give anything away. But this little outburst of rage was definitely worth probing further. Hinde tilted his head to one side and allowed his gaze to roam up and down Vanja's hair.

'It looks so soft. I wouldn't mind betting that it smells good too.'

Vanja looked at the skinny man sitting opposite her, with his thin hair and his watery eyes. What did he want?

Fourteen years.

Locked up for fourteen years.

She assumed that Hinde hadn't met very many women during that time. One of the psychologists he saw might be a woman, perhaps a member of staff in the library. But the idea of touching one of them was out of the question. So she could understand his request. His longing. But how strong was it? Could she use it to her advantage? She decided to take things one step further, at least.

'What do I get if I let you touch my hair?'

'Pack it in,' Sebastian said again, still with that sharpness in his tone. 'Don't talk to him.'

Without breaking eye contact with Vanja's challenging expression, Edward ran through the situation. This time there was something more than anger and impatience in Sebastian's voice; there was something protective. Were they lovers? She must be more than twenty years younger than him; the Sebastian Hinde had got to know in the late nineties had usually stuck to women his own age. But that could have changed, of course. However, there was nothing in their behaviour towards one another to suggest that they were in a relationship. On the contrary, Vanja exuded a certain coldness towards her colleague. There was no empathy in the looks she gave him, and her body language was negative. Perhaps they were just very good at hiding it? Worth finding out.

'Are you sleeping together?'

'We most certainly are not,' said Vanja.

'That's got nothing to do with you,' Sebastian said at the same time.

Edward was satisfied. Sebastian's answer, an anti-response in order to retain control. Vanja's answer, direct and prompted by emotion. Genuine. They weren't sleeping together. So why that protective tone? Was there more to gain here? He spoke to Vanja again. 'If you could just lean forward and lay your hair here . . .'

Edward turned his manacled hand upwards like a little bowl and squeezed his fingers together in a gesture which, when he did it, seemed almost obscene.

'Will you answer my questions if I do it?' Vanja pushed back her chair as if she was about to get up.

'For fuck's sake!' Sebastian spat out the words like an order. 'Sit down!'

Definitely disturbed by the possible scenario. Time to raise the stakes.

'Your hair, one answer. To any question you like.' Edward looked at her, his face shining with total honesty. 'Your breast, three answers.'

Sebastian got up with such force that the chair tipped over as he hurled himself across the table and grabbed hold of Edward's upturned hand. He squeezed the shackled fingers. Hard. It hurt, but Edward showed nothing. Pain was nothing new for him. He could control pain. The joy he felt at having gained a stranglehold on Sebastian's emotions was more difficult to conceal.

'Didn't you hear what I said?' Sebastian hissed. Close now. That dark glare just centimetres from Hinde's face. Hinde could feel his breath, feel the sweat on the palm of Sebastian's hand. He had won.

'Yes, I heard.' Edward relaxed his hand, which made Sebastian loosen his grip. Hinde leaned back. Satisfied. A little smile playing around the corners of his mouth. He met Sebastian's gaze with triumph in his eyes.

'Even if you weren't playing, you just lost.'

Vanja and Sebastian walked through the secure unit in silence. Sebastian's outburst had put an end to the session with Hinde. Edward hadn't said another word; he had simply sat back with that contented little smile on his face. Refused to take his eyes off Sebastian. They were now heading for the exit, escorted by a guard.

'I can look after myself.' Vanja broke the silence.

'Really? It would be nice if you demonstrated that.' Sebastian didn't slow down. He was still furious. Edward was right. He had lost. No, Vanja had made him lose. That was no less annoying, but different. Just because she didn't understand that you never gave Hinde anything. You didn't even bargain with him. There was an ulterior motive behind every suggestion he made, a betrayal behind every promise. Perhaps it was Sebastian's own fault. He hadn't prepared her properly, that was very clear. And that annoyed him too.

'I didn't get much of a chance, did I?' Vanja had practically broken into a run to keep up with Sebastian. 'The great Sebastian Bergman rushed in to protect the defenceless little woman.'

They had reached the exit, a heavy steel door with a small window in the centre. No lock or handle on the inside. The guard accompanying them did his best to appear uninterested in their conversation as he knocked on the door. On the other side a face appeared at the window and scrutinised them closely to establish that they were entitled to leave the unit and that there was no kind of threat involved.

Sebastian turned to Vanja for the first time since they had left the interview room and Hinde. 'Do you seriously think we would have found out anything if you'd let him touch your tits?'

'Do you seriously think I would have let him touch me?'

The door buzzed and then opened. Sebastian and Vanja left the secure unit and continued along the corridor. Vanja didn't know what annoyed her the most. There was a great deal to choose from, all relating to Sebastian. There was the fact that he'd underestimated her, that he had used the word 'tits' like some football hooligan, that he thought she needed protecting, that he was walking so bloody fast, that he had no confidence in her.

'I was playing along.' She caught up with Sebastian again. 'If you hadn't come charging in like some fucking knight in shining armour, it might have led somewhere.'

'No, it wouldn't.'

'How do you know? You jumped in straight away.'

'You can't play along with Hinde.'

'Why not?'

'He's much cleverer than you.'

Vanja slowed down, let him go on ahead. She watched him go and decided not to bother with any kind of rank order; she would simply hate everything about Sebastian. End of story.

192

Annika Norling had done her best to get Sebastian and Vanja to sit down on the sofas by the coffee machine while she went and told the governor that they wanted to speak to him, but without success. Sebastian marched past her desk, went straight up to the door and flung it open without knocking.

Thomas Haraldsson jumped in his chair. He felt as if he had been caught out, which surprised him. He looked up and immediately recognised the man who had stopped in the doorway; the expression on the man's face made it very clear that he couldn't make any sense of what he was seeing. His first words confirmed this.

'What the hell are you doing here?'

Haraldsson gave a small cough and sat up straight. Tried to regain something of the initiative, even though he had never had it. 'I'm working here now.'

Sebastian processed this information and quickly reached the only possible conclusion. The Västerås police had finally come up with a way of getting rid of Thomas Haraldsson, and had given him the boot. Whatever had happened, he now appeared to be working as a guard at Lövhaga. Haraldsson wasn't the first police officer to have followed that path. A change of career was often imposed because the individual in question was too violent, had acquired too many official warnings, or had proved unsatisfactory in some other way. It was rare for sheer incompetence to be the reason behind a step down, but if there was going to be a first time, Haraldsson had to be the prime candidate.

'Oh well, the police service isn't for everyone,' Sebastian said as he walked into the room. Vanja followed him, nodding a greeting to Haraldsson. A greeting which he didn't even notice. What did Sebastian mean, the police service wasn't for everyone? What did he think Haraldsson was doing there?

'Where's the boss?' Sebastian asked, settling down in one of the armchairs.

'What?' Haraldsson was even more confused now, if that were possible. He was sitting there behind his desk, wasn't he?

Vanja realised that no one had told Sebastian that Thomas Haraldsson was now in charge at Lövhaga, and that such a development was clearly beyond the bounds of his imagination. This could be interesting.

'So what are you up to?' Sebastian asked with a meaningful nod at the computer in front of Haraldsson. 'Surfing a few porn sites under his log-in? Was that how they got rid of you in Västerås?'

Haraldsson wasn't following this at all. There was obviously some kind of misunderstanding here. Apparently Sebastian didn't know who he was, or rather what he was.

'I work here,' said Haraldsson with a clarity which would have insulted a five-year-old.

'Yes, you said.'

'I work *here*.' Haraldsson patted the surface of the desk with the palms of his hands. 'This is my office. I'm the governor.'

Sebastian stiffened. 'You're the governor?'

'Yes. It's my first week.'

'How did that happen? Did they raffle the job?'

An entirely justified question, in Vanja's opinion, but even though she didn't think much of Haraldsson and his abilities, she knew that he was in a position to make their investigation considerably more difficult – which was the last thing she wanted now that she was certain Hinde was somehow involved in the murders. However, just like the last time they had worked together, Sebastian seemed completely oblivious to the fact that they needed to remain on good terms with certain people. She saw Haraldsson's expression darken at Sebastian's last comment, and decided to change the subject before Sebastian said something that would really offend him. Perhaps it was already too late.

'We've just spoken to Hinde,' she said, sitting down in the other armchair.

Haraldsson switched his attention to her and was met by a smile. 'I know. I approved the visiting order.'

'And we're extremely grateful for that; it made our work so much easier, but we need a little more information about Hinde.'

Vanja kept on smiling at Haraldsson, and saw his shoulders drop slightly as he relaxed. If Sebastian just had the sense to keep quiet now . . . He didn't seem to have fully recovered from the shock yet.

'I'm sure we can help you there,' Haraldsson said, 'but in that case I do have to ask what you're investigating.' He kept his eyes fixed on Vanja, attempting to look as determined as possible. He had no intention of putting a spanner in the works as far as Riksmord was concerned, but nor was he prepared to be treated as if he had no say in the matter. They might have been able to do that in Västerås, but it wasn't going to happen here.

His institution, his rules.

No, you don't, Vanja thought, keeping the smile in place. You don't need to know anything at all. She quickly ran through the options in her mind. Either she left Lövhaga with the information she wanted, or she would have to submit an application in order to get hold of it. This would take time and create unnecessary hassle. Vanja decided to give Haraldsson something, show willing.

'We are fairly certain that Hinde is involved in several murders we are investigating.' She could give him that. After all, it was only a matter of time before the press made the connection, she was sure of it.

'How could that be?' Haraldsson looked highly dubious, with good reason. 'He never leaves the secure unit.'

'We didn't say he committed the murders,' said Sebastian, who had recovered from the shock and had realised to his delight that he was now even more annoyed than he had been before they walked into the room. In fact, he was bordering on furious. A fantastic surge of energy flooded his body. 'We said he was involved; that's not the same thing.'

'May I ask what makes you think that?'

'Yes, but you won't get an answer.'

'We think he's had help from outside,' Vanja replied, immediately going against Sebastian. She could feel her colleague looking at her. 'Has anyone who was close to Hinde been released recently?' she went on, ignoring Sebastian's heavy, weary sigh.

'I don't know.'

'You don't know who's been released?' Sebastian got to his feet, too frustrated to sit still. 'What did you say your job was? Governor?'

'This is my first week in the post; I'm not fully up to speed with everything yet, that's perfectly understandable.' Haraldsson swallowed the rest of the sentence. He was defending himself when he had no reason to do so. Jenny was always telling him off about it, his bad habit of going on the defensive as soon as someone questioned him. The best thing was simply to ignore the unpleasant psychologist; he wasn't going to tell Haraldsson anything anyway. Haraldsson turned back to Vanja. 'I'll find out.'

He picked up the phone and made a call on speed dial. Sebastian headed for the door.

'Where are you going?' Vanja wanted to know.

Sebastian left the room without answering. He came out into the little waiting room with the two sofas, the coffee machine and Thomas Haraldsson's PA. She had introduced herself as Annika something-or-other. She looked up at Sebastian and smiled briefly before going back to her work. Sebastian gazed at her. Around forty years old, a few kilos overweight, emphasised by the tight top with a belt around the waist. Reddish hair, definitely not natural; the original mousy colour was beginning to reappear along her parting. Subtle make-up enhancing the roundish face, a pendant dangling between her breasts. Rings on two fingers, but no wedding ring. For once he didn't feel tempted in the least. He really couldn't imagine being interested in sex at the moment. However much he was actually trying right now.

'Is there something I can help you with?' Annika looked up again; presumably she had been aware of his silent scrutiny since he emerged from Haraldsson's office. Haraldsson, who had just confirmed that well-known hypothesis that most people climb one or two steps higher up the career ladder than their competence should allow.

Sebastian couldn't resist the temptation. 'Your boss said you're to bring him a coffee.'

'What?'

'Milk, no sugar, and you're to get a move on, he said.' Sebastian could see how annoyed she was. Perhaps not by the request for coffee in itself, but by the mention of the need to hurry things along. She got up with a restrained sigh and went over to the coffee machine between the two sofas. Picked up a plastic cup.

Sebastian decided to take things one step further. 'He doesn't want instant,' he said. 'Real coffee, from the cafeteria. In a proper cup.'

Annika turned to check if she had heard him correctly. Sebastian shrugged to indicate that he was only the messenger.

'Would you two like something as well, since I'm going anyway?' He could hear her struggling to prevent the resentment from coming through in her voice.

'No, we're fine, thanks.' Sebastian gave her a warm, sympathetic smile. 'If we change our minds we can use the machine.'

Annika nodded and gave him a look that said she thought Haraldsson could have done the same, then she left the room, slamming the door behind her. Sebastian went back into Haraldsson's office feeling slightly more cheerful.

His timing couldn't have been better. Haraldsson put down the phone, turned to his computer and started tapping away at the keyboard.

'As I understand it there's no one who is or has been particularly close to Edward Hinde. Roland Johansson was in the secure unit with Hinde, and they evidently had a certain amount of contact, but he's been out for almost two years.' He looked up at the screen and scrolled down with the mouse. 'Yes, two years in September.'

'No one else?' Vanja asked as she made a note of the name.

'He occasionally used to play chess with José Rodriguez in the library,' Haraldsson went on, tapping on the keyboard again. 'It says here that he was released just under eight months ago.'

'I'd like to take a copy of everything you have on them,' Vanja said, jotting down the second name.

'Of course; I'll get their dossiers printed off and you can pick them up from Annika when you leave.'

Vanja nodded her thanks; this had been easier than she expected. She was just getting to her feet when there was a tap on the door and Annika came in with a cup of coffee.

Sebastian pointed to Haraldsson behind the desk. 'For the boss.'

Annika went over and put the coffee down in front of Haraldsson without a word.

He looked up at her, pleasantly surprised. 'Thank you, that's very kind.' He took hold of the handle and turned the cup around a little way, as if to examine it. 'And in a china cup too, for once.'

Sebastian saw the dark look Annika gave her boss before she left the office. Maybe he should send her for a cake when they were leaving? Or perhaps that would be a step too far. He heard Vanja thanking Haraldsson for his help, and left the office with her.

When Riksmord had left the room Haraldsson picked up the coffee cup and leaned back in his chair. He took a sip. Delicious. Not the usual dishwater from the machine. He would ask Annika if she would mind fetching his coffee from the cafeteria all the time in future. But that could wait.

So Hinde was involved in several murders.

Several.

Plural.

Surely it had to be the serial murders he had read about in the papers. 'The Summer Psycho', as one of the tabloids had dubbed the killer. Four dead within a month. Stabbed, according to the press. A major investigation. An important case, and Riksmord thought Hinde was somehow involved.

Edward Hinde, in Haraldsson's secure unit.

He took another sip of the hot, delicious coffee. Riksmord were obviously looking for a murderer on the outside, but they had no idea who that might be. Did Hinde know? What if Haraldsson could help them? Even better, what if he could get Hinde to tell him what he knew? It would be no bad thing if he could be the one to provide the missing pieces of the puzzle in such a high-profile case. Perhaps he wouldn't always want to remain a prison governor. There were other posts available. Higher up. Haraldsson took another sip of coffee and decided to go and visit Hinde more often. Become his friend.

Gain his trust.

He could see the headlines.

He could already hear the praise.

It was after lunch by the time they gathered in the Room again. Sebastian had been home for a shower. He still hadn't got over his failure at Lövhaga. Not only had he not found out anything, but Hinde had won. A straight knockout. Sebastian had gone over the entire meeting in his head as he stood in the shower, and had come to the conclusion that it was actually Vanja's fault. Not because she had started bargaining with Hinde – they might have been able to turn that around, not to their advantage but at least into a no-score draw. The problem was Vanja herself. Who she was. His daughter. Sebastian had walked into the meeting with secrets. When he had met Hinde in the past, there had been nothing he felt he needed to hide. He could play his hand, react as he wished, make decisions on the spur of the moment without being afraid that the man on the other side of the table would find out more than he ought to know. That was no longer the case. If you were going to keep up with Hinde, then you had to be able to use the whole playing field. If there was a tiny area where you were unwilling to go, then you could count on the fact that Hinde would steer the conversation in that direction. This time not only did he have secrets to keep from Hinde, but from Vanja too. An impossible situation.

Torkel's fault.

Or his.

He should have said no.

He shouldn't have gone to Lövhaga with Vanja, he should have gone with Billy.

Pity he didn't think of that until he was in the shower.

Sebastian sat down next to Ursula. The Room was hot and sticky, with a stuffy smell. Someone had opened the window, but it didn't help at all. There was no air conditioning in the Room;

it was merely connected to the ordinary ventilation system, which struggled to cope with the heat in summer.

When they were all sitting down Billy started the projector on the ceiling and switched on his laptop.

'I've found both men who were released from Lövhaga; it wasn't difficult, we've kept tabs on them pretty well.'

He pressed a key and the picture of a man aged around fifty appeared on the wall. Ponytail. Broad face, broken nose, and a red scar running over his left eye and down his cheek. The man looked like a caricature of a career criminal.

'Roland Johansson. Born in Gothenburg in 1962. Two attempted murders and aggravated assault. Substance abuse. Held in Lövhaga from 2001 to 2008. Moved back to Gothenburg after serving his sentence. I spoke to his liaison officer. They were away together when the second and third murders were committed. Coach trip to Österlen with Narcotics Anonymous.'

'Is he using again?' Vanja chipped in.

'Not according to his liaison officer, but he does attend meetings on a regular basis.' Billy glanced down at his notes. 'He doesn't have an alibi for the first murder, but yesterday morning he was definitely in Gothenburg, again according to the liaison officer.'

Torkel sighed. Johansson definitely sounded like yet another person they could eliminate from the investigation. 'Who's his liaison officer?'

Billy leafed through his papers. 'Fabian Fridell.'

'What do we know about him?'

Billy understood why Torkel was asking. All Johansson's alibis were provided by the same person. It was unlikely that two different people had committed the murders, but Johansson might have some kind of hold over Fridell, forcing him to provide an alibi.

'Not much. Nothing on record as far as I could see, but I'll check him out.'

'Good.'

'And I'll speak to some of the others who were on that coach trip.'

Torkel nodded. No doubt Roland Johansson had been ambling around Österlen visiting breweries and painting in oils by the sea, or whatever Drug Addicts Anonymous did on their coach trips. But the sooner they knew for certain, the sooner they could eliminate him.

'I've requested his fingerprints and those of the other guy from records,' Ursula stated. 'So we can compare them with those found at the crime scenes.'

'Good,' Torkel replied. 'We'll run both a forensic check and an activity check on both of them.'

'I can take Fridell,' Billy said.

'How did Johansson get that scar?' Sebastian wondered.

Billy looked through his papers again, quickly and eagerly. He wanted to appear keen. 'It doesn't say. Is it important?'

'No. Just curious.'

Billy brought up the next picture. A younger man, Latin-American appearance. Large gold hoop in each ear.

'José Rodriguez, aged thirty-five. Held in Lövhaga since 2003. Assault and rape. Lives in Södertälje.'

'That's where the Focus was stolen,' Vanja said.

'Exactly. When I made that connection I contacted the local force and they went to speak to him.' Billy was pleased that he was one step ahead. He went on: 'According to them, Rodriguez can't remember what he was doing on the dates in question. Evidently he's a pretty serious alcoholic, at least from time to time.'

He shut down the laptop, went over to the board and pinned up hard copies of the pictures they had just seen.

Torkel turned to Sebastian. 'What did you get out of Hinde?'

'Nothing.'

'Nothing?'

Sebastian shrugged his shoulders. 'He's lost weight and he wanted to touch Vanja's tits, but that was about it.'

'But he does know something about the murders,' said Vanja, choosing to ignore what Sebastian had just said.

Torkel looked at her enquiringly. 'And how do you know that?'

Now it was Vanja's turn to shrug. 'A feeling.'

'A feeling?' Torkel pushed back his chair with some force and stood up. He started pacing up and down the room. 'So I have a man who claims to be an expert in serial killers in general and Edward Hinde in particular, and he gets fuck-all out of a face-to-face meeting.' He scowled at Sebastian, who met his gaze with equanimity before reaching for a bottle of mineral water. Purely out of consideration for Torkel's blood pressure, he chose not to respond. Torkel was usually the epitome of calm, but sometimes he erupted. All you could do was wait for it to pass. Sebastian opened the bottle and took a swig.

Evidently Torkel had finished with him, because he turned to Vanja. 'And then I have an investigator who has a *feeling* that Hinde is involved. A feeling! What shall we do next? Get someone to draw up his fucking horoscope?! Bloody hell!' Torkel stopped and slammed both hands down on the table. 'Women are dying!'

The room fell silent. From outside they could hear the faint sound of traffic, which no one had noticed until now. A wasp buzzed in through the window, but seemed to change its mind; it banged into the glass several times before finding its way out. Nobody moved. Everybody kept their eyes fixed on some neutral area where they could be sure of not meeting anyone else's eye. Except for Ursula, who looked at each of them in turn, apparently pleased not to have come under fire herself. Sebastian took another swig of mineral water. Billy adjusted a photograph which was already perfectly straight. Vanja started picking at a fingernail. Torkel remained standing by the table for a little while, then he walked very deliberately back to his place, pulled the chair towards him and sat down. If anyone was going to break the oppressive atmosphere that had descended, it would have to be him. He took a deep breath. 'If I arrange another meeting with Hinde, is there any chance that you might get something this time?'

'Possibly if I go alone,' Sebastian replied.

Vanja reacted immediately. 'Oh right, so it was my fault we didn't get anywhere?'

'That's not what I said.'

'You said you'd do better without me. How the hell am I supposed to interpret that?'

'I couldn't give a toss. Interpret it however you like.' Sebastian finished off the bottle of mineral water and belched gently due to the carbon dioxide, which made his tone more unpleasant than he had intended.

Vanja turned to Torkel. 'Do you think this is working? Do you?'

'Vanja . . .'

'Do you remember what we said we were going to do if it wasn't working? We said we were going to kick him out.'

202

Torkel sighed. He had lost his temper, and now there was a bad atmosphere within the team. The question was whether it had arisen out of frustration because they still knew nothing about the perpetrator, or whether it was because they had let Sebastian in again. Torkel didn't know, but he had to bring them back together, if only temporarily.

He slowly got to his feet. 'Okay . . . let's all calm down. It's hot, we've been working hard, it's been a long day, and it's not over yet.'

He went over to the board and gazed at the pictures before turning back to face the others. 'We need to get close to this man. We need to catch him. Ursula, compare the fingerprints and DNA with our records on Johansson and Rodriguez.'

Ursula nodded, got up and left the room.

'Vanja, go over to Södertälje and see if you can improve Rodriguez's memory.'

'Shouldn't we wait and see what Ursula comes up with?'

'The car that has presumably been following Sebastian came from the same place. At the moment that's enough to warrant paying a little more attention to Rodriguez.'

Vanja nodded. 'But he's not coming with me.' She gestured in Sebastian's direction without looking at him.

Torkel sighed. 'No, he's not going with you.'

★ ★ ★

'I just don't understand you.'

Torkel and Sebastian walked into Torkel's office.

'You're not the only one.'

Sebastian went and sat down on the sofa, while Torkel perched on the edge of the desk.

'You fight to come back, and once you're in, you seem to be doing your level best to get kicked out again.'

'Are you really thinking of getting rid of me just because I've trodden on a few toes?'

'It's not about that. Not anymore.'

'I couldn't have known that Annette Willén was going to be murdered.'

'I'm taking a big risk, keeping you in this investigation. You have links to all four victims. Imagine what that's going to look like to those upstairs.'

203

'Since when did you care about that kind of thing?'

Torkel sighed wearily. 'I've always cared about that kind of thing, because that's what gives my team the freedom to act on their own initiative. I know it doesn't matter to you, because you always do exactly as you please. But I'm telling you for the last time: sort yourself out.'

Sebastian thought over what he had done, what he had said, how he had acted since he joined the investigation. He quickly reached the conclusion that he had behaved exactly as he always did. He said what he thought, and didn't tiptoe around pretending to be eternally grateful. But he really didn't want to be kicked out. He could be close to Vanja if he stayed, but that wasn't the only reason. It wasn't even the most important thing anymore. If someone had asked him a couple of days ago what would diminish his interest in Vanja, his obsession with her, he would have said 'Nothing'. But he would have been wrong. Now something else was at the forefront of his mind, overshadowing everything else – even Vanja. Four women had died because of him.

'I really will try,' said Sebastian sincerely. 'I don't want to leave.'

Torkel got up and closed the door. Sebastian looked at his colleague with a certain degree of scepticism as he sat down in the armchair opposite. Now what?

'What's going on with Billy? He seems to be trying to move up a step or two,' said Sebastian, hoping the therapy session would be forgotten if he shifted the focus to someone else.

'You're changing the subject.'

'You noticed.'

'I'm happy to talk about Billy. Some other time.' Torkel leaned forward and put his hands together as if he were about to start praying. A bad sign, Sebastian thought. A listening stance.

'What's happened, Sebastian? You always used to be selfish and unpleasant and self-important, but since you came back . . . It's as if you're at war with everything and everybody.'

Torkel fell silent. The question hung in the air. What's happened? For a second Sebastian wondered what it would be like if he actually told Torkel. About Lily. About Sabine. About a happiness he had never known before or since. About the wave that had taken everything away from him. What harm would it do? It might even give him a bit more room for manoeuvre within the team.

Torkel would feel sorry for him, he was sure of it. Genuinely sorry. He would care in a way that nobody else had cared since it happened. Not that Sebastian had given anyone the chance to show they cared, but still.

A Torkel who interpreted everything Sebastian did as a reaction to grief could be very useful.

It was his joker.

His get-out-of-jail-free card.

He had no intention of playing it until it became absolutely necessary, but he knew he had to come up with some kind of answer for Torkel. He knew exactly what to say. He would tell the truth.

'I feel responsible.'

'For the murders.' A statement, not a question.

Sebastian nodded.

'I can understand that in a way,' Torkel said. 'But you're not to blame for their deaths.'

Sebastian knew that. Logically, he knew that. Emotionally it was a completely different matter. It still felt surprisingly good to talk about it. Perhaps he could have discussed it with Stefan instead, but he wasn't sure if Stefan was still his therapist after what had happened. Sebastian had called him and actually left an apology on his answering machine, but Stefan hadn't called back. And that was before Stefan even knew that Annette had been murdered. If Stefan found out that she had been killed because she had spent the night with Sebastian, their relationship would almost certainly be beyond repair. It was probably time to look for someone new to talk to, but until then, Torkel would have to do.

'The latest one, Annette. I slept with her just to annoy my therapist.'

'And what were your motives for sleeping with all the rest?'

Sebastian was surprised by the question, and by Torkel's relaxed attitude. He had been expecting a condemnation. Perhaps more of a gentle rebuke, given the fact that Sebastian was clearly affected by what had happened, but still a condemnation of sorts. Torkel's moral compass was extremely well calibrated.

'What do you mean?'

'Correct me if I'm wrong, but you're not out there looking for Miss Right, are you? All these women have just been some kind

205

of . . . distraction.' Torkel leaned back in his armchair. 'You're a user. You don't care about the women. Not before, not afterwards.'

Sebastian didn't even try to deny it. It wasn't exactly breaking news.

The first three victims, the women from his past, gnawed away at him, but there was a limit to how far you could rewind the tape, how far back in time you could regret your actions. But Annette . . . that was different. She had got under his skin.

'She had such low self-esteem, Annette. She was desperate for someone to make her feel good about herself. It was so easy . . .'

'You've got a guilty conscience.' Once again a statement, not a question.

Sebastian had to think about that. It was so long since he'd had a guilty conscience he wasn't sure what it felt like. 'I suppose so.'

'Would you have felt like that if she hadn't been murdered?'

'No.'

'In that case, it doesn't count.'

Harsh, but true. The exploitation, the conquest didn't bother him at all. But she had died because he had had a bad day. That was difficult to ignore.

'Are you in touch with any of the women you've been with?' Torkel took the conversation in a new direction. Moving forward.

'There are almost forty years between the first and the last. I can't remember even a fraction of them.'

Torkel caught himself wondering how many partners he had had. Two wives, four or five girlfriends before the first wife. Four, really. A few between his marriages. And then Ursula. Maybe double figures. He didn't need to make much of an effort to remember all their names. But of course in Sebastian's case he would have to multiply that by twenty, perhaps thirty. Perhaps even more. Memory lets us down.

'What I'm trying to say,' Torkel went on, 'is that if you do what you can to prevent a repetition, that might help. Both you and us.' He got up, signalling that the conversation was over. 'But if you don't remember them, it can't be helped.'

Sebastian stayed where he was, gazing into space.

Thinking.

He did remember some of them . . .

Vanja was gazing out over the centre. It could have been anywhere. But it was Hovsjö. One of the thirty-eight regions earmarked by the government in 2009 for 'additional attention' in order to 'combat a sense of exclusion', Vanja recalled. 'An investment' in 'vulnerable areas'. Which was all a more elegant way of describing a suburb where there were more problems than solutions. Vanja had no idea whether this additional attention had achieved anything, but it certainly didn't look that way.

Her GPS had guided her to Granövägen. A few metres up ahead it was possible to turn left into Kvarstavägen, which was where the pale blue Ford Focus had been stolen from six months earlier. José Rodriguez was suddenly a lot more interesting.

Vanja had parked, got out of the car and looked up at the brown eight-storey building. Found the right entrance and the right apartment. Rung the bell. No one answered, so she had tried the neighbour opposite on the same floor; Haddad was the name on the letterbox. A woman of about forty-five had opened the door. Vanja showed her ID and asked if the woman had seen José Rodriguez, or knew where Vanja might find him.

'I should think he's probably in the square,' the woman said with hardly any trace of an accent.

'Does he work there?' Vanja asked, picturing a lively market like the one in Hötorget in the middle of Stockholm.

The woman in the doorway smiled as if Vanja had said something really funny. 'No, he doesn't work.' Her tone as she uttered those four words made it clear what she thought of her neighbour.

Vanja thanked the woman for the information and set off towards the centre on foot.

A hairdresser's, a restaurant, a food store, a van selling burgers and the like, a pizzeria, a newspaper kiosk and a clothes shop. All spread out, with an expanse of concrete between them. A real wind tunnel in the autumn and winter, Vanja suspected, but at the moment the sun was beating down, making the square live up to the concept of a stony desert. A few people were sitting on one of the benches in the shade outside the clinic. A skinny Alsatian dog lay panting on the ground and the two beer cans being passed between the men and women on the bench told Vanja this was probably a good place to start looking for Rodriguez. She headed towards the bench. By the time she was about ten metres away, all five occupants had turned their attention to her. The only one who seemed completely uninterested was the dog. Vanja got out the photograph of José Rodriguez as she took the last few steps into the shade beneath the overhanging building.

'Do you know where I can find this man?' She held out the picture. There was no point in trying to conceal the purpose of her visit. They had probably sussed out the fact that she was a police officer as soon as she set foot in the square.

'Why?' A grey-haired man of indeterminate age who was holding onto the dog's lead looked up at her after a quick glance at the photograph in her hand.

'I need to speak to him,' Vanja replied, sticking to the direct approach.

'Yes, but does he want to speak to you?' The grey-haired man again. Both front teeth were missing, so the question came out with a slight lisp. It made him sound almost sweet. It crossed Vanja's mind that it must be a little difficult to command respect when you sounded like a six-year-old with a deep voice. Perhaps that was why he had the Alsatian. To compensate.

'I think he can make that decision.'

Obviously not the answer they wanted. As if on command they all went back to what they had been doing before she turned up. It was as if she had ceased to exist. Vanja sighed. She could walk around the square showing people the picture and asking questions until she got lucky, but it was hot, she was tired and she wanted to go home. She reached into the front pocket of her jeans and took out a hundred-kronor note. 'I just want to know where he is. He'll never know how I found out.'

'He usually hangs out down by the holiday camp,' a skinny, long-haired man in a denim jacket said immediately, reaching for the money with a grubby, shaking hand before the others even had time to exchange a glance to decide whether or not the price was right.

Vanja held the note out of reach. 'Where's that?'

'Down there.' The long-haired man waved his hand in the direction Vanja had come from. 'Down by the lake – what's it called . . . Tomatstigen . . .'

The name of a street. That would have to do. Vanja gave him the money and he quickly stuffed it in his pocket, seemingly oblivious to the disapproving looks from the others.

In the car Vanja entered Tomatstigen into the GPS and saw that it was indeed fairly close by, but if she was going to take the car all the way it would mean a considerable detour.

Instead she drove down into Kvarstavägen, parked as close as possible, then walked through a small copse of trees down to the neighbouring residential area and the holiday camp. The buildings were more like summer cottages than basic chalets. The gardens were well cared for; these were not a collection of tool sheds stuck in a corner. Each house must have measured twenty square metres, with garden furniture, barbecues, hammocks and other comforts to enjoy when the occupants weren't busy with their plants. Vanja had no desire whatsoever to get closer to nature, at least not in that way. Growing things, weeding, digging, thinning out – none of that was for her. She just about managed to keep her pot plants alive. But a place like this was pretty at this time of year, with flowers and greenery everywhere, and bees buzzing behind every fence.

Vanja crunched along the gravel track leading down towards the lake, scanning the area as she went. This didn't feel like the kind of place that would tolerate down-and-out drunks wandering around and spoiling the idyll. Had she been conned out of a hundred kronor back in the square? She had reached the edge of the development and decided to go back to the car when she saw them. Several people on and around a bench on the tarmac path running along the edge of the forest. The distinctive bags from the state-owned alcohol monopoly lay on the ground. It was a fairly large group; eight or ten people, perhaps. Two dogs this time. Vanja quickly made her way towards them. As she got nearer she could see that the man and woman closest to her were eating apples, presumably stolen from some handy garden.

She took out the photograph and got straight down to business. 'I'm looking for José Rodriguez; have any of you seen him?'

'I'm José Rodriguez.'

Vanja turned to her right and found she had to look down to meet the eye of the man in the picture. She suddenly felt unutterably weary. Weary and furious. This just couldn't be happening.

'How long have you been in that thing?'

'Why?'

'How long?'

'I got hit by a car six months ago, maybe a bit longer . . .'

Vanja let out an audible sigh and stood there for a moment to gather her strength before she turned and left.

'So what did you want?' the man shouted after her. Vanja merely waved dismissively without looking back, and kept on walking. She took out her phone and tried Torkel on speed dial. Engaged. She ended the call and tried Ursula instead.

Ursula was in the staff dining room staring blankly at a portion of fish gratin as it rotated in one of the microwaves. Late lunch. Or early dinner. So that she could say she'd already eaten if Micke called. For some reason she just didn't want to leave work and go home.

To Micke.

To yet another evening of playing happy families.

Her thoughts were interrupted by the sound of her mobile, which she had placed on the table. She walked through the dining room; someone had worked very hard to make it less impersonal and sterile. There were red checked cloths on the six oblong tables, matching the curtains and woven wall hangings. The white plastic chairs had been furnished with cushions, and a border stencilled with flowers ran all the way around the walls. The same floral pattern was repeated here and there on cupboard doors and on the white goods in the kitchen area. The harsh fluorescent lights had been replaced by individual lamps suspended above each table, along with a certain amount of spot lighting. Three troughs containing houseplants, plus an aquarium by the door, vouched for the fact that the room was 'not only a place to eat, but a space which can provide a period of harmony and restoration', as it had said in the staff bulletin following the renovations. How much had that cost? Ursula had never felt particularly harmonious or restored after eating in the dining room. Full, perhaps, but that applied to the old room too.

She picked up her phone and looked at the display. Vanja.

'Hi.'

'It's me,' she heard Vanja say; she sounded slightly out of breath, as if she was walking fast.

'I know. How's it going?'

'It's not.' Vanja almost spat out the words. 'The locals who checked out Rodriguez managed to tell us that he was an alcoholic, but they missed the tiny detail that he's in a fucking wheelchair.'

Ursula couldn't help smiling. Her confidence in the local police was virtually non-existent. This merely served to confirm her impression that in those cases where they didn't actually hamper an investigation, they certainly didn't do anything useful. She wondered if this was a good time to tell Vanja that they had already eliminated Rodriguez as a possible perpetrator. Neither his fingerprints nor his DNA matched those found at the crime scenes. She decided to leave it till later. It sounded as if her colleague had had enough setbacks for one day.

The microwave pinged; her fish was ready. Ursula went to get it.

'Look on the bright side – you had a nice little trip to Södertälje.'

As Ursula opened the door of the microwave and took out her plate, she heard someone come into the dining room. She turned around and saw Sebastian leaning on the doorpost. Her expression remained unchanged as she went back to her dinner and the phone call.

'I'm not coming back in today,' Vanja said. 'Can you let Torkel know?'

'Of course. See you tomorrow.'

Ursula ended the call, slipped the phone into her pocket and went back to the table with her plate. She glanced at Sebastian in passing. 'That was Vanja. She said hello.'

'No, she didn't,' Sebastian said matter-of-factly.

'No, she didn't,' Ursula confirmed, sitting down. Sebastian didn't move. Ursula started eating in silence, wishing she had something to read, something to look at. Why was he just standing there? What did he want? Whatever it was, she was sure she wouldn't be interested. She was convinced he should no longer be a part of the team. She didn't even dare to think about what would happen if the press made the connection between the victims and a person who was participating in the investigation. There was no way Torkel could have cleared his decision with the top brass, she was sure of it. If this went wrong, he might not keep his job. He was risking a great deal for Sebastian. She wondered whether Sebastian felt any kind of gratitude, whether he was even aware of the gamble Torkel was taking. Probably not.

She had things she wanted to think through. Private things. Like why she didn't want to go home. Whether Torkel was an option tonight as well. She was hesitant. After their last night together, while they were lying in his bed, Torkel had talked about Yvonne and some new man in her life; Ursula had forgotten his name, but she had got the feeling that Torkel was fishing, sounding her out to see if there could be something more between them.

Something more permanent.

No doubt she had only herself to blame; she had broken two of the rules she had established for their relationship, so perhaps it was hardly surprising if he thought she might be willing to revise her attitude to the third rule as well. But he was wrong.

'How are things with Micke?' Sebastian asked in a casual tone of voice, as if he had been reading her mind. Ursula gave a start and dropped her knife, which fell onto her plate and then the floor with a clatter.

'Why do you ask?' she snapped as she bent down to pick it up.

'No reason.' Sebastian shrugged. 'Just making small talk.'

'You never make small talk.' Ursula put her fork down next to the knife she had picked up, and got to her feet. She had lost her appetite. Did he know something about her and Torkel? If so, that wasn't good. Not good at all. The less Sebastian Bergman knew, the better. That applied to everything. He had the ability to turn the most innocent information against a person. And if he thought he could use it to his advantage, he wouldn't hesitate to do so.

Sebastian came into the room, pulled out the nearest chair and sat down. 'There's something I've been thinking about . . .'

'Mhm,' Ursula replied with her back to him. She dried her hands on a tea towel and turned to leave.

'Sit down for a minute.' Sebastian gestured to the chair opposite. 'Why?'

'Because I'm asking you.'

'I haven't got time.'

As Ursula was walking past Sebastian, he grabbed her wrist. She stopped and gave him a look which made it clear that he needed to let go right now. He didn't.

'Sit down. Please.'

Ursula jerked her hand away and looked at Sebastian. His tone of voice was different somehow, with no hint of teasing or superciliousness, and there was something in his eyes that told her this was important. Not because he had something to gain, but for some other reason.

Something real.

Something significant.

And he had said 'please', a word she hadn't thought was even in his vocabulary. She sat down, but perched on the very edge of the chair, ready to leave immediately.

'I've been speaking to Torkel,' Sebastian began, a little hesitantly.

'Oh yes,' Ursula said defensively, more and more convinced that she wasn't going to like what Sebastian had on his mind.

'About the fact that the four victims have had a relationship with me,' he went on without looking her in the eye. 'A sexual relationship.'

Ursula suddenly realised where the conversation was going. It wasn't about her and Torkel at all, but was heading for a topic she had even less desire to discuss.

'If there's a possibility that this might continue,' Sebastian went on, his voice quiet and serious, 'if more women are in danger . . .'

'I can take care of myself,' Ursula interrupted him, leaping to her feet.

'I know that, it's just . . .' Sebastian looked up and met her gaze with candour and sincerity. 'I don't want anything to happen to you because of me.'

'That's very kind of you,' Ursula said, keeping her tone neutral as she headed for the door. She turned back to face him before she left the room. 'It would have been even better if you'd shown me just a modicum of the same consideration at the time.'

She turned away and disappeared.

There was a knock on the door of the cell. Hinde put down the book he had been reading, sat up on his bed and quickly looked around the room. He hadn't left anything out, had he? Nothing that might give him away? A glance at the desk, the small bedside table and the single shelf, and his survey was done. The one advantage of having a small cell was that it was easy to check. Nothing on show that shouldn't be there. He swung his legs over the edge of the bed as the door opened and Thomas Haraldsson stuck his head in.

'Good evening, am I disturbing you?'

Hinde was rather taken aback by this everyday greeting, which sounded as if Haraldsson had just popped in to see a neighbour at home, or a colleague in the office next door at work. He presumed that this personal approach was meant to signify that the governor was not here on official business, but for some other reason. This could be interesting.

'No, I was just reading.' Hinde went for the same friendly tone. 'Come on in,' he added with a wave.

Haraldsson stepped into the cell and the door closed behind him. Edward looked at him in silence. Haraldsson was gazing around as if this was the first time he had been inside one of the cells in the secure unit. Edward wondered if his visitor would stick with the polite phrases from the outside world and tell him what a lovely place he had here. Amazing what you can do with a bijou space.

'I'm off home soon, but I thought I'd just pop in and see you,' Haraldsson said, completing his brief inspection of the cell. It was so small. How did they stand it?

'Off home to Jenny,' Hinde commented from the bed.

'Yes.'

'And the baby.'

'Yes.'

'How far gone is she now?'

'Eleven weeks.'

'Lovely.'

Edward smiled at Haraldsson, who pulled out the only chair and sat down. Enough of the small talk.

'I was just wondering,' Haraldsson began, 'how did it go with Riksmord?'

'How did they say it went?' Hinde asked, leaning forward.

'They didn't say much at all.' Haraldsson thought about it. What had he actually found out from Vanja and Sebastian after their meeting with Hinde? They thought he was involved in a number of murders, but they could have told Haraldsson that without even seeing Hinde. They hadn't said a single thing about the meeting itself, it struck him now.

'They didn't really say anything . . .'

Hinde gave an understanding nod. Haraldsson briefly considered telling him about his negative experiences of Riksmord in Västerås, putting himself on the same side as Hinde, so to speak, but then it occurred to him that the man on the bed didn't know that he used to be a police officer. Nor did he need to know. In fact, it was better if he didn't know. Better if he thought Haraldsson was just an ordinary harmless desk jockey.

'How do you feel the meeting went?' he asked instead.

Hinde appeared to consider the question. He rested his elbows on his knees and supported his chin on his linked hands.

'It was rather disappointing, to be honest,' he said thoughtfully.

'In what way?'

'It wasn't much of a conversation.'

'Why not?'

'I made them an offer which they didn't accept.'

'What kind of an offer?'

Hinde straightened up, apparently searching for the right words. 'There were certain . . . things I wanted, and I said that if I was given those things, I would answer one or more of their questions. Truthfully.'

He glanced at Haraldsson to see if he was nibbling at the bait, but the man on the chair looked confused more than anything.

'Mutual favours,' Hinde explained. 'Like a game, you could say. I've got something they want, they've got something I want, why just give it away? But Sebastian refused to play.'

Hinde met Haraldsson's eyes. Had he been too clear? Was it too obvious where he was going with this? After all, his guest had once been a police officer, until quite recently in fact. Would a warning bell start to ring? Apparently not. Edward decided to go all the way.

'I could make you the same offer.'

Haraldsson didn't answer immediately. What was Hinde offering? Information in return for what? He would find out if he went along with the game. But why was he making the offer? To gain advantages for himself, of course. Privileges. Of course it could also be that he was simply bored, and took every chance that came along to make his everyday life less ordinary, more stimulating. Haraldsson quickly went through the pros and cons in his head.

The advantages were self-evident. Hinde would answer his questions. Any questions. This would give him a unique insight and knowledge. In the best-case scenario he would find out enough to solve four murders.

The disadvantages? He didn't know what Hinde would want in return for his answers. But if he didn't say yes, he would never find out. If it was something that was against the rules, or something he couldn't go along with for any other reason, he could simply say no. Put a stop to it.

It couldn't go wrong.

Haraldsson nodded. 'Fine. What did you have in mind?'

Edward had to make a real effort to resist the impulse to let out a smug little laugh. Instead he gave Haraldsson a big, warm smile and leaned forward, almost confidentially.

'I'll tell you what I want, and when I've got it, you can ask any question you like, and I'll answer it.'

'Truthfully.'

'I promise.'

Hinde held out his right hand to show that they had an agreement. A handshake. All that was necessary between men.

They shook hands, then Edward shuffled back on the bed, leaned against the wall and drew his feet up onto the mattress.

Relaxed. Friendly. Play down the situation. He studied Haraldsson between his bent knees. What should he begin with? He needed to get an idea of how keen the man on the desk chair was.

'Have you got a photograph of your wife?'

'Ye-es . . . ?' Hesitation in his response.

'Can I have it?'

'What?' Haraldsson asked, looking slightly bewildered. 'Just to look at, or do you want to keep it?'

'Keep it.'

Haraldsson hesitated. This didn't feel good. Not good at all. This wasn't what he had thought Hinde would ask for. A longer spell in the exercise yard. Better food. Greater freedom on the computer. A beer, perhaps. Things that would improve and enhance his time in Lövhaga. Not this. What would Hinde want with a photo of his wife? According to the reports he was sexually inactive, so the idea of him masturbating over a photo of Jenny seemed unlikely.

'What do you want it for?'

'Is that the question you want to ask?'

'No . . .'

Haraldsson was beginning to feel stressed. Should he put a stop to this right now? Could he?

It was only a picture.

Riksmord were convinced that the man on the bed was involved in four murders. If Haraldsson played his cards right, he could virtually solve the case himself. Hinde was stuck in Lövhaga. There was nothing he could do. Haraldsson didn't even need to inform Riksmord. He could go higher up, straight to the top with his information. Keep all the glory for himself. Solve the case while others were at a loss.

It was only a picture.

He took his wallet out of his back pocket and opened it. Behind clear plastic on one side was a picture of Jenny, taken in a hotel room in Copenhagen about eighteen months ago. You couldn't see much of the room, the picture had been trimmed to fit in the wallet, but Jenny was radiant. So happy. Haraldsson loved that picture. It captured exactly who Jenny was. But it was still on his memory card; he could print off another copy.

It was only a picture.

And yet he couldn't quite shake off the feeling that he was making a big mistake as he placed the photograph in Hinde's outstretched hand.

'Are you involved in the recent murders of four women?' Haraldsson asked as soon as the picture had a new owner.

'Define involved,' Hinde replied, glancing at the photograph in his hand. Just over thirty. Slim. Smiling. Brunette. He could absorb all the details later. He put the photo down on the book on his bedside table.

'Do you know about them?'

'Yes.'

'How?'

Hinde shook his head and leaned back against the wall once more. 'That's question number two, Thomas. But just to show you how much I appreciate the fact that you've come to see me, I will answer the question without asking for anything in return.' He met Haraldsson's eyes. Saw anticipation, hope. He was keen, there was no doubt about that. 'Riksmord told me about the murders,' he said eventually.

'But before that?' Haraldsson went on eagerly. 'Did you know anything about them before that?'

'The answer to that question will cost you.'

'Cost me what?'

'Let me think about that. Come back tomorrow.' Hinde lay down and reached for his book. The photograph of Jenny slid down onto the table as if he had forgotten it was there. Haraldsson realised the conversation was over. He wasn't satisfied, but it was a start. It could definitely lead somewhere. He got up, went over to the door and left the cell.

★ ★ ★

On the way back to his office, Haraldsson made two decisions.

First, he wasn't going to tell Jenny that he had given a photograph of her to Edward Hinde. He couldn't quite work out how he would explain it. He would print off a new copy as soon as possible and replace the old one.

Second, he decided to regard today as a success. He had been faced with difficult choices, but had made the right decision. Taken a step in the right direction.

'That went well,' he said to himself out loud in the empty corridor. He thought it sounded a little bit as if he were making too much of an effort to convince himself, so he cleared his throat and said it again.

Louder.

More firmly.

'That went really well.'

In his cell, Edward Hinde was lying on his bed, studying the photograph of Jenny Haraldsson and thinking exactly the same thing.

Vanja was driving too fast. As usual. She felt full of impatient energy. She would go out for a run when she got home. It would be light for a few more hours yet, and it was already a little cooler.

She didn't really want to go running.

She really wanted to work. Make some progress. Get somewhere. A month after the first murder, and they were still fumbling in the dark. Hinde was involved, but how? The victims were linked to Sebastian, but why? Revenge, of course. But what if Sebastian had never become a part of this investigation? After all, it had been by no means certain that he would ever work with Riksmord again. In that case they might never have made the connection, found the link between the victims. It wouldn't be much of a revenge if the focus of that revenge never even noticed. Or had Hinde been counting on Sebastian's involvement, sooner or later? Was that why it was so important that the murders were exact copies? That they screamed out Edward Hinde? So that Riksmord would be forced to consult Sebastian, and he would then understand the connection?

And now that Sebastian was an active part of the investigation and had grasped the personal implications, did that mean the murders would stop?

So many questions.

No answers.

Vanja put her foot down. The needle on the speedometer touched a hundred and forty. She wanted to put the wasted hours in Södertälje behind her as quickly as possible. But were they wasted, or was she the one who had wasted them? She couldn't shake off the feeling that she had allowed her disappointment and impatience to affect her work.

She switched her phone to hands-free and made a call.

★ ★ ★

Billy was standing in the kitchen chopping broccoli, peppers and onions when the phone rang. Maya was frying chicken on one hotplate while toasting cashew nuts over a low heat on another. The chicken was supposed to be cooked in a wok, but Billy didn't own a wok. He had been given the frying pan for Christmas by his parents many years ago. He had used it more since midsummer than he had ever used it before. Maya liked them to cook together.

'Hi, Billy speaking,' he said, jamming the phone between his chin and shoulder as he carried on chopping.

'Hi, where are you?' Vanja was calling from the car; Billy had to strain to hear her voice over the noise. Her hands-free and his awkward grip on the phone didn't exactly help.

'At home. Where are you?'

'On the way back from Södertälje. Rodriguez is in a wheelchair as a result of a car accident, so it can't be him.'

'Hang on, let me put you on speakerphone.' He mouthed 'Vanja' at Maya as he pressed the appropriate key and put the phone down on the worktop. She nodded as if she had already worked that out. 'Okay, I can hear you again.'

'What's that hissing noise?'

'The frying pan, I expect.'

'What are you doing?'

'Cooking.'

'Really? You're cooking?'

'Yes.'

There was silence at the other end of the line. Billy could understand Vanja's surprise. He was a major consumer of fast food and ready meals; 7-Eleven and a range of frozen-food counters kept him alive. It wasn't that he couldn't cook, he just wasn't interested, and thought that the time it took to prepare a meal from scratch could be put to much better use. However, his total indifference wasn't something he wanted to go into while Maya was listening. He had a vague memory of listing cooking as one of his hobbies early on the morning of midsummer's day.

'What was it you wanted?' Billy pushed the vegetables to one side with his knife and glanced at Maya, who was listening to the conversation with interest. He started to finely chop a red chilli.

'I wondered if you could find out when the accident was? The one that put Rodriguez in a wheelchair.'

'Didn't he know?'

'I didn't ask him. I was so furious that the local police hadn't mentioned it, I just walked away. But of course he could still have something to do with the theft of the Ford, couldn't he? He lives very close by.'

Billy stopped chopping. She was ringing to ask him to look something up. A simple task that everyone, anyone, could do. From the corner of his eye he saw Maya shaking her head. Billy put down the knife and leaned closer to the phone.

'Hang on, have I got this right? You forgot to ask when the accident was, so you want *me* to check it out?'

'Yes.'

'I'm at home.'

'I don't mean now – you can do it tomorrow.'

'Why can't you do it tomorrow?'

Silence once more. Billy knew why. Vanja wasn't used to being contradicted or questioned. At least not by him. Well, there was always a first time, he thought; she might as well get used to it.

'You're better at finding that kind of thing than I am. It'll be quicker if you do it,' Vanja said; Billy thought he could detect a hint of annoyance in her voice.

What she said was certainly true, but it wasn't enough of an argument. For far too long he had accepted the role of some kind of administrative right-hand man within the team. But not anymore.

'I'll show you how to do it.'

'I know how to do it.'

'Well, you do it then.' Billy glanced at Maya, who responded with an encouraging smile.

'Okay . . . fine,' he heard Vanja say tersely. Then there was another silence, and after a second the sound of the car disappeared as well. Vanja had ended the call. Billy picked up the phone and slipped it into his pocket. Maya came over and squeezed his arm.

'How did that feel?'

'Good.' Billy paused for a moment, and decided to be straight with her. 'And a little bit petty, if I'm honest. I could do it in no time.'

'But she knows what to do?'

'Yes, but the thing is, now she's mad at me for something insignificant.'

Maya squeezed between the worktop and Billy and wound her arms around his neck. She looked deep into his eyes. 'The next time she asks you to do something, you can do it. It's not about refusing to help one another, it's about Vanja not taking you for granted.'

She gave him a soft kiss and stroked his cheek before returning to her pans.

Ursula was sitting at her desk. She was trying to work, but it was impossible to concentrate. Her mind kept taking her back. Not to the conversation in the dining room, but further back.

To the past.

To the two of them.

They had first met in the early autumn of 1992. Sebastian Bergman, the profiler who had trained in the USA, was due to give a lecture at the University of Gothenburg on signature behaviour and what crime scenes can reveal about serial killers. Ursula was working at the national forensics laboratory in Linköping, and had applied to attend the lecture as part of her ongoing professional development. It had been interesting and informative. Sebastian had been in his element − charming, knowledgeable, spontaneous − and the audience had listened attentively, keen to know more. Ursula sat right at the front and asked several questions.

They had had sex in his hotel room afterwards. She wasn't expecting it to turn into anything more than that. Their professional world was quite small, and she had heard the rumours about Sebastian. So she went back to Linköping. To Micke and Bella, who had just started school. Micke took care of all the preparations for school, and was home early in the afternoon so that their daughter wouldn't have to spend too long in day care. Ursula worked. As usual. Life went on. As usual.

Micke hadn't had a drink for over a year. He had his own company, and worked as much as he wanted to. They had a house in a good area, they were comfortable financially, Bella was happy at school, Ursula had a stimulating career, Micke was sober. A middle-class, suburban existence. A good life. As good as it got, she presumed.

Then one day when she was on her way home, someone shouted to her in the car park. It was him. Sebastian Bergman. She asked what he was doing there.

Meeting her.

Hopefully.

She was pleased to see him. Pleased that he had come to her. More pleased than she wanted to admit. She rang Micke and told him she had to work late. They went to a motel. They were in Linköping, anyone could come along, someone might see them and recognise them. Ursula didn't care.

Sebastian's lecture tour was over. He was due to start back at the university later in the term, but at the moment he was free. He might as well spend the time in Linköping. If she wanted him to.

For almost two months they had seen each other as often as possible. Sometimes at lunchtime, sometimes before she started work in the morning. Usually in the evening and at night. He was always available. Always keen. She was the one who decided where, how often and how long. It suited her perfectly.

In December she had suggested to Micke that they should move to Stockholm. She wanted to apply for a post with Riksmord. She had been thinking of changing jobs for a while, she was tired of working at the lab. Tired of not being an active part of the hunt; she missed the adrenaline, being there at the conclusion of a case, the capture. Riksmord had just appointed a new boss, Torkel Höglund, a man about whom she had heard a lot of positive reports. It was time to do something new, take that step.

It wasn't only because of Sebastian. The fact that they would end up working in the same place if she did get a job with Riksmord was a bonus. A welcome bonus, but that wasn't the reason why she wanted to move. She wasn't some little schoolgirl who fell head over heels in love and let her feelings dictate her actions. She knew perfectly well that it could end at any time. But the close proximity and the fact that they would see each other every day might also mean that it turned into something more, something deeper. For the first time she felt that she was capable of a different kind of relationship. A relationship where she would be able to relax, where she would no longer need to keep her distance, as she had always done in the past.

From Micke.

From Bella.

From everyone.

Besides which, her sister lived in Mälarhöjden, and her parents in Norrtälje. Perfect if they needed someone to look after Bella for a weekend. There was every reason to go, and no reason to stay.

Micke didn't agree.

His company was well established in Linköping, and his client base was in the west of Sweden. What was he supposed to do in Stockholm? Start all over again? And what about Bella? She'd been at school for a term, made new friends, kept her old friends, and she loved her teacher. Was it right to tear her away from such a secure environment? Ursula maintained that children make new friends wherever they go, and that of course Micke could run the company from Stockholm; it would just mean a few more business trips, a few more nights away from the family. But all the time she was trying to persuade him, there was one thought in the back of her mind: it wouldn't be a disaster if Micke and Bella didn't come with her. It would give her peace and quiet to explore what was happening. Whether it was time for a permanent change.

She was in luck. Micke came up with the idea that she should move on her own, and that they should live apart – for a while at least. He didn't want to stand in the way of her career, and if other people coped with commuting at weekends, surely they could do it too?

Ursula protested dutifully, but not for very long. She talked to Bella, promised to come home as often as possible. Bella was upset, of course. It was a big adjustment, a bit like a divorce, but Ursula was certain that she would have been much more distressed if it had been Micke who was leaving. In Bella's world, the right parent was staying.

Ursula got the job and moved. She found a two-room apartment in Södermalm, but spent as much time at Sebastian's place as at her own, if not more. At work they were totally professional; no one would have suspected that they were anything more than colleagues. Outside work it was beginning to feel as if they were becoming more and more established together. They did things that two work colleagues might well do; they went to the theatre, to the cinema, to restaurants, but they also started spending time with Ursula's sister and her husband. The four of them would have dinner together. Ursula still went back to Linköping almost every weekend, but it felt more and more as if she was leaving something behind rather than going to something. It didn't feel as if she was going home. The relationship with Sebastian meant much more to her than it did to him, she was certain of it. Sometimes it frightened her how much it meant. In the spring she finally dared to put it into words in her own mind.

She was in love.

For the first time in her life.

★ ★ ★

Ursula got up from her desk. She was getting nothing done, and sitting there thinking about events that had happened almost twenty years ago was pointless. Time to go. Home, perhaps. Away from here, at any rate. Roland Johansson and José Rodriguez had both been eliminated as possible perpetrators. The prints and the sperm found at the crime scenes came from someone else. That didn't necessarily mean that the two men weren't involved in some other way – the car that had been used to follow Sebastian had been stolen just a few hundred metres from where Rodriguez lived, after all – but a decision on whether to pursue this angle, and if so how, could be left until tomorrow. Ursula passed Torkel's office on the way to the lift, and looked in. Empty. A pang of disappointment. Not that she knew what she would have done if he'd been there, but it would have been nice to round off the day sitting on his sofa, perhaps deciding to have dinner together. She was hungry. Her meal had been interrupted. By the man who was standing further down the corridor, apparently waiting for her. Ursula walked past him without so much as a glance.

'See you tomorrow.'

'I'll walk you to your car,' said Sebastian, setting off by her side.

'Don't be ridiculous. There's no need.'

'Don't start. I want to.'

Ursula sighed, walked over to the lifts and pressed the button. Sebastian stood beside her in silence. After thirty seconds the doors slid open and Ursula stepped inside, followed by Sebastian. She pressed P and fixed her gaze on the metal doors.

'I was thinking about Barbro,' Sebastian broke the silence. 'Maybe I ought to tell her as well.'

Ursula didn't speak. She decided to pretend she hadn't heard him.

'I don't know where she's living now,' Sebastian went on, and Ursula thought she could detect a hint of apology in his voice. 'She might have got married and changed her name . . .'

'I've no idea.'

'I thought maybe you two might have . . .'

'No,' Ursula snapped. 'We haven't.'

Sebastian fell silent. The lift stopped and the doors slid open. Ursula stepped out into the underground car park. Sebastian followed her. Ursula marched purposefully towards her car, the sound of her heels echoing on the bare concrete. Sebastian looked around as he remained a few steps behind her, watching out for any change, any movement. The car park was deserted. Ursula unlocked the car from a distance of a few metres; when she reached it she opened the back door, threw her bag inside, then opened the driver's door. Sebastian was standing by the front bumper.

'Right then, goodnight. Take care.' He turned and lumbered back towards the lift. Ursula considered for a moment. Not that she really thought it was necessary, but just to be on the safe side . . .

'Sebastian!'

He stopped and turned around. Ursula left the car door open and went over to him. He looked at her with a mixture of puzzlement and curiosity.

'You must never, under any circumstances, tell anyone about you and me.' Ursula was whispering, which paradoxically sounded almost louder than normal speech as it bounced off the walls. 'Never.'

Sebastian shrugged. 'Okay.' He hadn't said anything to anyone for the last seventeen years, so he could probably keep quiet for a while longer. Evidently Ursula interpreted the shrug and one-word answer as an indication that he didn't think it was important.

'I mean it. I would never forgive you.'

Sebastian looked at her. 'And have you ever forgiven me?'

Ursula met his gaze. Was there a wish there? A hope? 'Goodnight. I'll see you tomorrow.'

She turned and went back to the car. Sebastian remained where he was until she had left the car park.

It was going to be a long evening.

Storskärsgatan 12.

An address that was forever imprinted on Sebastian's memory. This was where the letter he'd found in his parents' house had led him. This was where he had gained a daughter. Again. He pushed open the door and stepped into the darkness of the stairwell. This was the second time he had been inside the apartment block. The last time he'd walked up these stairs he had been full of nervous anticipation, while at the same time he had tried to tell himself that he could be disappointed. This time . . . In many ways it was worse. He reached the third floor. Eriksson/Lithner on the door. Sebastian took a deep breath and let the air slowly filter out through his lips in a long sigh. Then he rang the bell.

'What are you doing here?' was the first thing she said when she opened the door and saw who it was. Anna Eriksson. Her hair was shorter than last time. Some kind of bob. Same blue eyes. Same high cheekbones and narrow lips. Scruffy jeans and a checked cotton shirt that was big enough to belong to Valdemar.

'Are you alone?' Sebastian asked, quickly deciding to skip the niceties. He was really asking whether she might have a friend in the apartment; he had seen Valdemar leave five minutes ago.

'You weren't supposed to come here again.'

'I know that. Are you on your own?'

Anna seemed to understand the implications of his question. She took a step forward, effectively blocking the doorway. After a quick glance at the stairwell behind Sebastian to check that he didn't have company, she lowered her voice to a hiss. 'You can't come here! You promised to stay away from us!'

He had never done that, as far as he could recall. Promised. He had left with an unspoken agreement that he would never

230

get in touch with Vanja, Valdemar or Anna again, but he hadn't promised. And in any case, the situation had changed.

'I have to talk to you.'

'No!' Anna underlined the word with a shake of her head. 'It's bad enough that you were working with Vanja. I don't want anything to do with you.'

Sebastian reacted to the tense. *Were* working. Evidently Vanja hadn't mentioned that he was back on the team. At least not to her mother.

'This isn't about Vanja,' he almost pleaded. 'This is about you.'

He saw the woman in front of him stiffen. For a brief moment Sebastian could see what the last few months must have been like for her. She had lived with the lie for thirty years. Not just lived with it; it was the foundation stone of her entire existence. Thirty years. Long enough to almost start believing it herself. Definitely long enough to think she was going to get away with it. To think she was safe. And then he turned up. The person who could bring everything crashing down. Everything she had built up. Everything she had. Everything. Now here he was again, in spite of the fact that he wasn't supposed to come back. Things could only get worse.

'What about me?' Her tone was purely defensive now.

Sebastian decided he wouldn't even try to soften the blow. 'You could be in danger.'

'What? Why?' Confusion rather than fear. The question was whether she had even taken in what he had said.

'May I come in?' Sebastian said, as gently as he could. 'I'll say what I've come to say, then I promise I'll go.'

Anna stared at him as if she was trying to work out whether he was lying. Whether there was some other, hidden purpose behind his visit. Whether yet more unpleasant surprises might be lying in wait.

Sebastian met her gaze as sincerely and openly as he could. 'Please,' he begged. 'It's important; I wouldn't be here otherwise.'

Anna sighed, looked away and stepped to one side. Sebastian walked past her into the apartment. With one final glance at the stairwell, Anna followed him and closed the door.

Outside on Storskärsgatan, about thirty metres from number 12, the tall man was sitting in his car. A new car. Somebody had got rid of the Ford immediately after Sebastian Bergman had come racing towards him in the street outside police headquarters. He now had a silver Toyota Auris. He didn't know what had happened to the old car, or where the new one had come from. Stolen, presumably. There had been a message on fygorh.se telling him where and when to pick it up. He had gone along at the appointed time and sure enough, it had been standing in the exact spot with the keys in the ignition. He could start following Sebastian again, but from a greater distance this time. Not quite so visible behind the wheel. He was more careful, but Sebastian didn't appear to be looking for him. Not once had he looked around or taken detours which would have made it difficult to follow him. For a moment the tall man had got the idea that this might be a trap. That the psychologist's lack of interest in his surroundings and the absence of any obvious impact on his movements might be because other officers were shadowing him in order to get a glimpse of the man who had been following him. But that didn't seem to be the case. If it had been, the tall man would have noticed by now.

They had found number four. In the apartment. The newspapers had made a big thing of it. The tall man had bought all the morning and evening papers that day. They were lying next to him on the passenger seat. He was longing to get home so that he could read them. Grow. When he saw the rapid updates on the internet, he realised that he needed to expand and refine the ritual which accompanied the saving of everything that had been written about him.

She hadn't been entirely straightforward, number four. She was a new acquaintance, as far as he could tell. Bergman had been picked up by his psychologist on the hill outside the apartment block where Vanja Lithner lived, and they had gone off to some kind of meeting. Bergman had emerged about two hours later and jumped in a taxi with the woman who was to become number four. They had driven to her apartment. The tall man had followed them into the stairwell and managed to work out which floor they had gone to, but it had been impossible to say which apartment. While Sebastian was inside with the woman, the tall man had gone back to his car and started searching. He had made a note of the names on the letterboxes on the third floor. It didn't take him long to ascertain that there was only one single woman on the right floor. Annette Willén. There was of course a slight risk that Sebastian had picked up some grass widow, and that he was in bed with one of the married or cohabiting women the tall man had found. But it was most likely to be Annette Willén, and that was where he intended to start.

Sebastian had left the building at about five o'clock in the morning. He looked worn and tired, the tall man noticed as he watched him until he was out of sight. Time to make sure. There was no margin for error. The tall man had got out of the car, entered the building, walked up three flights of stairs. This was where things got tricky. Ringing a doorbell at this time of the morning could attract unwelcome attention. A neighbour might wake up and peer through their peephole, and he wouldn't even know about it. But how else could he be certain? He knocked gently. No reaction. He knocked again, a little louder and longer this time. Movements from inside. Footsteps.

'Who is it?' said a sleepy voice from the other side of the door.

'I'm sorry to wake you, but I'm looking for Sebastian,' the man said quietly, turning his face away from the peephole as much as he dared without looking suspicious.

'Who?' The woman obviously wasn't fully awake yet.

'Sebastian Bergman. He's supposed to be here.'

'Hang on a minute . . .'

Silence for a few seconds. The amount of time it took for Annette Willén to discover that she was alone. That was enough for the tall man. She had gone to look for Sebastian, therefore he must have been there. That was all he needed to know. He had already taken a step away from the door when the woman spoke again.

'He's not here. He's gone . . .'

Even through the solid wooden door he could hear her surprise and disappointment. She sounded as if she might burst into tears.

'Okay, sorry to disturb you.'

The man had hurried down the stairs before Annette got the idea of opening the door to speak to him. Like who was he and how did he know that Sebastian had been there? The tall man had no business inside the apartment. Not yet. First of all he had to report back and receive his orders. Then he would return.

He had gone home and been given his orders. She was to be number four.

The tall man had driven to the apartment block, parked a reasonable distance away and strolled back with the black sports bag over his shoulder. Up three flights of stairs, knocked on the door again. Annette had been at home, but hadn't opened the door. Wanted to know who it was.

'It's me. I was here this morning looking for Sebastian . . .' The tall man had a plan to get her to open the door. He always had a plan. A new one for each victim. It was pretty obvious that this morning's departure hadn't been a result of mutual agreement. Sebastian had crept out while she was asleep. Left her. Abandoned her. He would make use of that.

'I work with him,' the tall man went on quietly, his lips close to the door. 'He feels a bit bad about this morning. Sneaking off like that.'

Silence from the other side of the door. At least she hadn't told him to go to hell.

'He's not very good at . . . the morning after. But if I could come in, perhaps I could try to explain.'

'Has he sent you?' Indignation in the voice.

The tall man laughed as if she had said something not only amusing but unthinkable. 'No, no – he'd go mad if he knew I was here.' It was important to show that they were on the same side. The two of them against Sebastian Bergman. 'He's an idiot in certain situations.'

No response. Had he gone too far? But then the security chain had rattled and the door had opened.

The tall man was inside.

★ ★ ★

Now he was on Storskärsgatan. Again. Sebastian had been there on a number of occasions. Not inside, but outside. Mostly on Thursdays when Vanja Lithner was there visiting the people who must be her parents. Anna Eriksson and Valdemar Lithner. But today Sebastian had waited until Valdemar Lithner left the building, then he had gone in. Was he sleeping with Vanja's mother? It was possible. Anything was possible. He had never managed to work out the connection between Sebastian and this family. He wasn't having a sexual relationship with Vanja, the tall man was sure of that, which was why he had never reported back on the time Sebastian spent outside her apartment block.

The tall man leaned forward and looked over at number 12. He hoped Sebastian would soon come out. Admittedly it was high summer, but the darkness would soon come. Like in the cellar. When the naked light bulb had gone out.

Anna Eriksson's head was spinning. She had read that phrase several times in various books, but she had never really been able to imagine it. Now she understood exactly how it felt.

Someone was killing Sebastian's former lovers. The murders she had read about. She was one of Sebastian's former lovers.

She could die.

She had argued that nobody knew about them. But he said he'd been followed. So did this mean more people knew about them? And about Vanja?

She could die. This was insane.

Sebastian was sitting next to her on the sofa. She hadn't offered him anything when he came in. He definitely wasn't staying. But he was still here.

On her sofa.

In her living room.

In her life.

Which from the moment he arrived had become unimaginably complicated. She realised she was sitting there in silence, simply staring into space. Unseeing.

Sebastian leaned a little closer. 'Did you understand what I said?'

Anna nodded slowly and transferred her gaze to his face, as if to confirm that she was answering the question. 'Yes, but that's crazy. No one knows.'

'I thought no one knew about the others either. But if he found them, he can find you.'

Anna nodded again. It had been more than twenty years since Sebastian had been with two of the women. All the victims were in the Stockholm area. Family and friends around them. And yet they still died. The threat was real. The anxiety made her stomach churn. It almost felt like cramps. Oddly enough it seemed as if the realisation that she could be in mortal danger was still overshadowed by the consequent fear that someone somewhere could have worked out the truth about her daughter.

'So someone might know about Vanja as well?' Anna asked, her voice little more than a whisper.

'There's no reason to think so, and that's not what this is about.' Sebastian paused. He gave in to an impulse; he reached out and took her hand. 'You need to disappear for a while.'

Anna jerked her hand away as she got to her feet. He wasn't allowed to touch her. To console her or try to make her feel better. This was all his fault. If it turned out that she needed help, Sebastian Bergman was the last person she intended to ask.

'I can't just take off.' She took a few rapid steps across the floor and spread her hands in a gesture which underlined the fact that this just wasn't an option. 'I've got a job. A family. A life.'

'And that's exactly why you have to leave.'

Anna stopped dead. In the middle of the room. He was right, of course. Unfortunately.

'Isn't there someone you could go and stay with for a while?' Sebastian asked from the sofa.

'Well yes, I suppose so, but I can't just disappear, can I? What do I say to everyone? To Valdemar? And Vanja? What do I say to Vanja?'

'Nothing. You can't say anything to her about why you're going, because if you do she'll work it out.'

Anna nodded. Concentrated.

Sebastian got up and went over to her. 'Go and stay with someone,' he urged. 'Are your parents still alive?'

'My mother is.'

'Go and see her.'

'I don't know . . .' Anna left the rest of the sentence hanging in the air as she thought things over. She was starting to get her head straight. In sharp contrast to a few moments ago, her brain was firing on all cylinders now. Thoughts that had been whirling around in a meaningless mess now presented themselves with clarity, enabling her to dismiss them or give them further consideration.

'Would it seem all that strange if you went to stay with her for a week?' Sebastian asked, keen to get a definite decision before he left Anna.

'With no warning. Yes, it would. We don't exactly have that kind of relationship.' But in spite of her firm response, Anna had already begun to toy with a possible scenario.

Her mother could have phoned while Valdemar was out. Just now, this evening. Asked her to come over. Because she wasn't feeling too good, or because of something to do with the house – because she needed help, anyway. Valdemar would believe that. Then she could go. She would invent some story for her mother to explain her sudden appearance. A lot going on at work. At the end of her tether. Just had to get away from everything. If Valdemar rang, could her mother please be an angel and say that she was the one who had asked for Anna's help? She didn't want to worry him. Not when he was just getting over his cancer. Her mother would go along with that. Would lie for her sake. Anna could stay there for a while. Come back when they'd caught the murderer. Tell her mother she was feeling much better, and if the topic ever came up at a family dinner or at Christmas or something, she would simply laugh it off and say that her mother had misunderstood. Nobody would dig any deeper. It could work. It would work.

It had to work.

'You can't stay here,' Sebastian persisted. 'If anything should happen to you, if they found you . . . Then Vanja would find out. In the worst way imaginable.'

'I know, but I can't go tonight.'

'Why not?'

Because it didn't fit in with her plan. The situation mustn't appear too urgent, or Valdemar would insist on going with her. She would go tomorrow. It would still be a bit of a rush, but it was achievable.

'It's just not possible,' she said to Sebastian. She had neither the desire nor the energy to explain what she was planning. 'But I'll be fine. Valdemar will be home soon.'

'I could wait until he gets here.'

'No! I want you to go. Now. Right this minute.' Anna could feel herself regaining control after the initial shock. She would sort this out, just as she had sorted out every other problem that had arisen over the years. But Sebastian had to go. She grabbed hold of him and pushed him towards the hallway.

Sebastian realised there was nothing more he could do. He walked into the hallway. 'Don't open the door to anyone but Valdemar.'

'He's got a key.'

As Sebastian turned and saw Anna standing in the middle of the living room deep in thought, he suddenly realised how much trouble he had caused. It was only a couple of months since her husband had been told his cancer was in remission. How long had she lived with the knowledge that her life partner might die? Months? Years? And now he had turned up with yet another threat, bringing death into this cosy apartment once more.

'I'm sorry.'

Words he rarely used, but they were sincerely meant. He paused with his hand on the door handle. He really did want to know, and he could hardly be any less popular than he already was, or cause even more grief than he already had.

'Has he never asked?'

'Who?' Anna's thoughts were somewhere else altogether.

'Valdemar. Has he never asked who her father is?'

The expression on Anna's face made it clear that this was not a topic she wished to discuss. Not with him. Not with anyone.

'Once,' she said curtly. 'But I didn't tell him.'

'And he left it at that?'

Anna shrugged. 'He's a good man.'

'I've realised that.'

Silence. What else was there to say? Sebastian opened the door. 'I'm sorry,' he said again as he stepped out onto the dark landing.

'Yes, so you said.'

She closed the door behind him. Sebastian stood there for a moment, aware of how tired he was. Physically and mentally. This had been the longest day of his life, and it wasn't over yet. One more stop. One more. He set off down the stairs with a heavy tread.

The tall man was on the point of giving up when he saw Sebastian step out of the doorway further down the street, his mobile clamped to his ear. He slid down behind the wheel as far as he could without losing sight of his quarry. He was pretty sure the distance, the slightly reflective windscreen and the gathering dusk would make him impossible to spot even if Sebastian should look in his direction. But he didn't. He put the phone in his pocket and set off in the opposite direction. The tall man stayed where he was, watching him. Sebastian stopped at the crossroads; he looked as if he was waiting for something.

After five minutes a taxi pulled up. Sebastian got in and it drove off. The tall man turned the key in the ignition and began to follow. A little while longer. He could spare half an hour before duty called.

He was enjoying this. Not the pursuit in itself, but what it might lead to.

Number five.

Perhaps number six.

He had been given only the names and addresses of the first three women via the website. He had checked up on them, found out as much as he felt he needed to know about their lives, and chosen his time. Number four was different. Suddenly it had to be someone who had been with Sebastian Bergman recently. In order to make the pattern clear. It had worked. Riksmord had made the connection, he knew that. They had worked out the common denominator. The fact that Sebastian was involved in the investigation proved that. According to the Master, this should lead to Sebastian examining his conscience and attempting to warn some of his former partners. Not all of them, that would be impossible of course, but he ought to get in touch with those who were comparatively recent or who meant the most to him so that they could be protected. Was Vanja Lithner's mother one of them? Was that why Sebastian had gone there this evening? Could be. Worth reporting back, at any rate.

The taxi was driving along Valhallavägen. The wrong direction if Sebastian was going home. Was he going to warn someone else? The tall man couldn't suppress a smile. Perhaps he would be allowed to make the choice himself this time. To determine life and death. Him. No one else. He had been given that power. For that he would be eternally grateful.

Imagine if he had had it back then.

★ ★ ★

After the wedding and the move to the elegant apartment in the inner city, Lennart had become a frequent guest in their home, sometimes with his wife but usually alone. When Sofia and his father were going out, which happened quite often, Lennart would come and babysit.

He liked his 'grandfather'. They did his homework together, played cards, and he even tried to teach the older man how to play Nintendo. He hadn't yet made any friends at his new school, but Lennart often took him out on weekends. Skansen, Kaknäs Tower, Djurgården, the Royal Palace, places most of his contemporaries had already visited or at least heard of, but which were more or less unknown to him. Lennart also let him try out different things to see what he enjoyed. They went fishing, ice skating, berry picking, ten-pin bowling and to the adventure pool.

He really enjoyed those outings with his grandfather. His father and Sofia never wanted to come along. On the contrary, they seemed to appreciate the fact that he disappeared for a few hours now and again. Nothing was actually said, of course, but the years with his mother had given him an almost unique ability to read the moods of adults by interpreting glances and body language. It had come to him naturally as a way of avoiding problems. Adapting himself completely to her. Her wishes were always more important than his.

One day he had been picked up by Lennart as usual. Full of anticipation. They were going on a trip.

'Where are we going?' he had asked.

'You'll see,' was the answer.

They had driven along in silence. His grandfather seemed more tense than usual. Taciturn, almost brusque. He had tried to interpret in order to adapt, but he couldn't understand the signals. Lennart was giving off a new aura, a kind of reserve he hadn't come across before. So he sat quietly. It seemed to work well.

Out of the city. Smaller roads. Lots of twists and turns; sometimes he got the feeling they were driving back the way they had come, but he never asked. He had no idea where they were when Lennart turned down a narrow forest track which ended at a small brown wooden house in a clearing. A pitched green metal roof, with green window ledges and shutters.

Lennart had switched off the engine and they had both sat looking at the little house.

'What's this place?' he had asked.

'It's a lodge.'

'Is it yours?'

'No.'

'Whose is it?'

'That doesn't matter.'

'What are we going to do here?'

'You'll see.'

They had got out of the car and walked over to the lodge. It was summer. The forest smelled exactly as he expected a forest to smell on a hot, still day. A faint breeze soughed in the tree tops, but where they were walking there was no movement, thanks to the dense vegetation. Insects were buzzing. He thought he could just glimpse the shimmer of a lake through the trees. Perhaps they were going swimming?

A small flight of stone steps led up to a green wooden door, which Lennart opened. They walked into a narrow hallway. Wooden panels on the walls. A hat stand, a shoe rack on the floor. Even though there were no clothes hanging up and no shoes in the hallway, he got the feeling they were not alone. He couldn't see anyone, or hear anyone. It was just a feeling. He sensed a bigger room on the right and a small kitchen on the left, but Lennart had opened a door immediately to the left of the entrance and shown him a staircase leading downwards. To the cellar.

'What's down there?' he had asked.

'Go and see,' came the answer.

He had walked down the narrow stairs with horizontal wooden panels along the sides. At the bottom a naked bulb illuminated not only the staircase, but also the small room beyond. Half the size of the lodge, approximately. Wooden beams. Stone walls. No windows. Cold and damp. There was the smell of mould and something else, a faint metallic smell that he didn't recognise. Rugs on the floor. Otherwise empty. Nowhere to sit. Nothing to do. He was just about to ask again what they were doing there when he heard something that could only be footsteps from upstairs. More than one person. More than two. They seemed to be in a hurry. Creeping along in a rush. He was more puzzled than afraid as he turned to Lennart, who had stopped at the bottom of the stairs. His hand was resting on a black, old-fashioned light switch on the wall. Without a word he twisted it. An audible click was followed by darkness as the naked bulb went out. It was so dark that he couldn't tell whether his eyes were open or not. For a brief moment he thought he could see a strip of light right at the top of the stairs, and shadows slowly drifting in through the light only to be swallowed up immediately by the darkness. But he didn't know for sure. The image of the brightly burning bulb was imprinted on his retina, distorting and confusing. He blinked several times. Nothing but darkness. But he could hear footsteps coming down the stairs, he was sure of it. Footsteps and heavy, expectant breathing.

'Granddad . . .' he said.

But no one answered.

In the car on the way home Lennart had been exactly the same as always. Apologised if he had frightened him. It was just a game. A big boy like him could cope with a little game, couldn't he? Nothing had happened, had it? He had shaken his head. He had been scared. Of the noises. Of the darkness. But more than that . . . He didn't know how long he had stood there in the darkness, but when Lennart switched the light on again the room was empty. No sign of anyone else. In the car he wanted to say that he hadn't liked the game, hadn't liked it at all, but he kept quiet. Nothing had actually happened. And sitting in the car in daylight, he wasn't even sure that others had been there. Perhaps he had just got scared. Imagined things. He didn't dare ask Lennart. They stopped at McDonald's for ice cream, then they went and bought a new video game. By the time he got home things were more or less back to normal. He had been afraid, but the memory was fading. It was beginning to feel like a dream. Like something that had never really happened. From the years with his mother he was used to adapting quickly to new situations, changing moods, broken promises, parameters that suddenly changed. He had become a master at forgetting and moving on. He could do that now as well.

He and Lennart went on several more trips. At first he had been hesitant, hadn't wanted to go, but it had been just like before. They had done things that were fun. Good things. The memory grew more and more faint. Disappeared, until he genuinely couldn't remember it anymore.

Until they ended up at the lodge again.

Months later. Reluctantly he walked with Lennart towards the brown wooden house in the clearing. Granddad was holding his hand. Pulling him along, more or less. Heavy legs. Hard to breathe. Into the hallway again. Into that special silence which is created only when several people are trying not to make a sound. He thought he could feel their presence in the rooms he couldn't see. Waiting. Down the stairs. The naked bulb. Lennart by the light switch. The darkness. The rapid, creeping footsteps from above. This time he didn't look at the bulb before it went out, which meant he was able to see more clearly by the faint light that seeped in when the cellar door was opened. People. Of course. Naked. Wearing animal masks. He definitely saw a fox and a tiger. Or did he? He wasn't sure. It was very quick. He was afraid. The door was open for only a few seconds. Then the darkness.

The creeping footsteps.

The breathing.

'Who are they?' he had asked quietly in the car on the way home.

'Who?' Lennart flipped the question back.

'The people in the masks.'

'I don't know what you're talking about,' Lennart replied.

After the second time he didn't want to go out with Lennart anymore. Not anywhere. Never again. He talked to his father about it. Couldn't he just stay at home? His father wouldn't hear of it. It was important to keep in with their new relations. Lennart had only one grandchild; of course he wanted to spend time with him. He should be pleased that he had a granddad who was so interested in him. Invested so much time and money in him. Pleased and grateful.

He tried to explain that he really didn't want to go. He was informed that this was of no consequence. He was going. End of discussion. He wasn't really surprised. Not even upset. He should have known. It was exactly the same as it had been with his mother. His feelings didn't count.

What other people wanted was always more important.

And so the excursions continued. Most times everything was just the same as usual. Normal activities among normal people. But at regular intervals, which it seemed to him were getting shorter and shorter, they would visit the lodge. He started trying to work out what he had done differently on the occasions when they ended up there. Was it his behaviour? Perhaps it was actually his fault? He became more and more conscious of everything he did, from the moment he found out his grandfather was picking him up until they were sitting in the car. If it was an enjoyable trip he did exactly the same things the next time. If he ended up at the lodge, it was probably because of something he had missed. Everything became significant. The way his bed was made. The way his clothes were folded. Nothing must go wrong. The way the food was arranged on his plate. The amount of time he spent brushing his teeth. The smallest mistake, the least thing done differently, could mean that he would find himself in the darkness in the cellar. The number of steps he took from his bedroom to the kitchen on the way to breakfast. The order in which he packed his gym bag. His life became more and more ritualised. He heard Sofia talking to his father about something called 'compulsive behaviour' one night when they thought he was asleep.

She sounded worried. His father promised to have a word with him.

He had done so a few days later. Asked what the hell was going on. So his son told him. About the lodge. About the people who looked like animals. Who at first had just crept around in the darkness, frightening him. But who now did other things. Who were everywhere. Around him. On him. Inside him.

His father didn't believe him. People who looked like animals! He tried to explain the business with the masks, but he got all

245

mixed up. Stammered. Became embarrassed. So where was this lodge? He didn't know. They seemed to take a different route each time. He would lose concentration when he realised where they were going. Everything became kind of blurred. It was in the forest. In a clearing. His father grabbed hold of him. His expression was serious. He must never speak of this again. Did he understand that? Never. Why couldn't he just leave things alone? Why was he trying to ruin everything now that life was finally good in every way? He was frightening Sofia with his peculiar behaviour. What if she grew tired of them? What would they do then?

His father reminded him of what had happened to his mother. She had been ill too, imagined things, got confused about reality. Perhaps it ran in the family. If he carried on like this, they might have to send him away. Lock him up. He didn't want that, did he?

He never said anything else to anyone about what happened in the lodge.

But it happened again.

And again.

It stopped a few weeks after he turned sixteen, when Lennart died. He had a big smile on his face all the way through the funeral, imagining that he had killed him.

The taxi stopped and Sebastian got out. Vasastan. Ellinor Bergkvist. The tall man already knew about her, but he would include her in his report again now that Sebastian had renewed contact with her. He looked at his watch. Even if Sebastian had time to visit one or two more before it became too late, he had to stop his surveillance at this point. He put the car in first gear and sped past the taxi, which was still stationary. He hoped he would be allowed to choose. If so, he would go for Anna Eriksson. The fact that Sebastian worked with her daughter would be a bonus.

Sebastian walked up the stairs to Ellinor's apartment. He hesitated before ringing the bell. This would have to be quick. She had held his hand, got him to eat breakfast and sent flowers on his name day. She was definitely not someone Sebastian intended to get to know better.

In, explain the situation, out. That was the plan. He would give her no opportunity to misinterpret the reason for his visit. He took a deep breath and rang the bell. The door opened wide before he had a chance to take his thumb off the button. Ellinor smiled at him.

'I saw you through the window,' she said, stepping to one side. 'Come on in. I've missed you.'

Sebastian sighed to himself, fighting the impulse to turn around and leave. Run. Forget the whole thing. But no, he had to tell her. For his own sake.

In, explain, out.

He stepped into the hallway.

'I haven't missed you. That's not why I'm here.'

'But you're here anyway.' Ellinor gave him a slightly roguish wink as she leaned past him and closed the door. 'Take your coat off.' She gestured towards the hooks on the wall.

'I'm not staying.'

'But surely you can come in for a little while?'

Ellinor's expression was hopeful. Sebastian thought briefly, and decided that his errand wasn't really something that ought to be tackled while standing in a hallway. Not even when it came to Ellinor Bergkvist. He kept his coat on, but followed her into the living room. The windowsill crowded with pot plants. Sofa, armchairs, coffee table with a shelf for magazines underneath, a bookcase on one wall with a small number of books. A few

247

ornaments lined up, souvenirs from trips abroad perhaps. No photographs. Two pedestals with large green plants on either side of the door.

'Can I get you anything?' she asked when he had sat down on the sofa.

'No.'

'Are you sure? How about a coffee?'

'No.'

'I've bought some real ground coffee since you were last here, and one of those cafetière things.' She used her right hand to demonstrate pushing the plunger down in the pot.

'I don't want any coffee! Thank you. I need to talk to you.'

'What about?'

Was there a hint of expectation in her voice? Could he detect a hopeful little smile? He had no idea what she thought he had come to tell her, but there was no point in trying to soften the blow. He took a deep breath and embarked on the explanation he had prepared.

Four women had died. *(Yes, she'd read about that.)*

They had all had a sexual relationship with Sebastian. *(What a coincidence!)*

It was possible that someone had been following him for quite some time, so there was a risk that the murderer also knew about their one-night stand. *(What did he mean by that?)*

She could be in danger.

Ellinor perched on the edge of one of the armchairs and gazed at him, her expression serious. 'You mean he might come here?'

'There is a risk of that, yes.'

'What shall I do?'

'The best thing would be to go and stay with someone. Get away from here for a while.'

Ellinor clasped her hands in her lap and seemed to be considering what he had just said. Sebastian waited. Just as with Anna Eriksson, he wanted to be sure that Ellinor understood the gravity of the situation before he left, and that she was actually intending to leave the apartment.

'Who shall I go and stay with?'

All he knew about Ellinor was what he had found out after the talk on Jussi Björling, and they hadn't really touched on the

248

issue of who she should go to if she suddenly had to leave her home. She knew he couldn't possibly know the answer. And yet she asked him anyway. That bothered him. Of course.

'How the fuck should I know? There must be someone, surely.'

'I don't know . . .'

Ellinor fell silent. Sebastian stood up. He had done what he came to do. He had warned her. What she did with that information couldn't possibly be his problem. And yet he found himself almost feeling sorry for her. Her question suggested that there was no obvious place for her to go in an emergency. Was she really so alone? He had no idea. And he didn't really care. But she looked so small, perched on the edge of the armchair with her hands clasped.

'You could go to a hotel if there's nowhere else.'

Ellinor nodded without speaking. Sebastian thought for a second. Could he just leave? There weren't really any rules of etiquette to determine how long you ought to stay after you'd told someone their life was in danger. If there had been, he would have ignored them anyway. But should he stay? Have that cup of coffee? No, it would be misinterpreted. She would read something into it. Half an hour in the kitchen wouldn't make her any less lonely. Forget the coffee. He would stick to the plan.

'I have to go.'

Ellinor nodded again and got to her feet. 'I'll see you out.'

They went into the hallway. Sebastian opened the door and stopped. He felt as if he ought to say something, but he couldn't work out what. There was no point in warning her again. She had grasped the seriousness of the situation, he could see that from her face. He set off down the stairs and heard the rattle of the security chain as she closed the door behind him.

★ ★ ★

Ellinor leaned against the door and smiled to herself. Her heart was beating faster. Her legs were trembling. He had come back. Of course he had. Ellinor went into the living room and sat down on the sofa in the spot Sebastian had just vacated. She could still feel a little of the heat from his body. It made her feel warm inside, not just because of the physical warmth he had left behind, but because of his consideration. All this talk of not letting anyone into the

249

apartment and being wary of strange men who might approach her; what was all that if not a roundabout way of saying that he didn't want her to see anyone else? That she belonged to him?

She leaned back. Thought she could pick up his smell. He was shy. You wouldn't have thought it; he hid it so well behind that rough, boorish exterior. She had given him a couple of opportunities to say what he really wanted, to come out with the real reason for his visit, but he hadn't been able to do it. Instead he had come up with that ridiculous story.

She couldn't stay there.

She had to get away.

Ellinor had struggled to maintain her serious expression. Play along. She really wanted to leap out of the armchair and give him a hug, shake him and tell him she understood. But she would let him do it his way. Ellinor smiled to herself once again. The fact that he found it so difficult to tell her that he wanted her with him was quite sweet, really. But she understood. She understood him so well. Twin souls, that was what they were. She closed her eyes and luxuriated in the sensation of sitting where he had been sitting. She could indulge herself for a few minutes.

Ursula slid down into the warm water. She rested her head on the edge of the bath and closed her eyes. Tried to relax. It had been a shattering day, to say the least. The case had taken a turn that no one could have predicted. No one on the team was untouched by it, but Ursula felt that she was probably affected more than the others.

The connection with Sebastian brought back memories she had deliberately striven to erase. Memories she had consigned to oblivion. And now they came surging forward, unannounced and unwelcome, making her feel tense and irritable.

Suddenly she gave a start. Was that a noise? From downstairs? She lay motionless in the water, listening carefully, but she heard nothing more.

Fantasies.

Ghosts.

Micke wasn't at home. He had gone out for dinner with some clients. It could be late. Would be late. She hadn't been invited. She rarely was. Micke didn't go in for the type of client entertainment that required a wife by his side. Which was fortunate. To be perfectly honest, she wasn't particularly interested in his job. Things were going well and he was happy. She didn't need to know any more than that.

She had still felt hungry when she got home. She had eaten a bowl of cereal with yoghurt in the kitchen, and made a cheese and sliced pepper sandwich with Danish rye bread. When she had eaten she had gone into the living room with a cold beer to watch TV, but she hadn't been able to concentrate. Sebastian Bergman. The memories kept coming back. Feeling restless, she had switched off the television and decided to have a hot bath. She had checked that all the doors were locked and all the windows properly closed before she went up to the bathroom. She placed a bath bomb containing essential oils in the bath and turned on the taps. While the bath was filling she got undressed and put on her dressing gown. On her way back to the bathroom she had hesitated briefly, then shook her head; the idea was crazy. But she had still got out her service weapon and taken it into the bathroom with her. It was lying on the lid of the toilet. She would be able to reach it easily before someone could force the lock on the bathroom door. She pushed the thought away.

Stupid.

Nobody would come. She wasn't in any danger. She was safe. For the simple reason that no one could possibly know that she and Sebastian had had a relationship. They had been so clever. Well, there was one person who knew: her sister Barbro. She and her husband Anders were the only people Ursula and Sebastian had spent time with outside work.

One summer's day when they were laying the table on the patio, Barbro had asked Ursula straight out, 'What's going on with Sebastian?'

Ursula had looked across at Anders and Sebastian, who were standing over by the barbecue with a beer in their hands. Out of earshot.

'What do you mean?'

'I mean what's going on with Sebastian?'

'We work together, we get on well.'

'Are you sleeping with him?'

Ursula hadn't replied. Which of course was a reply in itself.

'And what are you going to do about Micke?' Barbro had asked in the same tone of voice as if they had been chatting about the weather while she carried on setting out the cutlery.

'I don't know.'

'When was the last time you were in Linköping?'

'The weekend before last.'

Barbro's eight-year-old daughter Klara had emerged from the house with a bowl of salad. Barbro had taken it and patted Klara on the head, giving Ursula a meaningful look at the same time. 'Thanks, sweetheart.'

Klara went back indoors.

'You think I'm a bad mother.'

'I just think you should finish one thing before you start on the next.'

They hadn't discussed it again. Not during the rest of that evening. Not later. Never again, in fact. Ursula had thought about the conversation a great deal in the days that followed. Why didn't she finish with Micke? What she had with Sebastian was something she had never experienced before. It was much more than the sex. He was clever, and he appreciated the fact that she was clever. He didn't back away from an argument. He lied when it suited him. He made sure he always kept a tiny distance between himself and everything else, including her. He was closer to himself than to anyone else.

He was like her.

She loved Sebastian, although she wasn't at all sure that it was mutual. They were together a lot, but not all the time. She wanted to see him more often than he wanted to see her. They had sex, spent the night, but never discussed moving in together. They never talked about a shared future. Was that why she didn't split up with Micke? It would move the goalposts. As long as she was married and went home at regular intervals, there could be nothing more than there already was between her and Sebastian. But if she suddenly became available, told him what she wanted, how she felt, what would happen then? She wanted to find out, and yet she didn't. Things were good between them, she told herself, while at the same time she longed for something more permanent. A commitment. But if she were to make such a demand, would she lose Sebastian? That was the risk.

During the autumn, she and Sebastian saw each other less and less often. Micke had more to do because of work, which meant he found it more difficult to manage on his own in Linköping, and for a few months he was drinking too much again. Ursula was needed at home. She took some time off work and moved back. Once she was there, she realised what her absence had done to her relationship with Bella. Sometimes she felt as if her daughter regarded her as a stranger. Someone who had just stepped in to resolve the situation until her father came back. Micke stayed away most of the time. He always did that when he fell off the wagon. He didn't want anyone, least of all Bella, to see him then. Ursula did her best to keep things together at home and to fix her relationship with Bella, but she wanted to be somewhere else. Bella's grandparents had to take over more and more frequently. She blamed work. Went back to Stockholm. To Sebastian. But something had changed. It was hard to put her finger on exactly what it was, but things weren't the same. Was it because they weren't seeing each other so often? Or was it something else? After her third trip back, Ursula had the distinct feeling that he was being unfaithful.

Sebastian was Sebastian. She knew that. His reputation as a ladies' man was well known. But she had really believed that she would be enough for him. She had hoped so. But she had no intention of making do with her hopes and his words. After all, she was Sweden's top forensic technician.

After a weekend with Sebastian she had taken a sheet from his laundry basket. A sheet that bore clear traces of sexual activity. She had taken it to the lab at Linköping and asked one of her former colleagues for a favour. She wanted to run a DNA test. The colleague quickly realised this wasn't part of any police investigation; he was understandably reluctant to get involved, but allowed her to use the lab. So she did it herself. It was simple.

She had collected Sebastian's DNA from some strands of hair in his hairbrush. The test result showed that one trace of DNA on the sheet came from Sebastian. Of course. But the other matched Ursula's DNA only at certain points. With growing horror Ursula realised what she was looking at.

It was elementary forensics. If the DNA profile didn't have exactly the same pattern, but was similar, it could well belong to a relative. The closer the relationship, the more similar the DNA profile.

These were very similar.

Like sisters.

She had confronted Sebastian, who had owned up immediately. Yes, he was sleeping with Barbro. As far as he recalled, he and Ursula had never promised to be faithful to one another. She'd been away for several months, more or less. What was he supposed to do, live like a monk?

She had walked away from him.

Maybe, just maybe, she could have coped with his infidelity. With a stranger. But not with Barbro. Not with her sister.

When she had left Sebastian she had driven straight out to Mälarhöjden. The whole family had been at home when she stormed in and confronted Barbro with what she knew. What was it she'd said about finishing one thing before you started on the next? Barbro had denied everything. Ursula had shown her the DNA report. Anders had been furious. Klara and Hampus had started crying. Ursula had left a home in chaos. That was the last time she had seen her sister. She eventually heard from her parents that Barbro and Anders had split up and moved away. She didn't know where. Didn't want to know. She had no intention of ever forgiving Barbro.

She had gone back to Linköping. To Bella. To Micke, who was back on his feet again. They had discussed the situation, and after a while Ursula had managed to persuade the family to move to Stockholm. She loved her job. She wasn't about to give it up just because Sebastian Bergman was a pig. They would be able to work together. She would make sure of it.

She had gone on ahead of the others and visited Sebastian. Spelled things out. They would work together. She hated him, hated what he had done, but she wasn't going to give up her job. She would not allow him to destroy anything else for her. If he as much as whispered to anyone else that they had been together, she would kill him. She had actually said that. And meant it. Sebastian had been uncharacteristically cooperative. He had kept his promise, hadn't breathed a word about their relationship to anyone, as far as she knew. Micke and Bella moved up to Stockholm. Life went on. It worked on every level. Her family. Her job. But nobody was happier than she was when Sebastian left Riksmord in 1998.

But now he was back.

Now neither hot water nor essential oils could make her relax.

Now she was lying here with a loaded gun on the toilet.

Now she was thinking about events she had spent several years trying to suppress.

Yes, Sebastian Bergman was back.

In the worst way imaginable.

Outside it was a perfect summer's evening, still light and warm, but as usual the inmates of the secure unit were making their night-time preparations. Some had already gone into their cells, but a few were still sitting in the common room. Lock-up was at 19.00. The inmates had thought this was rather early when they were informed that their evening activities were being curtailed by two hours, but their protests had been in vain.

Edward was always the last in the washroom. This evening, however, he was not alone, but had the company of the new arrival who did not yet understand the routines of the unit, and had turned up at quarter to seven two days in a row. His behaviour was annoying Edward, and he had already decided that when the opportunity arose he would make it clear that the washroom was his, and his alone, at this particular time. The veterans already knew this, and would silently leave the room just before he arrived. Hinde was standing in front of the mirror, gently washing his face. The washroom contained a dozen washbasins in front of a shatter-proof mirror which ran all the way along the tiled wall. On the other side, a little further down, were the showers and toilets. Edward contemplated his wet face and didn't even glance at the two warders as they walked past.

'Lock-up in fifteen minutes,' they called out before going into the common room to deliver the same message. Every evening was exactly the same, and Edward didn't bother to listen anymore. His routines were embedded in his body, almost down to the second, and he no longer needed a watch. He knew exactly when he was going to wake up, eat, read, shit, walk, talk and have a wash. The only positive aspect of this was that the identical pattern of each day gave him time to focus on what was important, what was significant, rather than everyday life; he got through that on autopilot by now.

Hinde picked up his black electric shaver. It was one of the few things he still disliked a great deal. He wanted to have a proper shave, but any kind of razor was out of the question in the secure unit. He longed for the day when he would feel the honed blade against his skin again. That would be freedom. Holding something sharp. That was probably what he longed for most. The metal blade in his hand.

He switched on the shaver.

In the mirror he watched as the staff turned off the wall-mounted TV and nodded to the three men sitting on the sofas in the common room to indicate that it was time. The same three as usual. They got up without making a fuss and headed off down the long corridor towards their cells. Behind them lay the only way in or out of the unit; he heard the click of the lock as the cleaner arrived. Same time as always. The inmates cleaned their own cells, but the communal areas had been contracted out. LS Cleaning. A long time ago the inmates had been expected to clean these areas as well, but that had stopped ten years ago after a violent dispute over who was actually supposed to be doing what. Two prisoners had been seriously hurt. Since then the work had been undertaken by a cleaning firm, but always after lock-up. The cleaner, a tall, thin man in his thirties, was pushing a big metal trolley containing all his equipment; he nodded to the guards as he wheeled it along the corridor. They greeted him cheerfully; they knew him. He had been cleaning there for some years now.

The cleaner pushed his trolley into the washroom, where he usually made a start. He stood a respectable distance away, waiting for Edward and the new inmate to leave. Everything according to the routine. All inmates must be in their cells with the doors locked before the cleaning could begin. The guards arrived a minute or so later. They looked at the men in the washroom.

'Come along, you two, it's time now.'

'It's only six fifty-eight.' Hinde calmly ran his hand over his newly shaved chin. He knew exactly what time it was. He still didn't condescend to glance at the guards.

'How do you know that? You haven't got a watch.'

'Am I wrong?'

Edward glimpsed a movement in the mirror as one of the guards looked at his watch.

'Less talk, more action.'

Which meant he was right. Edward smiled to himself. 18.58. Just over a minute left. He placed the shaver in his light brown toilet bag, zipped it shut and splashed his face one last time. Annoyingly, the new inmate was still standing there, showing no sign of leaving. Edward hated people who couldn't stick to the proper times. At any second the guards would tell them again, but Edward pre-empted them. He turned around and left the washroom with water dripping from his face. He walked over to the trolley and nodded to the cleaner.

'Evening, Ralph.'

'Evening.'

'What's the weather like out there?'

'Same as yesterday. Hot.'

Edward looked at the pile of fresh paper towels with which Ralph would shortly fill up the white plastic holders in the washroom.

'Is it okay if I take a couple of paper towels?'

Ralph nodded listlessly. 'Sure.'

Edward leaned forward and picked up the top three towels. At the same time the guards took a step forward. Their attention was focused on the new inmate. Not Edward.

18.59.

'Come on, you've got one minute!'

They stood tall, making themselves look big in the doorway just to show who was in charge. Edward ignored them completely. He was already on the way to his cell.

18.59.30.

Behind him he heard the guards walk into the washroom. He hoped they would give the guy in there something to think about. Something that hurt. Pain was the best way to learn, he knew that from personal experience. Nothing was more effective than pain. But this was Sweden. They didn't have the courage to exploit pain in this country. It would probably be a caution, a shortened break or the withdrawal of some other privilege. Hinde was afraid he was going to have to deal with the new guy himself. The guards wouldn't succeed. He became even more certain when he heard them launch into a loud discussion. He stepped into his cell with the three paper towels.

Perfect timing.

19.00.

The door closed behind him.

Edward sat down on the bed and carefully placed the paper towels on the bedside table. He loved this moment, when the routines of Lövhaga were replaced by his own. When the time became his. In two hours he would begin. Slowly he picked up the middle paper towel and opened it out, full of anticipation. Below the crease on the inside someone had written in faint pencil: '5325 3398 4771'.

Twelve numbers that represented freedom.

The last thing on his list was to get hold of Trolle and tell him to put a stop to his investigations. Sebastian had called from work and later from his mobile, but he had heard nothing all day. Now he let the phone ring and ring once more. He was starting to get worried. The mere thought that Torkel might sooner or later get in touch with his former colleague turned his blood to ice. And it would happen. In spite of everything, Trolle Hermansson had been one of the best officers involved in the Hinde case in the nineties. Torkel respected him in many ways. Not as a person, they were too different for that, but as a professional. Whatever you thought about Trolle, there was no denying the fact that he always got results. And Torkel was going to want to speak to him. Particularly if the investigation remained at a standstill. That was the secret of good police work. You turned over one stone after another, prioritised, started with those who appeared to be most closely connected to the investigation, then worked outwards. Further and further from the centre, until you had gone through every possibility. Then you started all over again. Trolle wasn't the hottest lead, but as time went by a good police officer would reach the conclusion that it might be worthwhile having a chat with him, and Torkel was a good police officer. One of the best, in fact. At some point in the future the Trolle-stone would be turned over. When that happened every dam might suddenly break, everything Sebastian was trying to hide might come cascading out and everything would be destroyed.

Because Trolle Hermansson couldn't be trusted.

After yet another unanswered call, Sebastian decided to go and see him. Just because he wasn't answering the phone didn't necessarily mean he wasn't home. Sebastian jumped in a taxi. It was a fraction cooler now, and he opened the window to get a little bit of fresh air. He could see people strolling along in their summery clothes; the city really came to life on these warm nights. Everyone looked so young and happy, all in groups of two or more. What happened to the old and the lonely and the depressed in summer? he wondered as he looked at them.

He was almost there when he spotted Trolle on the pavement on the other side of the street. He was wearing a big black coat, so he was hard to miss. Most of the people Sebastian had seen on the way hadn't been wearing coats or jackets, and those who had went for pale colours and light fabrics. Trolle looked as if he were equipped for the worst winter in living memory. Sebastian asked the driver to stop and stuffed a few hundred-kronor notes in his hand. He leapt out of the taxi and ran towards Trolle, who turned into Ekholmsvägen and out of his sight just a few hundred metres up ahead. He seemed to be on his way home. Sebastian ran after him. It was a long time since his heart and legs had worked so hard, and the hint of coolness he had felt in the taxi was long gone. He was sweating and puffing as he rounded the corner of Ekholmsvägen and saw Trolle step in through his doorway. Sebastian stopped to catch his breath. Now he knew where Trolle was, and from a purely tactical point of view he felt it was probably better not to turn up looking sweaty and desperate. He waited a few more minutes, then walked over to the apartment block.

★ ★ ★

Trolle opened the door after only two rings. He looked much fresher than the last time they had met, but the apartment behind him was still gloomy, and the same slightly unpleasant smell filtered into the stairwell.

'I saw from the phone that you'd called. I was just about to ring you,' he began, and surprised Sebastian by holding the door open to invite him in.

'We need to talk.'

'Evidently. I'm sure nine missed calls must mean something.'

Sebastian tried to smile disarmingly as he looked around the small, dark space. There were newspapers, clothes and mess lying all over the place. The blinds were closed, no curtains, the walls completely bare. It smelled of cigarettes, dirt and stale rubbish. Trolle showed him into the living room. The television was on with the volume very low; the only illumination was provided by some cookery programme featuring celebrities. The entire complement of furniture was made up of a sofa, on which Trolle appeared to sleep, and a glass table that must once have cost a great deal of money, but now served as a dumping ground for wine bottles, pizza cartons and an overflowing ashtray. The ceiling above the sofa was greasy and nicotine-yellow.

Trolle turned to Sebastian, noticed his critical expression and flung his arms wide. 'Welcome to my world. Once upon a time I lived in a white two-storey house in a swanky suburb. Now I live like this. Life is full of surprises, wouldn't you say?' Trolle shook his head and looked around, then went over to the sofa and pushed the grubby bedclothes to one side. 'Sit down. I've found something for you. Good stuff.' He gave a smile which could only be described as malicious. 'Really good stuff.'

Sebastian remained standing and shook his head. 'I don't want it anymore. I've come to ask you to stop digging.'

'Read it first. Before you decide.' Trolle bent down and picked up a white supermarket carrier bag, stuffed with what appeared to be papers. He held it out to Sebastian. 'There you go.'

'I don't want it. Get rid of it.'

'Read it anyway, it'll only take you about half an hour. Time well spent.'

Reluctantly Sebastian took the carrier bag. It probably only weighed a few hundred grams, but it felt considerably heavier in his hand.

'Okay. But you have to stop now. I'll give you the money, and then you have to promise me that you'll never tell anyone I asked you to do this. You and I have never even met.'

In spite of the gloom, Sebastian saw a glimmer in Trolle's eyes. A glimmer of interest. That couldn't possibly bode well.

'And who would be asking me?' Trolle looked at him with curiosity. 'What's going on, Sebastian?'

'Nothing. I just want you to promise me that you won't say anything.'

'No problem.' Trolle shrugged his shoulders. 'But you know me. Promises mean nothing.'

'I'll pay you double.'

262

Trolle shook his head and turned away from Sebastian with a gusty sigh. 'I helped you, and now you want to buy me off? Who do you think I am? I thought we were friends.'

'If we're friends, just promise me you'll keep quiet. And stick to your word,' Sebastian countered sourly.

'Why don't you tell me the truth instead?'

'If anyone finds out about this, it will be a total disaster for me. Total.' Sebastian gazed pleadingly into Trolle's implacable eyes.

'Why? Who is she, this Vanja? Why are you following her? Who's going to start asking questions? I want to know.' For the first time Trolle looked sincere. 'Then I'll stop. But not until then.'

Sebastian looked at him. He was screwed whichever way he looked at it. If he lied it would end in disaster. Trolle would probably go straight to Vanja out of sheer cussedness. If Sebastian told the truth, he felt as if he would never be safe again. But at least it would give him a little more time.

'So what's it to be?'

Sebastian thought frantically. The truth might already be in the white plastic bag. Trolle might already know. If Sebastian lied, it could make things worse. He made up his mind. 'She's my daughter. Vanja is my daughter.'

He saw at once that Trolle hadn't known.

But now there was nothing more to hide, so he told Trolle everything.

All of it.

When he had finished he felt a kind of peace. He felt lighter. So did the plastic bag. The secrets had been weighing him down more than he realised.

Trolle looked at him in silence. 'Bloody hell,' he said eventually.

He sank down on the sofa. He seemed to be thinking. He looked up at Sebastian. His tone of voice had changed completely; the teasing note had gone. 'What are you going to do?'

'I don't know.'

'I think you have to let her go. Stop what you're doing. Things can only end badly.'

There was a sincerity in Trolle's words that Sebastian really appreciated. He nodded in agreement. 'You're probably right.'

'Look at me,' Trolle went on. 'I didn't let go. I wouldn't listen to anyone.' He paused and looked over at a framed photograph on the windowsill. Two young boys and a girl, and a woman in the middle scribbled out with black ink. 'Now all I have left is a picture of them.'

Sebastian didn't say anything. His expression was sympathetic as he looked at Trolle.

'If you fight too much, you destroy what you have,' Trolle said quietly, almost to himself.

Sebastian went over and sat down beside him. He wondered briefly whether he ought to mention that there was a difference between following someone at a distance, and trying to frame your ex-wife's new boyfriend for possession of Class A drugs and kidnapping your children, but he refrained. Trolle had lowered his guard. He wouldn't appreciate it if Sebastian exploited the situation.

'I haven't told anyone else about this,' he said instead.

'I realise that.'

What Trolle did next surprised Sebastian. He took his hand. Clasped it in a kind, comforting, intimate grip. They looked at one another. Then Trolle leapt to his feet, his heavy body full of energy again.

'If someone has been following you, as you say, then you've just led him to Anna Eriksson.'

It was obvious when Trolle said it, and yet it hadn't occurred to Sebastian. When Torkel had said that he perhaps ought to try to warn some of the women he had slept with, he had meant by telephone, of course. But after the conversation with Ursula, Sebastian had become determined to visit them in person, for some reason. Somehow it felt like the least he could do. It had never crossed his mind that someone might still be following him. After almost being run down by the blue Ford outside Riksmord, he had somehow dismissed the idea. The man had been spotted, caught out, it was over. It had never occurred to him that his pursuer might carry on, possibly in a different car.

'Do you think so? But I've already warned Anna. She's planning on leaving town.'

'Was that what you were doing when you were round there this evening?'

'Did you see me?'

Trolle nodded, but there was something else on his mind. 'I saw someone else too. I didn't think about it at the time; I just

264

happened to notice. But now you tell me you've been followed . . .'
Trolle didn't complete the sentence.

Sebastian began to feel anxious. 'What? You didn't think
about what?'

Trolle had gone pale. 'Twice when I've been there and you've
been there, I've seen a man sitting in a blue Ford Focus. I just
assumed he was waiting for someone.'

Sebastian jumped up. 'That's him. He's the one who's been
following me.'

'He was there tonight as well. But in a different car – a silver
Japanese job.'

'What did he look like?'

'Hard to say. He was wearing sunglasses.'

'And a cap?'

Trolle nodded.

They ran out to look for a taxi. Sebastian wanted to go straight
to Storskärsgatan, but Trolle insisted they make sure they weren't
being followed first. In spite of the fact that they couldn't see a
silver car anywhere, they mustn't take anything for granted. They
found a cab and jumped in the back seat. Trolle directed the driver,
changing their destination, making him drive here and there, and
once they got into the city centre he insisted they use bus and taxi
lanes as much as possible. He was constantly checking behind them,
and it was half an hour before he was satisfied.

They were alone.

Eventually he directed the taxi to Karlaplan, and they walked
the last bit.

Storskärsgatan was deserted. A man with a dog was walking in
the park a short distance away, but he was heading in the opposite
direction.

Trolle turned to Sebastian. 'Stay here. He'll recognise you.'

Sebastian wanted to protest, but didn't know how, so he said
nothing. He stared up at the apartment where he knew Anna and
Valdemar lived. There was a warm glow from the windows, but
he couldn't see anyone. How could he have led the danger here?
He was an idiot!

'Do you understand?'

265

Sebastian nodded without taking his eyes off the apartment. Trolle looked calm. His eyes were sparkling; Sebastian had never seen him so alive, so focused.

'I'll check up there too, I promise,' said Trolle.

Sebastian withdrew into the shadows by one of the buildings on the corner and watched him go; he was glad he had confided in his former colleague. Trolle walked slowly along the short street. He looked as if he was out for an evening stroll, but Sebastian could see that he was carefully checking every car he passed. Sebastian looked up at the apartment again. Suddenly felt the weight of the carrier bag in his left hand. Trolle had refused to take it back, so Sebastian had had no alternative but to take it with him.

It was strange how quickly things could change. A few days ago Sebastian's only aim had been to hurt the two people living up there. Now he wanted to save them. He saw a bin a few metres away and was about to go over and throw the bag away when he saw Trolle heading back towards him, on the other side of the street this time. He was ambling along and chatting on the phone, but he was still checking every car. As he came closer Sebastian was able to pick up snippets of the conversation.

'I understand that, and of course if you're happy with your pension provision, then . . . Okay, thank you. Goodbye.' He ended the call and slipped his phone in his pocket as he walked past Sebastian.

'Come on, let's not hang around here.'

Sebastian quickly joined him. They turned off towards Valhallavägen.

'She's at home. Valdemar's there too.'

'What are we going to do?'

'*We're* not going to do anything. You're going to go home. I'll keep an eye on things here.'

'But . . .'

'No buts, Sebastian.' Trolle stopped and moved closer to him. Placed his hands on Sebastian's shoulders. 'Trust me. I'm here for you, Sebastian. We'll sort this out together. You can ring me any time.'

He gave Sebastian an encouraging pat on the shoulders and turned away. Headed back towards Storskärsgatan. Sebastian remained where he was. His feelings towards the man walking away from him were a mixture of trust and something approaching love. He didn't usually allow himself to feel those emotions towards anyone. Not him. Not Sebastian. He had always been able to manage on his own. But not anymore.

He would be eternally grateful to Trolle. He would be his friend, properly this time.

He went home. He was absolutely exhausted; he took off his jacket and trousers and fell into bed. He didn't throw away the carrier bag. He just couldn't bring himself to do it. It was too heavy, when it came down to it. He left it by the bed.

Didn't look inside.

Not tonight.

Not yet.

Torkel was sitting in the kitchen with Yvonne. He had refused a glass of wine, but had accepted a beer while Yvonne got on with packing for a trip to Gotland the following day. She and the girls had rented a small cottage on the western side of the island for a week, and both girls had decided at the last minute that there were things in Torkel's apartment that they absolutely had to take with them. He had gone home, gathered up the essential items and brought them round in a bag.

'What time do you sail?' he asked, taking a swig of his beer.

'Half past nine.'

'Do you need a lift?'

'Kristoffer's taking us.'

Torkel nodded. Of course he was.

'Will he be coming over while you're there?'

'No, why do you ask?'

'I was just wondering.'

Yvonne paused briefly in her packing and looked at him with curiosity. 'Do the girls talk about him?'

'No.'

Torkel tried to remember whether his daughters had even mentioned Kristoffer's name while they were with him, but he couldn't recall a single occasion. They didn't talk much to him at all. Not as much as he would have wished. Maybe that wasn't so strange. When they got divorced he and Yvonne had opted for joint custody without even needing to discuss the matter, but the girls spent far more time with Yvonne than with him. His job made a strict every-other-week schedule impossible. He was often away, and when he was at home it didn't always suit the girls to stay with him. They now classed being with Yvonne as 'home'; when they were with him they were 'at Dad's'. Yvonne was closer to the girls than he was. It was slightly painful, he couldn't deny that.

'Vilma thought that might have been why I left her birthday party early,' Torkel went on, 'but I explained that it was work.'

'You mean she thought you were leaving because Kristoffer was here?'

'Yes. She was afraid I might find it awkward, I suppose.'

For a moment it looked as if Yvonne might ask 'And did you?', but she went back to her packing instead.

'So how are things with you?' she asked in a deliberately casual tone. If she had been wondering what he thought about her new relationship, there was no hint of it in her voice.

'So-so. We've found a connection between the victims, but I've brought Sebastian in again, so it's all a bit difficult.'

'That's not what I meant.' She stopped what she was doing and looked him in the eye. 'Have you met anyone?'

Torkel thought about it. The question was the same one his daughter had asked a few days ago. But this was Yvonne. The answer could be different. He could tell her the truth.

'I don't know. There's someone I see occasionally. She's married.'

'Is she going to leave him?'

'I don't think so.'

'And is that going to work?'

'I don't know. Probably not.'

Yvonne just nodded. For a moment Torkel thought he would like to go into things a little more deeply. Tell her how lonely he sometimes felt. How much he wanted what he had with Ursula to become something more. There weren't many people he could talk to about this. No one, in fact. But the moment had passed. Yvonne changed the subject and they chatted for a little while longer about everyday matters and the forthcoming trip. Torkel finished his beer. After quarter of an hour he got up, said goodbye to the girls and wished them all a good trip, then set off home.

It was still hot outside even though it was after ten o'clock at night. Torkel enjoyed the walk home to his empty apartment. He took his time. Wondered whether to slip in and have another beer somewhere on the way. Delay his return home. He was lost in his own thoughts when a door suddenly opened out onto the pavement, and he almost crashed into the person who emerged. A person he recognised.

'Micke! Hi.'

'Hi. Hello. Hi . . .' Micke looked surprised. His eyes were darting from side to side, as if he couldn't quite place the man in front of him, in spite of the fact that he had met Torkel on a number of occasions.

'So, you've found your way to Söder,' Torkel said in an attempt at humour.

'I've been visiting a friend.' Micke nodded at the door which had just closed behind him. 'Watching the match.'

'Oh yes, which match was that?'

'Er, it was some . . . I don't really know, we weren't paying all that much attention.'

'Right.'

Silence. Micke was trying to look past Torkel. Anywhere but at him.

'Well, I'd better be getting home.'

'Okay. Say hello to Ursula from me.'

'Will do. Bye.'

Micke walked away. Torkel watched him go; was it his imagination or had Micke seemed a bit strained? He felt his stomach contract.

Did Micke know?

Did he know that Torkel was sleeping with his wife? In that case surely he would have confronted him, Torkel thought. Been furious. Or at least overtly unfriendly. He had seemed uncomfortable more than anything. There must have been another reason why Micke was in such a hurry to get away from him. It had nothing to do with him and Ursula. Convinced he was right, Torkel continued on his way. There was a restaurant on the corner, and the tables outside were busy. He would have that other beer. Maybe something to eat as well. He wasn't in a rush to be anywhere else. After all, no one was waiting for him.

As always Edward worked until one o'clock in the morning. That was his routine. It gave him four whole hours. Two hundred and forty minutes of pure, undisturbed time to himself. The silence in his cell was liberating. The only sound was the hum of his laptop, an older model with a fairly loud little fan, but it had been approved by the powers that be because it had neither a modem nor wi-fi. It was incapable of communicating with the outside world. Was. Imperfect tense. A good idea that had been set out in the policy document relating to the supervision of criminals, but one that had become redundant the day mobile broadband became available everywhere in the form of a small oval plastic device complete with a pay-as-you-go card and a USB port. A twelve-digit code, and suddenly the whole world was accessible.

The day the modem was smuggled in to Edward and he connected with the outside world for the first time was the best day of his life, or at least the best since he had been locked up in Lövhaga. Before he was deprived of his freedom there had been many happy hours. But that was in another era. Before this one. Edward divided his life into before and after. It was a good way of looking at his existence. Before and after the key changes that affect every life.

Before and after Mother.

Before and after Sebastian Bergman.

Before and after Lövhaga.

Before and after the modem.

Once he got the modem, those two hundred and forty minutes each night became extremely productive and enriching. He only used it after lock-up, and then not all the time. Out of habit he always logged on between 21.00 and 01.00. During that period the risk of a sudden cell check was negligible. Hinde just couldn't understand why this was allowed to happen. The rules actually stated that all unannounced cell inspections should be irregular, unexpected and impossible to predict. And yet they never took place between 21.00 and 06.00. Or at least they hadn't for the last six years. The reason for this idiotic course of action, he quickly worked out, was the same budget cuts that had led to an earlier lock-up. It used to be 21.00, now it was 19.00. The number of day staff had been cut; there were more of them, and they used to work through until nine o'clock in the evening. Now the night staff came on duty at seven. In order to save even more money, the number of night staff, which was already smaller, had been reduced, which meant that surprise inspections were effectively out of the question. Until the day when some sensible individual spotted this anomaly and reorganised the rota or increased the number of night staff, the situation would remain the same.

Each night he hid the small piece of plastic in the air vent behind his bed. He had managed to unscrew the grille with the handle of a coffee spoon. Using that same spoon he had spent many a long night before the arrival of the modem chipping out a little space inside the vent, in the brick wall just to the left of the opening. Then he had transformed the space into a secret compartment by fashioning a slim cover to match the rest of the bricks, which he could place in front of it. So even if someone opened the air vent, against all expectation, there was nothing to see.

These days it took him on average two minutes to get out his beloved little white modem. This evening it was slightly quicker, because he was feeling so inspired. He connected to the internet and as usual began on what had been his start page for a long time.

fygorh.se.

New material awaited him. He really did love the internet. You could find anything there if you really wanted to. If you knew what or who you were looking for. If you had two hundred and forty minutes every day.

Every week.

Every year.

Outside darkness was falling, but the apartment was filled with light. When Ralph got home from work he had meticulously followed the ritual, and now every light was switched on. He had reported on the evening's activities, and was now sitting at the big white table in the sparsely furnished living room. The only thing in front of him was the black folder. He had started sorting out his press cuttings once again. He worked calmly and methodically. He was simultaneously exalted and exasperated by his needs. He loved to feel the power of the bold headlines, the appeal of the black and white pictures, but at the same time he was irritated by the fact that they seemed to have an adverse effect on his discipline, to a certain extent. He didn't usually behave like a child in a sweet shop. He had spent a long time learning to suppress his needs and urges, but the internal pressure was immense. He blamed the fact that he had not yet found the optimum filing system. The perfect ritual.

Cut out, gather up, place the remainder of the newspapers in the recycling sack; that part was quite satisfactory. But the rest – into the envelope, into the drawer – had its flaws. He would have to modify it. Improve it.

He wanted to see them, hold them, touch them.

He had bought a folder. At first he had thought of filing everything purely in date order; each day would have its own pocket. But eventually he had decided that each newspaper should have its own separate section, so that it would be easier to follow the course of events from the point of view of a particular publication. But there was something missing. Something wasn't right. Tonight he was reorganising the material once more, this time according to size. Full-page spreads first, then three-quarter pages and so on in descending order. He discovered to his delight that there

273

was nothing smaller than a quarter-page. It was clear that he was a major news story.

That he meant something.

That he was being noticed.

He was happy with the new system; it felt right. He closed the folder and got to his feet. It was filling up. More and more newspapers were writing more and more extensive articles. Tomorrow he would buy another folder. Or possibly two. Definitely something more upmarket. It was no longer appropriate to keep his collection of cuttings in ordinary, cheap folders. He needed to upgrade. Demonstrate its value to himself and to the Master.

Be proud.

He went into the bathroom to make his preparations for the night. Flipped over the little timer that was fixed to the wall. He had found it in a little antique shop in the Söder district of the city. The timer itself was attached to a blue piece of wood, and above it were the words: 'For two whole minutes the sand will run – brush every tooth, and then you're done!' The perfect aid to facilitate and maintain the power of the rituals. He brushed his teeth thoroughly until the very last grain of sand had trickled through, and finished off as always with dental floss. He used it morning and night; he liked his mouth to be really clean. He loved the taste of blood from his gums, and pulled the white thread back and forth five times beside each tooth, until he was bleeding in several places. He rinsed his mouth and contemplated the blood-coloured water he spat into the washbasin. Rinsed and spat again. Less blood this time, but still a faint red tinge to the water as it trickled away. He didn't know if it would have been less red after a third rinse. He had never rinsed his mouth more than twice.

He heard a brief ping from the laptop in his bedroom. Ralph knew at once what it meant. A new message from the Master. The computer alerted him each time a new update was added to fygorh.se. He didn't really want to rush straight into the bedroom; he wanted to have a wash first.

The Master preached patience. He must remember that, he thought. Cherish the place inside where things were done in the correct order.

The rituals.

The foundation.

He wet his hands under the running water, pressed the soap dispenser twice, worked up a lather by rubbing his hands six times in each direction, then rinsed it off with an equal number of rubs underneath the tap. Then he washed his face with the same degree of thoroughness, dried himself according to the ritual, and finished off with the creamy moisturiser.

Then he was ready for the Master.

The message was brief and concise. A new task.

He was not allowed to choose. But it didn't really matter. The Master had chosen the same one.

Anna Eriksson.

She was next.

She was number five.

Trolle had slept for only four hours when he was woken by the alarm clock. In spite of this he felt surprisingly alert, and got up from the sofa immediately. It felt strange; he usually slept for at least nine hours a night and still woke up feeling significantly more tired. He opened the blinds and gazed out at the morning sun, which was already warm. It was a long time since he had been up before six. Once he had done it every day. When there was a dog to walk and children to take to nursery and school. A wife to drive to work with. All those things that hadn't seemed like life at the time, but had in fact been exactly that.

The things you didn't miss until they were gone.

Trolle didn't bother with his morning cigarette; he went to look in the fridge instead. It was, as he had suspected, virtually empty. He drank the last of the milk straight from the carton and decided to buy breakfast from the 7-Eleven. He needed to keep in shape now. Be sensible about his diet and his sleep. He had no idea how long his contribution would be needed, but sleep could quickly become a rare commodity. The challenge was to remain alert while fighting off the boredom that went hand in hand with long surveillance operations; it was easy to nod off under those circumstances. And there would be no one to relieve him.

He was completely on his own this time.

That was why he had gone home at one thirty this morning. Up in Anna Eriksson's apartment all the lights had gone out hours before, and after giving the matter careful thought Trolle had made the judgement that the chances of the murderer striking in the middle of the night when the husband was at home were significantly less than those of an attack after Valdemar had left the following morning. So far all the murders had taken place when the woman was alone, and Trolle could see no reason why that particular element should change. But it was only a risk assessment, not an exact science, and he didn't inform Sebastian of his decision. Sebastian would never accept the risk; his emotional link to the case was too strong and he would insist on Trolle staying there all the time. But he had to conserve his strength. He would need it today, and he would be forced to make difficult decisions all the time, free from emotional constraints, based on an assessment of acceptable risk.

He also needed to sort out some equipment: a car and a gun. He had rented a car over the internet, and had tried to get hold of a pistol. It had gone very well; Rogge would try to get hold of one during the day. But Trolle didn't want to be completely unarmed, so he went back to the kitchen, pulled out a chair, opened the cupboard above the fridge and rummaged around behind several old packets of macaroni. Found what he was looking for. A stun gun wrapped in a plastic bag. A black Taser 2 which he had bought online a few years ago. He checked that it was working; there was a flash between the poles and he put it in the pocket of his big coat with a degree of satisfaction, knowing that it was more effective than people suspected. He had tried it out one night on a well-built individual who had gone down like a felled tree as soon as it touched his neck. Trolle decided to buy new lithium batteries as soon as he had the chance, just to be on the safe side, but the ones that were in it would do for now.

He left home. Bought a large coffee and a roll on the way. Took a taxi to the car rental firm which was on the way into town; it opened at six thirty. First of all he was given a white Nissan Micra, but he swapped it for a dark blue one. White was too noticeable. He didn't want to be seen. He called at a garage and stocked up on cigarettes, dextrose, water and biscuits. It was likely to be a long day, and he wasn't sure when he would get the opportunity to buy more provisions.

At quarter past seven he was in position outside the Eriksson/Lithner apartment; this was ten minutes before the time Valdemar usually left home to travel to work on the subway. He found a parking spot with a good view of the building, pushed his seat as far back as it would go and settled down. Realised he hadn't even thought about alcohol during the course of the morning. It was a good feeling, and he celebrated with a little water straight from the bottle.

Fifteen minutes later Valdemar emerged from the building; he was wearing a suit and walking quickly. On his way to work, presumably. From what Trolle had seen in the past he usually wore a suit when he was working, and the speed at which he was moving suggested that he was late. He soon disappeared from view. Anna was now alone, he assumed. He would make sure she stayed that way. Sebastian had told him she was intending to leave Stockholm; it was Trolle's responsibility to make sure she got away safely. He stared at the other parked cars, looking for any sign of movement. Saw nothing. He picked up his mobile.

Anna Eriksson got out her suitcase. She had lain awake until the early hours. Sleep was impossible. The whole situation was so absurd that she didn't really know what to think. But she now knew that certain things were true. She was in danger. She hadn't really grasped the whole picture, but she had clearly understood that it was serious, both from Sebastian's ashen, pleading face and later from her daughter's brief comments about the murders.

Anna had called Vanja an hour or so after Sebastian had left, because she wasn't sure if what he had told her could possibly be true. After all, he could have had some reason of his own for wanting her out of the way. She wasn't sure.

Vanja had sounded stressed. Couldn't talk for long. Anna pretended that she was worried about what she had read in the paper. Tried to get as much as possible out of Vanja without revealing the real reason for her call. She didn't get far. Police confidentiality and the ability to separate her work from her home life were important to Vanja, and she stuck rigidly to both.

But what Anna did find out terrified her.

Yes, Sebastian was working with Riksmord again. 'I don't understand why he's even allowed to stay on,' Vanja had said.

'Surely he's not involved, is he?'

'Yes, he is. I can't tell you how. Anyway, you wouldn't believe me. No one would believe me.'

So it was true. Anna tried to end the call without betraying her sudden panic.

No one would believe me.

Anna believed her.

Anna knew.

Anna had called her mother right away. Made up a story. Her mother was surprised, but pleased that she was coming.

Then work. She explained that she needed some time off. Family problems, she said. It was fine. She was popular at work, and they were concerned about her rather than taking issue with her absence.

She reassured them. It was nothing serious – just something she needed to sort out with her elderly mother – but it might take a while.

After that she had packed enough clothes for a week. She had rung Valdemar and asked him to come straight home. She didn't want to be alone. She had told him that her mother wasn't feeling too good, and that she was thinking of going to stay with her for a while. He suggested going with her, but she talked him out of it. This was her mother, and it was ages since they had spent time together. It was nothing serious. In fact, it was more or less a reason to get away from work, go and see her for a while . . . He swallowed the lie without even noticing it.

Probably because she was a good liar. Really good. She wondered when that had happened. She used to think that honesty was so important.

But that was when the truth didn't hurt.

So many times she had wanted to tell Vanja the truth.

So many times she had been on the point of doing so.

But the lie which had started out as a convenient, protective device had been fed by thousands of tiny white lies, until it had become the reality.

From the start, Valdemar had wanted to tell Vanja the truth once she was old enough to understand, but Anna had kept putting it off. She had constantly postponed the revelation, weeks, months, years, until the weight of the truth was so great that it would crush everything. Until it was quite simply too late.

'You're the only father Vanja needs,' she had eventually told her husband, and they had left it at that. They had grown so close, Vanja and Valdemar. Was it because he had made that extra effort? Was it so no one could ever question his commitment, his love? Whatever it was, it had worked. Vanja loved Valdemar more than she loved Anna. More than she loved anyone.

They complemented each other so beautifully. Over time Valdemar had given up protesting, and he had become complicit. Because he loved Vanja like his own daughter.

But one day a few months ago he had appeared at her door. Sebastian Bergman.

With some letters from a time long gone.

She had said no and closed the door. Hoped he would just disappear.

That hadn't happened.

He had been working with Vanja in Västerås, Anna discovered. And now he was working with her again.

Vanja disliked him intensely. That was the only positive point, and the only thing that was still protecting the truth. Everything else was sheer chaos. Anna had a secret within the secret. She was the only one who knew that Sebastian was Vanja's father. She had always kept that information from Valdemar.

Tried to protect him.

Or perhaps she hadn't trusted him.

He wasn't like her. He had more of a problem with liars. So the only time he had asked who the father was, she had said that it was irrelevant. That she had no intention of ever telling anyone, and if that was a problem for him, for them, he should put an end to their relationship there and then.

He had stayed. Never asked again.

He was a good man.

Better than she deserved.

Now she might be in mortal danger, and still she had to lie. Perhaps it served her right. Perhaps that was how it would end.

The telephone rang. The sound made Anna jump. Another cold call, trying to sell a broadband package this time. She quickly said no and put the phone down. She thought she recognised the voice. From yesterday. The man who had called so late, wanting to talk about pensions. She stopped dead. Did she really recognise the voice? She went cold all over, grabbed the receiver again and looked at the caller display to see if it gave a number for the person who had called.

Withheld.

Both just now and last night.

Did it mean anything? No doubt she was just being paranoid. But she couldn't shake off the feeling that there was something about the voice. It had sounded the same both times: quite old, weary, slightly hoarse, not at all the way cold callers usually sounded. They normally had young, positive voices, keen to offer something. Not this one. He wanted something else. He gave up too easily. As if the fact that she had answered was enough for him. As if he were satisfied with the knowledge that she was at home.

Anxiously she went over to the window and looked down at the street. Saw nothing. But what would she be looking for? She went to the front door and locked the seven-lever mortice deadlock. Left the key in the door.

Decided to finish packing and call a cab.

She might as well go to the station right away.

Ralph had spent the last ten minutes trying to find a parking place. He drove past Storskärsgatan via De Geersgatan a couple of times on his quest. The first was a dead end and the second was a one-way street, so he had to drive around in a big circle via Värtavägen in order to get back. He hated the fact that he was so obviously driving round and round. The same silver car driving past over and over again could attract the attention of some nosy neighbour. And yet there was no alternative. He needed the car. Preferably parked as close as possible. It made him feel less exposed. It meant there was less time during which he could be identified. That was the advantage of residential areas; parking wasn't a problem. In general this new target seemed much more troublesome than the first three. He had had less time for observation. He had been able to log their activities over a period of several days, but the limited results available on this occasion suggested that the safest time was in the mornings between seven thirty and eight thirty, after her husband had left and before she travelled two stops by bus or walked to the care home where she worked.

At the same time, he was more courageous now. Better. Stronger. Before the first one he had been overcome by nerves several times, and had aborted his mission because of small disturbances: a neighbour's window was open, a cyclist passed by just as he was getting out of the car, a child started crying somewhere. A couple of times he had simply lost his nerve altogether and gone home.

But by the time he got to number three things were getting easier, and with the last one, the Willén woman, he had begun to improvise, to be braver. All within the prescribed framework, of course, but he had allowed the situation to take its course, trusted his instincts. It had been a liberating feeling, which made him feel even more strongly that he was up to the task. He was an experienced man now. A man with power. On a mission that few people would accomplish as well as him. If anyone.

Many of the separate elements were actually more challenging than he could have imagined when they were no more than advanced fantasies. The first time he had cut through the throat he had felt sick. The sound of the skin as it was torn apart was strange and unexpectedly fleshy, and the blood that spurted out was so hot and sticky that he panicked for a moment. But he had started to get used to it. Developed his abilities. The last time he had actually dared to look her in the eye as her life drained away. A potent feeling. If there was a God, which he very much doubted, that was probably how he regarded us. A being free of those surging emotions that clouded the judgement. It would be like observing the death throes of an ant. Interesting. But no more than that. It was just a person; the ritual and the task were more important than all of humanity.

The aspect that still caused him the greatest problem was the sexual element. He knew he needed to do it. Had to do it. It was part of the ritual. But he didn't enjoy it. To tell the truth, he could only just manage it. It was demanding and repulsive. He found it difficult to maintain his erection. Too many noises, too difficult to push his way in. He didn't even like women. They were too curvy, with their flabby breasts and bottoms and their smells.

Around him.

On him.

Inside him.

That part took all of his concentration. He didn't like being close to anyone. Not in that way. Not at all. But he couldn't miss it out. That would be cheating. A defeat. Failing to follow in the footsteps of the Master.

He turned into De Geersgatan for the third time, but still couldn't find anywhere to park. He was starting to get worried about the time. He should already be inside the apartment, well under way. He had been to one of the DIY superstores on the outskirts of the city, one of those that opened at six o'clock in the morning, and had bought a pair of white overalls. He needed an excuse to get into her apartment, and turning up as a painter who was going to do the stairwell seemed like a good idea. He had also bought a few cheap tins of paint and a cap which he could pull right down over his face. It should work.

★ ★ ★

Trolle had noticed him the second time he drove past. The same car, the one he had seen before. Japanese, silver. The driver wearing sunglasses and a cap. Seemed to be looking for a parking space. Close to Storskärsgatan. Trolle put down the bottle of water and his hand instinctively went to his pocket. The Taser was there. He took it out. The black plastic was warm, and it felt comfortable in his hand. His pulse rate increased, and he tried to think through his options. Calling the police was one of them. He had never had any problems with Torkel. On the contrary; throughout his decline and fall, Torkel had never judged him. He hadn't agreed with everything Trolle had done, but that was hardly surprising. Some things had been completely crazy. But even so, Trolle had always felt supported by his colleague. They didn't see each other anymore, but that was hardly Torkel's fault. It was Trolle who had withdrawn, but somewhere deep down he had convinced himself that they still respected one another.

However, a call to Torkel would put Sebastian in a precarious position.

Why was the man picked up outside the apartment block where Vanja's mother lived?

And what was Trolle doing there?

He really didn't want to do Sebastian any harm. Not now that he knew how alike they were. It was almost as if he could atone for his own mistakes if he sorted this out.

But however he looked at things, Sebastian's secret would be in danger. He had to intervene. Simply chasing the man would mean that he would get away, and other women would be at risk. Trolle had to act. Take him out. Then work out a plan.

It was up to him.

And only him.

It felt really good. Better than for a long, long time.

The car drove past for a third time, and Trolle made up his mind. He was holding all the trump cards. The man in the silver car didn't know about him. He had the element of surprise on his side. He started the car and slowly pulled away a couple of minutes later. Parked illegally on a crossing a few metres further down, on De Geersgatan.

Got out of the car and walked back.

Now there was a parking space available for someone who was looking.

He was convinced the man in the Toyota would take it.

★ ★ ★

Ralph spotted the space when he was still on Värtavägen. It was perfect. Only thirty metres from the entrance to her building. But if he was unlucky somebody else would grab it, so he put his foot down and shot through the traffic lights on Valhallavägen just as they turned red. A quick right turn, then right again. He slowed down; he didn't want to attract unnecessary attention. The space was still there. He parked carefully. Looked around. Everything was quiet and peaceful. He was annoyed at being late; it was almost eight o'clock. He felt for the Mora knife in his belt. It wasn't the one he would use later; the carving knife was wrapped in its plastic bag inside his sports bag as usual. But a smaller knife was useful at the start. As soon as the door opened. A hand over the mouth, a knife to the throat. Shock and mortal fear. It usually worked. He felt the painter's overalls were a good disguise, because he could carry the knife quite openly. Craftsmen always had a knife.

He undid his seatbelt and was about to get out of the car when the passenger door was yanked open and someone got in. An old man. He looked scruffy, with longish grey hair and a big black coat. But his eyes were burning. He wanted something. In his hand he was holding a black plastic object that looked like a broken torch.

'It's over,' the man said, trying to press the peculiar object against Ralph's neck. He heard an electrical fizzing and a faint ticking sound; he brought his right arm up in a reflex action and managed to knock aside the attacker's arm. The old man wasn't as quick as Ralph. The black thing that was making a noise hit the headrest, and he suddenly realised what it was.

The little blue flashes.

The electrical buzzing.

A stun gun.

With renewed strength he tried to push the man's arm against the back of the seat.

Trolle swore and was just about to make an attempt to free his arm when the tall, thin man struck him with his left hand. The blow caught his mouth; it didn't really hurt, it just made him even more furious. He realised that his attempt to take the driver of the silver car by surprise had completely failed, and that he was suddenly in an extremely vulnerable position. He was in no condition to engage in close combat. He had to finish this quickly. He struck out twice in quick succession with his own left hand; one blow missed, the other caught the man on his cheek. He groaned and his head fell forward a fraction.

Trolle managed to free his right hand and pressed it against the man's body. Enough was enough. He couldn't fight in a fucking car. He pressed the trigger once again and waited for the Taser to do its job. In his peripheral vision he saw the man's left arm shoot out towards his stomach. He tried to block the blow, but missed. It didn't matter, this would soon be over in any case.

The man's blow landed first. It was incredibly painful. So painful that Trolle lost all his strength in an instant, and the Taser fell uselessly from his grasp.

How had that happened?

The pain exploded as the man struck again. Everything started to go black, and Trolle realised what was happening.

The man wasn't punching him.

He was stabbing him.

He did it again.

The whole of Trolle's lower body suddenly felt warm and wet. He was on the point of losing consciousness, but he managed to look down at the man's hand. It was holding something, and something was welling up out of Trolle's belly.

The first something was a knife.

The second something was his own intestines.

The last thing he saw was the knife going in again.

Ralph saw the blood and guts surging out and landing on the man's lap. It looked bizarre, but he carried on stabbing. He had to be sure. The old man in the passenger seat let out a long, rattling sound before he suddenly fell completely silent. Eventually he slowly toppled forward onto the dashboard. Ralph suspended his attack, but remained on high alert. One single movement from the intruder and he would begin again. But there was nothing. The silence inside the car was palpable. The sleeves of his white overalls were blood-red. The car stank of blood and intestines.

His mind was racing.

What had happened? Who the hell was the dead man sitting beside him? Was anyone else going to turn up? He looked around anxiously, but the street appeared to be deserted. There was no one heading towards his car, no one paying them the slightest attention. The old man could hardly be a police officer. They didn't use a Taser in a situation like this. They used real guns. But somehow his own identity, or at least his plans, had become known. Because the dead man wasn't sitting in his car just by chance.

'It's over,' he'd said. You didn't say that if you were going to rob someone. You said that if you were intending to stop someone. The Master had been right. He had been careless in some way. Given himself away. Perhaps Sebastian Bergman was behind this. Perhaps he was a more worthy opponent than Ralph had thought. He had realised that Ralph was shadowing him. Had run towards him outside the police station. Perhaps changing cars hadn't been enough.

But that still didn't make sense.

If Sebastian had something to do with the fact that there was a dead man sitting in his car, then the man should have been a police officer. Sebastian was working with them. And there should have been more of them. A lot more. He was top priority. He was the most important case they were working on. So where were the rest of them?

He couldn't really come up with any answers.

Ralph looked anxiously around again. Saw a movement from the building where he ought to be right now. A taxi pulling up. He slid down out of sight. Saw Anna Eriksson come out of the main door carrying a suitcase. She got into the taxi. He ought to follow her, but realised this would be impossible. He had to change his clothes. Dump a body. Get rid of the car.

He had failed.

He had let the Master down.

He would have to face the consequences.

Vanja was already in a bad mood when she arrived at the station. To tell the truth, she had gone to bed in a temper the night before, and woken up furious this morning.

It wasn't even half past seven, but it was already a bloody awful day.

As if it wasn't enough that they were getting nowhere with the case, which she found incredibly frustrating, Sebastian Bergman was still an active part of the investigation. She just couldn't understand why. How could someone who had had a relationship with all four victims be allowed to remain part of the inner circle? Even if Torkel was right when he claimed that Sebastian's involvement might prevent further murders now that Edward Hinde had got his attention, it was still completely indefensible. If this came out, Torkel was finished. Not even he would be able to survive the media firestorm. But that wasn't the only thing that had put her in a bad mood. What really infuriated her was that Torkel seemed to prioritise Sebastian above everyone else in the team. He wasn't that fucking fantastic. Besides which, he got on her nerves. She couldn't relax when he was around. He kept on looking at her in a funny way. She felt as if she was being watched. He had an adverse effect on her work. She hated him.

And yesterday she had ended up in Södertälje, a trip which had been a total waste of time.

She hated Södertälje as well.

Then, when she asked Billy for a little bit of help, what had he said? 'Do it yourself.' What the fuck was that all about? Since when did you respond to a request for help within the team with 'do it yourself'?

Back in her apartment after the pointless jaunt to Södertälje, which had cost her a hundred kronor on top of everything else, she had had a shower, made tea and sandwiches and settled down

289

to stare mindlessly at the TV. She wasn't going to sit down at the kitchen table with her case notes as she usually did. She was going to unwind. Relax.

She couldn't do it.

She definitely couldn't do it after Anna had called her very late to explain that Gran was ill and she was going to stay with her for a few days. Of course Vanja had wanted to know what was wrong with her grandmother, and had been told it was nothing serious. But why would Anna take time off work to go and stay with her if it wasn't serious? Anna was hiding the truth. Just as she had done when Valdemar got sick. She had kept quiet about test results, played the whole thing down. Vanja had had to go to her father to find out how things really stood. He told her everything. Anna had lied to her. Vanja hadn't been at all happy about that. Admittedly Anna was probably just trying to protect her daughter, but regardless of her motives, the lies hadn't exactly brought them closer. And there was already a distance between them; she called her mother Anna, but she called Valdemar Dad. That said something.

It was something that Vanja would have to discuss with Anna at some point, the fact that she didn't like the lies within their relationship. On the phone last night she had felt like saying she would go with her mother to visit Gran. But she couldn't take time off. Not right now. She couldn't leave work when they had got nowhere in over a month. No, that wasn't strictly true; they had made some progress. They had found the link to Hinde. But she wouldn't be allowed to follow up that lead. Sebastian would be doing that. Torkel had already made his decision.

Bloody Torkel.

Bloody Sebastian.

Bloody everything.

She had switched off the television and gone out. Just for a walk, initially. To get some fresh air, clear her mind, tire herself out. But then she had slipped into her local pub as she was passing. Had a beer, then a few more. Hooked up with some guys and gone on somewhere else. Bumped into people she knew. Had a few more beers. And then someone had started ordering shots. It might have been her. For a brief moment she had considered taking one of the guys home with her, but in the end she had resisted the temptation. She still hadn't got to bed until well after two. Quite tipsy. Drunk, in fact. Not like her at all.

Her alarm clock went off at the usual time. And now, after barely four hours of drunken sleep, she was at work. More bad-tempered than hungover, but it certainly wasn't a good combination.

She sat down at her desk and switched on the computer. Started searching for Rodriguez. Found him, but there was nothing about where or when he had been involved in the accident that had put him in a wheelchair. She would just have to keep looking. But first she needed coffee. Caffeine and a painkiller would work wonders. She went into the staff dining room, took a mug out of the cupboard above the sink and made a cappuccino before returning to her desk. She opened the top drawer and took out a box of Ipren. Swilled down a tablet with a sip of coffee. She was just about to get back to work and start expanding her search when Billy came in. The strap of his shoulder bag was across his chest, and he was carrying a cycling helmet. Billy had a bike with twenty-four gears. Made from the same material as a spaceship, or something. Hi-tech. Of course. Vanja's had three gears. She never used it.

'Hi, how's things?' Billy said as he shrugged off his bag at his desk.

'Fine,' Vanja replied without looking up. She did her best to look as if she was concentrating really hard in order to avoid any further conversation. It didn't work.

'What are you doing?' Billy wanted to know, coming around her desk to have a look. He was hot, she noticed. The sweat was pouring down his cheeks and neck. He tilted his head to one side and dried himself with the sleeve of his T-shirt.

'I'm trying to find out when Rodriguez ended up in a wheelchair.'

Billy felt a slight pang. The truth was that if Vanja hadn't already been there, Billy would have started the day by digging out the information she wanted. Maya thought he had done really well yesterday. But although it felt good to put his foot down from time to time, so that people stopped taking him for granted, he had felt guilty all evening.

'Where are you searching?'

'Why?' Vanja took her eyes off the screen and looked up at him. 'Do you want to help?'

Billy hesitated. This was a new situation. Vanja wasn't asking for help. She was asking if he wanted to help. Billy went for the safe option and came back with a question of his own. 'Do you need help?'

'No.'

Vanja went back to the computer and started tapping away. Billy stood there for a moment, unsure of what to do next. She was in a bad mood, there was no doubt about that. Because of him, presumably. With a certain amount of justification. Should he just let it go, hope it would pass? He decided he would be a little nicer than usual to Vanja today. He didn't like it when they fell out.

'Would you like a coffee?' A little puff on the pipe of peace couldn't do any harm, surely.

'I've got some, thank you.' She pointed to her cappuccino.

Billy nodded to himself. He should have noticed. One more peace offering left. An outstretched hand that he knew she would take.

'Her name is Maya.'

'Whose name is Maya?'

'The girl. The theatre girl . . . My girlfriend.'

Vanja looked up as if she was expecting more. Billy had nothing to add. He had been prepared for a battery of questions. He had decided to answer them all, except for mentioning what Maya did. After yesterday's telephone conversation Vanja would immediately put two and two together, and that would be it for Maya. Shit, when did everything get so difficult? Vanja was still looking at him encouragingly. He was beginning to feel a bit stupid. As if he had said it as some kind of boast.

'It's just . . . I just thought you might want to know . . .'

'Okay.' Vanja went back to her computer. Not interested in his girlfriends. She really was in a foul mood. Perhaps he wasn't the only reason after all.

'Right, well, I'm going for a quick shower.'

'Okay.'

Billy stood there for a couple of seconds, then left the office. It was going to be a hard day.

Edward was sitting in the library.

For a comparatively small institution, Lövhaga had a big library. There were probably a number of reasons for this. The high level of supervision required by the inmates. The desire to strengthen the patients' intellectual development, to make them grow as people. The belief that books and knowledge would make them better in some magical way. And of course the thing that lay behind most human buildings: self-interest. The more impressive the library, the more inmates who regularly spent time in there improving themselves, the higher the grade the institution was able to achieve in internal reports. The logic was depressingly simple: an impressive library equals expert and proactive leadership.

Hinde had witnessed the results of such logic after the great cleaning riot. A few months later the library was extended signifi-cantly, and acquired an upper floor where the emphasis was on the humanities. As if future riots among inmates from the former Yugoslavia who were suffering from post-traumatic stress syndrome and had been convicted of repeated crimes of violence could be prevented by the acquisition of *The History of the Renaissance* in twelve volumes, or writings on philosophy and the history of ideas.

There was a range of both non-fiction and novels, but you had to search hard to find the real treasure. It had taken Edward quite some time, but now he was sitting upstairs as usual reading one of his favourite books. It was a detailed account of Napoleon's march across the Italian Alps in 1797. At the time Napoleon had just been made a general and had been dispatched with all haste to defend France's allies against the Habsburg dynasty. It was during these glorious battles that he demonstrated the strategic skill that would take him all the way to the heart of history. Edward had read the book many times before, but not for the descriptions of the troops, the battles, the problems with provisions or the politics behind it all. No, in the middle of the book there was a chapter which was intended to give a deeper insight into Napoleon as a person, and which mainly concerned his relationship with his mother, Letizia Bonaparte.

A strong mother.

A domineering mother.

Hinde felt he had discovered Napoleon's secret in this chapter. He could see the little boy who wanted to achieve so much for one reason, and one reason alone: Letizia. She must have been a difficult woman to deal with.

Edward left Letizia for a moment and looked around. He knew it was two or three minutes past twelve, and there would soon be a shift change in the library. The guard on the upper floor went down to the small reception desk right next to the entrance on the ground floor; he would leave the library with his colleague as soon as their relief arrived. Their replacement always arrived alone, and stayed downstairs, which was larger and busier. When the second guard arrived ten minutes later, one of them would come upstairs.

Hinde put down the book. Carefully moved his chair closer to the railing so that he could get as clear a view as possible of what was happening down below.

As usual Hinde was alone on the upper floor. The other inmates no longer went up there, at least not while Edward was around. They obediently remained downstairs. That was the way things had been for a long time, and sometimes it felt as if the management had spent millions and built the entire upper floor for the use of just one person.

A wonderful feeling.

It had taken a few weeks of intensive effort after the ostentatious opening before the others fully grasped the unwritten rules. At that time Edward had been helped significantly by his well-built friend Roland Johansson; he missed having Roland by his side. Roland had a unique ability to persuade others. He was completely unafraid, and was never held back by banalities such as empathy or compassion. At the same time he had displayed something of a soldier's loyalty towards Edward, and had always been there, silently supportive. Roland didn't say much, but Edward had gently worked on him until he found the way in via his childhood and the series of betrayals that had shaped him. Alcoholic parents. One foster home after another. Disruption and insecurity. An early acquaintance with crime and drugs. The usual sordid mess that applied to ninety per cent of those he was so unhappily forced to live with at the moment. But the difference between Roland and the others was that Roland was intelligent. Extremely intelligent. Hinde had sensed this almost at once, and had tested his IQ with the help of one of the books in the library. Roland scored 172 on the Stanford-Binet scale: 0.0001 per cent of the population came out at higher than 176. Hinde had double-checked using the Wechsler scale, and got roughly the same result. Roland Johansson was unique, and to Edward he was a godsend. A forgotten, gifted boy tempered to steel by a hard life and by people who constantly let him down. Someone who had never been seen for what he really was. Until he met Edward. Mental stimulation replaced the chemical variety, and Edward began coaching him for his future role. Following his release, Roland had kept a low profile. No crime, no drugs. He had waited for the signal. Edward's treatment had been more effective than twenty years of society's inept efforts. He gave Roland an identity, a belief in himself. That was better than all the books in the world, however many volumes they came in. Edward was pleased to have such a loyal henchman on the outside, but he missed him in here, partly because their friendship had become important to him, and partly because his position of power in Lövhaga had been weakened without Roland. Instead, Edward had been forced to lean on Igor, the triple murderer. Igor was at least as effective when it came to muscle, but unfortunately he was bipolar, which meant he was unreliable.

Edward saw the relief guard enter the library downstairs; slightly later today, but within the margin of error. He stopped and exchanged a few words with his colleagues. All three of them laughed at something, then with a farewell pat on the shoulder the other two went for lunch. In the doorway they met a cleaner in blue overalls pushing his trolley along, on his way into the library. They nodded to him. The cleaner nodded back. Ralph. Dead on time. As always. Edward saw Ralph pause for a brief chat with the guard who had just settled down behind the desk. Then Hinde slipped over to the lift. He stayed behind the bookshelves to make it look as if he was searching for a particular book, but the guard downstairs took no notice of him. Fourteen years without incident had made them feel safe. Spoiled.

'I'll make a start upstairs,' he heard Ralph say.

'Start wherever you like,' the guard replied calmly.

Hinde heard Ralph quickly push his trolley towards the lift and press the button. The doors opened immediately and Ralph got in with his trolley.

They would have approximately nine minutes before the second guard arrived and one of them came upstairs. They very rarely met in this way; it was only in exceptional cases, if they really needed to talk about something. When the internet wouldn't do. It was a security measure which Edward had introduced. It was of the utmost importance that their meetings didn't become too regular. They must never follow a pattern that the guards might notice, arousing their suspicions. But today they needed to talk. Ralph had sent a worrying message via fygorh.se. Someone was on to them. A man was dead. A man Hinde knew, at least if the driving licence Ralph had found on him was correct.

Trolle Hermansson.

One of the police officers in that stuffy interview room. An inspector in those days. The most aggressive of the three he saw most often during the intense interrogation.

Not a police officer any longer.

So what was he doing outside Anna Eriksson's apartment?

It must have something to do with Sebastian. It had been Sebastian, Trolle and Torkel Höglund in the interview room back then. Sometimes they took it in turns. But it was always one of those three. And now one of them was dead. The one who wasn't a police officer any longer. It must have something to do with Sebastian Bergman. He was the only one who would involve an old ally. He must have been doing his own thing. If the rest of Riksmord had known of Ralph's existence, they would have sent in the special operations unit. Not an old ex-copper. An old ex-copper all by himself.

Edward positioned himself by the bookshelf closest to the lift. Ralph wheeled out his trolley and placed it in front of the lift doors to prevent them from closing. Then he picked up a brush and went over to the other side of the shelf, opposite Edward. He made a few brisk movements with the brush. He was whispering, but could barely hide his agitation.

'I put the body in the boot like you said.'

'Good.'

'The car is out in Ulvsunda, on the industrial estate. Bryggeri-vägen. But I can't work out how he found me.'

Edward shifted two books so that he could look at his disciple. He gazed at him steadily. 'You must have been careless. Someone followed you.'

Ralph nodded, ashamed of himself. Looked down at the ground.

Hinde went on: 'Anna Eriksson? What happened to her?'

'She's gone.'

Edward shook his head. 'She was to be the next one, wasn't she?'

'Yes.'

'What have I always said? Planning. Patience. Determination. Anything else leads to carelessness and defeat. We're losing right now – you do understand that?'

Ralph didn't dare look at him. He was so ashamed. The strength he had felt when he touched the newspaper cuttings ebbed away. 'But why weren't the police there?' he asked quietly. 'I don't understand. Why some old man?'

'Because the police don't know.'

'What do you mean?'

'Perhaps someone suspected that you might strike. In that particular spot. But not the police.'

'Who?'

'Who do you think?'

'Sebastian Bergman?'

Edward nodded. 'It has to be him. But for some reason he didn't want to tell his colleagues that Anna Eriksson could be the next victim. Why?'

'I don't know.'

'Neither do I. Not yet. But we have to find out.'

'I don't understand . . .' Ralph dared to look up at the Master, who met his eyes with an expression of utter contempt.

'Of course you don't. But think. You said he'd been following her. For a long time.'

'Who?' Ralph was confused.

'Vanja Lithner. Anna Eriksson's daughter.' Edward paused. Ralph still didn't get it. Obviously. Idiot. But Edward was beginning to understand more and more. The solution to the mystery lay with Vanja. The blonde woman whose breasts he wanted to touch. He hadn't attached much importance to her visit to Lövhaga the other day. But then he found out that Sebastian had been following her. Why? Why had he been following an officer from Riksmord for weeks, months, before he was brought into the investigation? It had to be relevant. The feeling that it was significant grew stronger when he thought back to the events in the visitors' room. Sebastian had felt the need to protect her. That wasn't like Sebastian Bergman. As a general rule he kept his relationships with other people to a minimum. He just didn't care about them. But he cared about Vanja. Why? Edward had to start digging, exploring. Probing.

Ralph was standing there in silence, looking around nervously.

'No problem, there's plenty of time.' Edward gave him a reassuring smile. 'I want you to go home and check up on the whole family. When did Anna meet Valdemar? When was Vanja born? I want to know everything. Her friends. Where she went to university. Everything.'

Ralph nodded. He still didn't really understand, but he was relieved that Edward was no longer exuding contempt.

'Okay.'

'Today. Now. Tell them you don't feel well, and go home.'

Ralph nodded eagerly; he had been so afraid that his failure would mean the end for him. That what he had begun would simply disappear. Come crashing down. It would be the worst thing that could possibly happen. Because he had tasted it. Real life.

'Then will you give me the next one?' suddenly came flying out of his mouth.

The unexpected question annoyed Edward. Had he already lost control of the worm standing in front of him? He had given this pathetic weirdo everything. Created him. And now he was standing there trying to negotiate. He would show him. But not yet. He needed him at the moment. Until he knew. Until he was sure. So he smiled warmly instead. 'You're so important to me, Ralph. I need you. You can have another if you want. Just as long as you sort this out first.'

Ralph immediately calmed down. Realised that he had probably gone too far. Asked for too much.

'Sorry. I just wanted . . .'

'I know what you want. You're keen. But remember: patience.'

Ralph nodded obediently.

'I shall await your report,' Edward said, then turned and went back to his table, to Letizia Bonaparte and her son.

Ralph wheeled his trolley into the lift and went down.

The second guard walked in less than a minute later.

Perfect timing.

Jennifer Holmgren yawned.

Not because she was tired, nor because of a lack of oxygen. She was just seriously bored, standing there on the lawn sloping down towards Lejondal Lake. She was facing not only the leader of the police search team, who was just going over the key points, but also a large yellow two-storey house with an enormous veranda facing the lake. Next to her were several police officers, most of them from Sigtuna, like her. Jennifer suppressed her yawn and silently went over the points she needed to remember.

Lukas Ryd.

Six years old.

Missing for several hours. Three, his mother hoped. More, his father thought. At any rate, Lukas had not been in his bed, nor anywhere else in the house, when his parents woke up that morning, about three hours ago. They had gone to bed at half past midnight, so the truth was that the kid could have been gone all night. Nobody knew. The doors had been closed when they woke up. Closed but not locked.

Jennifer could feel herself beginning to sweat in her uniform. The sun was beating down mercilessly on her back. This was her first missing person. After four terms at the police training academy, she was now in her second month as a trainee in Sigtuna. The town wasn't what you might call crime central. There was plenty to do, that wasn't the problem. She had checked the statistics. During 2009 the crime rate in Sigtuna had been higher than the average throughout the country: 19,579 reported crimes per 100,000 inhabitants. The national average was 10,436. But it still didn't feel like the most exciting place in Sweden to be a police officer. And Jennifer wanted excitement. Obviously she wanted to make a contribution to society and to help people, but that wasn't her main reason for joining the police. When she applied she had toned down her dreams of action and excitement and demonstrated a more mature, realistic view of the profession, but during the entire course of her training she always excelled when it came to activities that were physically demanding and/or involved some kind of close combat or the use of guns. There hadn't been much of that since she arrived in Sigtuna. She had stopped speeding drivers in the thirty zone outside a school. She had dealt with reports of break-ins, criminal damage, theft and minor assault. She had carried out random breathalyser tests, sat in reception, and produced more passports than she would have thought possible.

Police work, absolutely.

Action and excitement, not so much.

Two months that felt like two years. That was why she had felt a small surge of excitement when she first heard about Lukas Ryd. A little boy. Missing. He might have been abducted. She had silently nurtured that hope until they arrived and established the facts.

Lukas's little Bamse the Bear rucksack was missing. Two cans of Coca-Cola and a packet of alphabet biscuits had also disappeared.

The kid had run away from home.

Or maybe it wasn't even that exciting.

He had woken up, felt like a picnic, and hadn't wanted to wake his parents.

So ordinary. So banal. So boring.

Jennifer Holmgren knew that this was probably the wrong attitude, but come on! He'd come home when he got too cold or too bored.

Unless he got lost, of course. There was plenty of forest around here. But at this time of year that thought didn't exactly produce a rush of adrenaline either. As far as the temperature was concerned, finding him wasn't a matter of urgency. That left quarries and lakes. Jennifer had thought of that as soon as she saw the garden. The boy could have wandered down to the lake and fallen in, but the family didn't have a jetty and the lake wasn't tidal, so if he had drowned he ought to be lying there in the shallow water.

Jennifer was allocated a search area a kilometre away. A small forest track on the other side of the main road. She felt a faint stirring of hope again. She had dismissed the idea of a planned kidnapping. The parents didn't seem to be rolling in money, in spite of the relatively large house overlooking the lake, but what about a random abduction somewhere along the main road? A little boy walking along in the ditch. A dirty old man. A paedo.

Not that she wished the child ill, or wanted him dead. Absolutely not. She really did hope that nothing had happened to him. But a bit of action, a bit of excitement . . . A tip-off about a suspect vehicle, the search, gradually closing in, the discovery, the strike, the arrest.

That was why she had joined the police. Not so that she could go for a brisk walk in the forest on a hot summer's day, searching for some kid who fancied a snack. She might as well have been a classroom assistant in a nursery, in that case. Okay, that was unfair, they didn't lose kids. Well, not often, but the principle . . .

She set off along the forest track. It looked as if it ended at a gravel pit or something similar, according to the map. Perhaps Lukas had got stuck in the gravel. Clambered up one of the heaps, then the loose stones underfoot had begun to shift. Slide. The more he tried to gain a foothold, the lower he sank. Could that even happen in a gravel pit? She didn't know, but the thought of heroically seizing the tiny hand that was the only thing protruding from the immense gravel canyon, of pulling the boy free, clearing his mouth and blowing life into him as her colleagues finally arrived . . . She lengthened her stride. She glanced distractedly among the trees on either side. His parents thought he was wearing blue cotton trousers and a yellow T-shirt with a short-sleeved blue checked shirt over the top. That was what he had been wearing yesterday, at any rate. Like a little Swedish flag running around in the forest. Jennifer suddenly wondered why the kid had run away from home. If it wasn't just a case of a six-year-old fancying a little adventure, of course. Had he run away for a reason? Jennifer had been furious with her parents on a number of occasions while she was growing up, who hadn't, but she had never run away from home. Could there be something exciting there? If she found the boy, she could pump him for information. He was only six. Children were still afraid of the police at that age, weren't they?

Jennifer reached the gravel pit. She was thirsty. Drenched in sweat. Flies buzzing all around her. The others were calling in via the radio on a regular basis. She didn't really see the point of reporting in every five minutes to say you hadn't found anything; surely it would have been better if they'd agreed that whoever found the boy would shout.

She hadn't found him, anyway. She was just about to turn back when she caught a flash of metal behind the heap of gravel furthest away, on the edge of the forest. She screwed up her eyes and shaded them from the sun with her hand. She could see a windscreen and a broken headlight. A car. It seemed an odd place to park a car. Very odd. Suspicious.

A prostitute who had brought a client here?

Someone dealing drugs?

A body that had been dumped?

Jennifer undid her holster and slowly approached the car.

Billy had showered and got himself a coffee. He glanced over at Vanja when he came back to the office, but she didn't even look up when he walked through the door, so he decided not to disturb her again. He hoped she wouldn't bear a grudge; he didn't actually know if she did that kind of thing or not. They had never fallen out before, as far as he could remember. Disagreed, discussed, but never quarrelled. He decided to leave it for a while, then if the worst came to the worst he would just have to apologise later. It wasn't the end of the world.

He sat down at the computer, logged on, put on his headphones and started Spotify on his mobile as he brought up a text document. He had written it last night when he couldn't sleep. It was just a series of points, a way of structuring his thoughts. It was the case, from the beginning right up to now. Ideas and theories. He had never tried working like this before; he just wanted to see if it would get him anywhere. He leaned back and looked through what he had written.

One possibility was that someone was killing Sebastian's former lovers and copying Hinde as he did so without there being any link whatsoever between the murderer and Hinde. It might just be an idea that some lunatic had had in order to get his revenge on Sebastian.

Highly unlikely.

Because Hinde was involved in these murders in some way. Sebastian seemed sure of it, and Vanja had also had a distinct feeling that this was the case after she had met Hinde. So they could probably assume that Hinde was involved.

But he couldn't carry out the murders himself. That was completely out of the question. In which case, as far as Billy could work out, that left two alternatives.

The first was that Hinde had asked someone to do it. On some occasion. Someone he had met only once. He had told this person that he wanted all the victims to have something in common, explained what that was, and subsequently the killer had acted entirely alone. He had followed Sebastian, and that was how he had found Annette.

Possible, but not really credible.

The sticking point was that the murderer had deviated from his MO when it came to Annette's murder. Women from Sebastian's past were suddenly abandoned in favour of his latest conquest. Why? If you toyed with the idea that Hinde had supplied a list of relevant women, would the copycat really have deviated from that list? Started to improvise?

Again it was possible, but not credible.

The only remaining alternative was that Hinde was in constant contact with the murderer. That they were somehow able to exchange information. With the murder of Annette Willén, it became clear to Billy that this had to be the case. The murderer followed Sebastian, saw Annette and told Hinde, who gave the order to kill her. Or Hinde had given the murderer the task of finding a woman who was more recent, so to speak. So that the link to Sebastian became clear.

Credible, but unfortunately not possible.

Because Hinde had no contact with the outside world. Or did he? Billy had spoken to Victor Bäckman at Lövhaga and had been given the details of Hinde's internet activity over the past few days. He was intending to start there. It was possible that someone had inserted coded information into the pages Hinde visited – a code only Hinde could interpret. Like in some old spy thriller.

But how did he reply, if that were the case? He couldn't use chat rooms, comment, or send anything at all from the computers in the library. Which meant there was only one alternative . . .

Someone patted Billy on the shoulder. Torkel. He took off the headphones.

'Can we make a start?' Torkel said.

Billy gathered up a pile of papers from his desk, stood up and left the room. Vanja stayed where she was and closed her eyes tightly for a few seconds. She massaged her forehead with her index finger and thumb. The painkiller hadn't helped. She opened the drawer and took another tablet. Rinsed it down with coffee that wasn't even lukewarm any longer, and walked out into the corridor, where she almost bumped into Ursula. Sebastian was lumbering along a few steps behind her. Vanja ignored him.

'Good morning,' she said to Ursula.

'Hi. You look tired.'

Vanja nodded as she tried to come up with a suitable response. She didn't really want to advertise her midweek drinking binge. She went for an acceptable explanation for the dark circles under her eyes. Worry.

'My grandmother is ill.'

'Oh, I'm sorry,' Ursula said sympathetically. 'Nothing serious, I hope?'

'No. Anna's gone to see her. I'm sure she'll call . . .'

Sebastian smiled to himself. Anna had gone. Left the city. One less thing to worry about. He had thought about it a lot. What he had done. What he ought to have done. What he was going to do. If he had made a mistake and possibly led the murderer to Anna's apartment, the best thing would have been to post two police officers there to wait for the perpetrator. Smuggle them inside. Let Valdemar go out so that it would look as if Anna was home alone, then wait for the copycat to turn up. That would have been the best thing, the right thing, but it was impossible. How could Sebastian say that he was afraid that Anna might be next, when the victims had only one thing in common? It was out of the question. He would have to rely on Trolle. Who wasn't answering his phone. He hadn't picked up all morning. This was a cause for concern. Sebastian took out his mobile and tried Trolle again as he followed the others into the Room. No reply.

'Sebastian . . .' Torkel was giving him a meaningful look. 'We're ready to start.'

Sebastian put the phone in his pocket with a sigh.

Vanja reached for one of the bottles of water in the middle of the table; she opened it and drank deeply.

'Okay,' Torkel began. 'A quick update. Vanja, would you like to begin?'

Vanja quickly swallowed the last of the water with a little cough.

'I've managed to eliminate Rodriguez from the theft of the

car. The blue Focus was stolen two days after he cut across the E4 without looking where he was going. Drunk as a skunk, apparently.'

'Anything else?'

'Not as far as Rodriguez is concerned. There's nothing to indicate that he's involved in any way.'

Torkel nodded. A possible lead that had turned out to be a dead end. There had been a lot of those in this investigation. Too many. He turned to Billy. 'Billy?'

Billy straightened up in his chair and more or less continued his musings aloud, starting from where he had been interrupted earlier. 'I think someone is helping him.'

'Congratulations, Einstein.' Sebastian brought his hands together in a slow clap. 'It's pretty obvious that someone is helping him, isn't it?'

'I don't mean with the murders. I mean with information. Contact. I think he has help inside Lövhaga.'

They all leaned forward. Interested. Focused. This wasn't a revolutionary suggestion – they had sniffed around the idea before – but Billy might have a new angle. One that might lead somewhere.

'I've checked with Victor Bäckman, who's responsible for security out there,' Billy went on. 'None of those held in the secure wing are allowed to communicate via the computers. However, two of them are allowed to use the telephone. Their calls are recorded; I've got the print-outs here.'

He picked up five sets of perhaps fifteen pages each and passed them around the table. 'Names, addresses, phone numbers. There aren't many of them. One of them usually rings his girlfriend. The other usually rings his mother. There's the odd exception, but nothing regular. We ought to have a chat with them, though. The people they're calling, I mean.'

'Absolutely.' Torkel looked up from the list he had just been given. 'Vanja, could you sort that out?'

Vanja had to make a real effort not to show how surprised she was. The world had turned upside down. Billy was in the middle of a lengthy discourse about the case, mainly the more technical aspects, admittedly, but even so. He was pushing ahead. And she was supposed to sort out some uniforms to go and have a word with the people on the list he had given her. Her headache was getting worse.

'Of course,' she said quietly, staring down at the desk.

'Anything else?' Torkel was still looking at Billy.

'If it isn't one of the inmates, it could be someone who works there. I've requested staff lists and I'm going to run them against everything we've got.'

'I assume none of the guards at Lövhaga has a record?'

Billy shrugged. 'You've said that Hinde is manipulative. He's communicating with someone. I know it . . .'

'How can you be sure?'

Sebastian again. Genuinely curious this time.

Billy ran through his reasoning: the fourth murder was different.

Sebastian nodded. It was very unusual for a serial killer to change his MO, but for a copycat to do so was almost unthinkable. Unless Hinde had found a weak personality whom he could control. Someone for whom the killing was less important than pleasing Hinde. Not impossible. All they had to do was find him. Apparently Torkel had reached the same conclusion.

'Go through the staff. Get some help if you need it. Good work, Billy.' He turned to Ursula, who spread her arms wide in an eloquent gesture.

'As far as forensics goes we've got just as much today as we had yesterday. Or just as little, depending on how you want to look at it.'

Torkel nodded, gathered up the material he had brought with him and the papers he had been given during the briefing, and got ready to bring things to a close.

'What about Sebastian? Aren't we going to hear his input?' Vanja felt she had to take out her bad temper and her headache on someone. And who better than Sebastian Bergman? She leaned forward and fixed him with a defiant stare. 'What contribution have you made? Apart from keeping your trousers on, I hope.'

Torkel's phone rang before he had time to comment on Vanja's outburst. He chose to answer, knowing that Sebastian was perfectly capable of taking care of himself.

Sebastian gazed calmly back at Vanja. Should he tell her he'd actually tried to warn some of his former lovers? Done what he could to prevent a repetition? That he was intending to sit down with a phone today to try to get hold of several more? No. Partly because they would want to know who he'd warned, and partly because they would think it was incredibly stupid to start visiting these women when someone might still be following him. But nor did he intend to take any more crap. He had been badly shaken by what had happened, and Vanja had made the most of it. No sympathy, just contempt. Right now he didn't care who she was; it was time for Sebastian Bergman to rise again.

'I have indeed kept my trousers on. I might have unzipped my flies and had a little wank, but I presume that's okay with you?'

Vanja gave him a poisonous look and shook her head almost wearily. 'I hate you.'

'I know.'

Torkel ended the call and turned back to the group without any indication that he had heard the last exchange.

'A car has been found. Burnt out. It is, or was, a blue Ford Focus.'

'Where?'

Vanja, Billy and Ursula were all on their feet immediately.

'A gravel pit out in Bro. I've got the directions.'

'Let's go.'

Billy pulled up by the gravel pit behind Ursula's jeep. He turned off the engine and sat there for a moment. Watched as Ursula got out, opened the boot and took out her equipment in two large bags. Vanja was sitting next to him with her sunglasses on. Her head was lolling against the headrest, her breathing calm and regular.

When they had got down to the car park she had thrown him the keys. 'You drive.'

Since then she hadn't spoken. Not a word. He drove out of the city and they headed north in silence. When they had travelled a little way along the E18 he asked whether she minded if he put the radio on. No reply. He tuned in to The Voice. Snoop Dogg. She didn't protest, so he assumed she had fallen asleep. Just past Bro he turned right onto the 269 and with the help of the GPS found his way to the minor road leading to the gravel pit near Lövsta. And here they were. He shook her gently by the shoulder.

'Wake up, we've arrived.'

'I am awake.' Vanja sat up straight and stretched.

They got out of the car and walked towards the burnt-out Ford. The air was motionless between the heaps of gravel, insects buzzing everywhere. Vanja guessed that the temperature must be around forty-five degrees. A uniformed female officer aged around twenty-five was standing just outside the area that was being cordoned off. Vanja went over to her as Billy continued towards the car.

'Jennifer Holmgren,' the officer said, holding out her hand.

'Vanja Lithner, Riksmord. You found the car?'

'Yes.'

Vanja looked over at the Ford Focus. Or what was left of it. It was just about possible to tell that it had been blue in the odd place that the fire hadn't reached. Otherwise it was ash-grey. The tyres and the bumper had melted, as had the whole of the interior. The doors and the roof had buckled from the heat. All the glass had shattered. The boot was open, and the bonnet was missing. Perhaps something in the engine had exploded. Ursula would tell them, if that was the case. She was walking around taking photographs from every possible angle.

Vanja turned back to Jennifer. 'Did you touch anything?'

'Yes, I opened the boot.'

'Why did you do that?'

Ever since Jennifer had reported her discovery and been told that she was to stay where she was and wait for Riksmord, she had been contemplating the fact that her real reason for opening the boot – that she was hoping to find a dead body as the result of some kind of transaction between criminal gangs – wasn't exactly going to cut it. She had realised that Riksmord would think searching for the victim of an execution in a sunny gravel pit outside Sigtuna was at best utterly stupid, and at worst professional misconduct. Even if two dead bodies had been found in the boot of a burning car on the E6 in Halland a few years ago. Jennifer would have given anything to be in the patrol car that was first on the scene back then . . . Today the boot had been empty, but while she was waiting she had come up with a much better reason to explain why she had opened it.

'We're looking for a missing six-year-old. I just wanted to make sure he hadn't hidden in there, or something. It's so hot,' she added.

Vanja from Riksmord nodded. A nod which told Jennifer that her explanation had not only been accepted, but had also impressed Vanja a little.

'Nothing else?' Vanja wanted to know.

'No. Why are you interested in this car? Has it been involved in something?'

Vanja looked at her uniformed colleague. There was no mistaking her tone: anticipation bordering on excitement.

'Have you found the child?' she asked, avoiding the question.

'What child?'

'The one you were looking for.'

'No. Not yet.'

'In that case I think you should carry on looking for him.'

Vanja ducked under the police tape and went to join Ursula and Billy.

Jennifer watched her go. Riksmord. That was where she ought to be. As soon as she had finished her placement in Sigtuna, she would put in her application. How old was that Vanja? Thirty, maybe. Five years difference. And she didn't exactly seem new to the job. If she could do it, so could Jennifer. And she would. But first of all she would find Lukas Ryd. There was an area not far away known locally as the Marchland which sounded promising.

★ ★ ★

Vanja went over to the burnt-out car and looked inside. A total mess of melted plastic, burnt wires and distorted metal. Ursula was still taking photographs, but she was usually able to form a quick assessment of the most important elements at a crime scene. Vanja straightened up. 'Anything?'

'A very powerful accelerant. No sign that there was anyone in the car.' Ursula lowered the camera and met Vanja's gaze across the roof. 'I don't want to pre-empt things, but don't get your hopes up.'

Vanja sighed. The number plates were burnt beyond recognition, impossible to read with the naked eye. They didn't even know if it was the right Ford. They could be standing here wasting valuable time because somebody couldn't be bothered to take some old wreck to the scrapyard.

'I'll take a walk along the track to see if I can find anything.' Obviously Billy was thinking along the same lines. There wasn't much for them to do here. Not at the moment, anyway.

'Like what?'

'I don't know. Something. Anything. We don't all need to stand around here staring.'

He walked away from the car, ducked under the tape and set off. Vanja stayed where she was. With hindsight it had been a little hasty of all three of them to come rushing over, but they were so desperate for a breakthrough. They really needed something, and they had hoped that this would be it. But there wasn't much here. No chance of finding footprints. No witnesses. No CCTV cameras. Ursula would deal with the car. So what else was there to do? There was no point in them all standing around staring,

312

as Billy had said. But somebody had to do it, and apparently that was her job. Bloody hell, it was hot.

★ ★ ★

Billy walked along the track, scanning the surrounding area as he went. He didn't really know what he was looking for, or what he thought he might find. If they were lucky, their perpetrator had made a mistake out here. He hadn't allowed for the fact that they would be called in. Perhaps he had thrown away an empty petrol can that might lead them to a service station with CCTV cameras . . . Wishful thinking, no doubt, but at least searching along the forest track beat staring at a burnt-out car along with a bad-tempered Vanja.

He had gone about eight hundred metres without finding anything and had almost reached the main road. A hundred metres further on, on the left-hand side by the crossroads, was an isolated house made of red-painted wood, with white eaves and window frames. Solid stone foundations. Steeply pitched tiled roof. Two cars in the drive. A three-wheeler and toys in the garden. Definitely someone living there. Worth a visit. Billy turned off towards the house, but he had gone no more than a few steps before he heard a rustling sound in the trees behind him to the right. Billy spun around and instinctively placed his hand on his gun, but relaxed when he saw a woman aged around forty coming towards him with a dog on a lead. Some kind of setter. Brown. Long-haired. Hot. Tongue dangling like a tie.

'Are you from the police?' asked the woman as she stepped up onto the road a few metres away from Billy. The dog was panting and tugging at the lead, wanting to come and say hello.

'Yes.'

'Why are you here? I've been seeing officers around all day.' The woman and the dog came over to Billy, who bent down and patted the excited animal on the head.

'Some of them are looking for a child who's gone missing.'

'Who's missing?'

'I don't know. A little boy from the local area. I'm here because a burnt-out car has been found up at the gravel pit.'

'I see.'

313

'Do you live around here?' Billy asked, straightening up. The dog was starting to show a bit too much of an interest in his hands, licking them like mad. Lack of salt, presumably.

'I live there.' The woman pointed to the red house on the crossroads.

'What's your name?'

'Carina Torstensson.'

'I'm Billy Rosén. Do you know anything about it?'

'The car?'

'Yes.'

'No.'

'It ended up here at some point between ten o'clock yesterday morning and . . .' Billy broke off. They didn't actually know when the car had been driven to the gravel pit. It was cold, so that excluded the last ten hours, but otherwise it could have been dumped at any time. He shrugged. '. . . Some time during the night. You didn't see anything unusual during that period?'

Carina was already shaking her head.

Billy gave it one last try. 'Perhaps when you were out with the dog . . . Did you notice another car? Someone who didn't really seem to belong here?'

'I met a man when I was out picking mushrooms.' The head shaking was replaced by a pensive nodding. 'That was yesterday.'

Billy took a deep breath. At last! Somebody who had seen something. So far he had been like a bloody ghost, but Carina Torstensson had seen someone.

When she was out picking mushrooms.

In the heat of high summer.

In July . . .

Carina noticed his doubtful expression.

'The chanterelles have started to come through. It's a bit dry at the moment, but the late spring was quite wet, so there are a few . . .' She looked up at the clear blue sky. 'But of course a little more rain wouldn't go amiss.'

'This man you met . . .' Billy decided not to write her off just yet, and led her back to the matter at hand.

'He came from up there.' She gestured over her shoulder with her thumb.

'From the gravel pit?'

'Yes.'

'Do you remember what he looked like?' Billy dug out a pen and a notepad, and opened it at a clean page.

'Tall. Not dressed for the forest. Leather jacket. Long hair in a ponytail. A big scar over one eye.'

Billy stopped writing. A big scar. Like Roland Johansson.

'Was it his left eye? Running down over his cheek?' Billy used the pen to show her what he meant on his own face. The woman nodded. Billy made a note.

'Did you see where he went after that? Did someone pick him up?'

'No, he got on the bus.'

'Which bus?'

'The 557. To Kungsängen. It goes from over there.' She pointed down the main road and Billy saw a bus stop about fifty metres from Carina's house.

'Do you remember what time this was?' He was almost holding his breath. If they could get a time they could find the bus, the bus driver, and a possible destination. Carina thought about it.

'Quarter past, twenty past twelve. He must have caught the twelve twenty-six.'

'Thank you!' Billy had to suppress the impulse to give her a hug. 'Thank you!' He put away his notepad and broke into a run.

★ ★ ★

He didn't have to run far. After only a few hundred metres he met Vanja in the car. She slowed down beside him and wound down the window as he caught his breath.

'Where are you going?' he asked.

'Ursula's fine on her own back there; we're not doing anything useful.'

'Okay . . .' Billy got in, fastening his seatbelt as Vanja moved off. 'Roland Johansson has been here.'

Vanja glanced over at him, and Billy felt the car slow as she instinctively lowered her speed. Surprised.

'The guy who was in Lövhaga at the same time as Hinde?'

'Yes.'

'How do you know?'

'I met a woman who lives just by the crossroads.' He pointed out the red house, which they were about to drive past. 'She saw him here. Yesterday.'

'Did you go off to interview witnesses?'

Billy was lost for words. He had expected a whole lot of questions from Vanja. About the case. About Johansson, about the witness. Instead she was wondering why he had left the gravel pit, with a hint of criticism in her voice.

'No, I went to check out the track, and I bumped into her.'

'And you asked her about the car?'

Billy sighed. The information he had was good news.

Big news.

Possibly crucial news.

Get your priorities straight, he thought.

'No, I was just walking along the road.' Billy did his best to keep the irritation at bay, but he could hear the exaggerated care in his explanation. 'She was out with her dog and she asked me what we were doing here and I told her and then she said she'd seen a man with a bloody great big scar who was coming from the direction of the gravel pit at the right time. What was I supposed to do? Ask her to keep quiet until you were there to hear it as well?'

'Oh no, you seem to be doing your own thing these days anyway.'

Vanja turned left onto the main road and put her foot down. More criticism. For what, exactly? For the life of him he couldn't work out what he had done wrong. He had refused to help her with a search, but that was all. He was ambitious; he wanted to develop. To change. He decided to tackle the issue head on.

'What's the matter with you?'

Vanja didn't answer; instead she gave every appearance of concentrating on the road.

'As soon as I don't do exactly what you say, or do something on my own initiative, you go crazy,' Billy persisted. 'Do you feel threatened?'

'By what?' A touch of amusement in her tone. As if she had suppressed a little laugh at a ridiculous idea.

Billy straightened up in his seat. 'By me,' he said sharply. 'Are you scared I'll turn out to be better than you, or what?'

This time she didn't bother to suppress it; she let out a short, harsh laugh. 'Oh yes. Absolutely. Got it in one.'

Her gaze was still fixed on the road. Billy thought he detected a tiny smile at the corner of her mouth, but he wasn't sure. There was, however, no doubt about the irony in her response.

'What do you mean by that?' This time he didn't try to hide his annoyance. Why should he? He was furious.

'By what?'

'By that tone of voice and "Oh yes. Absolutely. Got it in one".'

Vanja didn't answer immediately. There were a number of options. She could keep quiet, ignore his question. She could brush him off, apologise if she had sounded unkind, say that hadn't been her intention.

Or she could tell the truth.

'I meant that I'm not scared you'll turn out to be better than me.'

'And why not?'

'Because that will never happen.'

Billy leaned back in his seat. He could have carried on asking "why?" and "why not?" for a while longer, but what would be the point? Vanja had made it perfectly clear what she thought of him as a police officer. There was nothing more to be said. Vanja was obviously of the same opinion.

They drove on in silence.

As he pulled out onto the motorway and put his foot down, Haraldsson realised he was going to be seriously late for work. Although it didn't really matter. He didn't have to clock in, after all. He was the boss. It was July. He could use a bit of flexi-time. In advance, so to speak.

The alarm clock had gone off at the usual time, but Jenny had rolled sleepily over to his side of the bed and snuggled in under the covers. Tucked her head in the hollow between his neck and shoulder, wrapped her arm around him. Her pregnancy wasn't showing much, but Haraldsson thought he could feel the slight roundness of her stomach against his body. There was a life inside her. Their child. Half him, half her. Though he hoped the child would be more like Jenny: 70/30, perhaps. She was so beautiful. In every way. Warm, thoughtful, wise, funny. She was everything that was good. Sometimes he just couldn't believe how lucky he was to have her. He loved her so much.

He had told her that. This morning. She had responded by hugging him even more tightly. One thing had led to another. They had made love. Afterwards he said it again.

'I love you.'

'I love you too.'

'I've got a surprise for tomorrow.'

'Shh . . .' She had put her finger to his lips. 'Don't say any more. I don't want to know.'

Tomorrow would be their fifth wedding anniversary. He had the whole day planned. First of all he would give her breakfast in bed: tea, toast with raspberry jam and cheese, scrambled eggs and crispy bacon, melon with strawberries dipped in chocolate. He would be late for work tomorrow as well, he realised. Later in the day, when Jenny was at work, she would be picked up by car and taken to a luxury spa for a range of treatments. At the same time some men were coming round to plant an apple tree in the garden. An Ingrid Marie. Jenny liked apples that were slightly sharp, and at the nursery they had said an Ingrid Marie would be perfect. And it was a pretty name, too. If they had a daughter, they could call her Ingrid Marie. Ingrid Marie Haraldsson. He was really excited about tomorrow.

Five years.

Wood.

And she was getting a tree. A tree from which they could pick apples in the years to come. It would blossom every spring, and every autumn they could rake up the leaves together before the first snow. Ingrid Marie and her brothers and sisters would be able to climb it. Being careful, of course. In his mind's eye Haraldsson could see himself and Jenny sitting in the shade of the apple tree when they were older. Old. The children and grandchildren visiting. Taking bags of fruit home with them to make jam and juice. Unless of course they had already taken cuttings from the tree to plant in their own gardens. This was a gift that would bring them both benefits and joy for the rest of their lives together. A gift of love. Jenny would be thrilled.

But that wasn't the end of it. In the evening a chef was coming round. He would serve them a three-course menu with wine, and then clear up the kitchen afterwards. All Jenny and Haraldsson had to do was relax. Think about each other.

Nothing could go wrong.

His mobile rang. Abba. 'Ring Ring'. He glanced at the display before he answered. Work. What now?

'Haraldsson.'

'Where are you?' Annika. His PA. He made a mental note to have a little chat with her. Something appeared to have gone slightly wrong with their relationship. He thought he had been encouraging, praising her initiative. That business of fetching his coffee from the dining room, for example. He had made a point of mentioning it and suggesting that she might like to carry on doing that.

'I'm on my way. Did you want something?'

'You have the monthly meeting with the psychologists.'

Shit, he'd forgotten that. The governor and the medical staff had a meeting on the last Wednesday of every month. Haraldsson had intended to postpone it, which was why he hadn't put it in his diary. He wanted to be a bit more familiar with things before they met for the first time, but he hadn't quite got around to moving the meeting. Now it was too late presumably.

'Where is it?'

'Here. In twenty minutes.'

Haraldsson glanced at his watch. He wouldn't be there for at least half an hour.

'In that case I'll be there in plenty of time,' he said, ending the call. Annika would tell everyone he was on his way and that he would be on time. He had half an hour to come up with a reason for his late arrival. Something to do with the traffic, that was probably the easiest. Road works, perhaps. One lane closed. Long queues. He would apologise, but of course it was impossible to plan for these things. Nobody would bother to check. He turned up the radio and put his foot down.

Billy and Vanja were sitting in the canteen at the bus depot waiting for Mahmoud Kazemi, who had been driving the bus in question the previous day. The woman they had spoken to on reception had told them he would be back in less than ten minutes, and that he then had a fifteen-minute break. Billy had asked what happened if they needed to speak to him for longer than fifteen minutes, and had been informed that they would need to travel with him on the bus if that were the case. The bus couldn't be late, and there was no possibility of arranging a swap or a substitute driver at this stage. Billy decided the interview wouldn't take longer than quarter of an hour. He had no idea what Vanja thought. They hadn't spoken since their conversation in the car.

The woman on reception showed them into the canteen. A functional space. Not all that shabby, not all that new. Sit down, have a break, eat. Nothing to tempt the employees to a longer break than necessary. A mixture of sweat and the smell of fried food in the air.

Billy sat down at one of the tables as Vanja went over to the coffee machine.

'Do you want one?'

'No thanks.'

Vanja shrugged and waited with her back to him as the machine filled a paper cup. Then she came and sat down next to him, presumably because it would look very odd if they were sitting at separate tables when Mahmoud arrived. She drank her coffee in silence, and Billy said nothing.

A man in his forties appeared in the doorway. Height perhaps a hundred and eighty-five centimetres. Dark hair, moustache, brown eyes looking at them rather nervously.

'They said you wanted to speak to me.' Mahmoud jerked his thumb in a vague backward movement to indicate who 'they' were. Vanja guessed he meant the woman on reception.

'Mahmoud Kazemi?' Vanja said, getting to her feet. Billy followed suit.

'Yes. What's this about?'

'Vanja Lithner and Billy Rosén; we're from Riksmord.' Both of them showed their ID; Mahmoud glanced at the cards without interest. 'We'd like to ask you a few questions about your shift yesterday.'

The man nodded and the three of them sat down. Vanja pushed a photograph of Roland Johansson across the table to Mahmoud. 'Do you recognise this man?'

Mahmoud picked up the photograph and looked at it carefully. 'Maybe . . .'

Vanja felt a stab of impatience. Roland Johansson looked like a member of some Hells Angels chapter, with half his face sliced open. If you'd met him, you'd remember him. How could Kazemi be in any doubt? He might not be sure about the time, but he must know whether or not he'd seen him.

'He might have got on your bus yesterday,' Billy said helpfully. 'Out at Lövsta.'

'Lövsta . . .'

'Between Stentorp and Mariedal.'

Mahmoud looked up from the photograph and gazed at Billy with a slightly weary expression. 'I know where it is. I drive the bus there.'

'Sorry.'

The room fell silent. Vanja took a sip of her coffee.

Mahmoud Kazemi studied the picture for a little longer, then put it down on the table and nodded firmly. 'He did get on. I remember, because he smelled.'

'Smelled of what?' Vanja wanted to know.

'Smoke. As if he'd been burning something.'

Vanja nodded encouragingly as she wondered whether certain people had a better memory for smells than for something they'd seen. She couldn't believe the bus driver hadn't recognised Roland Johansson as soon as he saw the picture. 'Do you remember where he got off?'

'Brunna.'

'Have you seen him out in Lövsta before?' she asked.

'No.'

'Are you sure?'

'No, but I think I would have remembered him. With that big scar.'

Vanja chose not to comment; they had got what they came for.

Vanja and Billy thanked Mahmoud for his help, and gave him their phone number in case he thought of anything else. They left the bus depot and walked back to the car without speaking. Mahmoud had led them to Brunna. They had a time, they had a place. With a bit of luck these new leads wouldn't end there. They would go back to the station and carry on.

Another car journey.

The same deafening silence.

Sebastian couldn't decide which feeling was the strongest.

A full stomach, tiredness, or impotent rage.

After Vanja, Billy and Ursula had left he had spent the better part of an hour wandering around the offices. Drunk far too much coffee. Tried to summon up the energy to do what he had said he was going to do.

Make those calls.

Eventually he hadn't been able to put it off any longer. He went into the Room. Closed the door. He would be left in peace there; it was only the Riksmord team who used it. The team he was still a part of. Time to prove it. Do something. Do what he could.

He had started by sitting down with a pen and paper and racking his brains. Where should he begin? He couldn't possibly go back ten or twenty years. He didn't remember them. That was just the way it was. He didn't remember their names, what they looked like, where they lived, who they were. The fact that the murderer had gone for Annette Willén didn't necessarily mean he wanted to be sure that Riksmord had made the connection with Sebastian. It could just as easily be that Hinde, who Sebastian was convinced somehow lay behind all this, was simply unable to find any more women from his past, and had therefore been forced to take someone more recent.

So he focused on that angle himself.

There were still plenty.

And it was still difficult.

After another hour he had six names written on his pad. Six women he had slept with since he got back from Västerås at the end of April. In Stockholm, or at least not too far away. Six whose names he actually remembered. Or five. He had a Christian name and a vague idea of which part of the city one of them

324

lived in, but only the part of the city when it came to a seventh. With the help of the computer he managed to find their phone numbers – something he never asked for when they met. If they wanted to give it to him he would take it, but threw the piece of paper away immediately.

He pulled the pad towards him and took a deep breath. Then he came up with a reason to put off the difficult conversations for a little while longer. Trolle. He still hadn't got hold of Trolle. He tried his number. No reply. Left his fifth or sixth message. Picked up the pad again and made a start.

It turned out to be an object lesson in futility. One of the women who answered insisted he had the wrong number. They had never met, she said. Two refused to speak to him when he explained who he was. Simply slammed the phone down, didn't pick up when he rang again. One listened, but when it came to explaining the situation, telling her what had happened, Sebastian's courage failed him. He couldn't be the one to tell them their lives were in danger. Not over the telephone. So he ended up issuing a vague warning about being careful. Not letting in any strangers. He must have sounded completely incoherent and slightly crazy. Towards the end the woman had asked what he actually wanted. He had put the phone down and didn't even attempt to call the last name on the list.

He couldn't do it over the phone.

He just couldn't.

But he couldn't go and see them in person either.

There was nothing he could do.

What contribution had he made? Vanja had asked. The answer was simple and depressing. None. He had to see Hinde again. That was where the solution lay. That was where he would find something he could work with, something he could understand. He had to see Hinde.

He leaned back in the chair, stretched his legs out under the table. Closed his eyes.

He was tired. He hadn't been able to settle last night after all that business with Anna. He had toyed with the idea of going back and keeping Trolle company, but had decided against it. He had gone to bed and gazed idly at the television until he fell asleep at around half past two.

The dream had woken him before five. His right hand tightly clenched. His nails had pierced the skin in two places, and blood was seeping out. He straightened his fingers and felt the cramp slowly ease. He lay there for a while, wondering whether to invite the dream back in. He did that sometimes. Allowed it to regain a foothold. Enjoyed every second of the unadulterated feeling of love which it encompassed and conveyed, in spite of everything.

Sometimes he needed it.

Needed to feel Sabine. Close by. Her little hand in his. Remember her smell. The way she ran towards the water on her eager little legs. Hear her voice.

'Daddy, I want one of those too.' Her last words to him when she saw another little girl playing with an inflatable dolphin.

He needed to feel the weight of her as he carried her. Her soft hands against his sun-warmed, stubbly cheeks. Hear her laughter when he almost stumbled.

Until the noise came.

The roar.

The wave. That would take her away from him. Forever.

★ ★ ★

The door of the Room opened and Vanja, Billy and Torkel walked in. Sebastian gave a start and almost slid off his chair.

'Were you asleep?' Torkel asked without a hint of a smile as he pulled out a chair and sat down.

'I was trying,' Sebastian replied, sitting up straight. He looked at the clock. Quarter of an hour had disappeared. He still didn't feel too good.

'What have you been doing to wear yourself out?' Somehow Vanja managed to include the answer 'nothing, as usual' in her question, so Sebastian didn't bother to reply.

'Where's Ursula?' he asked instead. He assumed they were about to have some kind of meeting.

'Still at the gravel pit, I presume,' Torkel said. 'I haven't heard from her.'

He turned to Billy and Vanja, who were sitting on the other side of the table in silence. They looked at one another, but neither seemed particularly keen to speak.

326

'You do it,' Billy said curtly, leaning back in his chair. It was almost as if he was making a point.

'Why?'

'It's probably for the best.'

Sebastian watched the pair with growing interest. Those two hadn't just been out working this morning, that much was clear. Something else had happened. In spite of the brief exchange, it was impossible not to notice the chilly atmosphere between them. Interesting.

Vanja shrugged and quickly ran through what had happened since they left the station. The car at the gravel pit, the witness, Roland Johansson, the bus driver, Brunna.

'We checked Brunna.' Billy took over without being asked. 'There's no Roland Johansson living there, and no one who has their post redirected there.'

'But a car was reported stolen from there yesterday.' Vanja again. 'A silver Toyota Auris. The time fits.'

'That's the one!' Sebastian burst out. Slightly too loud and slightly too enthusiastically, he realised as everyone turned to look at him.

'How do you know?' Vanja put into words what all three of them were thinking; Sebastian could see that.

He swore to himself. He knew because Trolle had told him that the person who was following him was driving a silver Japanese car. He knew because Trolle had seen it outside Anna Eriksson's apartment block. But what he knew and what he could tell them were two completely different things. He couldn't say anything about Trolle and Anna. Nor was there any way he could reasonably know that the Toyota was linked to their investigation.

The others were still staring at him, waiting for an answer.

'I don't know,' Sebastian said quietly. He cleared his throat. His voice mustn't let him down if he was going to get out of this one. 'I don't *know*, obviously,' he repeated. 'It was just . . . a feeling.'

'A feeling? Since when did you pay any attention to feelings?'

Torkel's question was justified. He knew Sebastian better than anyone in the Room. He might come up with theories and hypotheses, some of them incorrect as it would later transpire, but they were always based on a solid foundation of facts. Possible, credible. Through all the years Torkel had worked with him, Sebastian had never offered an assumption based on a feeling.

Sebastian shrugged. 'Roland got off the bus in Brunna, the car was stolen there, Roland is somehow mixed up in all this. Everything fits. It . . . fits.'

Silence. Vanja shook her head. Billy was staring straight in front of him; it almost looked as if he hadn't been listening. Torkel's expression made it clear that he thought Sebastian was talking rubbish, and it looked as if Torkel was wondering if there was a reason for this. Sebastian was just about to expand on his explanation when Torkel appeared to lose interest in him, and turned back to Vanja and Billy instead. 'It's a coincidence we can't ignore. Put out a call for the Toyota.' He nodded to Billy.

'Already done,' Billy said with a quick glance at Vanja.

'Good. I've spoken to Roland Johansson's liaison officer in Gothenburg, Fabian Fridell.'

'And what did he say?' Sebastian pretended to be more interested than he actually was. Anything to compensate for his reaction to the silver Toyota.

'He hasn't seen Johansson for a few days.'

'What does that mean?' Vanja demanded. 'Two days? A week?'

'Our friend Fabian was extremely vague on that point.'

'Someone's threatened him.'

It wasn't a question.

'That's the feeling I got,' Torkel said with a nod.

Silence fell once more as everyone around the table allowed this to sink in. Billy was the one who summarised what they were all thinking.

'So Roland Johansson is involved in some way, but forensic evidence from the crime scenes rules him out as the perpetrator, and he has an alibi for the second and third murders.'

'Then again, his alibi is Fridell,' Vanja chipped in. 'If Fridell has been threatened, that could be a lie.'

Billy shook his head. 'I've checked with some of the others who were on the trip to Skåne. Roland Johansson was definitely there.'

'So we're looking for more than one person,' Torkel established.

'But Hinde is directing the whole thing,' Sebastian said, keen to make sure they didn't lose focus in the light of this new information. 'I know it.'

'You know it?' Vanja said with an infuriating smile. 'Or is it just . . . a feeling?'

'Shut up. You know it too. Everyone in this room knows it.' Sebastian got to his feet and started pacing. 'I've never met Roland Johansson. There's no reason for him to want to get revenge on me. But he's linked to Hinde. Everything is linked to Hinde.' He stopped and turned to Torkel. 'What's happening with my request for a visit?'

'The last time it took two days.'

'Have you told them it's urgent? That it's important?'

'What do you think?' Torkel spoke to Billy and Vanja: 'Where do we go from here?'

'I've sent uniformed officers to speak to the recipients of those calls from Lövhaga,' Vanja replied. 'We should hear something soon.'

'I noticed the list of all the staff on the secure unit has arrived,' Billy said. 'I'll make a start on that right away.'

Sebastian realised that Torkel was now looking at him. For a moment he couldn't work out what was going on, but then he grasped that he was also expected to answer the question.

'I'll carry on with what I was doing,' he managed.

Nobody asked what that was. The meeting came to an end. Sebastian was the last to leave the room. So they were looking for a silver Toyota instead. And Roland Johansson. Trolle already knew about the Toyota, but he ought to be told that another person was involved. It could be important.

Sebastian rang Trolle's number on his way out.

Still no reply.

He had broken his own rule, which was to use the computer only after lock-up. Immediately after lunch he had closed his door and quickly linked up to the internet. He should be safe for half an hour. He just had to do it. He needed to have his suspicions confirmed. When he read Ralph's email it was as if time stood still; he sat in front of the computer staring at it. He didn't know if five minutes passed, or ten, or twenty. It didn't matter. They could confiscate the computer now.

He already knew all he needed to know.

Anna Eriksson had married Valdemar Lithner eighteen months after Vanja was born. He had been at university in Gothenburg during the autumn when Anna got pregnant. There was nothing to suggest that he even knew her at that time. He was on a work placement in Essex when Vanja was born. What new father would do such a thing? He hadn't moved to Stockholm until Vanja was six months old.

And then there was the birth certificate Ralph had managed to find.

Father unknown, it said. Two simple words. What woman would put that, then marry the same man eighteen months later? It was unthinkable.

It was more likely that Anna knew exactly who the father was, but that he didn't want to take on the responsibility. A man who had simply gone from one woman to another. A man who had dumped Anna and gone off to the USA, because that was what he wanted to do.

Sebastian Bergman.

That would make sense of the fact that he was following Vanja, watching her from a distance, not daring to make himself known. His need to protect her during their recent interview.

330

The circumstantial evidence was strong, but he had to be certain. He must not get this wrong. He needed to know whether Anna Eriksson and Sebastian Bergman had met in the past. Whether they had had a relationship in 1979. Anna Eriksson hadn't been a student at the University of Stockholm, so it wasn't that straight-forward. But Ralph had found a link between the two of them. On Facebook, of all places.

Hinde couldn't believe how much information certain people gave on there. Quite freely. With the lowest security settings, which meant that anyone could go in and just start looking through everything. Karin Letander was one of those people. She had been one of Sebastian's students in 1979, and loved posting photographs from the past, when she and her friends were young and beautiful. The happiest days of her life, as she put it. Her entire folder of photographs, which was substantial, was open to anyone who visited her page. Including Ralph. To make things even easier, Karin had sorted her pictures by the year, and had spent a considerable amount of time writing banal little comments under each one. For someone who was searching for the truth, it was an absolute goldmine.

The 1979 folder contained five pictures.

The most important photo had been taken at what appeared to be a party in Sweden. It showed Karin, Sebastian and a woman Hinde didn't recognise. Anna Eriksson. They were all smiling at the camera, and Sebastian's hand was resting on the woman's shoulder. The caption read: 'Autumn party at uni. Anna Eriksson was there too. I wonder what happened to her?'

Yes, what did happen to her?

Well, now there was one person who knew. He had just found the final piece of the puzzle that transformed a nagging suspicion into the truth.

It all fitted. She must have got pregnant in the early autumn of 1979. Perhaps it was even something to do with that party.

He got up. He couldn't sit still, however hard he tried. The crack he had been searching for had turned into a fissure as deep as an abyss. Big enough for amazing possibilities. Great achievements. The perfect revenge. It made his head spin, and the entire plan had radically altered.

Including his own role.

Vanja Lithner was Sebastian's daughter.

This was now perfectly clear to him. It was one of the best days in his life, and a real before-and-after moment.

Before the knowledge about Vanja.

After the knowledge about Vanja.

And now Edward was needed. Edward, and no one else.

Ralph was in the way now. He had been useful during the journey. The information he had just supplied was crucial. But he was still no more than a little worm who didn't have the courage to look Hinde in the eye. A little boy in an elongated body who had recently started trying to take on a role he couldn't fulfil. Hinde had become aware of Ralph's growing self-confidence when he suddenly discovered that hyperlinks and quotations about the current spate of murders had been inserted all over the place on fygorh.se, among all the randomly selected material. There was something on every page.

Media attention had never been important to Hinde. It was banal, one-dimensional and provided no real satisfaction. But it had an effect on Ralph. He had become like a teenager who wanted to be seen. Proactive. Seeking acknowledgement. Admittedly it was a natural progression, and Edward had always known that a change would take place. But the speed of Ralph's journey had surprised him. He used to kneel before Edward, but now he was worshipping another god: the limelight.

He remembered their first encounter. Ralph had managed to mumble that he had read everything that had been written about Hinde. He felt that they were alike. That they had a great deal in common. Hinde had politely encouraged further conversation. The tall, skinny man in front of him showed such obvious signs of submissive weakness that Hinde had immediately seen how easy it would be to lead him. He didn't know where, not at that point. But he had started working on Ralph right away, and the result had surpassed all his expectations. Ralph told Hinde about his sick mother – that was obviously what they had in common. Hinde had briefly considered punishing Ralph at once because he had called Edward's mother sick, but had restrained himself. The opportunity to administer punishment was always there, while the opportunity to manipulate someone in exactly the way you wanted was considerably more difficult to come by. Ralph had talked about his 'grandfather', about the lodge and the people wearing animal masks. Yet another thing they had in common. The abuse. Edward had let him carry on. Ralph would never understand that however much they had in common, it would always be overshadowed by the differences between them.

Throughout his entire life, Ralph had never got his own way. Hinde always got his own way.

But at the same time, Ralph was out there. One of his representatives in the real world. His source of information for the great plan.

Invaluable in the short term.

In the long term – eminently replaceable.

At that moment it came to him. The idea. In its simple clarity Hinde saw the perfect use for the worm. The place where someone who was prepared to bend and bend yet again could be most useful in the new landscape Edward saw before him. It was perfect. It just had to be done in the right way. The way that would cause Sebastian the greatest amount of pain.

He began by giving Ralph another task.

There weren't many left.

He wanted to keep one for himself.

So it would have to be Ellinor Bergkvist.

Planning. Patience. Determination.

The three most important words for him right now. Nothing could be allowed to go wrong this time. The long kitchen knife, the nightdress and the nylon stockings were neatly packed in the black bag waiting in the hallway. Food and drink in a carrier bag next to it. The digital camera was in his pocket, along with the smaller, razor-sharp Leatherman mountain knife. He had changed into a blue polo shirt and beige chinos. The same clothes he had worn for the first four murders. Well-dressed, but anonymous. When he went to take Anna Eriksson, that was the first time he had worn a disguise. He had felt that he needed it. His planning time had been minimal, and he had to strike within a certain period. She didn't live alone, and might have been warned. He had had to make sure she would let him in. Hence the disguise. He had deviated from the ritual. Punishment had followed. The fat man had turned up.

Ralph had gone to the barber's around the corner as soon as he received Ellinor's name through fygorh.se. He didn't want a haircut. He had his hair cut exactly every ninety-one days. Rituals. He just wanted a different style. That was frightening enough. He changed his cap for one in the same style, but a different colour; he tucked it in his back pocket and hooked his sunglasses into the open neck of his polo shirt instead of wearing them. At least he had them with him. He was not breaking the ritual. He was modifying it.

He gazed at himself in the bathroom mirror and hated the way he looked. He ran his hands through the unfamiliar, well-groomed hair. It felt oddly sticky and coarse. The hairdresser had informed him that it was some kind of product that would enable him to slick his hair back. She had persuaded him to buy two

334

jars to be on the safe side. He smiled at himself and his new look. Tried to like it. Told himself that now he looked more like one of those cool guys who hung out around Stureplan rather than the tall skinny man nobody noticed. That it was an improvement. It wasn't. But it was all in a good cause. Nothing could be allowed to go wrong this time. Nothing. The man he idolised had forgiven him and given him another chance. Because it was important to Ralph. The Master cared about his feelings. No one had ever done that before, and he had no intention of betraying that trust. If it meant making minor changes to what he was wearing and perhaps a new hairstyle, those were small sacrifices compared with the bigger picture. The important thing was to get it right from now on. Obviously he needed to be more careful.

He had no idea how much or how little those who were on his trail might know, but the more hours that passed since the man in the car died, the safer he felt. If they had known his identity, they would have been knocking on his door by now. There wouldn't be any kind of surveillance operation. They would come for him straight away.

The Master had taken four. He was on the way to his fifth. Soon he would be making history. The thought made him pull himself together. Take control of himself and his feelings. Realise how important it was to remain calm.

Outside it was a little cooler than it had been for the last week, and he walked quickly towards the subway station, which was about ten minutes away.

He didn't like having to use a different form of transport, but he didn't dare use his own green Polo. He had parked the silver Toyota in Ulvsunda as per instructions, but the Master hadn't said anything about a new car in his short message. Somehow he was the one who had access to stolen cars. Ralph merely received instructions on where to pick them up and where to leave them. Someone else took care of that side of things; Ralph had no interest in who that might be. The Master had several people working for him, he knew that. But this time there had been no mention of a new car, so he would have to take the subway to and from Vasastan. On the way he called in at a flower shop. Bought twenty red roses and asked the florist to create a romantic bouquet, complete with a little card. He wrote a simple message:

'Forgive me. Love, Sebastian.' He liked that. It felt good to link Sebastian even more clearly with the woman who would soon be dead. Ralph decided he would leave the bouquet on the kitchen table, with the card clearly visible to the police. He wished he could see their expressions when they found a dead body in the bedroom and a romantic bouquet in the kitchen.

This was all according to the ritual, he convinced himself. He always left clues behind. This was just another clue. In a different way. The Master would appreciate the gesture, he knew it.

Ralph paid for the flowers and went back out into the sunshine. He must look like a man in love, he thought. A cool guy buying a bunch of red roses for the woman he had just met. He removed the sticky label from around one of the stems: Västertorp Floristry.

Clues, yes.

But only those he chose to leave.

That was planning.

Ellinor Bergkvist had spent the day doing all kinds of different things. She had called work and arranged to take the leave she was owed. Watered all the plants in her apartment and asked the widow Lindell on the third floor to keep an eye on them while Ellinor was away. Fru Lindell had persuaded her to stay for coffee and cakes, and they had sat chatting for almost an hour. It had been very pleasant, but after a while Ellinor began to feel that she still had a lot to sort out at home.

You couldn't just drop everything for a man, however wonderful he might be. You had to make sure you left your home in good order. Particularly if a neighbour was going to be wandering around the place while you were away.

So she gave the apartment a thorough clean. Vacuumed, dusted, wiped down surfaces. Cleaned the windows. Changed the sheets and plumped up the cushions on the sofa. Emptied the fridge and decided to move all the plants out onto the balcony so that there would be no reason for fru Lindell to go anywhere else.

When she had finished, she sat down on the sofa with a small glass of her favourite cognac. She had had the bottle for several years, and only treated herself to a drop on special occasions. It was from a small producer and was expensive but good. It made her feel special and exclusive in a world of simple rewards. A world that didn't know how to take pleasure like her.

To live like her.

To love like her.

The days had been intense since Sebastian Bergman had come storming into her life. She needed a little while with herself and her thoughts before she moved on. She sipped slowly, and just sat there.

A little bit of time to herself. In the moment.

Before her life continued.

Ralph got off the subway at Odenplan. He wasn't sure if that was actually the closest station for Västmannagatan, because he travelled on the green line too infrequently to be certain, but that was how it had looked on the map. There weren't many other travellers on the platform, and he quickly emerged from the depths. Crossed the main road and headed west. Västmannagatan ought to be a few blocks away. He had never been there on foot before. As he walked along he thought about how to proceed. He took out his mobile and called Ellinor's number. She answered on the third ring.

'Ellinor Bergkvist.'

Ralph ended the call immediately. She was at home. He knew she lived alone in her apartment, and he had managed to get hold of the entry code for the outside door of the block the day after Sebastian's first visit, when he had helped an elderly lady inside, so at least the first hurdle was taken care of. But after that he would have to improvise. As in the case of Anna Eriksson the planning was inadequate, which bothered him. But the alternative was to keep her under surveillance for weeks, or at least days, and he knew the time was no longer available. They had moved into a new phase. Everything must happen faster. Decisions as well as actions. He ought to be able to cope. He would cope. He was experienced now. On the verge of making history. He was the inoffensive delivery man from the flower shop, bringing a gift. What woman wouldn't open the door to him?

'Forgive me. Love, Sebastian.'

He smiled as he thought about his plan.

He reached the front door and his final destination, but walked past without stopping. He went up to the little park and sat down on one of the dark green benches for a while. Looked around. Nobody in the vicinity as far as he could tell. Nobody paying any attention either to him or to the front door. A rubbish truck drove slowly past, but disappeared around the corner. Ralph got up, holding the bouquet so that it covered most of his face.

Walked back slowly. Not too fast. He mustn't appear stressed. Mustn't be noticed.

He must be nothing more than a bunch of roses.

A gift of love on the way to a woman.

The code was 1439. He double-checked on his mobile, where he had made a note of it to be on the safe side.

1439. Correct.

The door swung open by itself. It had an automatic mechanism to make life easier for the elderly and those with pushchairs. He didn't like it. It made his entrance too grand, too theatrical, as if he were walking onto a stage. He moved quickly into the large foyer and stood there for a while, pretending to search for a name on the list of residents even though he knew exactly where she lived. Fourth floor. Three neighbours. The automatic door closed behind him, and the silence inside the building was a relief as the sound of the traffic died away. He felt as if he was invisible, standing there in the pretty white foyer with its ornate Greek-inspired statues in the neoclassical style. The roses fitted in.

Red and white.

The colours of love and innocence.

It was poetic for death to arrive in this way.

He decided to go up in the lift. Once he had reached the fourth floor he would leave the inner gate open so that the lift couldn't move, and anyone who needed to move around the building would have to use the stairs. That would enable him to hear if anyone was on their way up or down, and give him time to act. It could all come down to seconds in the end.

The lift wasn't there, so he pressed the worn black button above the word CALL. The machinery jerked into life with a mechanical thud. He peered up the shaft through the black gate and saw that the lift was on the fourth or fifth floor. It began to descend with irritating slowness.

The critical moment would be from the time she opened the door until he was inside the apartment with the door closed and the woman under control. It must be accomplished in just a few seconds, and as quietly as possible. The acoustics in the stairwell would amplify every sound. He took out the Leatherman knife. Flicked it open and concealed it in his right hand behind the roses.

★ ★ ★

Ellinor walked around the apartment one last time. Decided to leave the balcony door open a fraction so that it wouldn't smell stuffy when fru Lindell turned up. She would be there this evening, if Ellinor knew her as well as she thought she did. She flicked the catch so that the balcony door was still locked, but with a tiny gap. Then she was happy. The apartment was in perfect order.

She opened the front door and stepped out with her keys in her hand. Locked up behind her. Saw the lift pass her floor on its way down. Typical. If she had come out a minute earlier she could have stopped it. Now she would have to wait. She wheeled her little black cabin case, which she had bought with a staff discount, over to the lift. She was pleased with the case. It was both practical and fashionable. The lift continued its slow descent. They had discussed having it renovated at the last residents' meeting, but had shelved the issue. Its old-fashioned open style was charming, with its lattice gate and dark wood, but from a practical point of view it left a great deal to be desired. Ellinor and some of the others had suggested a faster, more modern model. One where you just pressed the button and waited. With this one you had to wait until it stopped before you pressed.

★ ★ ★

Ralph stiffened as he heard a door open above him. He wasn't sure which floor the sound had come from. He was able to rule out the first floor immediately, it was higher up than that, but because of the acoustics it was impossible to be any more accurate. He listened hard, but the hum of the lift was the only thing he could hear. He waited for the sound of footsteps on the stairs, but none came. So the person in question was presumably waiting for the lift. Just like him. Now he had to keep his cool. He raised the bouquet slightly so that he was just a body whose face was concealed by roses, and tightened his grip on the knife. At long last the lift arrived; it stopped with a small dull thud followed by a sharper metallic click from the locking mechanism. He opened the door as quietly as he could, but he didn't really know what to do. There were two options: abort or go on up.

He decided on the latter. He could always abort at a later stage. First of all he would force the person up there to act. He held the door open so that the lift couldn't go anywhere. The building was silent. You could have heard a pin drop.

A minute or so passed. Ralph had time to think through the alternatives many times. Too many. Perhaps the best thing would

340

be to abort his mission after all. Come back in a while, start all over again. He was just about to let go of the lift door and leave when he heard the person upstairs start walking down. The footsteps were rapid, and sounded as if they were fast approaching. The decision was instantaneous. There was no going back. He stepped into the lift.

★ ★ ★

Ellinor was annoyed. This was just typical. She didn't actually have anything against using the stairs – exercise was good – but the problem was the suitcase. It was a bit too heavy to carry all the way. And then there was that article she'd read, which had stated very clearly that walking down the stairs wasn't good for you. Bad for the knees, apparently. Walking up was beneficial, but you should avoid walking down. But now she had no choice. She couldn't wait any longer. Annoyingly, the lift began to move when she was halfway to the third floor. For a moment she considered turning around and going back up. Then again, she might as well carry on; she could take the lift from the floor below, if it stopped there. She went down the last few steps and stood by the lift. With a bit of luck it would be Robert Andersson from the third floor. He usually came home around this time. At long last the lift arrived, and she stepped aside to let Robert out, if it was him. But it wasn't Robert, it was a taller man. She saw beige trousers, a blue polo shirt and a big bunch of roses that covered his face. The lift didn't stop, it just carried on going up. Ellinor smiled to herself. Someone upstairs was going to receive a beautiful bouquet. Love gave her fresh energy, and she decided to carry on down the stairs. She couldn't stand around here all day, waiting for lifts.

★ ★ ★

Not again. Not again. Not again.

Instinctively he thought of pressing the emergency stop button. But by the time the thought was ready to be translated into action, he was already half a metre above the third floor, and would just be stuck there, trapped between floors. Through the lift doors he could see Ellinor trotting down the stairs. Away from him. He had made too many changes to the ritual. She was getting away. The powerful, sweet perfume of the roses suddenly turned his stomach.

He yanked open the door when he reached the fourth floor and started to run. Threw caution to the winds. He couldn't fail this time. If that meant taking major risks, then so be it. How he was going to be able to carry out the ritual was a question he would address later. First he had to get hold of her. He realised at once that he could no longer hear the sound of her footsteps because of the noise his own feet were making. He stopped for a second, and soon heard her again. She couldn't be far away. A floor below him. He set off again.

The second floor flew by. He tried to take two steps at a time on the next flight, but had problems with his balance. It was difficult with his sports bag, plastic bag, and the flowers. He almost slipped, used the banister for support and regained control. Threw away the roses when he reached the first floor, and carried on running. He finally reached the stylish foyer he had started from a few moments ago.

It was empty.

The door was open, so she must have just gone out. He hid the knife in the palm of his hand and rushed outside. She must be close. Very close.

There she was. Walking towards Norra Bantorget. Eight, ten metres away. Alone on the pavement, but there were cars passing all the time. A little way ahead he could see a couple of mothers with their pushchairs. It was impossible for him to do anything now. He would just have to follow her. Try to find a more suitable opportunity, make sure he didn't lose her.

His breathing caught up with him and he realised how much he was sweating. He slowed down and carefully snapped the knife shut. Put it back in his pocket. Gave her a bit of a head start.

Patience. Determination.

That was what he needed now.

He could see her. And he wasn't going to let her go.

She belonged to him.

★ ★ ★

Ellinor was trying to find a taxi. There were usually one or two outside the hotel on Norra Bantorget, so she headed in that direction. Not that she travelled by taxi very often. She enjoyed walking, particularly when the weather was good. If this had been

342

an ordinary day, she would have walked all the way. But today was a special day; today she had a destination she wanted to reach as soon as possible.

A taxi was coming towards her; it looked as if it was free, and she quickly raised her arm to hail it. She was delighted when it braked and stopped right in front of her. She picked up her case and jumped in the back. Saw a tall man a short distance away staring at her; he walked out into the street after they had driven past him. He seemed to be looking for a taxi as well, she thought as she looked back and noticed him trying to flag down a cab heading in the opposite direction; it didn't stop. She smiled. She had been lucky to get this one.

It was definitely her lucky day.

She asked the driver to take her to Östermalm.

To love.

Sebastian Bergman had been ringing Trolle all day. His disquiet had grown with each unanswered call. It would soon be more than sixteen hours since they had parted company outside Anna Eriksson's apartment block. They had never been closer than at that moment, and the warmth Sebastian had felt made his anxiety all the more palpable. Particularly as Anna was now safe. He should have heard that from Trolle, if nothing else. That had been the whole point of his former colleague's presence outside her apartment.

To protect her.

To protect Vanja.

To protect the secret.

But Sebastian didn't know what else he could do, apart from continuing to try Trolle's number.

He focused on the approaching meeting with Hinde in order to clear his mind. Apart from that, he was no use whatsoever as a member of the team. Vanja was absolutely right. He set off to look for Torkel. He needed to get the meeting with Hinde arranged as soon as possible. Edward Hinde was the key. Sebastian's earlier distaste had vanished, and he was positively longing to confront Hinde alone, without needing to worry about Vanja. He would win the next encounter. Go for a knockout.

Torkel wasn't in his office. According to his secretary, he was in a board meeting upstairs. Sebastian stomped up one flight of stairs and walked over to the window of the big conference room they used. Torkel was sitting in there with a number of others. Obviously top brass. Some of them were even wearing those stupid white uniforms with gold epaulettes. Sebastian hated police officers with gold epaulettes. They were as far removed from real police work as it was possible to be. They never went anywhere near a crime scene; they only appeared on TV or in some conference room with a bottle of mineral water in front of them. Like now. Sebastian plonked himself down just outside the window. Torkel hadn't seen him. Or at least he wasn't letting on that he had. Sebastian's frustration grew, and when he had been sitting there for fifteen minutes, he could contain himself no longer. He got up and flung open the door of the conference room.

'Afternoon. Are you sitting here trying to solve the murder of Olof Palme?'

The room fell silent, and everyone stared at him. The odd face was familiar from the old days, but Sebastian didn't recognise most of them. However, the one person he did know well got to his feet.

'Sebastian, the door was closed for a reason,' Torkel said, suppressed rage in his voice. 'We're in a meeting.'

'I can see that. But I have to see Hinde. Today. We can't wait any longer.'

'The visiting order hasn't arrived yet. I'm doing my best to hurry it up.'

'Do more than your best. Get it sorted.'

'We're not going to talk about this now, Sebastian.' Torkel looked around apologetically before turning back to Sebastian. 'I'd like you to leave, please.'

'If I can just have that visiting order I'll disappear immediately. Promise.'

Sebastian looked at the collection of people around the table. Most of them met his gaze with a mixture of surprise and contempt. He realised he was completely in the wrong, but he just couldn't play by their stupid rules anymore. Lives were at risk. Not just his own.

'I'm sure your smartly dressed friends want to solve this case before he cuts the throat of a fifth victim. I'm the key.'

He saw Torkel's eyes flash. Obviously he had gone too far. A woman sitting on Torkel's right got to her feet, slowly and deliberately. Sebastian recognised her as the national chief of police.

'I don't think we know each other,' she said in a voice that could cause frostbite. The civilised way of saying: 'Who the hell are you?'

'No, we don't,' Sebastian replied, firing off his most winning smile. 'But if you can help me sort out that visiting order, you might get the chance.'

Torkel marched over to Sebastian and grabbed him by the arm. 'Excuse me. Back in a moment.'

He dragged Sebastian out and shut the door behind him.

'What the fuck are you doing? Have you lost your mind? Do you want me to throw you out?'

'Why is it taking such a long time? Is Haraldsson being difficult?'

'I have no idea! It doesn't bloody matter! We just have to wait. You're not a police officer, so it takes a little while. If you don't like it, you can piss off right now.'

'Oh, sure. You can threaten me with that as often as you like. I'm the only one who can put a stop to the murders. You know that.'

'Your expertise and your invaluable insights have certainly been a great help so far.'

'Sarcasm isn't really your thing.'

There was a short silence. Torkel was breathing heavily.

'Okay, let me put it this way. Go home. You cost too much.'

'I'll work for free.'

'I wasn't talking about money.'

Sebastian met Torkel's eye and swallowed the comment that was on the tip of his tongue.

'I'll let you know when the visiting order arrives.' Torkel opened the door and went back into his meeting. Sebastian could hear him apologising before the door closed and Torkel's voice became an indistinct murmur.

For a second Sebastian wanted to go back in. Make himself look even more ridiculous.

But that would have been a step too far. Way too far.

He had done enough damage as it was.

For once he did as Torkel said and went home.

It took him a while. He had to check first to see if anyone might be following him. A silver Toyota, above all, but he regarded every car that drove past or was parked by the pavement with a certain degree of suspicion. He peered into every single one. The murderer had switched cars once, and he could do it again. He zigzagged home, went round in circles, and took plenty of time. Only when he was absolutely convinced that no one was following him did he walk through the front door of his apartment block on Grev Magnigatan. Climbed the stairs, went inside and sat down on the bed in his room.

His anxiety about being followed. The secrets. The double dealing. Trolle. The women. Vanja. Everything was taking its toll on him, making him act irrationally, and if he carried on like this there was a risk that he wouldn't be allowed to see Hinde at all. An organisation like the police service was only prepared to accept a certain level of conflict without results, he was well aware of that.

He lay down on the bed. Closed his eyes and tried to switch off. The apartment was silent and still. It was nice just to lie there. He tried to breathe quietly and meditate, as Lily had once taught him.

Deep breaths. Regular. Slow. Find the stillness.

He had loved Lily so much. The memory of her was always just behind the image of Sabine, its contours softer and fainter, but always there like a shadow. He knew why she was number two. Because he was ashamed. He had let go of their daughter. Lost her to the sea.

The feelings of loss suddenly overwhelmed him, the steady breaths immediately replaced by the ragged breathing of grief. He felt persecuted. By himself and his memories. He could never be free of them.

Sitting up, he caught sight of the plastic handles of Trolle's carrier bag sticking out from under the bed. It was here too, the proof of who he really was. Half hidden under the bed were the documents, ordered and paid for by him, that could besmirch Vanja's parents. What had they actually done to him? Nothing. Anna had simply tried to protect her daughter from a man who was capable of anything. Valdemar knew nothing, Anna had said. That was doubtless true. But in spite of the fact that both of them were innocent, he had wanted to hurt them, punish them. They weren't even his real opponents. That was down to him, and him alone.

His own worst enemy.

He slowly picked up the bag from the floor. He ought to burn it. Destroy it. He had no right to their lives. He barely had the right to his own life. If only he knew where to find some matches. In the kitchen, perhaps. He went in and started with the drawers. Cutlery in the top one. Various kitchen utensils in the second. No matches. Pot holders and table mats that he never used in the third. Suddenly the doorbell rang. He looked towards the hallway in surprise. He couldn't remember when that had last happened. Probably somebody wanting to sell him something. Or Jehovah's

Witnesses. The bell rang again. He decided to ignore it; he was busy and he couldn't be bothered to get rid of them. But then he heard the voice outside.

'Sebastian. Open the door. I know you're in there.'

It was her. Ellinor Bergkvist. This couldn't be happening. What was she doing here?

'Come on, Sebastian, open this door!'

She rang the bell again. For longer this time. Persistent. Could she really know he was in there? With Ellinor that didn't seem impossible. Another ring.

'Sebastian!'

With a curse Sebastian left the kitchen, threw the plastic bag under the bed as he was passing the spare room, marched into the hallway and yanked the door open. Tried to look as annoyed as possible. It wasn't difficult. Not with Ellinor Bergkvist standing on the landing. She had a black cabin case with her and she was smiling happily and expectantly at him.

'Here I am,' was the first thing she said. As unequivocal as her smile.

His response was equally unequivocal. 'What the hell are you doing here?'

'I think you know that.' She raised her hand as if she wanted to touch him, stroke his cheek perhaps. Sebastian instinctively took a step back. Ellinor carried on smiling at him. 'Can you take my case?'

Sebastian shook his head. 'I asked you to leave the city for a while. Until the murderer has been caught.' He looked at her, his expression serious. 'Don't you understand? You're in danger.'

Her reaction was to pick up the suitcase herself and push past him into the hallway. He let her. Or, to be more accurate, he didn't have time to stop her. Ellinor had a talent for taking him by surprise. She put down the case.

'Am I really in danger?' She stepped forward and closed the door behind her. Turned to face him. Came very close. With those green eyes he found so hard to resist. 'Or is it just that you want me here?'

Once again she reached out to touch him. This time he let her. He didn't really know why. There was something about Ellinor that he couldn't quite put his finger on. He could smell her breath. Sweet and fresh, as if she had just been sucking a lozenge. Always ready.

'The way I want you?' she went on as she caressed his cheek, his neck, slipped her hand inside his shirt. He was annoyed and turned on at the same time. He had met a lot of women, but never anyone like her. She just didn't listen to him. Whatever he said, she transformed it into something else. Something positive. For her. She was the fixed point in a universe all of her own.

He tried again. 'What I said was true. I didn't make it up.'

'I believe you,' Ellinor said in a teasing tone which suggested the exact opposite. 'But I might just as well stay with you instead of sitting all alone in some hotel room.' She took his hand and placed it on her breast. 'This is much nicer, and much cosier.'

Sebastian tried to gather his thoughts. Ellinor was showing clear signs of stalker tendencies. The hand-holding on that first evening, the flowers and phone call on his name day, the way she had interpreted his warning. She might not be ill in the medical sense of the word, but her connection to Sebastian was definitely unhealthy. He ought to throw her out.

'We've only made love at my place,' Ellinor whispered into his ear.

'We haven't made love anywhere. We've screwed.'

'Now don't you go spoiling this with ugly words.' She gently bit his earlobe. She smelled of soap. Her skin was soft and warm, and he allowed his hand to slide up over her breast, around the back of her neck, her throat. He ought to explain that he definitely hadn't just made the whole thing up as some crazy scheme to get her to move in. That she had to listen to him. Understand that he was serious.

But if that was what he wanted, why was he standing here carrying on like this in the hallway? Why was he pulling her close and leading her towards his bedroom? Those green eyes were to blame.

It was their fault.

Because there was something about her.

She always got past his resistance.

★ ★ ★

He lay in bed afterwards as she inspected the apartment. He actually felt more relaxed than he had for a long time. He hadn't been to bed with anyone in the apartment since Lily. He had always played away. Surprisingly enough, he felt no guilt. The usual post-coital angst was conspicuous by its absence. Reluctantly he realised he was lying there listening to Ellinor as she wandered around. She sounded happy. He smiled as he heard her cheerful exclamations about the number of rooms and the possibilities.

'What a big room! This would make a wonderful dining room!'

At least they hadn't done it in his and Lily's bed, he told himself. And this place had never been their real home. They had spent a lot of time here, but when they got married they had moved to Cologne.

'You've even got a library!'

There really was something special about the woman who was exploring the rooms he never used these days. She was fascinating in a way he couldn't really define. However firmly he pushed her away, she kept on coming back. Like a bouncy ball that absorbed the energy from his push. This wasn't what he had had in mind when he went to the talk on Jussi Björling and met her. Then again, a lot of things that had happened since then had been unexpected, to say the least. Things he had actually managed not to think about for a while. Whatever you might say about Ellinor, one fact was undeniable. She took his mind off everything.

After a few minutes she came back. She had put on his shirt without doing up the buttons. Her red hair was glowing, and she looked like a woman in a French film. Feminine and irresistible. It almost felt as if she had seen the same film. She got into bed, tucked her legs underneath her and looked at him.

'This place is huge.'

'I know.'

'Why don't you use it all?'

'It's for you.'

Her eyes shone, like a child on Christmas Eve. 'Really?'

'No, but whatever I say, that's what you'd hear anyway.'

She nudged him playfully, ignoring his nasty remarks as usual. They didn't seem to have any effect on her whatsoever. 'We'll get this place sorted, I promise.'

'*We* won't get anything sorted. You can stay here for a couple of days. But then you have to move.'

'Of course. We'll take it slowly. If you don't want me here, I'll leave right away.' She straddled him and kissed him on the mouth.

She must have seen the same film.

'Okay, good. I don't want you living here.'

She smiled at his attempt. She wasn't listening. 'But why not? You're worried about me, you said so. If I'm here, you can keep an eye on me. And you need me.'

'I don't need anybody.'

'Don't lie, darling. You do need someone. It's blindingly obvious.'

He didn't know what to say. She was right. He did need someone, but not her. Definitely not her. She didn't wait for his reply; she went into the kitchen to make them both coffee. He lay in bed listening to her. She was whistling as she hunted for the coffee.

Nobody had done that before.

But that wasn't the worst thing.

The worst thing was that deep down he liked it.

'Edward Hinde wants to speak to you.'

Annika poked her head around Haraldsson's door. He looked up from the folder he was reading in one of the room's two armchairs. 'Lövhaga 2014, Visions and Aims' it said on the front. Haraldsson was only on page two of the thirty-page document, and on the table in front of him was a notepad on which he was jotting down the phrases he didn't understand and the areas in which he needed to acquire more background knowledge and information. He had covered almost half a page so far. Twenty-five per cent of the text was virtually incomprehensible. For that reason he was delighted to have the opportunity to put the whole thing to one side and turn his attention to more important matters.

'Does he?'

'Yes, one of the guards rang. As soon as possible.'

'I'll go straight over.'

Haraldsson almost leapt out of the chair and left the room. At last. He had wanted to go over to the secure unit several times. Just pop in. But it was a balancing act. He mustn't seem too eager, but he didn't want to lose touch either. Lose the closeness that had grown between them. But now Hinde had taken the first step. Taken the initiative. It was a good sign. Haraldsson had been hoping they would soon meet again. He couldn't delay the visiting order for Riksmord any longer. They had to be allowed an interview. But Haraldsson wanted the opportunity to get in there first. To break the case. Imagine if Hinde gave him something crucial. Imagine if he ended up not only celebrating his wedding anniversary tomorrow, but also reading in the morning paper that the serial killer who had been terrorising Stockholm had been caught. Perhaps it might say that unconfirmed sources indicated that the key pieces of the puzzle had been supplied by staff at Lövhaga.

In the best-case scenario his name would be mentioned. Yesterday *Expressen* had made the connection between Edward Hinde and the recent murders. It didn't suggest that Hinde was involved in any way, but someone had obviously leaked the fact that there were similarities in the MO. They were pushing the copycat angle today, Haraldsson had noticed on the internet. The victims from the nineties were front-page news all over again. There had also been a fact box about Hinde, a quick recapitulation of what had happened back then.

The murderer had been caught, and the person responsible for solving the case worked at Lövhaga, where Hinde was incarcerated.

It would be massive.

He was still smiling as he walked into Edward Hinde's cell.

'You look happy.' As usual Edward was sitting on the bed with his back to the wall, his knees drawn up. 'Has something nice happened?'

The desk chair had been pulled out and was facing the bed. Haraldsson sat down. He couldn't really start talking about his hopes for their meeting, and at the same time he wanted to keep Hinde in a good mood; he seemed to have appreciated the small talk they had indulged in so far. And Haraldsson had several reasons to feel happy.

'It's our wedding anniversary tomorrow. Jenny and me.'

Which reminded him . . . Haraldsson quickly glanced around to see if he could spot the photograph of his wife anywhere. It didn't seem to be on show. Just as well. What if the staff saw a photo of the governor's wife stuck on the wall of Hinde's cell?

'That's nice,' said Hinde. 'How many years?'

'Five.'

'Wood.'

'Fancy you knowing that! Not many people do.' Haraldsson was genuinely impressed. He had looked it up on Google several months ago.

'You'd be surprised at how much I know,' said Edward, realising he sounded rather more smug than he had intended.

'You should be on one of those TV quiz shows.'

'Yes . . . but I don't think that's going to happen.'

'No.'

Hinde looked on with amusement as Haraldsson fell silent. A plan for the future had begun to take shape. In order for it to be absolutely foolproof, he needed a number of items. Thomas Haraldsson could supply most of them. His two hundred and forty minutes on the computer tonight would provide the rest. Edward had already known that it was Haraldsson's wedding anniversary tomorrow. Just as he had known for a long time that the new governor used to be a police officer. He had carried out a thorough search when he heard that Lövhaga was to have a change of leadership. If Haraldsson hadn't brought up the wedding anniversary himself, Hinde would have tried to lead the conversation in that direction. Now he didn't need to.

'So how will you be celebrating?' he asked with sincere interest in his voice. 'Your wedding anniversary,' he quickly clarified.

'Breakfast in bed to start the day, then I've spoken to her boss at work and arranged for her to have a few hours off. She'll be picked up by car before lunch and spend the afternoon at a luxury spa.'

'Where does she work?'

'It's a firm called BDO; they're accountants. Then we're having a special dinner in the evening.'

'So it's a day full of special treats.'

'And she's getting an apple tree too. An Ingrid Marie. For our garden.'

'You're very thoughtful.'

'She's worth it.'

'I'm sure she is.'

The two men fell silent again, but the silence was in no way embarrassing or awkward. Haraldsson suddenly realised he was almost happy sitting here. It surprised him how pleasant it was, chatting to Hinde. He listened. Really listened. Apart from Jenny, Haraldsson couldn't think of anyone he knew who was so genuinely interested and so . . . encouraging. But even though he had managed to establish a real rapport with Hinde, he must remember the purpose of his visit.

'As I'm sure you understand, I have some questions I would like you to answer.' He hoped he hadn't been too direct. Too pushy. He didn't want to give Hinde the impression that they were meeting just so that Haraldsson could make use of him.

Clearly this was not a problem; Hinde lowered his legs from the bed and leaned forward. 'Excellent, because there are some things I would like.' Edward smiled disarmingly and spread his hands wide. 'It's a win-win situation.'

'Yes,' said Haraldsson as he returned the smile, convinced that he was the one who had the most to gain. Which Hinde would agree with. Because he also had the most to lose.

★ ★ ★

Two things.

It transpired that Hinde wanted two things, neither of which Haraldsson had with him. Nor could he get hold of them inside Lövhaga, at least not without attracting a whole lot of unwelcome questions. So he had left the cell, gone back to his office and told Annika that he was going out for a while. He had taken the car and driven down to the little shopping centre.

Two things. Two quick visits to two shops. On the way back he glanced over at his purchases lying on the passenger seat and tried to work out why Hinde wanted them. He also wondered whether it might be wrong and unethical to give them to him. He decided it wouldn't be. Both were completely innocuous products. It wasn't as if he were giving Hinde access to weapons or anything like that. One was a common drug available over the counter without a prescription. And the other was a vegetable. A root vegetable, possibly. Haraldsson wasn't sure.

He pulled into his personal parking space, picked up the bags and went straight over to the secure unit. He had to stop himself from breaking into a run. He felt as if he was just minutes away from the resolution. He had carefully worked out what he was going to ask Hinde. Evidently he was going to be allowed two questions today. That should be enough.

The guards opened the door of the secure unit and one of them accompanied him to Hinde's cell. Haraldsson had slipped the two small bags under his thin jacket; there was no point in arousing curiosity about what he was delivering to a convicted serial killer. Hinde was still sitting on the bed where Haraldsson had left him. He waited until the door was firmly closed before he broke the silence.

'Did you get them?'

355

Haraldsson took out the bags from under his jacket and put his hand inside one of them. He moved over to the bed and slowly, almost dramatically, placed the jar from the supermarket on the bedside table. Hinde glanced at the item and nodded.

'What did you want to ask?'

'Do you know who killed those four women?'

'Yes.'

'Who?'

Hinde closed his eyes and breathed deeply. Tried to hide his disappointment. How was this possible? Haraldsson had had plenty of time to prepare for this meeting. He had had the opportunity to make the most of the questions he asked. So why hadn't he asked 'Who killed the four women?' as his first question? Hinde knew the answer. The new governor had merely confirmed Hinde's views on those working within the prison service. It wasn't an area that attracted the brightest brains in society. At least not when it came to those who were allowed to leave at the end of the working day. Hinde gave a little sigh. This was too easy. The challenge was non-existent. It was boring.

'"Who" is another question,' he said, with almost exaggerated clarity.

Haraldsson swore silently. This wasn't going according to plan. The first question was supposed to provide him with a name and the second with a location where the police – once Haraldsson had tipped them off – would find the murderer. He had been too eager. Now he would only get a name. But that would be enough. It was more than Riksmord had. It would still be crucial information. He would still be the one who solved the case.

Haraldsson took out the bag from the chemist's. He didn't know much about the contents of the bottle. He had never used it himself. It seemed rather disgusting. He hesitated for a moment with the bag in his hand. Somehow this felt the same as when he had handed over the photograph of Jenny: a niggling unease that he was doing the wrong thing. That he was making a mistake. He made a snap decision and tossed the bottle across to Hinde.

'Who killed them?'

Silence. Hinde carefully studied the little bottle before looking up at Haraldsson. He seemed to want to delay his answer like the jury in some courtroom drama. Build up the tension.

'A man I know,' he said eventually.

'That's not an answer.' There was an almost childish disappointment in Haraldsson's voice. As if he was five years old and had opened a packet of Saturday sweets only to discover that it was full of vegetables.

Hinde shrugged. 'I can't be held responsible for the fact that you're asking the wrong questions.'

'I asked you who it was.'

'You should have asked what his name is.'

Silence. Very deliberately Hinde leaned forward and placed the bottle on the bedside table. Haraldsson followed the movement with his eyes. His gaze rested on the little bottle. Perhaps he should take it back. God knew Hinde hadn't earned it. Admittedly Haraldsson had phrased his first question badly, but Hinde had simply wriggled out of the second one.

'There's something else I'd like.'

Haraldsson shifted his focus. A request, a question. It wasn't too late to walk away a winner. 'And what would that be?'

'I want to ring Vanja Lithner at Riksmord tomorrow.'

'Why?'

'I want to speak to her.'

'Okay. What's the name of the man who killed those four women?' Haraldsson could hardly sit still on his chair. It was so close now.

Edward slowly shook his head. 'You're not due any more answers.'

'I've agreed that you can phone Vanja Lithner, haven't I?' That was it, Haraldsson just couldn't sit down any longer. He got up and took a step towards the bed. 'That's worth another answer.'

'But you asked me why I wanted to ring her. I told you. Truthfully.'

Haraldsson stopped dead, deflated. His 'why?' had been a pure reflex. It wasn't even a question. It was obvious that Hinde wanted to speak to her, otherwise he wouldn't have asked for permission to ring her, would he? That didn't count. Hinde was cheating. But Haraldsson could fight back when necessary. The gloves were off now.

'You can forget that phone call,' he said, underlining his words by pointing a finger at Hinde, 'unless you give me a name.'

'Don't break a promise you've made, Thomas. Not with me.'

Suddenly Haraldsson saw a different Hinde, in spite of the fact that he hadn't moved a muscle or raised his voice. His eyes had darkened. There was an intensity in his words that Haraldsson hadn't heard before. There was a threat in his voice.

Mortal danger.

Haraldsson got the feeling that the last thing the four women Hinde had murdered had seen before they died was the man sitting in front of him now. He edged towards the door.

'I'll be back.'

'You're always welcome.'

The old Hinde was back as he calmly leaned forward and quickly spirited the bottle and jar into the bed, out of sight. The metamorphosis happened so fast that Haraldsson wasn't sure whether what he had seen had actually happened, but a glance at the gooseflesh on his forearms confirmed that it had.

'You will get your name,' Hinde said quietly. 'When you do one last thing.'

'What's that?' Haraldsson was whispering too.

'Say yes.'

'To what?'

'You will understand when and to what. Just say yes. Then I will answer one more question.'

With a final brief look at Hinde, Haraldsson left the cell. That hadn't gone according to plan. Not at all. But he had one more chance. Say yes. What could Hinde possibly mean by that? What did he want with Vanja Lithner? What was he going to do with the things Haraldsson had given him? Many questions. Too many for Haraldsson to be able to concentrate on 'Lövhaga 2014, Visions and Aims'.

He decided to make use of his flexi-time again and go home. To Jenny.

Sebastian woke at five. He had slept better than expected. The dream had woken him as it always did, but it lacked something of the devastating power it sometimes had. He relaxed his right hand and stretched cautiously. She was lying beside him.

He slid out of bed and put on his underpants. Went to see if the newspaper had arrived. The doors to all the other rooms were wide open. The way she had left them. With a certain measure of reluctance he went to close them. He hadn't been inside three of the rooms for several years, so he couldn't help taking a quick look before he closed the doors. It really was a beautiful apartment, if you looked at it with fresh eyes. Her eyes. Particularly when the low morning sun shone in through the big windows. But the open doors and the rooms beyond belonged to another life. A life he didn't want to be reminded of. The fact that Ellinor had forced her way in was enough of a change. The rest of his life would remain untouched and intact.

Last night they had talked about everything possible. He and Ellinor. In the kitchen. She had told him about Harald, her ex-husband, who had come home one day and announced that he wanted a divorce. Just like that. He had met someone else. It had obviously been immensely painful. It had made her doubt herself, she said. That was a few years ago. She had tried internet dating for a while, but hadn't met anyone. It was so difficult. What about him? Why was he alone? Sebastian had successfully managed to dodge the question. He had let her do most of the talking while he sat there with a cup of coffee listening to her banal nonsense and her women's-magazine analysis of sex and relationships. Oddly enough he didn't hate every word as he usually did. Presumably he was weak and at a low ebb because of everything that had happened, but however he looked at things he came to the same conclusion.

He liked having her there.

She laughed a lot, kept a normal, easy conversation going and didn't take much notice of him. It was strange to have someone around who wasn't really affected by his snide remarks. It made him feel less compelled to continue. She was entertaining. She brought ordinary, everyday life into his apartment. He wasn't sure he wanted anything to do with it, but it was a diversion. Something new.

He put the morning paper down on the table, picked up his phone and rang Trolle. Still no reply. The anxiety returned. Why wasn't he answering? Something must have happened. Suddenly he felt a strange urge to crawl back into bed with Ellinor. Press the pause button on reality. Ignore everything. He suddenly realised what she was to him. She was someone to hold when things got difficult. Who was always pleased to see him. Who forgot all the unpleasant things he said to her.

He realised with great clarity why he didn't feel guilty when he thought about Lily.

Ellinor was like a pet.

Some people got a dog, but he had ended up with Ellinor Bergkvist.

Satisfied that he had defined their relationship, he made coffee and read the paper. He went to the 7-Eleven around the corner and bought breakfast for them both and lunch for Ellinor. He didn't want her to have to go shopping for food; he wanted her to stay indoors to be on the safe side.

She was sitting in the kitchen wearing his shirt when he got back.

'Oh, you've been out and bought breakfast for us! You're so sweet.'

He started unpacking the food. 'I don't want you to go out. You have to stay in the apartment.'

'Aren't you overdoing things a little bit?' She came over and kissed him on the cheek, then jumped up and sat on the worktop. 'I mean, I'm not going to disappear just because I go out for a little while.'

Sebastian sighed. He hadn't the strength to argue with her. 'Can't you just do what I say, please? Please.'

'Absolutely. But in that case you'll have to do some shopping for dinner on your way home. I'll make a list.' She jumped down. 'Pen and paper?'

Sebastian pointed to one of the drawers under the worktop where she had been sitting. Ellinor opened it and took out a black pen and a small notepad. She sat down at the table and started writing.

'Pasta, fillet steak, salad, shallots, brown sugar, balsamic vinegar, veal stock, cornflour. Tell me if you've already got any of this.' She broke off. 'You've got butter, I presume? What about red wine?'

'I don't drink.'

Ellinor looked up from her list with a surprised expression. 'Not at all?'

'Not alcohol, no.'

'Why not?'

There were reasons. A few years ago he had spent a few months trying to avoid the dream with the help of booze, and had almost ended up an alcoholic on top of everything else. He was a person with an addictive personality. He had problems when it came to setting limits. Nothing she needed to know.

'I just don't,' he replied with a shrug.

'But if you're passing, can you get a bottle of red for the sauce? You don't mind if I have a glass?'

'No.'

'Would you rather have potatoes instead of pasta?'

'I don't care.'

'Okay. Is there a dessert you particularly fancy?'

'No.'

'In that case, I'll decide.'

She carried on writing. He carried on with breakfast. Normality and everyday life. He had never gone shopping with a list in his entire life. But then he had never met anyone like Ellinor before either.

Sebastian had decided to take a walk; he strolled through the city up to Kronoberg and arrived at Riksmord before everyone else. He sat down in the Room and waited for the others. He picked up the phone and rang the number he had now tried countless times. In spite of the fact that there was still no answer from Trolle, this gave rise to less anxiety within his body. After breakfast he had gone back to bed with Ellinor. From a purely sexual point of view, they were extremely well suited. It wasn't love. Definitely not. But it was something. Love hurt. This didn't.

Before he left, Ellinor had laid out a fresh shirt and asked him to have a proper shave. Life was strange. His recent journey had been so intense that soon nothing would surprise him. But he needed to find Trolle. The question was how he should go about it. Could he get Billy to help? He didn't have to tell the whole truth, but could let his colleague know that he had gone to see Trolle when he realised he was being followed. Asking an old friend for help wouldn't sound too far-fetched. Billy was usually pretty good at keeping secrets, and his relationship with Vanja seemed somewhat strained at the moment, so there was unlikely to be a leak in that direction. It was obvious that Billy had started trying to work his way up in the hierarchy, and Vanja was fighting back. She would never admit it, of course, but it was clear to Sebastian that she thought Billy had started to get above himself. A group always worked best when everyone accepted their role and didn't question the role of others. That was why he had never been able to fit into a group; questioning was his life blood. Billy had actually impressed him, and had proved himself to be a pretty good police officer. He had also helped Sebastian off the record in Västerås when it came to finding Anna Eriksson and getting hold of her current address. He could be a useful ally in the search for Trolle.

Sebastian was intending to call at Trolle's place after the morning briefing. If he didn't find anything there he would have a word with Billy. Satisfied with his plan, he went and got himself a coffee from the machine in the dining room. Gathered his thoughts and promised himself he wouldn't fall out with either Vanja or Torkel today. He needed to protect his presence within the team, to be cooperative rather than confrontational.

Thirty minutes and two cups of coffee later, the others came trooping in. They hardly looked at him, even though he was wearing a clean shirt. Wouldn't the two women notice something like that, if not the men?

Ursula went first, turning to face the others as she placed the folder she was carrying on the table. 'Shall I make a start? I've got the autopsy report on Annette Willén.'

'Carry on,' Torkel said.

Ursula laid out several enlarged photographs of Annette's mutilated naked body. The wound in her throat gaped at them. This was the first time Sebastian had seen her dead, and it affected him more than he had expected. It was difficult to make the emotional leap between the image he had of her in life, in that dress, warm and desperate for love, and the way she looked in the photographs. Ursula took out yet another close-up of the slashed throat.

'Trachea and carotid artery severed. One blow and a sharp movement outwards. Exactly like the others.'

'Would she have felt much?'

Ursula looked at Sebastian. There was no doubt that his question came from the heart. She answered without a trace of empathy.

'It was very quick. She choked before she bled to death, so the end came quickly. Relatively quickly.'

Sebastian didn't answer. He looked even paler. Ursula addressed herself to the others. He deserved to suffer.

'It's difficult to determine the exact time of the attack. She was lying in direct sunlight. But if Sebastian left her at five, then the murderer definitely turned up very soon after. The preliminary estimate is between five and ten a.m.'

'So he followed Sebastian to her apartment?'

'That's a reasonable assumption. Particularly as we now know that Sebastian was being followed.'

The room fell silent, a silence evoked by the proximity between Sebastian and the murderer. Sebastian searched feverishly for some memory of that fateful morning. Had he seen anyone? Anything? Met anyone on the stairs? Heard a car door slam and turned to look? Caught a glimpse? But there was nothing.

'I didn't see anyone, but then again I wasn't looking either.'

'No, I assume you just wanted to get away as quickly as possible. Cosy breakfasts don't seem to be your thing,' Vanja said acidly. Sebastian lowered his gaze. Didn't want to respond. Wasn't going to respond. Wasn't going there again. Cooperation not confrontation.

Torkel joined in with the discussion. 'We'll send out some uniforms to conduct fresh door-to-door enquiries now we've narrowed down the time frame. One of the neighbours might have seen someone hanging around.'

'Ideally in the vicinity of a blue Ford Focus,' Billy chipped in.

'Where are we up to with the cars?' Torkel asked.

'We didn't get any more from the Focus, and the Toyota has passed a number of congestion-charge pay stations; the most recent was yesterday morning . . .'

There was a knock on the door and a young constable came in, looking stressed. 'Excuse me, but there's a phone call for you, Vanja. Apparently it's important.'

'It'll have to wait, we're in the middle of a meeting.'

'It's from Lövhaga. Edward Hinde . . .'

They all stiffened. For a second they thought they had misheard.

'Are you sure?' Vanja asked, sounding dubious. 'Edward Hinde?'

'That's what he said.'

Vanja pulled the phone on the table towards her. 'Put him through, please.'

The young constable quickly turned and left the room. Vanja leaned forward, waiting for the call. The others also edged closer. It was as if the cream-coloured plastic object on the table had become the room's centre of gravity, drawing them all towards it. Billy stood next to Vanja with one hand on the speaker button; at the same time he placed his mobile next to the loudspeaker with the other hand. They all waited in silence. Only Sebastian stayed where he was, a little distance away. He was frantically trying to work out what was going on. Why was Hinde on the phone? What was the purpose behind his call? Should he try to stop it? This didn't bode well, he felt instinctively. As usual, Hinde was ahead of them.

He acted.

They reacted.

Never the other way round.

The sound of the telephone made them all jump, even though they had been waiting for it. Billy pressed speaker phone and the recording function on his mobile simultaneously. A soft rushing sound came through the loudspeaker. Someone was on the other end. Suddenly Hinde was there with them. Subconsciously Vanja leaned forward even more, as if she were trying to hear if he was really there in the silence.

'Vanja Lithner . . .'

The answer came quickly and clearly. 'This is Edward Hinde. I don't know if you remember me.'

It was definitely him. The well-modulated voice. Calm, focused, and behind the self-possession the certain knowledge that he had the advantage. This was obviously his next move. Sebastian could see him in his mind's eye. The smile, the cold watery eyes, the telephone held close to his mouth.

Vanja attempted to sound equally composed. 'I do, yes.'

'How are you?' Hinde's tone was relaxed, intimate. As if he were ringing an old friend for a chat.

'What do you want?' Vanja almost hissed. 'Why are you calling?'

They heard Edward laugh out loud.

'Vanja, this is my first telephone call for a very, very long time. Can't we spin it out a little?'

'I thought you weren't allowed any calls.'

'They made an exception.'

'Why?'

Sebastian took a step towards Vanja. He was asking himself the very same thing. Someone at Lövhaga had done a deal with Hinde. And had undoubtedly come off worst. He felt that this conversation should be brought to an end right now. Hinde's tone was too playful, too familiar. Too self-satisfied. There was something about it that scared the shit out of Sebastian. That was his daughter, having a conversation with a man who always had a plan. Who always carried it through. Torkel saw that Sebastian was about to move forward, and stopped him with a keen glance.

Sebastian hesitated. His mandate was weaker than ever. He had lost Torkel's trust. He gave his temporary boss a pleading look, but Torkel shook his head. Meanwhile the conversation continued.

'I have information you ought to be aware of.'

'I'm listening.'

'Just you. Because I presume the others are listening at the moment.'

Vanja looked enquiringly at Torkel, who gave her a quick nod in response. In all probability Edward knew that Vanja would never take the call alone, and lying felt like more of a risk.

'That's right.'

'The information I wish to pass on is for your ears only. But perhaps you won't be allowed to come and see me again?'

'Why do you say that?'

'Sebastian seemed very protective of you. It was almost as if he thought you wouldn't be able to cope with me on your own. Is he there?'

Sebastian answered without asking Torkel's permission. Went and stood next to Vanja.

'I'm here. What do you want?'

'Vanja can come over and have a little chat with me, can't she? Please?'

'Why? If you've got something to say, you can say it now.'

'No. Only to Vanja. Face to face.'

'Never,' Sebastian heard himself saying.

But it was too late. There was a clatter as the phone was put down and the rushing sound disappeared. The connection had been broken. Hinde was gone. Vanja got to her feet with a determined expression on her face. Sebastian immediately realised where she was going.

'No, Vanja. Don't do it. Don't go there.'

She looked at him crossly. 'Because?'

'He won't give you anything. He just wants attention. I know Edward Hinde.'

'Hang on a minute. We suspect he's involved. He rings and offers information. Are we just supposed to ignore that?'

'Yes.'

Sebastian looked at her, his eyes pleading. As if that would make any difference. He could feel the whole thing slipping through

366

his fingers, but he had to fight. He knew that he couldn't let go, not under any circumstances. Not again. Vanja must not go there. No way.

'Is it because he didn't ring you? Is that the problem? The fact that he might want to tell *me* something?!' Vanja met his eyes, every bit of her ready for battle.

'No – it's dangerous!'

'What the hell are you talking about? I can take care of myself.' She turned to Torkel for support. Which was immediately forthcoming. She was almost taken by surprise.

'You can go. We might as well find out what he wants.'

'But what about the visiting order?'

'I'll sort it.'

'Oh, so *now* you can sort it,' Sebastian muttered.

Torkel pretended he hadn't heard.

'I can fix you up with a wire,' Billy said, heading for the door. Vanja stopped him. 'No. If he notices he might clam up.'

'He's not going to say anything important anyway,' Sebastian said, determined not to give up. 'He's just going to go all round the houses. Talking a load of crap . . . Lies.'

Vanja interrupted Sebastian. 'In that case you two *do* have something in common.'

'Vanja . . .'

Sebastian watched her as she walked towards the door. He was terrified; she was on her way to Hinde. To the Monster. He couldn't give up; his final words to her were a feeble appeal.

'At least let me come with you.'

Her response was anything but sympathetic. She didn't even look at him. 'Sorry, you weren't invited.' And with that she walked out.

Sebastian suddenly had the feeling he would never see her again. That all his efforts to reach her had been in vain. He slumped down on a chair. The others looked at him, uncomprehending. They already knew how self-centred Sebastian was, but his reaction to the situation still seemed extreme. For Torkel it was the final straw. Sebastian had really lost the plot. He seemed to regard the fact that Vanja was going to see Hinde on her own as some kind of personal defeat. It reminded him a little of the moment when Sebastian had told him he had slept with all the women who had been murdered. Torkel had seen the same mixture of panic and sorrow in his eyes. It had been understandable on that occasion, but not now. Now it was merely unacceptable. The very idea of wanting to stop Vanja, the best police officer on the team, from obtaining information was overstepping every conceivable mark, irrespective of whether it was because he didn't think she could do it or because he thought he should have been the chosen one.

Sebastian looked at them, especially Torkel; he could see the lack of understanding in their eyes, but hadn't the strength to explain. They would never be able to grasp the whole picture anyway; it was too complex. Sebastian stiffened. What if that was the explanation? What if Hinde knew? He turned to Ursula.

'Can I borrow your car?'

She shook her head. 'No, Sebastian.'

'Can I borrow your fucking car?!'

Ursula looked in astonishment at Torkel, who also shook his head. 'That's enough now, Sebastian.'

Sebastian was furious. 'Not for me. Give me the keys!'

'Sebastian, we can't go on like this,' Torkel began.

'Fine! Good!' Sebastian broke in. 'Kick me out! I couldn't give a damn! But give me the fucking car keys!'

After another glance at Torkel, who responded with a resigned shrug, Ursula reached for her bag, which was hanging on the back of the chair. She dug out the car keys and tossed them to Sebastian.

He almost ran out of the room.

He had to find a way to stop Vanja.

He just didn't know how.

He ran through the open-plan office, normally an oasis of calm. Those who were working there stared at him with curiosity, but he didn't care. He hoped that she had had to wait for one of the lifts down to the car park, and that he would catch up with her by taking the stairs. By the door leading out of the office he crashed into two women carrying takeaway coffees. One of them dropped hers, but Sebastian pushed past her without stopping and tore open the door. His feet flew down the stairs, and he counted the floors as he went. Third, second, first; there were two floors of parking spaces and he hoped Vanja had parked in her usual spot on the upper level. He flung open the heavy grey metal door. Ran in among the cars. The car park was almost full. He heard an engine spring into life a short distance away, and ran in that

368

direction. Then he saw her. She was just pulling out, heading towards Fridhemsplan.

'Vanja! Wait!'

Presumably she hadn't seen him. Or she was just ignoring him. At any rate, she kept on going. He watched the car disappear. Looked around. Realised that he didn't know what car Ursula drove. Or where she had parked it. He looked at the key in his hand. Volvo. He ran, pressing the button on the black ignition key in the hope that the lights on one of the cars would flash and show him the way. No luck. He dashed around the car park, pressing the button over and over again. After a while he heard the click. The car was at one end, as far from the exit as possible, and it responded to his constant pressing with reassuring flashes. He raced over, opened the door and got in. Fumbled with the key for a moment before he managed to start the car.

Foot to the floor, the tyres screeching as he swung around.

He still didn't have a plan.

Except to drive as fast as possible.

To stop her.

Haraldsson's morning had been everything he'd hoped it would be.

The alarm went off at six twenty, and he got up right away. Jenny was fast asleep on her side of the bed. He closed the bedroom door quietly, pulled on a T-shirt and a pair of sweat pants and went downstairs. The feeling he had as he headed for the bathroom reminded him of the way he used to feel as a child coming up to Christmas and birthdays: a bubbling happiness, knowing that an utterly perfect day lay ahead. He went to the toilet and had a quick shower, then went into the kitchen. He began by melting a bar of chocolate in a bowl over a pan of boiling water, then dipped the strawberries he had bought on the way home yesterday. He placed them on a dish to allow the chocolate to set, then got out the toaster and frying pan. Toasted and fried. Bread and bacon. Sliced the melon. Cracked four eggs, mixed in the milk and melted butter in the frying pan. Made more toast. Switched on the kettle and put a tea bag in a cup. Took cheese and raspberry jam out of the fridge. Set everything out on the biggest tray they had. Feeling very pleased with himself, he checked that everything was as it should be. Finally he went out to the car and opened the glove compartment. Removed a little red box. A ring. Gold, with a diamond and two rubies. He hadn't given Jenny a present the morning after their wedding. He hadn't actually realised that it was expected of him. Jenny's friends and his female colleagues had been very surprised to hear that Jenny hadn't received anything. Or as Margareta in the Västerås police had put it: 'So Jenny ended up with nothing after her wedding night.' As if the fact that she had gained Thomas Haraldsson as her husband didn't count. Jenny had never mentioned it. Never breathed a word of disappointment, or hinted that she had missed the traditional gift. But now she was going to have her present. Five years too late. But better late than never.

Haraldsson hurried back indoors and placed the little red box on the tray. Perfect. He picked up the tray and went upstairs.

She was awake when he walked in. Smiling at him.

He loved her so much.

'Happy anniversary, darling,' he said, putting the tray down on the floor before leaning forward to kiss her. She wrapped her arms around his neck and pulled him close.

'Happy anniversary to you too.'

'I've made breakfast.'

'I know, I heard you.' She kissed him.

He picked up the tray as she plumped the pillows and arranged them against the wall. They sat in bed side by side and ate their breakfast. He fed her with strawberries. She loved her ring.

Just as he had expected, he was late for work.

Annika was already there when he arrived. Of course.

'Sorry I'm late,' Haraldsson said as he walked into her office, whistling. 'It's my wedding anniversary.'

He didn't need to apologise to Annika, of course; it was just a way of being able to talk about the fact that he had something to celebrate. He wanted everyone to know. Annika looked mildly interested.

'I see. Congratulations.'

'Thank you.'

'Victor rang a little while ago,' Annika went on. 'He's sent an email, and he'd like an answer as soon as possible.'

'What did it say?'

'You can read it,' Annika said, with a nod in the direction of Haraldsson's office. 'On your computer,' she added, just to be on the safe side.

'Can't you print it out? That would be quicker; my computer isn't switched on yet.'

'Okay.'

'Good – could you bring it in, please?'

Without waiting for an answer he went into his office, shrugged off his jacket and sat down behind his desk. He switched on the computer and picked up 'Lövhaga 2014, Visions and Aims'. He just had time to open the folder before Annika knocked on the door, came in and handed over his print-out.

'Thank you.'

Haraldsson put the folder to one side and read the email.

Dear Thomas,
With regard to Edward Hinde's phone call, which you approved yesterday.
(By the way, this is something we need to discuss; I would prefer to be
consulted when an inmate's security arrangements are changed.) Apparently
the call this morning means that Riksmord will be coming to speak to
him later today. This is not a problem as far as I am concerned, but as
usual you will need to approve a visiting order.

Yours sincerely,
Victor Bäckman

Thomas read the email again. Hinde had called Vanja Lithner, and now she was coming to Lövhaga. Today.

This didn't feel right.

It didn't feel right at all.

Haraldsson stood up and hurried out of his office.

Edward Hinde was sitting in his usual place reading on the upper floor in the library when he heard footsteps coming up the stairs. A wave of irritation swept over him. Was it the new inmate? If so he would have to have a word with Igor in the very near future so that Igor could explain to the new guy that there were rules which must be followed. His rules.

But it wasn't the new guy. It was Haraldsson. Edward closed the book about Napoleon and put it to one side. Haraldsson nodded to the guard who was standing a little way off, pulled out a chair and sat down opposite Edward. He leaned forward across the table, an eager expression on his face.

'I want to be there,' he whispered. Edward didn't know whether this was because they were in a library, or so that the guard wouldn't hear them. It didn't matter.

'Be where?' Hinde wondered in all honesty.

'I want to be there when you speak to Vanja Lithner.'

'I don't think so.'

'This is non-negotiable. I am *going* to be there.' Haraldsson emphasised the point by almost slamming his fist down on the table. He stopped himself about a centimetre from the surface.

372

Because they were in a library, Hinde assumed. There was no real reason why Haraldsson should be concerned about the guard hearing a thud from their direction.

'I don't think so,' Hinde repeated calmly.

'In that case I won't allow you to see her.'

Edward's eyes darkened, but Haraldsson was prepared for that. He had his reason at the ready.

'I never promised that you would be allowed to see her,' he said somewhat smugly. 'I said you could make a phone call, not that you could see her. That will cost you an answer.'

In his mind's eye Hinde saw himself stand up, quickly lean forward, grab hold of Haraldsson's head and slam it down on the table. Before the governor or the guard had time to react he saw himself move around the table, yank back Haraldsson's head, place the palms of his hands on Haraldsson's temples, and twist. Heard the sound of his neck breaking.

However tempting the picture might be, he wasn't going to do it. Still, it was time to show who was in charge here.

'You seem to be an ambitious man, Thomas,' he said quietly, but with an intensity that made every syllable hit home. 'Correct me if I'm wrong, but I think this job means a lot to you.'

Haraldsson nodded, not entirely comfortable with the direction this conversation was taking.

'I have your . . . gifts in my cell,' Hinde went on. 'How will you explain to the board that you smuggle things in for me?'

'I shall deny it.'

'And will anyone believe you?'

'They'll believe me more than they'll believe you.'

Edward remained motionless, apart from his eyebrows, which shot up enquiringly. 'Really?'

'Yes.' Haraldsson looked into those dark, searching eyes and wished he was as certain as he hoped he sounded.

'So if I reveal our little agreement, the fact that I tell you everything I know in return for the things I want, they'll believe you and not me.'

'Yes.' Haraldsson could hear from his voice that his wish hadn't been fulfilled.

'And how will you explain the items I have?' Hinde asked in a perfectly ordinary tone of voice, which contrasted sharply with the intensity of his gaze.

'Someone else gave them to you.'

'And you're prepared to gamble your entire career on that?'

Haraldsson sat in silence. He felt like a chess player who had only his king left, while his opponent had suddenly acquired another queen.

'If they don't believe you, it won't just be a question of losing your job. You might be behind bars when the baby arrives.'

Haraldsson leapt to his feet and went down the stairs without a word. Edward grinned. The plan was progressing nicely.

★ ★ ★

Haraldsson stormed back to his office. That hadn't gone according to plan at all. Now he would have to approve the visiting order. Hinde would see Vanja Lithner without him. But he would make sure he spoke to Vanja immediately afterwards. Force her to tell him what had emerged during the meeting. He could do that. It was his institution. His rules.

For a moment he toyed with the idea of going to Hinde's cell and searching for the photo of Jenny, the jar and the bottle. But what reason could he give if someone found him in the empty cell? An unscheduled search. He would never do that himself. It wasn't his job. It would just look suspicious. And what if he didn't find the items? No, the best thing would be to allow Hinde to have his meeting, and then to pump Vanja for information. It wasn't an ideal situation, but what he did with the information he gleaned would be key. Vanja would have to report to Torkel. He could go higher up immediately. There was still hope.

It could still be an utterly perfect day.

She was expected.

The guard opened the gate as soon as he saw her. There was only one way into Lövhaga, and that was via the small security post. On her first two visits she had had to show her ID at the window, but now they recognised her and waved her through straight away. She walked along the path towards the main building, past the high fence topped with barbed wire. On the other side lay the open section. She could see some of the inmates sitting outside enjoying the sun in the exercise yard. It was obviously far too hot to play football; they had taken off their tops and were lying there relaxing. One of them sat up to look at her.

'Are you coming to see me?' he shouted, flexing his muscles.

'You wish!' she replied and continued to the second gate set in the second fence, which was also topped with barbed wire. This was the barrier separating the secure unit from the other buildings. This time the guard insisted on seeing her ID, and she had to hand over her gun. But he was also expecting her.

'That was quick,' the guard said. 'They said you probably wouldn't be here until about twelve.'

'There was hardly any traffic.'

'Haraldsson asked me to take you straight in.'

'He's not going to be there, is he?' She couldn't hide her displeasure at the thought.

'No, but he asked me to let him know when you arrived.' The guard locked her gun in the grey safe, took out the key and called his colleague over the radio. 'Edward Hinde's visitor has arrived.'

Vanja nodded to him and went to wait on the gravelled area outside the security post. After a few minutes another guard came to collect her. He led her to a huge reinforced door and opened it for her. They passed through two more security doors, turned left down a corridor and went up some stairs. They didn't seem to be heading for the same room as last time, although it was difficult for her to tell exactly; the interior of Lövhaga looked the same everywhere. Institutional pale blue, and poor lighting. Finally the guard stopped.

'Wait here. As you're alone we need to make sure he's properly secured before you go in.'

Vanja nodded, but a part of her was wondering if they would have had the same concerns about security if she had been a man. Probably not. But perhaps it was hardly surprising. Hinde definitely had a particular relationship with women. Even though she was convinced that she could take care of herself, she was grateful. She respected danger, although she would never admit to anyone that she was slightly nervous. She went into a small waiting room and sat down on a sofa. The room was dark and stuffy; the only light came from a small barred window high up. She leaned back on the hard sofa. Tried to calm her nerves. Everything had happened at top speed today. The meeting that had been interrupted by Hinde, and the rapid, unexpected trip to Lövhaga. And then there was Sebastian's behaviour. He really had overstepped the mark today, and seemed to have lost the plot completely. Torkel had called a few minutes after she left to tell her that Sebastian had gone after her in Ursula's car. Vanja had switched on her blue light, and fortunately there had been no sign of Ursula's car in her rear-view mirror.

She was glad that Sebastian wouldn't be with them for much longer. That was the only positive aspect of this situation. She could understand that Sebastian was extremely stressed by what had happened. However cold and emotionally disturbed he might be, it was obvious that this had had a significant effect on him. But it was still crazy to allow him to remain anywhere near the investigation. She would never be able to understand why Torkel, whom she still respected, had defended him for such a long time. But she hadn't known Sebastian in his glory days. That had to be it. She hadn't seen him at his best. Because Torkel was no idiot. Apart from this error of judgement, he was the best boss she had ever had, and she decided not to make too big an issue of what had happened. Sebastian's book had actually impressed her once upon a time. So he had had something. But not any longer. And now Torkel realised that too.

At long last.

She had to concentrate on stopping the murders and rebuilding her relationship with Billy. She missed him. Could Billy's new girlfriend have something to do with the fact that he was no longer satisfied with just handling the technical aspects of the investigation, which was what she and the rest of the team used him for? Perhaps it wasn't an unreasonable point of view. Vanja had taken him rather too much for granted, and she hadn't always asked for his opinion. At the same time, they always used to be honest with one another. That was the part she didn't really understand. Why was this happening now? Why was he discontented, and why hadn't he said anything? Vanja had believed and hoped they had that kind of relationship. Obviously not. She decided to have a proper chat with him as soon as she got the chance.

She heard a door open and went out to have a look. The guard was back.

'He's ready now.'

She followed him, feeling tense. She straightened her shoulders and tried to look as relaxed as possible. She had only met Hinde once, but there was one thing she had clearly understood. He saw through people. Read them. She couldn't go in there looking nervous or tense.

She would just have to bluff her way through.

This was a different room. Smaller than the one they had used the first time. No windows. The same grubby pale blue walls as in the corridor. It felt like a cell that was no longer used. Two chairs and a table in the middle, nothing else. Hinde was sitting with his back to her, his hands and feet shackled to the sturdy metal table, which in turn was screwed to the floor. The police would never be allowed to go so far with someone they were holding in custody. The suspect's lawyer would see to that, if nothing else. But there were no lawyers here. This was Lövhaga. And this wasn't a normal interview. The stringent security measures had presumably been something Haraldsson had insisted on if the meeting was to go ahead. She wondered how Hinde had managed to arrange it at such short notice. Sebastian still hadn't received his visiting order. So Hinde must have given Haraldsson something. The thought that Haraldsson might be able to influence the investigation in any way was not a pleasant one.

Hinde remained motionless, in spite of the fact that he must have been aware of her presence in the room by this stage. The only sound came from the shiny chains which clanked as he gently moved his hands.

The guard handed her a small black box with a red button. 'Panic alarm. I'm just outside. Knock when you're done.' Vanja took the alarm and looked at it with a certain degree of scepticism. The guard smiled. 'Just to be on the safe side. According to the rules there should actually be two of you. And Haraldsson wants to see you immediately afterwards. He wants a report.'

'Of course.' She nodded, even though she had no intention of giving Haraldsson anything. Not until she knew more about his role in all this.

The guard closed the door firmly behind him.

Vanja looked once more at Hinde's motionless back. 'Here I am,' she said.

He replied without turning around: 'I know.'

Vanja walked around the table, keeping her distance. Met his gaze for the first time. He looked up at her with a friendly smile, as if he were sitting in a restaurant with a cup of coffee rather than shackled to a table in a locked room.

'I'm so glad you came. Please sit down.' He nodded at the chair opposite.

She ignored him. 'What do you want?'

'I don't bite.'

'What do you want?'

'A little chat. I don't see women anymore. So if I get the chance, at least I have to try. You would do the same if you were me.'

'I could never be you.'

'I'm not as terrible as Sebastian says. There are reasons for everything.'

Vanja took a step closer to him and raised her voice. 'I'm not here for a little chat. I'm here because you said you had something to tell me. But that seems to have been little more than crap.'

She turned and walked back to the door. Raised her hand to summon the guard.

'You'll regret it if you do that.'

'Why?'

'Because I know who killed those women.'

Vanja lowered her hand and turned to face him. 'How do you know?'

'You find things out in here.'

'Crap.'

'You know that I know.' For the first time Hinde turned and looked straight at her. 'You saw it in my eyes the last time you were here.'

Vanja stiffened. Was he just guessing, or had he really seen some kind of reaction from her on her previous visit? Had he sensed the realisation she had only registered as a feeling? If he had, then he was better at reading people than anyone she had ever met. Better and more dangerous.

'If you knew last time we were here, why didn't you say anything?'

'I wasn't sure. I am now.'

'How come?'

'I spoke to the person in question. He works here. He confessed. He was boasting, actually. He idolises me. Can you imagine?'

'No. What's his name?'

'First of all there's something I'd like to know about you. Something personal. Are you more like your mother or your father?'

'I have no intention of talking about personal matters with you.'

'It's only a question.'

'But what kind of a bloody question?'

Vanja walked around him again. He followed her with his eyes. The smile had disappeared. His expression was still friendly, but at the same time horribly intrusive. She could feel him trying to get inside her head. Read her. Examine her.

'I'm just interested, that's all. I was most like my mother, that's what people said when I was growing up.'

Vanja shook her head. 'My father, I think. Who's the murderer?'

Hinde looked at her, then closed his eyes. He deliberately moved away in his mind for a second and took a deep breath. Visualised the man. Her father. Tried to see the unbroken genetic line between the man he hated and his daughter, standing here with him in this room. He had to make a decision. Should he tell her? Expose the dirty little secret which was almost too obvious

379

once you knew it? She had his eyes. His restless energy. He wanted nothing more than to take that away from her. Break her down. Defile her. He had to remind himself that slow and steady wins the race.

Planning. Patience. Determination.

The cornerstones.

'I agree,' he said dreamily, opening his eyes. 'I think you're most like your father too.'

'Last chance, then I'm leaving. Give me a name.'

Hinde nodded to himself and leaned forward. 'I wasn't just winding Sebastian up when I said I wanted to touch you,' he said in a quiet, meaningful voice.

Vanja stood over him, her arms folded. 'You are never going to touch me.'

'Perhaps not. But I have something you want. In my experience people are prepared to go quite a long way to get what they want. Wouldn't you agree?'

He opened his right hand, which up to that point had been clenched in a fist. On his palm lay a tiny, neatly folded piece of paper that was no bigger than a thumbnail.

'Here he is. Just a metre or so away from you.' He smiled at her once more.

Suddenly he bent down with lightning speed and picked up the piece of paper in his mouth. Straightened up and showed her the note, firmly clasped between his front teeth.

'It will take two seconds to swallow it,' he said through his gritted teeth. 'Then it will be gone forever, and I won't say another word. Am I still not allowed to touch you?'

Vanja was still standing there with her arms folded, her eyes fixed on the little scrap of paper.

'Not your breasts. Just your hair,' Hinde went on. 'That's not such a big sacrifice for you to make, surely?'

He very deliberately opened his left hand and raised it towards her. It lifted a few centimetres before the chain stopped it. His fingers moved urgently, enticingly.

'Please, Vanja. Put your hair here.'

Vanja didn't know what to do. Could that piece of paper really provide the answer they had been seeking for such a long time? Or was it just a trick? Sebastian had warned her against playing along with Hinde's games, and it was one piece of advice she actually felt inclined to follow.

'How do I know you're not lying?'

'I always keep my promises. You will know that if you've done your homework. The choice is yours.'

He gave her a big smile, the note still clearly visible, the fingers of his left hand still beckoning playfully.

Vanja quickly tried to analyse the situation. It was extreme in every way. The risk that the whole thing was a trap was considerable, but at the same time she couldn't help feeling that Hinde was telling the truth. She didn't see how this could lead to a simple hostage situation. Hinde was firmly shackled. She had the panic alarm. The unease she had felt initially was now tempered with a strange curiosity, almost recklessness. If she turned and walked away, she might regret it forever. Because if that little piece of paper between Hinde's teeth was the solution, then it would be worth it. If Hinde was telling the truth, not only would she be saving the lives of future victims, but she would be the one who had succeeded in getting crucial information out of Edward Hinde. All on her own. Just her. Nobody else. That would make Sebastian's presence in the team superfluous from now on. Because if she could solve this case, why would they ever need Sebastian Bergman again?

She moved her left thumb onto the alarm button. It would take a fraction of a second to press it. Perhaps thirty seconds before the guard was in the room. Hinde couldn't move his right hand across to hold her. One hand. She would be able to pull away easily. It might cost her a clump of hair, but she would be able to do it. She would be exposing herself to a comparatively low level of risk for a minute or so.

She decided to play along. She slowly bent forward, keeping as far away as possible from Hinde while allowing him to reach the ends of her hair with his left hand, if he stretched as far as the chains would allow. She heard the metallic rattle just before his fingers touched her blonde hair. She met his eyes. What was it she could see there?

Anticipation?

Happiness?

His fingers gently caressed the soft, silky hair. It was finer than he had imagined. It felt lighter in his hand. He picked up the scent of a fruity shampoo. Leaned forward a fraction so that he could breathe in the aroma. Suddenly he wished that she was the one chained to the table instead of him. Wished he had greater freedom of movement so that he could feel her. Properly. He got more excited than he had expected, and had to struggle to hide his feelings. His mother had also had blonde hair. Longer than Vanja's. But it hadn't been as soft. This hair made him want to pull it. Hard. But he couldn't have everything. Not at the moment.

Planning. Patience. Determination.

This would do for now. Reluctantly he withdrew his hand and spat out the piece of paper, which landed in the middle of the table. His expression was as gentle as he could make it as he looked at her.

'You see, I do keep my promises.' He leaned back and lowered his hand to show that he was done. Vanja straightened up and grabbed the note. Without unfolding it she headed for the door.

'See you again, Vanja.'

'I very much doubt that.' She banged on the door. 'I'm done here!'

The guard opened the door after a few seconds and she left the little room. Hinde sat there motionless; he could still remember the scent of her.

I always keep my promises, he thought.

See you again, Vanja.

She didn't want to show the guard the note, so asked where the toilets were. The visitors' facilities were one floor up in what seemed to be a purely administrative area. The depressing colours were the same as everywhere else in Lövhaga, but at least the toilets had been cleaned recently.

Vanja sat down on the closed seat and unfolded the piece of paper. There was a name, written in pencil in capital letters: RALPH SVENSSON.

She thought she recognised it. Not the surname, perhaps. But Ralph, with ph at the end. She had read it somewhere. But where? She took out her mobile and rang the person who might know. Billy. He answered almost right away.

'Hi. Can you check out a name for me? Ralph Svensson. Ralph with a ph. If that's okay?' she added.

'Did you get the name from Hinde?'

Billy didn't even appear to have heard her final caveat. She could hear him tapping away on the keyboard.

'He says that's the murderer. I think I recognise it from somewhere.'

'Me too. Hang on.'

Billy went quiet. The tapping continued. Vanja's fingers drummed a nervous tattoo as she waited for him to come back. The question was how reliable the tip-off would turn out to be, but she couldn't worry about that right now. The priority was to investigate it thoroughly. Find out everything they could about Ralph Svensson. Billy came back. She could hear straight away that he was excited.

'He's not an employee, but he's on the list of those who have a pass into Lövhaga. He works for a cleaning company, LS Cleaning. We've already checked him out, but there was nothing on him.'

'Find out all you can. I'll ring from the car. Tell Torkel.'

She ended the call and stood up. Flushed the toilet and washed her hands just to be on the safe side before she left. The guard was standing a short distance away, and immediately tried to attract her attention.

'All done?'

'Absolutely. I have to go.'

'But what about Haraldsson? I've already told him we're on our way.'

'Tell him he can ring Riksmord if it's important. I'm running late.'

Vanja set off towards what she hoped was the way out. She didn't have time for idiots anymore.

Billy rang back before she had even retrieved her gun. He spoke quickly, and she could hear Torkel in the background.

'Torkel wants to know how reliable this is. Do you think we have reasonable grounds for taking Svensson into custody?'

'I don't know how reliable it is. Hinde gave me a name. Haven't you found anything?'

'Not really. Born in 1976. Lives in Västertorp. No record. Has been working for LS Cleaning for seven years. I spoke to his boss, who has nothing but praise for him. The only possible lead is that he was offered a cleaning job at a hospital closer to home last year, better pay and better hours, but he turned it down. Said he was happy at Lövhaga.'

'Is he here now?'

'No. Went off sick at lunchtime yesterday.'

Vanja nodded and turned away so that the guard, who was busy with the safe, wouldn't hear what she said. 'Has he had access to Hinde's section?'

'Yes, he's worked in both the open section and the secure unit.'

'That should be enough. He's been named as a suspect and we have evidence of possible contact.'

She heard Billy speaking to Torkel. He was soon back on the line.

'Torkel is talking to the prosecutor right now about searching Svensson's place. He needs to know exactly what Hinde told you.'

'He didn't say much. Just that this Ralph had confessed to him. Boasted about the murders. Apparently Hinde is his idol.'

'Perhaps Hinde is just trying to set him up.'

'Maybe. But I think it's him. I don't think Hinde was lying.'

'Anything else?'

'No.'

There were certain things that nobody else needed to know. The details of her meeting with Hinde definitely fell into that category. How she had acquired the information. It wouldn't have any influence on whether or not they got a search warrant in any case.

'Why is he helping us? Did he tell you that?' Billy wanted to know.

Vanja didn't say anything for a moment. She had been so carried away by the fact that Hinde *had* got in touch with them that she had completely ignored the entirely justified question as to *why* he had done it.

'No. Because he's a law-abiding citizen?'

'That doesn't sound very likely, does it?'

'Is it important?'

'Maybe not.'

'If it turns out to be significant, then we'll find out.' She turned to the guard, took her gun and slipped it into the holster. 'Call

384

me when the search warrant comes through. I'm heading back to Stockholm now.'

She ended the call and thanked the guard for his help. He pointed to the big door.

'There's a man out there who's been asking for you. He doesn't have a visiting order.'

Vanja knew who it was.

For a second she thought she actually preferred Haraldsson.

There were idiots, and then there were idiots.

Sebastian was standing next to Ursula's car, looking up at the high walls and the grubby buildings. He had parked just outside the main gate, as far to the side of the road as he could get. That had been his compromise. The staff had come out and he had had a heated discussion with them. They claimed that he was impeding the movement of traffic in and out of Lövhaga, and that not only did he not have police ID, he had no visiting order either. Sebastian then pointed out that they were brainless desk jockeys and insisted that he needed to get in. After a few minutes of yelling they had eventually shaken their heads and gone back inside, leaving him there.

He paced nervously back and forth across the road. Kicked at the gravel along the kerb in frustration. Picked dandelions and flicked the heads off the stalks with his thumb, just as he used to do when he was a child. He needed to blot out the thought of Lövhaga's absurd bureaucracy by engaging in simple physical actions, and above all he needed to suppress his anxiety about Vanja. Those idiots behind the fence wouldn't even confirm that she was in there, in spite of the fact that he could see her car. They let him stay where he was, but nothing else. It was just like the rest of his life right now. He was stuck in a no-man's-land where nobody could even be bothered to fight with him anymore.

He was slipping away from the centre of events. Joining the investigation was supposed to enable him to get closer to Vanja. To get a life. Perhaps even to solve the case, although that hadn't been his real motive at the outset. But all that was before Hinde. Before this turned into a personal conflict. Before all the gates began to slam in his face. Because it wasn't only the steel gate leading into

Lövhaga that was closed to him. He had called Torkel from the car, hoping he would somehow be able to persuade him to stop Vanja. He hadn't answered. Hadn't called back. Nor had Billy. And it was his own fault; he was the one who had managed to turn everyone against him. He couldn't blame anyone else, however much he might want to. At the same time his anxiety over the danger in which Vanja might find herself had diminished. She was sensible, and wouldn't take any unnecessary risks. Hinde wouldn't be interested in anything as banal as a straightforward hostage scenario. No, he always had bigger plans. The only question was what those plans might be.

Hinde knew the truth. Sebastian could feel it. That was why he had requested permission to see Vanja.

Was he going to tell her?

Or was that also too banal for him?

Sebastian hated not knowing. He started pacing again. Walked past the gate and peered in. Suddenly he spotted Vanja. She was hurrying across the yard towards her car. Should he call out to her? Wave? Should he just stand there? What did she know? He saw her glance in his direction, but she didn't react in any way. He might have been no more than fresh air. Her lack of interest cheered him.

She didn't know.

If she had known there would have been fury or disgust in her eyes, not total indifference. Perhaps that wasn't a cause for celebration under normal circumstances, but given the current situation it was the best possible outcome. He realised he was smiling to himself. Grinning, in fact.

She couldn't believe her eyes as she drove towards the gate. Was he really standing there blocking the road with a scornful grin on his face? She wound down the window and leaned out. 'Excuse me, you're in the way.'

'I want to talk to you,' he ventured.

'But I don't want to talk to you.'

She stopped the car a few centimetres away from him. He didn't dare move; if he did she would probably just put her foot down and disappear.

'I have to know. What did Hinde want?'

'He gave me the name of the murderer.'

The little smile that had been playing around Sebastian's lips until now vanished immediately. He hadn't expected this. 'What? What do you mean?'

'He said he knew who the murderer was. Someone called Ralph Svensson, apparently. He's a cleaner here at Lövhaga. We know he's had the opportunity to be in contact with Hinde.'

'And you believe Hinde?'

'I have no reason not to. We follow up every lead, don't we?'

'Why would he tell you?'

'The real question is why didn't he tell you? I mean, you're supposed to be the expert. The one who knew how to get him to talk.'

She couldn't keep the malicious pleasure out of her voice. She didn't even try. Without thinking, Sebastian walked up to her.

'And he had nothing to do with all this? Do you really believe that?'

'I'm a police officer. I don't have an opinion. I investigate. Excuse me.'

She put her foot down, the tyres gripped the road with a screech and the car shot forward. He jumped aside instinctively and watched her drive away.

Left behind again.

He was starting to get used to it.

While he was in the car on the way to Västertorp, where Ralph Svensson lived, Torkel received permission to search Svensson's apartment. After a long conversation on the telephone, Gunnar Hallén, the prosecutor, had finally given his approval. There was strong circumstantial evidence, but it was the evaluation of Hinde's testimony that was the problem. The fact that he had been sentenced to life imprisonment didn't exactly help in terms of his credibility. It had taken a lot of persuasion on Torkel's part, but Torkel knew that Hallén was going to give his permission when it came down to it. This was the kind of high-profile case that was absolutely crucial in terms of career prospects. Searching a property on slightly less than adequate grounds wasn't as bad as failing to act at all.

Torkel had asked Billy to organise an emergency response team to break down the door if necessary, and had got into the car with him shortly afterwards. He wanted to be on the spot, ready to move as soon as they got the go-ahead. There was no time to lose on logistics and transport. Vanja would join them in Västertorp as soon as possible. He didn't even bother calling Sebastian.

Billy parked in the turning area behind a number of red apartment blocks dating from the 1950s. Ralph Svensson's place was three hundred metres away, up on a hill closer to the small centre, which had had its heyday long ago. Billy made contact with the leader of the emergency response team, who promised they would be there in five minutes. Then he called Ursula and told her where they had parked.

Torkel walked around, gazing at the leafy surroundings and the freestanding apartment blocks. The warm breeze carried with it the smell of food and the sound of music from open windows.

He could hear laughter somewhere. A group of children were whooping as they cycled around a sandpit a short distance away.

Billy opened the boot and took out a bullet-proof vest which he began to put on.

Torkel looked at him enquiringly. 'We'll let the experts go in first.'

'I want to be there. It's our case.'

'Yes, it is. We don't need to break down doors to prove that.'

'Okay. I'll go in just as an observer.'

Torkel shook his head. Billy had definitely changed in the last few weeks. In the past he had been perfectly happy to play second fiddle, and to support both Torkel and Vanja on the IT side of things. Now he wanted to storm into an apartment with a gun in his hand.

'We will do what we have always done,' Torkel said firmly. 'They will secure the suspect. Then we will take over.'

Billy nodded, but didn't take off the vest. He looked like a defiant teenager.

Torkel walked up to him and placed a hand on his shoulder. 'Has something happened? It feels as if there's a certain amount of . . .' he searched for the right word, '. . . friction in the team. Mainly between you and Vanja.'

Billy didn't reply. Torkel kept his hand where it was.

'You need to talk to me about this. We're a team, but it doesn't always feel that way at the moment.'

'Do you think I'm a good police officer?' Billy looked candidly at Torkel. It was the first time Torkel could ever remember Billy referring to himself with the slightest hint of uncertainty.

'You wouldn't be working with me if you weren't,' Torkel replied.

Billy nodded. 'But if we're a team, why are we treated differently?'

'Because we are different,' Torkel said, as if it were the most obvious thing in the world. 'We have different strengths, different weaknesses. We complement each other.'

'And Vanja is the best police officer.'

'I didn't say that.'

'Okay, but if Vanja had put on this vest and wanted to go in as an observer, would you have stopped her?'

389

Torkel was about to respond with the self-evident 'yes' that was on the tip of his tongue when he hesitated, realising that perhaps Billy was right after all. Would he really have been as firm with Vanja? Probably not. Because she was a better police officer? Probably.

He didn't answer.

Which was answer enough.

Ralph had just sat down at the computer and started to log in to fygorh.se. He would send a message to the Master. Confess his failure. He had waited outside the front door of Ellinor's apartment block until dark yesterday, hoping that she would come back. She hadn't.

He was worn out when he got home. Followed his usual routine and switched on all the lights in order. Then he stopped. At a loss. The sports bag and the food. What should he do with them? Unfortunately it seemed that he would have to come up with a ritual for when he had failed. He thought it over for a while, then came to the conclusion that the best and most natural course of action was to go through the preparation ritual, but in reverse order. He removed the chlorine bottle from the carrier bag and replaced it in the cupboard under the sink, put all the food and drink back in the fridge, then folded the bag and put it away in the cleaning cupboard. Went into the bedroom. Unpacked the nylon stockings and the nightdress and placed them in the top drawer. Then he stopped. He really ought to put the sports bag in the space between the clothes now, but in that case what should he do with the knife? It hadn't been used, but with all the setbacks of the past few days his need to follow the rules to the letter felt so much greater. He decided to take the bag into the kitchen. There he removed the knife, rinsed and washed it, dried it and put it back in the sports bag with a fresh three-litre plastic bag. He threw the old one in the cupboard under the sink and went back into the bedroom. Now he could put the sports bag away in the top drawer and close it. All done.

He fell into bed, exhausted. The room was bright and warm; the hundred-watt bulbs in every corner took away the shadows, every last scrap of the terrifying darkness, and calmed him.

He had slept for a couple of hours. Woken from his dreamless sleep and tried to get going. He had spent the morning looking for Ellinor Bergkvist. She wasn't at work, and they had refused to say when they thought she might be back. He had tried calling Taxi Stockholm to ask if they could tell him where the cab with the registration number JXU346 had dropped the woman who had been picked up on Västmannagatan at about four o'clock yesterday afternoon. This was not the kind of information they were prepared to give out just like that, and when they asked who he was he had hung up. He hadn't found her. He had failed.

Ralph typed in his username and password. A message. From the Master. Sent during the night.

The message was brief and concise.

'You are me now.'

That was all it said. Ralph got up and walked around the room, confused but somehow excited at the same time. He had been elevated to the status of an equal. There was no other way to interpret it. He felt a glow inside; he hadn't expected this at all.

But what did it mean? Was he no longer to receive orders from the Master? Was he to act completely on his own initiative? Evolve under his own steam?

He was lost in speculation when he heard something that sounded like a minor explosion from the front door. Seconds later, black-clad figures wearing helmets came storming in, carrying what looked like automatic firearms pointing straight at him.

'Police! Get down on the floor!' screamed the figures. With lightning speed Ralph threw himself at the computer, grabbed hold of it and hurled it at the wall. Shards of plastic and electronic components flew everywhere. He rushed forward and stamped on the remains of the computer until burly men came and forced him to the floor. He didn't even struggle as they bent back his arms and snapped on the handcuffs. He looked at the broken computer in front of him. He had protected the Master.

They were rough. But it didn't matter. In fact, Ralph was suddenly suffused with a feeling of calm. This feeling grew as more black-clad figures entered the room and carried him out of the apartment. He had reached the next phase, and now he understood the full import of the Master's message.

You are me now.

Indeed he was.

Vanja arrived just as the emergency response team drove off with Ralph Svensson. From her car she had seen them lifting a tall, skinny man wearing a polo shirt and grey trousers into the back. He wasn't even struggling, he was just lying motionless as the four officers carried him. Vanja watched them disappear before she got out of her car. She slammed the door and walked over to the apartment block. She was angry, and the sight of Billy wearing a bullet-proof vest and smiling at her from the doorway didn't exactly help.

'We got him, Vanja. It's him.'

'Why couldn't you have waited for me?' She walked towards him. 'It was my tip-off. It was me who got the name out of him.'

Billy's smile vanished immediately, to be replaced by the coldness she had encountered before. 'Speak to Torkel. It was his decision.'

He walked away. Left her standing there. A short distance away she could see Torkel with the leader of the emergency response team. They were deep in conversation, and the other officer was gesticulating. They seemed to be going through the operation. Vanja set off towards them, but changed her mind. She didn't have the strength to fight with Torkel as well. And his decision had been the right one. She would have done the same if it had been up to her. The important thing was to act quickly, not who did what.

The professional side of things was just one aspect. The other was personal and was related to her position within the team, everyone's roles, and the division of responsibility. Everything that had been so clear and straightforward before this case. She watched as Torkel and the other officer shook hands and said goodbye.

'Well done, Vanja,' Torkel called as he walked over to her.

'Thanks. How sure are we?'

393

'Ursula is in there now. She's doing a preliminary assessment on her own to avoid any risk of contamination, but it looks like a goldmine.'

'Really?'

Torkel nodded calmly. He seemed relaxed, and Vanja realised that he was already convinced they had the right man. She felt some of her irritation ebbing away; this was something to celebrate. They might just have solved the case.

'Ten identical nightdresses, nylon stockings, a leather folder full of newspaper cuttings about the murders,' Torkel went on. 'A knife that seems to match the wounds. And a wall covered in pictures of the victims.'

'But that's brilliant,' Vanja said; she was astonished. Was it really going to be that easy to tie Ralph Svensson to the murders?

'Absolutely, and she's only just started. The DNA will take a day or so, at least for a preliminary result.'

Vanja nodded, and they looked at each other with something approaching affection. Both of them felt the weight of this moment. It was a beautiful day. The sun was shining beyond the long shadow cast by the building where they were standing, making the grass look soft and inviting. It felt as if they were walking into the sunshine. Away from the shadows in which they had found themselves for such a long time.

'I'm sorry we took him without you,' Torkel said kindly. 'But we couldn't wait.'

'I understand that,' she said without hesitation. 'It was a good decision.'

Billy came up to them. He had taken off the bullet-proof vest. 'Ursula says it will be a few hours at least before we can go in.'

The other two nodded, but said nothing. They stood there together in silence, gazing out at the sunshine and greenery.

Like a team.

The way things used to be.

The sound of Billy's phone broke the silence. His new girlfriend, they realised from the softness of his tone. He moved away to discuss their plans for the evening.

Torkel turned to Vanja. 'Hallén is going to want to hold a press conference this afternoon. I'd like you there.'

'But you usually deal with that kind of thing,' she said, surprised.

394

'I know, but I want you to do it. It's thanks to you that we've cracked this.'

She smiled at him. Knew exactly why she had applied to work with Torkel Höglund and Riksmord. Because he was a good boss. Because he understood people. Understood that everyone needed to feel involved.

Sebastian had arrived at the police station around one o'clock. Looked for Torkel and the others. Nobody could tell him where they were. Eventually one of the uniformed officers he usually said hello to told him they were out on an operation. To the south of Stockholm, apparently, and it had gone well. Frustrated, Sebastian had called every single member of the team. Started with Torkel and worked his way down. None of them answered. He got an idea and headed for the remand centre, which was next door to the station, to see if he could find any of them there. Perhaps they were on their way to arrest this Ralph Svensson, whose name Hinde had given to Vanja for some inexplicable reason. No one there. No one who was prepared to tell him whether anyone was on their way in either. He was back in no-man's-land.

He went outside. Up to Fridhemsplan and the supervised entrance to the underground car park. He knew they would probably use it when they got back. Sat down on the grass a short distance away and waited. The guard stared at him suspiciously from his booth, but didn't challenge him. Sebastian was in a public area, and had done nothing illegal. A middle-aged man in a crumpled jacket, who lay down in the overgrown grass after a while. To the Securitas guard he must have looked like an alcoholic who had been heading for Kronoberg Park but who had run out of steam and flopped down on the first patch of grass he found. Only the bottle was missing.

He felt utterly worthless. A first-class degree, years of further study at institutions which included the FBI's Quantico Academy in the USA, a bestselling author, one of the Swedish police service's top profilers for a number of years, and yet the only hope he had left now was that the others would happen to drive past and that in some magical way he could become part of the investigation again. That was his only plan, the only solution he had managed to dig out of his enormous toolkit of knowledge. To stick with it.

His mobile rang. He grabbed it eagerly. It might be one of them. It wasn't. It was a number he recognised, but not a number that had ever called him.

His home number.

He answered.

It was Ellinor. Of course.

He thought about taking out his frustration on her, yelling at her, letting her feel his pain. But she sounded so happy he couldn't do it.

'Sorry, darling, I know how difficult it can be when someone rings you at work. But I'm a bit worried that you might be cross with me.'

'Why?'

'Because I left the apartment.'

'Why did you do that?' His anger turned into anxiety. Perhaps with no justification. If the operation had been a success, if Ralph was the one they were looking for, then the threat had been removed. She could go home. Move out. He could kick her out.

'Well . . . I didn't actually leave the building.'

'What? So where did you go?'

'I went to see the neighbours. I thought I'd introduce myself.'

Sebastian was lost for words. All the negativity he had felt from the start was suddenly replaced by a strange feeling that he was always a part of some parallel universe when it came to Ellinor. They were fundamentally, totally incompatible. They had nothing in common. There was no way they could ever have a relationship.

'I don't have anything to do with my neighbours,' he said tersely.

'No, that's what they said. They were ever so curious about you. Anyway, you need to do some more shopping. We need to add to the list.'

'I don't understand.' He sat up in the grass.

'You mustn't be annoyed, but I've invited our next-door neighbour to dinner. Jan-Åke. His family are away. He's a doctor, like you.'

'I'm not a doctor. I'm a psychologist.'

'So you need to be home by five,' Ellinor went on as if she hadn't heard the correction, 'and call me when you're in the shop. It'll be lovely. Or are you cross?'

Sebastian groped for his anger, for the words that would hurt her so much she would simply disappear. But he couldn't find them. They were hard to get hold of. Her world was so much softer. So much nicer. In her world he was worth something.

'I'm doing this because I love you, you know that, don't you? You can't live like a hermit when you've got such a beautiful apartment. I'm not having it. Will you be back by five?'

'Yes.'

'Kiss kiss.'

'Kiss kiss,' he heard himself reply. Then she was gone.

He got to his feet, feeling confused. Dinner with a neighbour he hadn't even spoken to in twenty years. But that wasn't the worst thing. The worst thing was that he was actually looking forward to it. A little bit. There was a place where he was still the centre of attention. A place where he was still wanted.

A place he hadn't had for a very long time.

A home.

Occupied by a very strange woman, admittedly, but even so. A home.

Prosecutor Hallén was so carried away that he forgot how to do up his tie for a moment. He wanted to go for the French knot he rarely used, and after a couple of attempts he managed it. He had called his wife and asked her to record the news on both SVT and TV 4. With a bit of luck there might even be a special broadcast, but he had no control over that; he could only hope for the best. As far as he was concerned, the big question – whether they had arrested the right person or not – had been answered. The initial evidence was overwhelming. Perhaps they should have waited for the results of the forensic investigation, but that wasn't realistic. News of the arrest would leak out, and the press conference would put a stop to the spread of rumours. And it would also show results.

Torkel Höglund and Vanja Lithner had arrived, bringing photographs taken inside the suspect's apartment. They were terrible and disturbing. The man had a photo wall with thirty-six pictures of each victim, apart from the first woman; there were only thirty-four pictures of her. Hallén felt slightly unwell when he looked at the photographs. The women alive, tied up, wearing a nightdress. Only seconds from death.

'It's him,' he said, then he looked away, out over the small conference room. 'I don't need to see any more.'

They went down to the press room on the first floor. Before they even got there they could see that the press conference would be well attended. On the street there were outside-broadcast cars from every major TV channel, and at reception there was a queue of journalists waiting to get in.

Hallén turned to Torkel. 'I'll give a brief introduction, you run through the course of events, then we'll take questions together if that's okay.'

'Fine.'

Hallén pushed back his shoulders and made his way through the sea of curious journalists. Vanja smiled as she watched the prosecutor moving ahead of them. He nodded in recognition at the crowd of faces, completely unfamiliar to her. She knew Torkel hated this kind of thing. It was obvious from his body language. Shoulders hunched. Chin practically on his chest. He probably knew most of these people too, but he didn't acknowledge anyone. His entire body signalled that he wanted this over and done with as quickly as possible so that he could get back to work. Vanja herself felt a growing sense of excitement. She could enjoy this, she realised. With a bit of luck this might not be the only occasion on which she was involved. If Billy was going to start trying to reposition himself within the team, perhaps she could move too?

She noticed Sebastian standing a short distance away. His expression was weary and resigned. He had been waiting for them by the entrance to the car park when they got back from Västertorp. Had stared at them as they drove in. At first Vanja had hoped that Torkel would ignore him, but her boss wasn't as childish as she was. They had stopped, Torkel had opened the car door and briefly informed Sebastian that they had arrested Ralph Svensson and would shortly be holding a press conference. Sebastian was welcome to come along if he was interested in the details. Then he had closed the door and they had driven off.

He might not be as childish. But he was effective. Vanja realised that she didn't want to have Torkel against her. Ever.

Ralph looked around the tiny cell. So this was what it looked like inside the Kronoberg remand centre. He had walked past and wondered many times. Now he knew. A bed, a table and chair, a toilet. The furniture was made of pale pine, the walls in two colours, with yellow at the bottom and pale grey on the top. Perhaps it didn't look like much to the outside world, but inside he was fizzing with excitement. From the street there was something threatening about the anonymous, bunker-like building right in the middle of Kungsholmen. The exterior revealed no secrets, it was merely a wall concealing the stories within. But once you were inside you could feel them. The memories impregnating the walls.

This was where they had brought the Master, once upon a time. Ralph didn't know which cell he had occupied. But that didn't matter. He was following in the footsteps of the Master.

He had been asked to undress, and the guards had issued him with grey standard-issue clothes made of faded cotton. They checked his mouth and anal orifice for any illegal substances. Made him take a shower. He had loved it. He knew that their harsh, meticulous approach could mean only one thing.

They feared him.

He was important.

He was someone.

He could see it in their eyes, hear it in the way they spoke to him. They had already started checking on him every five minutes through the little aperture in the steel door. Either they were afraid he might commit suicide, or they were simply curious. It was of no significance to him. He relished their curiosity, and suicide wasn't something he had even considered. That would be a defeat. This was where it began. The real contest. Soon they would come and open the door and take him for his first interrogation. No doubt it would take a day or so. That was what had happened to the Master when he was in here. They would want to be fully prepared, to confront the suspect with irrefutable evidence. Knock him off balance right away. But he was ready. There was just one thing he was desperately hoping for. That it would be Sebastian Bergman sitting opposite him in the interview room. Imagine that. Meeting the man the Master himself had met.

They would dance together, he and Sebastian. For a long time, he hoped. Like the duel Sebastian and Hinde had once fought.

Ralph smiled to himself. He had come so far. Learned how to deal with the blood, the knife, the screams. Now he would learn how to face his opponent for real. He suddenly felt exalted in a way he had never felt in his entire life.

Sexually.

His body was actually throbbing, and he found it difficult to sit still. He touched his penis. It was hard. He didn't care if they were watching him through the door. He was thinking of just one thing. If Sebastian wasn't sitting opposite him in the interview room, he would be very disappointed.

In a number of ways.

The press conference had begun. The noisy buzz of conversation stopped as soon as the prosecutor began his introduction. Sebastian had positioned himself as close to the door as possible. He went through his options. It was obvious that he had been removed from the case. At the same time he was more convinced than ever that the people up there on the podium were not seeing the whole picture. The idea that Hinde would content himself with this was unthinkable. It wasn't in his nature.

The prosecutor ended his somewhat vague speech, which seemed mainly concerned with highlighting the decisive action taken by himself and the prosecutor's office. Torkel took over. As always, he was direct and to the point. As if he wanted to get out of there as soon as possible.

'At twelve forty-five today we apprehended the man we suspect is responsible for the series of brutal murders of women in Stockholm and the surrounding area. He was taken into custody at his home, where we have also secured what we believe to be vital evidence of the suspect's guilt.'

Sebastian saw Vanja straighten up to look out over the assembled representatives of the press. She met his eyes. Didn't look away. This was obviously a moment she would remember. His daughter. She really was like him, the way he had been in his glory days. A powerful gaze that only grew prouder the more people he had in front of him. He understood how she was feeling. More than she would ever know. She was the one who should be speaking. Not Torkel. She was born to it. One day she would get the chance. The question was whether he would be there to hear her. Even though he knew they were wrong, or at least were refusing to see the whole picture, he couldn't help feeling a certain pride in her. They were so alike, when it came down to it.

403

'We have found the murder weapon, traces of blood and a number of items which can be linked directly to the crimes. We also have DNA from the crime scenes which will now be compared with that of the suspect,' Torkel went on.

One of the keenest journalists got to his feet. He looked as if he couldn't wait any longer. Sebastian recognised him as one of *Expressen*'s most experienced hacks. What was he called – Weber?

'What do you have to say about the rumour that Edward Hinde may be involved in the murders?' he burst out.

Torkel leaned towards the microphone and spoke as clearly as possible. 'I don't want to pre-empt the investigation, but at the moment we are acting on the assumption that the perpetrator acted independently. We can, however, confirm that he was inspired by Edward Hinde's past crimes.'

This seemed to be the trigger for a barrage of fresh questions. The other journalists stayed on the same track.

Hinde. Hinde. Hinde.

No doubt that would make the best headlines. A copycat. Inspired by the great Edward Hinde. That was the way they all wanted it to be.

Clear and simple.

But it was never that simple. Both Sebastian and Edward Hinde knew that.

Sebastian had heard enough. He wasn't interested in simplifications. He walked out. Vanja hardly even glanced in his direction. He realised that he had to find out the truth for himself. Find out Edward Hinde's real reason for giving the name of the murderer at this particular moment.

Riksmord and the media would be satisfied with Ralph Svensson.

He wasn't.

404

The morning had been everything she had hoped it would be.

Thomas's alarm clock had gone off at six twenty. He got up right away. She pretended to be asleep until he had quietly closed the bedroom door. Jenny stretched out in bed. Five years. Married. They had been together for over eight years. They had never been unhappy, but she didn't think they had ever been happier than they were now. She knew this was largely down to the pregnancy. That and Thomas's new job. He hadn't been happy in his old job. Or rather, he had been happy until they acquired a new boss. Kerstin Hanser. She had stepped into the post Thomas had been so sure he would get. Work meant a great deal to her husband.

He wanted to be the best.

He wanted others to realise he was the best.

Sometimes Jenny got the feeling that the reason so few people seemed to reach this conclusion was because Thomas simply wasn't the best. Perhaps he wasn't even that good on every occasion. There was nothing wrong with his ambition, but sometimes he made life unnecessarily complicated. Tried to hide his faults and failings, which paradoxically became increasingly apparent the more he struggled to conceal them. But he had become much better at lowering his guard. Sharing his feelings. At home, anyway. She didn't know what he was like in his new job, but the fact that he had got the job was a gift from above. In the past he had felt inadequate, both at work and at home. Their disappointment at not getting pregnant had eaten away at both of them. At their relationship. Not that she had ever doubted they would make it.

Then he had been shot. In the chest, if you asked him. In the shoulder if you asked anyone else. But wherever the bullet had landed, the whole episode had been a wake-up call. For both of them. It made them realise what was important. It might sound banal, but it was still true.

The job was important, but it wasn't everything.

Children were important, but adoption was always a possibility.

The two of them, together – that was irreplaceable.

And now they were back on track. More than that. She was happy, and she was sure Thomas was happy too. She could hear him working away in the kitchen. To be honest, she knew exactly what the breakfast menu would look like. Every birthday and every wedding anniversary it had consisted of exactly the same things. Nothing wrong with that – she liked scrambled eggs, bacon, toast with raspberry jam, melon and strawberries dipped in chocolate, but it wasn't exactly a surprise. Thomas very rarely surprised her. He might have managed it today if she hadn't gone looking for a memory stick she thought might be in the car. It hadn't been, but she found a little red box that could only contain a piece of jewellery. A ring, to be precise. A beautiful ring. She would pretend to be surprised, but her happiness would be genuine.

She heard Thomas go out – to fetch the ring, presumably – and come back inside. Then she heard him coming up the stairs. She decided not to pretend to be asleep. The door opened and she smiled at him.

She loved him so much.

★ ★ ★

She got to work late.

It wasn't the end of the world. She had been working in the office all week. There was a lot to do, but she felt she was more efficient there than when she was out visiting clients, where the social aspect sometimes seemed to take up more time than the job itself. She was slightly behind with her studies too. The higher level accountancy exam was getting closer. The plan was to become a chartered accountant. At the moment she had a certificate, but that didn't mean a great deal. If she could pass this exam there would be more opportunities and a better salary. There wouldn't be any time to study this evening, though. She was pretty sure that Thomas had booked a table at Karlsson på Taket. He usually did.

Her thoughts were interrupted by a knock on her office door, which was ajar. She looked up to see a man wearing a taxi driver's uniform.

'Jenny Haraldsson?'

'Yes?'

'I've come to pick you up.'

'Sorry?'

'I've come to pick you up,' the man in the doorway repeated.

Jenny glanced at her diary, lying open on the desk. Nothing all day, apart from a note right at the top to show that it was her wedding anniversary.

'There must be some mistake . . .' She looked up at the man again. 'Where are you supposed to be taking me?'

'I think it's meant to be a surprise.' The man was smiling broadly.

The penny dropped as she heard the sound of delighted laughter behind him. Veronica and Amelia, her boss and her colleague, appeared in the doorway.

'Did you know about this?' Jenny asked them.

'It's a bit earlier than I expected,' said Veronica, glancing at her expensive wristwatch. 'But yes, I knew about it.'

'Me too,' said Amelia. 'And I'm so jealous!'

'Where am I going?' Jenny felt a stirring of anticipation.

'We're not saying a word.' Veronica adopted a serious expression. 'You just go off and relax, and we'll see you tomorrow.'

'I'll just finish up and get my things,' Jenny said to the driver.

She almost ran back to her desk. Picked up from work. And she hadn't had a clue. Thomas really had made an effort this time. She quickly saved and closed down the document she had been working on. Relax, Veronica had said. Last spring a leaflet from Hasslö Spa had come through the door at home. Jenny had said how nice it looked, and that she would love to go there. Had Thomas remembered? Fingers crossed. Jenny grabbed her jacket and handbag. This could end up being her best wedding anniversary ever.

'I'm ready.'

'Off we go then!' said the driver, indicating with a sweeping gesture that she should lead the way. He smiled again. He should do it more often, Jenny thought. It softened his otherwise hard features a little, and drew attention away from the ugly red scar running down over his left eye.

They left the office together.

Sebastian had got hold of Ralph Svensson's address from one of the officers standing outside the press conference. Obviously he hadn't officially been booted off the case yet, because the officer, who recognised Sebastian from Liljeholmen and the murder of Annette Willén, was happy to give him a quick update.

He had been involved in the operation at Svensson's apartment but didn't really have anything of substance to report. It had all happened very fast. The aim was to get the target out as quickly as possible. Everything had gone to plan, apart from the fact that Svensson had managed to throw his computer at the wall, destroying it. He had been taken into custody and, as far as the officer knew, had not yet been questioned.

For a moment Sebastian considered trying to arrange an interview with Ralph, but dismissed the idea. Nobody would be allowed access to the suspect without Torkel's permission; that was common practice. The likelihood of Torkel approving a meeting between Sebastian and Ralph Svensson was almost non-existent.

Instead he took a taxi to Västertorp. With a bit of luck he could at least get into the apartment and possibly find something. There was a patrol car parked outside, but no guard on the main door of the apartment block. He went up the stairs, but was stopped by a burly officer at the entrance to Svensson's floor.

It took a fair amount of begging and persuasion, but after a while Ursula appeared in the doorway in her spotless white protective clothing. She looked at him in surprise.

'What are you doing here?'

'I thought I might come in and have a look around. If you've finished?'

She shook her head. 'I don't even know what your position is as far as the investigation goes right now. Are you still with us?'

Sebastian shrugged. 'I don't know.' He was being honest; it was the only way to be with Ursula. 'But I want nothing more than to solve this, you know that. It's just that I have a different view on how to go about it.'

'You have views on most things, that goes without saying, but you're usually better than this. Much better.'

'I'm sorry about that.'

'It's not your fault. We should have kicked you out as soon as you made the connection between yourself and the victims,' she said drily.

'Can I come in? I can usually spot things that might be useful. I promise not to touch anything.'

She looked at him. There was something about Sebastian that was very touching. He had lost his usual footing and fallen on his face right in front of them. She had never seen him so weak. She sought his tired eyes, wanting to look into them.

'If you answer one question.'

'What's that?'

'Come inside.'

She nodded to the officer, who moved aside, allowing Sebastian into the apartment. It was light and sparsely furnished. The kitchen was on the left, and gave the impression of being used only rarely. The living room opened out on the right beyond the hallway; the furniture consisted only of a sofa and a large table. A torch lying on the table. Large floor lamps everywhere. It was hot, mainly due to the absence of either curtains or blinds, allowing the sun to shine straight in. Sebastian followed Ursula into the bedroom.

'He certainly liked things neat and tidy. Everything is in perfect order.' She opened the top drawer and showed him a pile of folded pale blue nightdresses, alongside unopened packets of nylon stockings. 'Creepy, isn't it?'

Sebastian nodded.

Ursula went on: 'If you look in there it'll turn your stomach.'

She pointed to a door which appeared to lead to a walk-in wardrobe or small storeroom. Sebastian started to move towards it, but she stopped him.

'Put these on.' She was holding out a pair of plastic shoe protectors. He bent down and slipped them on over his black shoes. She handed him a pair of sterile gloves. 'And these.'

'So what was your question?'

'Why did you sleep with my sister?'

He looked at her in astonishment. He could have spent a hundred years guessing what she wanted to ask him, and he would never have come up with this.

'I've always wondered,' she added.

Barbro. Such a long time ago. Why? What should he say? What could he say? Nothing. He shook his head.

'I don't think I can answer that.'

Ursula nodded to herself. 'Okay. I'm just trying to find a way to forgive you.'

'Why?'

'Because I have a feeling you need it.'

Their eyes met. Locked. She knew him well.

'But I could be wrong,' she said lightly. 'Take a look around if you like.'

She turned and went back to the kitchen. He watched her go, but still didn't know what to say. He would hurt her whatever he did, and that wasn't what he wanted.

He opened the door Ursula had indicated. The space inside was small. A bench along one wall with a printer on it. Boxes of photographic paper. A sheet of hardboard fixed to another wall. Sebastian went over to it. Four bundles of pictures were hanging from bulldog clips, with the numbers 1, 2, 3 and 4 circled in thick felt tip above them. As Sebastian got closer he could see what the pictures showed. His women. All four of them. Terrified. Photographed from what could best be described as the perspective of a god, with the photographer looking down on them. Telling them exactly what to do. Sebastian put on the gloves and took down the bundle under number three. Katharina Granlund. Naked and weeping in the first picture. Dead, staring straight ahead in the last. He flicked through the other bundles. Quickly. Didn't want to get caught up in the details. The final picture was the same each time. The knife that had sliced through their throats. Sebastian felt sick. He wanted to run away as fast as he could. As if his flight could undo what had been done. But he stayed where he was. Replaced the photographs. Looked away. Heard Ursula moving around in the kitchen. She was right. But she was also wrong. How could he ever be forgiven after these pictures?

411

He went back into the bedroom, mainly to get away from the horror. The small room looked much like the rest of the apartment. The only difference was the pale, neatly made single bed. Just as many floor lamps. Torch on the bedside table. Just as light. But after those pictures on the wall, the light was simply a lie. This was the darkest apartment he had ever been in. He looked inside the only wardrobe. Perfectly ironed shirts and trousers hanging in a row. Underneath, in wire baskets, batteries and torches were arranged with military precision. In more baskets below those lay socks and underpants.

Ralph Svensson had prioritised torches above his underwear. The fact that he had some kind of obsessive compulsive disorder was beyond doubt. The real question was how many diagnoses could be applied to him. If anyone even cared. Sebastian was no longer interested.

He picked up one of the larger torches. Pressed the black rubber button. The torch came on immediately. New battery. Ready for action. Ready to spread light all around. As he was about to put it back he caught sight of something that had been underneath the torch. Hidden. It looked like a driver's licence. Carefully he picked it up and turned it over.

A picture of Trolle Hermansson stared at him. The icy chill inside him was instantaneous. So was the pain. He had to look at it again. Read the words. Several times. And every time they said Carl Trolle Hermansson.

That was why he hadn't answered his phone.

That was why he wasn't at home.

He had found the person who was following Sebastian. He might even have saved Anna. But he had paid with his life.

There was no other explanation. Why else would Trolle's driver's licence be in this darkest of all apartments?

Once again, Sebastian had lost.

Everything he touched was torn from his grasp. Brutally and violently. That was the truth. The only truth, which made itself clear to him over and over again. For a long time he had tried to fight it, keep it away from him. Blamed everyone but himself. God, his mother, his father, Anna, Vanja – everyone, in fact, except the one person who was actually responsible. Because there was only one person carrying the guilt now. He replaced the torch carefully and slipped the driver's licence into his pocket.

It was over now.

He gave up.

Suddenly she was standing behind him. 'He had a computer as well. Billy's going to go through it. Since he threw it at the wall, there's bound to be something on it.'

He didn't reply. She turned to go back to her work.

'Ursula?'

She didn't reply, but she did stop.

'I think I do need forgiveness. But I don't know how that can ever be possible.'

'Nor do I, Sebastian. But those who know about these things say that honesty usually works best.'

She left the room.

He didn't say any more.

But he could feel Trolle's driver's licence in his pocket. The burden of guilt on his shoulders.

He would never be able to receive forgiveness.

Never.

★ ★ ★

He was sitting on a stone outside the apartment block when they pulled up next to the patrol car. He had been sitting there for a good half hour without moving. Holding the licence in his hand, as if that might lessen the pain. They got out and walked towards the building. Vanja first, followed by Torkel. They were in the middle of a discussion, talking excitedly. As if he wasn't there. Which was true, of course. He wasn't really there anymore.

Vanja seemed proud of her first TV appearance. 'Anna saw it on the news. She called from Gran's.'

'How is your grandmother?' Torkel asked sympathetically as he caught up with her. 'I heard she wasn't too well.'

Sebastian slowly got to his feet and put the driver's licence back in his pocket. Took out his police ID card instead. Went to meet them.

'She's much better. Anna's coming home,' Vanja replied.

'I'm glad to hear that.'

Only now did they appear to notice the man walking towards them. They stopped and waited for him in silence. No apparent emotion. As if they were encountering a memory they had already put behind them.

Sebastian was standing in front of them.

'We need to talk,' said Torkel.

Sebastian's intention was to make it easy for them. He held out the ID card he had been given at the beginning of the week. 'I'm going home now.'

'Okay.' Torkel took the card and nodded to his former colleague and friend.

'I'm sorry about everything.'

'At least we've got him,' Torkel said. He had no desire to quarrel.

Nor did Sebastian. But he had to warn them, even if they almost certainly wouldn't listen to him. 'Hinde isn't done yet – I hope you realise that.'

'What else can he do?' he heard Vanja say.

'I don't know. But he's not finished.' He pushed his hands into his pockets. Felt Trolle's driver's licence. 'But I am. It's your problem now.'

He moved to walk away, but couldn't quite do it. This was probably his last moment with Vanja. He wouldn't be following her anymore. The dream was over. Because that's what it had been. A dream. This was the only goodbye he would ever have. The last few minutes with the daughter he had never really had.

The daughter he had wanted so much.

He almost whispered to her, 'Be careful. Promise me you'll be careful.'

She couldn't understand his mournful expression at all. 'Do you really think it wasn't Ralph?'

'No, no. But do you know what worries me?'

'The fact that you didn't solve the case?' Her voice was as sharp as a knife. Still caught up in the conflict he had left behind.

'No. The fact that you refuse to see that Edward is behind the whole thing. He will never give up. Never.'

He walked away.

It wasn't much of a goodbye.

But it was all he would get.

Ralph Svensson.

One of the cleaners. So near, yet completely out of reach. The day was ruined for Haraldsson. Not even the prospect of dinner with Jenny could cheer him up. Riksmord must have got the name from Hinde. They picked up Ralph only an hour or so after Vanja Lithner left Lövhaga. Without speaking to him. Even though it had been one of the conditions for allowing her to see Hinde at all. She had broken an agreement. He should have known. You just couldn't trust anyone who worked for Riksmord. They constantly disappointed him. What could Vanja have offered him that immediately produced a name? Haraldsson had built up a relationship, proved himself ready to work with Hinde, delivered. What did she have that he didn't? The answer was obvious, but surely they hadn't . . . She couldn't have agreed to . . . Admittedly they had been alone in the interview room, but still. She didn't seem the type. A ringtone interrupted his thoughts. Abba. He picked up his mobile and looked at the display. A number he didn't recognise.

'Thomas Haraldsson.'

'Afternoon, Västerås Cabs here,' he heard a male voice say. 'You ordered a taxi for today.'

Haraldsson frowned. Were they ringing to confirm the booking? It seemed a bit late. He glanced at his watch. They were supposed to be picking Jenny up right now.

'That's right,' he said warily.

'We're at the pickup address, but there's nobody here.'

'Nobody there?' Haraldsson assumed the man meant that Jenny wasn't there. Anything else seemed highly unlikely. The company wasn't very big, but surely somebody should be there.

So naturally his next question was: 'Are you in the right place?'

'Engelbrektsgatan 6. Her colleagues said another driver came and picked her up earlier today.'

'So you sent two drivers?'

'No, that's why I'm calling. Did you book a different cab?'

'No.'

Haraldsson didn't understand any of this. Something had clearly gone wrong somewhere. He found it very difficult to believe that it could be down to him. The whole day had been meticulously planned. The driver passed him over to Veronica, who said exactly the same thing. A man had collected Jenny about an hour ago. He was wearing a taxi driver's uniform. A big guy with a ponytail and a scar over one eye. He'd joked about it being a surprise, so he must have been the cab Thomas had ordered.

Haraldsson ended the call none the wiser. The taxi firm must have messed it up, but in that case where was Jenny? He scrolled down to her name in the list of contacts and called her mobile. No reply. When the voicemail kicked in, he left a message asking her to call him. Ended the call. Rang home. The answering machine clicked on. He left the same message there, perhaps with a little more anxiety in his voice. Ended the call. Thought for a moment and went back to his desk. Opened his web browser and Googled the name of the spa. Found the number and called them. At least he got an answer this time. Jenny Haraldsson hadn't turned up yet. But there was still fifteen minutes to go before her booking; should they get her to call him when she arrived? Yes, Haraldsson said. They should.

He leaned back in his chair. He wasn't really worried, but it was unlike her not to answer her mobile. He let his mind wander, trying to find a thread that might eventually lead to an explanation for what had happened. Where she was.

The man who picked up Jenny had known it was a surprise, Veronica had said. Not many people knew that. Not even Västerås Cabs, it struck him. He had merely booked a cab to collect her from work. He hadn't mentioned that the person being picked up didn't know anything about it. The only person with whom he had discussed the surprise was Veronica, so that Jenny could have the afternoon off. She was the only one who knew.

She and Edward Hinde.

He went cold all over.

Could Hinde have anything to do with this? It seemed impossible. Unbelievable. He and Hinde had worked together. Hinde had got everything he asked for. If there was anyone who should be dissatisfied with the outcome of their conversations, it was Haraldsson. Why should Hinde go anywhere near Jenny? He had shown a certain amount of interest in her, that was true. Asked to keep her photograph. But Hinde was safely behind bars. Even if Hinde had been working with Ralph Svensson on the outside, as Riksmord seemed to believe, he too was in custody. Riksmord had arrested him almost an hour before Jenny was collected by the mysterious driver.

For a brief moment he toyed with the idea of confronting Hinde, but he decided against it. Firstly, it was unthinkable that Hinde could have had anything to do with Jenny's disappearance. Possible, he corrected himself. Possible disappearance. There was probably a completely natural explanation for what had happened.

Secondly, his direct confrontations with Hinde had turned out to be less than successful.

Haraldsson pushed away the frightening thoughts. He was being paranoid. He had spent too much time with Edward Hinde. That horrible man had managed to crawl under his skin. He tried Jenny's mobile again. Heard it ringing, no reply, voicemail. Haraldsson couldn't shake off the feeling that something was wrong. He picked up the 'Visions and Aims' folder again, but soon put it down. Opened his email inbox. There were a number of messages that needed answers, but he couldn't concentrate.

Someone had picked her up.

She had gone with this person and disappeared.

He couldn't just sit here and carry on as if nothing had happened. Even if he was pretty sure nothing had happened.

Haraldsson left his office and Lövhaga and went home.

Edward Hinde was sitting cross-legged on his bed. Eyes closed. Calm, steady breathing.

Focused.

Composed.

Turned in on himself.

As soon as he heard the first rumours about Ralph spreading through the unit, he had got to work. He had made it known in the vicinity of one of the guards that he wasn't feeling well, and was therefore going back to his cell for a rest. Once he was there he closed the door firmly behind him, slid under the bed and immediately began to unscrew the cover of the air vent. He worked quickly, well aware that this was the weakest point in his plan. It was highly unlikely that one of his fellow inmates would walk in uninvited, but if they did, it would be a distraction, nothing more. If a guard opened the door, though, that would be the end of it. The stress of the situation helped him. He had never before removed the cover in such a short time. He reached in and took out the fork he had stolen from the canteen yesterday, along with the jar he had got from Thomas Haraldsson.

Seven hundred and fifty grams of pickled beetroot.

Hinde replaced the cover, but didn't screw it in place. He got up, tucked the fork into his sock and slipped the jar of beetroot under his top. This was the next risky enterprise. Even if he kept his hands cupped around his stomach as if he was in pain, a watchful eye might spot the jar. But he had to go for it. Stooping slightly, he left the cell and hurried towards the toilets.

Hands around his stomach. Rapid, shuffling steps. A man in dire straits.

Once inside a toilet cubicle he took out the jar and placed it on the edge of the washbasin. He pulled out a thick bundle of paper

418

towels from the dispenser and spread them out on the lid of the toilet. Then he opened the jar, fished out several slices with the fork and let them drain off before laying them on the paper towels and beginning to mash them thoroughly. When there was nothing left but mush, he scooped it up with the fork and shovelled it into his mouth. Then he repeated the process until the jar was empty. It got quite difficult towards the end. Seven hundred and fifty grams of beetroot was more than he had thought. Before he left the toilet he picked up the jar and gulped down the remaining liquid. Then he rinsed the jar, tucked it under his top once more, slid the fork inside his sock and went back to his cell. He didn't bother hiding the jar this time, but simply placed it behind the desk. He sat down on the bed, drew his legs up beneath him and closed his eyes.

Planning. Patience. Determination.

He had now been sitting on the bed for about an hour. Roland Johansson should have completed his task in Västerås. Ready for the next job. High time for phase two.

Slowly and deliberately Hinde straightened his legs and stood up, only to slide under the bed once more and remove the bottle he had been given by Haraldsson.

Ipecac.

Two hundred and fifty millilitres.

He unscrewed the cap and knocked back the contents of the bottle in two gulps. It didn't taste good. But that didn't matter; he wouldn't be keeping it down for long. Before he left the cell he decided to hide the empty bottle and the beetroot jar in the air vent after all. It would be stupid to fail just because he had been lazy and careless. However, he could feel that he wouldn't have time to screw the cover back in place. His stomach was gurgling. He went out into the dayroom, still with his hands cupped in front of him. His jaws were tightly clenched and he could feel that he had actually started sweating. He stopped in the middle of the room.

Showtime!

When he felt the first indications that his stomach was beginning to cramp, he collapsed. Screaming. Everyone else in the room stopped dead, staring at him. Hinde clutched his stomach and writhed around on the floor. He took a breath so that he could scream again, but before he could make a sound the contents of

419

his stomach came up in a violent cascade of vomit. The inmates standing closest to him jumped aside in disgust. The guards who had begun to move towards him when he collapsed stopped dead, unsure of what to do. It was a well-known fact that the security staff knew very little about physical complaints. Hinde was counting on it, and those who were on duty today didn't disappoint him. They hadn't a clue what to do. Just as he had planned. He heaved again. Through tear-filled eyes Hinde saw to his immense satisfaction that what he had produced this time was thick and almost black in colour. The right consistency, the right colour. The beetroot had had time to react with his stomach acid, and most of the red colouring had disappeared. Unless you smelled it at really close quarters, it would be impossible to distinguish from internal bleeding. Hinde calculated that no one would want to stick their nose into the substance he now brought up for the third time, with slightly less violence than before. One of the guards was speaking into his two-way radio, summoning help, while the other seemed to be wondering how to get to Hinde without stepping in the contents of his guts. The cramps began to ease. Hinde breathed in through his nose and swallowed some of the vomit that had got stuck there. It tasted of beetroot and ipecac. He bent double and screamed with pain one more time, before switching tactics; he started rolling from side to side, whimpering helplessly. One of the guards came over, crouched down and gently placed a hand on his shoulder. Hinde coughed, struggling with what appeared to be severe pain.

'Help me,' he snivelled feebly. 'Please, help me.'

'We will,' said the guard.

Little did he know how right he was.

Haraldsson had got home in record time. Broken every speed limit and traffic regulation you could think of. His anxiety grew, pushing him on. He screeched to a halt in the drive, switched off the engine and leapt out.

The spa had been in touch. A different woman from the one he had spoken to earlier. Jenny Haraldsson hadn't turned up. Did he know if she had just been delayed, or . . . ? He told the truth; he didn't think she would be coming. The woman informed him apologetically that he would be liable for seventy-five per cent of the fee, since it was such a late cancellation. He didn't care. An unnecessary expense was the least of his problems. He unlocked the front door and stepped inside.

'Jenny!'

Silence. Without taking off his shoes he moved through the hallway.

'Jenny! Are you here?'

The same silence. He walked quickly through the living room, into the kitchen, glanced in the combined guest room and sewing room. Yanked open the door of the utility room and toilet.

Empty.

Silent.

He went back into the hallway and up the stairs. A few steps from the top he paused. Strange, how the brain worked. He hadn't been thinking about anything at all. The fear had pushed everything else aside. But now he suddenly remembered. Hinde and the four murders in the nineties. All exactly the same. The copycat, Ralph Svensson. 'The Summer Psycho'. Four women this time too. He had read about them. The MO identical.

Tied up. Raped. With their throats cut.

At home.

In their bedrooms.

Haraldsson looked up. At the bedroom. His and Jenny's bedroom. Where they had had breakfast and made love this morning. The door was closed. It wasn't usually closed. Why would they close it when no one was home? A small sound broke the silence, and Haraldsson realised it had come from him. A little whimper of pain. And fear. He had to force himself to carry on up the stairs. Step by step. When he reached the top he grabbed hold of the last part of the banister to stop himself from falling backwards. He couldn't take his eyes off that closed door. Couldn't get it out of his mind. Particularly now, at the height of summer, it would be far too hot to sleep in there at night if the door had been closed all day. She hadn't closed it. Why would she have closed it? He took a deep breath and let the air filter out slowly between tight lips before he was able to move forward. He jumped when he heard Abba. His mobile. He grabbed it without looking at the display.

'Haraldsson.'

He hoped it would be her. That he would hear her voice telling him that everything was fine, there had just been a silly misunderstanding.

'It's Victor Bäckman,' he heard on the other end of the line. Not her. Everything wasn't fine. The disappointment swept over him, and he had to use all his strength to stay on his feet. He couldn't speak, but there was no need. Victor carried straight on. 'Edward Hinde has collapsed in the dayroom; he brought up a lot of blood.'

'What?'

'He seems to be in a really bad way. We can't take care of him here. Something to do with his stomach, I think.'

'Okay . . .' Haraldsson heard what Victor was saying, but couldn't really understand why he was being told this right now. He was still finding it difficult to process the information.

'The ambulance will be here shortly, that's why I'm calling you. You need to approve a transfer to the hospital.'

'Do I?'

'Yes. Shall we transfer him?'

As if from nowhere, another thought came into his head.

An image.

A memory.

Hinde is sitting on the bed in his cell. Haraldsson is standing in the doorway. Gooseflesh on his forearms. Hinde's quiet voice.

'Say yes.'

'To what?'

'You will understand when and to what. Just say yes.'

'Are you still there?' Victor asked in his ear.

'What? Yes.'

'Do we transfer him? Yes or no?'

'Just say yes.'

Haraldsson tried to grasp the significance of what he had just heard, the connection he had just made. Hinde had known he was going to be ill. Had known that this conversation was going to take place. That this question would be asked. He must have done. But how? Was he just faking – or did it have something to do with the things Haraldsson had given him? Beetroot and a bottle from the chemist's. Some kind of South American name, that's what it sounded like. Icacaca . . . something. Why an illness, genuine or otherwise? Because he wanted to be moved. Get out. Escape. Should he warn Victor? Tell him about his suspicions?

'Just say yes.'

There was no scope there for a warning, an attempt to prevent something from happening. It was a simple exhortation to say one word. Give his consent. Obey orders. He tried, but he just couldn't get his head around the consequences. Couldn't weigh up the pros and cons. Everything was chaos. The bedroom door was closed. He took the last few steps. He had to know.

'Thomas? Are you there?'

Haraldsson placed his hand on the door handle. Took a deep breath. Closed his eyes. Prayed to a God he didn't even believe in. With a brief exhalation he pushed open the door. Quickly, like ripping off a plaster. Prepared for the worst, but at the same time not prepared at all.

The room was empty.

Jenny was still only missing.

'Yes,' he said. It sounded like a dry croak.

'What did you say?' Victor asked.

Haraldsson cleared his throat. 'Yes,' he repeated in a firmer tone of voice. 'Transfer him.'

'Okay. Where are you? Are you coming back later?'

Haraldsson ended the call. Put the phone back in his pocket. Stood in the doorway of his empty bedroom and began to weep.

Before Ursula finished for the day she felt she had to check with SKL, the national forensics lab in Linköping, that the two sterile packages containing DNA samples from the apartment had actually arrived. They had gone by special courier some hours ago, and the plan was that Torkel should be able to make use of a preliminary report when questioning Svensson the following day. She managed to get hold of the chief forensic pathologist, Walter Steen, who reassured her. Everything was looking good, SKL had started work already, and he would personally ensure that they delivered the necessary information the following day. That was enough for Ursula; she had known Steen for some time, and he was a man of his word. Satisfied, she left Ralph Svensson's stuffy apartment. The relief shift had just arrived, and she had a brief word with the two new officers in the stairwell, emphasising that no one but her was to be allowed access, at least not without her permission. She left them her home and mobile numbers to be on the safe side, and went down the stairs. It had been an incredibly intense day, and she felt weary in both body and soul. She stopped outside the main door and enjoyed the summery smell of warm grass for a while. In spite of the tiredness she was content. The apartment had turned out to be a veritable treasure chest, and she had found herself having to prioritise rather than engage in a thorough search. She still had many hours of work left, but she was convinced that they had already secured sufficient evidence to ensure that Ralph Svensson would be convicted of all four murders, with or without a confession. That was her real aim: to find evidence so strong that the suspect's own account no longer weighed so heavily. That was when she knew she had done a good job – when the truth became objective and measurable.

She set off towards her car, tentatively wondering whether to call Torkel. He and Vanja had called in after the press conference. They must have bumped into Sebastian outside, because the first thing Torkel had said was that Sebastian was off the case from now on. Vanja in particular seemed relieved. She was bubbling with energy, and spat out a few brief, brutal remarks about the impossible man she disliked so much. Ursula herself felt sad more than anything. Not because she thought Sebastian had brought anything to the table this time, but she remembered him from the old days, when he had possessed an amazing, innate power. The man who had left Ralph Svensson's apartment with his shoulders hunched was not the same man. Nobody should have to fall so far. So hard. Not even Sebastian Bergman. So she could never share Vanja's joy.

Before he left, Torkel had lingered in the hallway for a moment. She recognised the glow in his eyes from similar occasions when they were out on a job. It always appeared when they made a major breakthrough in an investigation; it was as if they could somehow hold on to the moment by being together.

But she wasn't going to let it happen this time. It didn't feel right, somehow. In some strange way, it was a completely different matter when they were in another town. It wasn't as serious. Admittedly it was more tempting now, but it was also slightly sordid. And then there was Mikael.

She got in the car and headed into the city without really knowing where she was going. Perhaps the compromise would be to go into work, but she didn't really want to do that. She decided to go home.

★ ★ ★

Mikael was there. He was sitting on the sofa when she walked in.

'You look tired,' she commented.

He nodded in response and got up. 'Coffee?'

'Please.'

He went into the kitchen and switched on the coffee machine while Ursula sat down by the open window. It was blissfully quiet outside, and she enjoyed hearing him bustling about in the other room. She had made the right decision. Rules were rules, and just because you'd broken them once, that didn't mean you had to do it again. She had to admit that there was something about Mikael that calmed her. He might not be the most passionate person in the world, but he always had time for her. That was worth a great deal.

'I heard on the radio that you'd arrested someone,' he called from the kitchen.

'Yes, I've spent the whole afternoon in the suspect's apartment.'

'Did you find anything?'

'Loads. He's guilty.'

'Good.'

Mikael came back into the living room.

'Come and sit down,' she said, patting the seat next to her on the sofa, but he shook his head.

'Not right now. We need to talk.'

She was taken aback. Sat up straight and looked at him. Mikael didn't often want to talk, or expect her to listen.

'Has something happened to Bella?'

'This has nothing to do with Bella. This is about us.'

She stiffened. His voice was different, somehow. As if he had practised what he was going to say. As if he had been preparing for this for a long time.

'I've met someone, and I want to be honest with you.'

At first she didn't understand what he was saying. Eventually she had to ask, even though she suspected she knew the answer already. 'I don't really understand; are you saying you've met someone else?'

'Yes. But we're not seeing each other at the moment. I didn't think it was fair on her. Or you.'

She looked at him in shock. 'You've been with someone else and now it's over?'

'I haven't been with someone else. We've seen each other a few times, and now I've put things on hold. For the time being. I wanted to talk to you first.'

She sat there, lost for words. She had no idea what to do next. Anger would have been the simplest option. Clean and cutting. But she couldn't find it. She couldn't actually find anything.

'Ursula, I really have tried lately, with the trip to Paris and everything. But I haven't got the strength anymore. I'm sorry. It's my fault.'

His fault.

If only it were that simple.

427

The ambulance from Uppsala turned into Lövhaga precisely eighteen minutes after the call to the emergency services. Fatima Olsson jumped out and went round the back to get the trolley. She was glad they had arrived. On the way to the hospital she would travel in the back with the patient, which meant she could avoid sitting next to Kenneth Hammarén. She didn't like him. For the simple reason that he didn't like her. She didn't know why. Maybe it was because she was born in Iraq, or because she was better qualified – she was an intensive care nurse, he was a paramedic – and therefore better paid, or because she was a woman. It could be a combination of all three, or there might be some other reason altogether. She hadn't asked. She had been with him for two weeks now, and she intended to speak to her boss as soon as she got the chance, and to ask if she could work with someone else in future. He was reasonably good at his job, but he was bad-tempered and always negative towards her. Took every opportunity to have a go, to correct her or to criticise what she was doing. It only happened with her. She had seen him with others, and his attitude had been completely different. It was definitely her. He just didn't like her.

Kenneth got out, always thirty seconds after her so that he wouldn't have to help. Fatima placed the emergency bag on the trolley, leaving the back doors of the ambulance open – they were inside the prison grounds, after all – and set off towards the secure unit where a guard was waiting for them at the door. As usual Kenneth led the way, five metres in front of her.

The dayroom was empty except for Hinde, who was still lying on the floor. One of the guards had placed a pillow under his head. The rest of the inmates were back in their cells. Fatima quickly assessed the situation. Middle-aged man. Violent vomiting,

428

the consistency of coffee grounds. Pain in the stomach, judging by the position in which he was lying. Possibly a bleeding ulcer. Definitely internal bleeding. Fatima bent down.

'Hello, can you hear me?'

The man on the floor opened his eyes and nodded feebly.

'My name's Fatima; can you tell me what happened?'

'I got a pain in my stomach and then . . .' His voice seemed to fail him. He made a vague, sweeping gesture in the direction of the vomit-covered floor.

Fatima nodded. 'Are you in pain now?'

'Yes, but it's a bit better.'

'You're coming with us.'

She gave Kenneth a challenging look, and they worked together in silence to lift the man onto the trolley and secure him. He didn't weigh much. He seemed very weak. They would definitely need the siren on the way back.

The guard who had been sitting with the man walked with them down the corridor to the waiting ambulance. He and Fatima got the patient into the ambulance without any help from Kenneth, and as Fatima began to close the doors the guard moved to climb in.

'What are you doing?'

'I'm coming with you.'

Edward lay there listening with interest. This was the part of the plan over which he had the least control. He had no idea what the arrangements would be when it came to accompanying an inmate being transferred to hospital. How many guards? Would they be armed? Inside the unit they had only batons and Tasers. Was it different during a transfer? Would there be a car following them? Two? Would they wait for a police escort? He had no idea.

He could hear the guard explaining to Fatima who Edward Hinde was, and that there was absolutely no question of the ambulance being allowed to leave without supervision. The guard who was now standing by his feet would be travelling in the back with Hinde and Fatima, and a colleague was on his way to sit with the driver. Two, then. Separate and possibly armed. But that still shouldn't cause any problems. At least there was no talk of waiting for the police.

The other guard came running and got straight in the front. His colleague jumped in the back and Fatima showed him where to sit. They closed the doors. Fatima knocked twice on the pane of frosted glass separating them from the driver's compartment, and the ambulance moved off. After just a few metres the siren was switched on. Hinde could feel the tension building inside him. So far everything had gone exactly according to plan, but the most difficult and risky part of the operation lay ahead.

Fatima spoke to him. 'Are you allergic to any form of medication?'

'No.'

'You've lost a lot of fluids and salts, so I'm going to put you on a saline drip.'

She turned around in the swaying ambulance, opened a drawer and with practised movements took out a drip which she hung on a hook above Edward. Then she got up, opened a cupboard higher up and took out a small cannula. She sat down beside him while at the same time applying a compress to a dispenser containing antiseptic. She quickly pressed the damp square to the crook of his arm.

'You'll feel a sharp prick.' Adeptly she inserted the cannula, taped it in place, straightened out the tube leading from the bag and fastened it to the cannula. Then she leaned forward to turn on the drip. Her breasts were right in front of Hinde's eyes. He thought about Vanja. The solution began to run into his vein.

'Okay, I really need to ask you a few questions. Do you think you could manage that?'

Edward nodded and smiled bravely. Fatima returned the smile.

'So what's your ID number?'

He didn't have time to answer; the ambulance braked sharply then stopped completely. Through the partition wall he could just about hear the driver swearing. He lay there on tenterhooks. It could of course have been some careless driver who had forced them to stop, but it could also be the beginning of his final step towards freedom. He saw the guard stiffen, on full alert, as Fatima apologised for the sudden braking. Edward looked around in the ambulance for some kind of weapon. Preferably a knife or something similar. Nothing. Besides which he was fastened to the trolley. He wouldn't be able to help. All he could do was wait.

★ ★ ★

Kenneth swore again and pressed the horn. Somebody must own the red Saab that had been so carelessly parked on the left-hand side of the road, making it impossible for them to get past. Just after a bend, too. Idiot. It was sheer luck that his reactions were so quick, otherwise they would have crashed straight into it. Kenneth sounded the horn again. Where was the fucking idiot who owned the fucking car? He couldn't be too far away. In which case he should have heard the siren. Seen the blue light. Typical. Only two hundred metres until they reached the main road, where he would have been able to edge his way past. There was no chance on this stupid little road. A fence on one side of the Saab. A deep ditch on the other. He sounded the horn yet again.

The man sitting beside him seemed nervous. Kept looking around. His hand resting on some kind of stun gun in his belt.

'What's going on?' Kenneth asked.

'I don't know. Can you go back?'

Kenneth shrugged and put the ambulance in reverse. He saw the man next to him unhook the two-way radio from his belt and bring it up to his mouth.

Then the world exploded.

★ ★ ★

In the back of the ambulance they suddenly heard, above the sirens, the sound of two shots and breaking glass. It seemed as if everything was happening at once. A shadow flew past the frosted window and something splashed all over it. Something dark. Running down the glass. The guard sitting next to Edward leapt to his feet. Fatima screamed, clamped her forearms over her ears, locked her hands behind her neck and bent forward. She's lived in a war zone, Hinde thought as he saw her reaction. He simply lay there contemplating the chaos that had broken out in just seconds. He heard three loud thuds against the side of the ambulance.

'What's happening?' Fatima yelled. The guard had the Taser in his hand, but nobody to point it at. Edward lay motionless. He had no intention of drawing attention to himself unnecessarily.

Suddenly the sirens stopped. Instead of a constant racket in the background, there was now total silence. A worrying silence. The guard turned his head, listening for noises from outside. Nothing. Fatima slowly straightened up and stared at the guard in shock.

'What's happening?' she whispered.

'Somebody's trying to get him out,' the guard replied, still on full alert.

Almost as if to confirm his statement, the back door was yanked open. Two more shots were fired. The first bullet went straight through the soft tissue immediately below the ribs, came out through the back and shattered the frosted glass. The second went into the middle of the chest. The guard collapsed. Fatima screamed. Roland Johansson pulled open the other door so that he could see her, and aimed his gun at her.

'No,' Edward said tersely.

Roland lowered the gun and climbed into the cramped space, which seemed to shrink even further with the huge man in there. In silence he began to unfasten Edward's restraints. Once Edward was free, he sat up. What he really wanted to do was run outside. Jump in the air. He had to exert every scrap of willpower to avoid losing control. It was so close now. He looked up at the saline drip. Reached up and unhooked it.

'I'll take this with me.'

No reaction. Fatima was in shock. She was rocking back and forth, staring into space. Roland held out his arm to offer Edward support as he got off the bed and stepped down from the ambulance. He was still weak from his little performance in the dayroom. Slowly they walked along the side of the ambulance. Stopped halfway.

'Will you be okay?'

'Yes. Thank you.'

Edward leaned against the vehicle. Roland left him with a pat on the shoulder and went to open the door on the passenger side. Without any apparent effort he pulled out the guard, who was slumped in a motionless heap. A bleeding wound in his throat just below the jawline and one below the collarbone, Edward noticed as Roland dragged the guard past him towards the back doors. Alive, but not for much longer. He heard Fatima scream as Roland more or less threw the dying guard into the back of the ambulance. Edward closed his eyes.

Roland went round the other side. When he shot the guard, the driver had tried to make a run for it, but he hadn't been anywhere near fast enough. Roland had caught up with him, grabbed him,

432

and banged his head three times against the side of the ambulance. Now he seized the unconscious driver, chucked him in the back with the others and climbed in after him. He ignored the guards. One was dead, the other dying. He unhooked the handcuffs from their belts and turned the driver over. Secured his hands behind his back, then turned to Fatima, who was still sitting on her chair beside the trolley.

'Your turn.'

Fatima shook her head, incapable of movement. Roland stepped over to her, pulled her up from the chair and pushed her down on the floor next to the others. She offered no resistance as he fastened her hands behind her back. He grabbed a blanket, got out and walked past Edward to the passenger door. He began to sweep out the shards of glass that were all over the driver's compartment. When he had got rid of the majority, he spread the blanket over the passenger seat, then helped Edward settle there with his drip. Before he closed the door he smashed the rest of the glass so that the window looked open rather than broken. With Edward taken care of he went over to the red Saab and took a roll of gaffer tape from the back seat. Returned to the ambulance and the four occupants in the back. Bound the ankles of the driver and the woman, just to be on the safe side . . . Roland finished off by winding the tape twice around their heads, covering their mouths. He jumped out, closed the doors, got into the driver's seat and turned the key. The whole thing had taken less than five minutes. No one had seen them. Nothing was moving. No sirens approaching. Only the sounds of the forest.

They set off. Edward glanced in the rear-view mirror and saw the red Saab getting smaller and smaller. They were putting it behind them. Leaving it. Just as he was putting Lövhaga behind him. Leaving it.

Now he could, he would, start looking to the future.

★ ★ ★

Roland was driving just above the speed limit. Edward was fairly sure that this road wasn't a high priority when it came to police speed checks, at least not in the case of emergency response vehicles, but it was stupid to take the risk. An encounter with the authorities wouldn't be the best idea for a number of reasons. They would want to know about the broken window. There were bloodstains in the driver's compartment. Roland wasn't wearing the right clothes. An observant police officer would notice all of those things. Oh well, they would cross that bridge if they came to it.

It was a beautiful day. The green shades of summer everywhere. Edward almost felt dizzy as he contemplated the billowing countryside opening out around him. So much space. The last fourteen years seemed even more limited and enclosed now that he had a different perspective. Now that he could see what he had been denied. He relished every fresh view that appeared along the twisting road. The wind tugged at his thin hair through the broken window. He closed his eyes again. Breathed deeply. Allowed himself to relax. The air seemed lighter. Different. Each breath made him stronger. This was how it felt to breathe as a free man. Roland slowed down. Edward opened his eyes. They had reached the E18. Half an hour, and they would be in Stockholm. He turned to Roland.

'Have you got a phone?'

Roland reached into his pocket and handed over his mobile. Edward keyed in a number from memory and waited for an answer.

Haraldsson was standing by the bedroom window. He had been standing there ever since he opened the door and found the room empty. He had walked over to the window, past the unmade double bed. What else could he do? Look for Jenny? Where? He had no idea. He was literally paralysed.

The fear, the terror, Jenny, the job.

In the garden the men planting the apple tree had started work. He saw them arrive. Watched them walk around the garden. Pointing and discussing. They agreed on the best spot and began to measure and dig. Fetched bags of compost. Just an ordinary working day. Ordinary lives, just a few metres away from him. A reality that made sense.

It was difficult to think clearly. What could he do? He couldn't be involved. Mustn't be involved. Jenny was gone. He was involved. But that didn't mean anybody else had to find out. Please, let nothing have happened to Jenny. His thoughts jumped and skipped like a needle on a scratchy old vinyl LP.

Hinde was being transferred. Had probably already left Lövhaga. He wanted to be transferred. Something was going to happen. What? Should Haraldsson alert the police? /skip/

Would that save Jenny? Jenny was gone. /skip/

What reason could he give for contacting the police? He could hardly say that he had carried out certain errands for Hinde, and that one of them had led to Hinde being allowed to leave the prison. That wouldn't just be career suicide. That would be a punishable offence. /skip/

Jenny. Where was she? She just couldn't be dead. What would he do? How could he live without her? /skip/

Hinde hadn't left Lövhaga, and Ralph had already been arrested at the time when Jenny disappeared. What did that mean? That Hinde was in contact with more than one person on the outside? /skip/

Ingrid Marie couldn't have a daddy in prison. /skip/

Should he tell someone? Could he tell someone? What reason would he give for his suspicions? Perhaps Hinde was actually ill. Perhaps he had gone to the hospital. In which case a warning that this might be an attempted escape would seem odd to say the least. And if he thought something like that might be on the cards, why had he given permission for the transfer? /skip/

'I've never killed a pregnant woman.' /skip/

What would happen if he contacted the police?

What would happen if he didn't?

His phone rang again. Haraldsson could feel his heart beating faster with hope as he took it out of his pocket. A number he didn't recognise. Not Jenny. He answered anyway.

'Haraldsson.'

'This is Edward Hinde.'

Haraldsson's mind went completely blank. It was as if all the thoughts that had been crowding his head before had been blown away.

'Where are you calling from?' was the only thing he could come up with.

'That doesn't matter. You did what I asked you to do, so you can have your question.'

Haraldsson heard every single word. Heard, but didn't understand.

'What?'

'I keep my promises, Thomas. You said yes, which was what I wanted, and for that I will answer a question.'

'What have you . . .'

'Wait, Thomas,' Edward interrupted him. Haraldsson immediately stopped speaking. 'I'm not telling you what to do,' Edward went on softly, 'but if I were you I would ask: "Where is my wife?"'

Haraldsson closed his eyes and saw flashing lights. He was afraid he might faint. He couldn't do that. If he passed out he would never know. Silent tears poured down his cheeks.

'Where is my wife?'

His voice only just held. Hinde began to tell him.

Every single window in the apartment was wide open.

But it was still hot.

Sticky.

Stuffy.

Vanja was sitting on the sofa, channel hopping. It was painfully clear that nobody broadcast their best programmes at this time of day. She switched off the TV, threw the remote control down beside her and picked up the special supplements that had come with both evening papers. *Expressen* had ten pages on the arrest of Ralph Svensson, with an exclusive on the first page adorned with a large picture of him. Unmasked beneath the banner headline: THE FACE OF THE SUMMER PSYCHO. At the top of the page it said 'The police suspect that this is' in significantly smaller letters. Ralph hadn't even been charged as far as Vanja knew, but he had already been hung out to dry by the press. Restricting the publication of names and photographs was out of fashion these days. The early identification of suspects was 'in the public interest'. Which meant that nobody was prepared to pay for a pixellated image. Besides the fact that she herself thought it was unethical, it also made their work more difficult sometimes. Identity parades suddenly became a lot less valuable when the suspect's face had been staring out from every front page.

The picture in *Expressen* was from Ralph's passport; it wasn't particularly flattering. He looked just as crazy as everybody else did in their passport photograph. Inside the paper his entire life story was laid out. His mother's illness, the fact that his father had remarried, his new mother, her kind relatives, the moves from one place to another, money, school, employment. They had found some classmates who remembered Ralph Svensson as quiet and withdrawn. A bit odd. Difficult to get to know. Spent most of his time alone. That might have been true, Vanja had no idea, but she wondered if the newspaper would have got the same response if they had called and said that Ralph Svensson had won the Nobel Prize, rather than that he was a suspected serial killer. It kind of fitted the image. The lone wolf. The recluse. The oddball. Vanja thought the former classmates, who almost certainly hadn't given Ralph a thought over the past twenty years, had simply bowed under the weight of expectation. After the exposure of Ralph's entire life, leaving aside any possible dreams, hopes, wishes and any other distractions that might just humanise him, the paper had just as much information about Edward Hinde. The journalists were lucky: Ralph was a copycat, so they could reprint the news from 1996 all over again. Vanja couldn't bring herself to read all of it. She tossed the paper aside and went into the kitchen for a glass of water. It was just after half past six. It would be another two hours before the sun went down, but at least the temperature outside was beginning to feel bearable. A balmy breeze found its way in through the open window.

She was restless.

A pleasant weariness normally came over her when they had completed an investigation, as if both body and brain were able to relax at last, after weeks of tension. She was usually happy to order a pizza, drink a little too much wine, and chill out on the sofa. But not this time.

They had brought in the right man, she was sure of it. Sebastian Bergman had been completely outmanoeuvred, which was another positive. She couldn't imagine that he would be able to worm his way in again. Torkel had made it clear that enough was enough, and even Sebastian seemed to have reached the same conclusion. Yes, it had been a job well done, taken all round. A good day. So why couldn't she relax?

Because things weren't right between her and Billy. Now the case was entering a less frenetic phase, she was able to focus on their damaged relationship. Ever since she had said in the car that she was a better police officer than he was, things had been strained. Not surprisingly. Before that, too, if she was honest with herself, but since her poisonous comment in the car it had been open warfare.

At least that was how it seemed to her. He had started whatever was going on between them, but she had escalated it all with her stupid remarks, and she would be the one who put a stop to it. But things couldn't carry on like this; Billy was too important to her. At this rate, one of them would end up asking to leave the team, and that was the last thing she wanted. She had to get the situation back to normal. She went back into the living room and picked up her mobile.

★ ★ ★

Maya opened the oven and took out the gratin of pork tenderloin. Billy put out the dish of couscous and sautéed vegetables. They were having an early dinner. Since he now had the evening off, they had decided to go to the theatre. It hadn't been his idea originally, but they had made the decision together. Billy didn't know the company at all; according to Maya they were an English theatre group called Spymonkey, who were performing on four evenings that week. Physical comedy drama, she said.

Billy couldn't picture it.

'Like a cross between Monty Python and Samuel Beckett.'

Okay, a reference he understood. He liked Monty Python. Some of it, anyway. Not all of it. It was a bit dated. But it was only fair that she choose what they were going to do. He had opted for the cinema last time, plus he had been working such long hours that they had hardly seen each other. He could put up with a couple of hours of British physical comedy if it meant being with her. He poured them both a glass of wine and sat down at the table. His eating habits had improved beyond recognition since he met Maya. He liked it. He liked a lot of things when it came to Maya. Everything, in fact. His phone rang and Billy checked the display. Vanja.

'I have to take this.'

'Okay. Don't be long.'

Billy went into the other room. He hadn't told Maya about his conversation with Vanja in the car. He liked both of them, and he wanted them to like each other. The chances of that would be significantly reduced if Maya found out about the exchange which had already destroyed so much. He sat down on the sofa as he took the call.

'Hi, it's me,' Vanja said.

'I know.'

'What are you doing?'

Billy thought quickly. How should he handle this? Tell the truth as far as possible, he decided.

'We're just about to have dinner.'

'You and Maya?' Was there a hint of distaste in the way she said the name? Had she emphasised the *y* a little too much? *Mayyyya*. Or was he just imagining things? Looking for problems? Possibly.

'Yes. Me and Maya.' He looked over towards the kitchen where Maya was sipping her wine. She was obviously waiting until he came back before she started eating. 'It's on the table; was there something you wanted?' Billy was doing his best not to sound dismissive.

'How about coming for a run?'

'Now?'

He hadn't been expecting the question. Hadn't thought she would want his company.

'In a while. After you've eaten. It's not too hot outside now.'

'I don't know . . .'

'I thought we could have a little chat. About us.'

Billy didn't answer immediately. There it was. The first step. Vanja had taken it. Billy looked over towards the kitchen again. Maya met his eyes and smiled, but at the same time her hand formed a mouth that was talking and talking. He smiled back and rolled his eyes to indicate that the person on the other end was babbling away, while he quickly went through the options in his mind. He wanted to go for a run. He definitely wanted to talk to Vanja. About their relationship. But he wouldn't have time to do that and go to the theatre. He didn't want to go to the theatre, but he did want to be with Maya. He wanted to drink wine and spend time with his girlfriend. He was going to have to make a choice. He and Vanja would sort out their problems, he felt sure. He knew it. But not tonight. He was going to choose Maya, and Vanja would just have to accept it.

'I'm sorry,' he said, and meant it. 'I can't.'

'So what are you going to do?'

Did she sound disappointed? This time he didn't think it was his imagination.

'We're going out. To see a play.'

'A play?'

He realised how it must sound. She knew his views on the theatre. He had chosen the worst thing he could think of, over her. That was how it sounded. But that wasn't the case. He might have been choosing Maya over her, but he didn't want to say that.

'Yes, we arranged it ages ago.' He had booked the tickets less than an hour ago, but it was time to abandon the truth. Save what could be saved.

'Okay. Some other time.'

'Yes.'

'Have fun. Say hi to Maya.'

'Will do. Listen, I really do want us to . . .' But she had ended the call. Billy wondered briefly if he should ring her back and finish the sentence. He decided to leave it for now, but he would definitely tackle the issue at work tomorrow. He would call her if she didn't come in; sometimes she took the day off after they had made an arrest.

Billy went back into the kitchen.

'Who was that?' Maya asked as she started to eat. She really had been waiting for him.

'Vanja.'

'What did she want?'

'Nothing.'

He sat down and picked up his glass of wine. It wasn't true. That wasn't what Vanja had wanted, that was what she had got.

This wasn't how he had imagined their wedding anniversary at all. Not at all.

After Edward Hinde's call, Haraldsson had raced out to the car and entered the GPS coordinates. The map quickly came up. Out past Surahammar and Ramnäs, left, into the forest, down towards Lake Öje. He had asked if Jenny was still alive, but hadn't received an answer. That was the second question; he was only allowed one, Hinde had said, and ended the call.

As he drove, Haraldsson tried to tell himself that there was no reason for Hinde to tell him where Jenny was unless he was going to be able to save her. The logical move would be to let her go; she had fulfilled her role as a means of pressurising Haraldsson. There was nothing to be gained by hurting her. But however hard he tried to convince himself, there was always, deep down, the knowledge that Hinde did not act logically, did not need reasons. That was why he had been sitting in Lövhaga for fourteen years.

He was a psychopath.

Haraldsson followed the GPS. The roads grew narrower and narrower, the forest more and more dense. Then he saw water between the trees, and the track came to an end. He parked next to an enormous rhododendron and got out of the car. A summer cottage. Built on the slope leading down to the lake. Many years ago, no doubt; no one would get permission to build so close to the shore these days. He walked over to the house and tried the door. Locked. He peered in through a window. The kitchen. There was obviously no water or electricity; he could see a wood-burning stove and washing-up bowls turned upside down on the small draining board. No taps, just a large metal bucket containing a ladle on a stool beside it. Picturesque, but empty.

'Jenny!' he shouted.

No reply.

Haraldsson carried on walking around the house, looking through each window in turn. Nothing. He stopped and gazed around. The garden wasn't very large, but it was a beautiful setting. Lawns on three sides. A badminton net on the one leading down to the lake. Garden furniture and a flagpole on another. Someone enjoyed the good life out here.

'Jenny!'

Somewhere high above the lake a bird answered him. Haraldsson could feel the panic growing. There was an outside toilet a short distance away on the edge of the forest; he went to check, but that too was empty. Apart from a cloud of buzzing flies. He closed the door and had just decided to break into the house when he noticed an unnaturally rounded hillock beyond the flagpole. A path through the blueberry bushes leading to it. Big stones sticking up between the long grass and the turf at the sides. A food cellar. Haraldsson hurried across. As he got closer he could hear the faint sound of banging. He stopped. Was it true, or just his imagination? No, someone was definitely banging. From inside the earth cellar. It wasn't very loud, but even so. Haraldsson was there in seconds. The sound grew louder as his hopes grew.

'Jenny!'

He ran around the small hillock and ended up outside a large dark wooden door. Turned the key and flung it open. A kind of lobby approximately a metre in length, then another door. The banging was loud and strong now. She was alive, at least. The thick stone walls had done a good job of muffling the sound before, but now he could hear it clearly. A key in the lock. Haraldsson turned it and opened the door.

Jenny was standing just inside, screwing up her eyes at the sudden brightness. He rushed in and hugged her.

Tightly.

She clung to him.

For a long time.

★ ★ ★

In the car on the way home she didn't say anything at first. She had been scared, of course. Terrified. It wasn't until the taxi turned down towards the cottage that she had realised something was wrong. The big man had grabbed her bag and forced her out of the car, into the earth cellar. She hadn't been able to think straight. But now she was safe, her thoughts brought questions with them. She needed to understand. Haraldsson hated lying to her, but right now things were too uncertain to allow him to tell her even a sanitised version of the truth. Instead he explained that he had spoken to his former police colleagues when he got the call from the real taxi driver, and apparently there was a gang who specialised in picking people up from their place of work and robbing them like this. The police thought they had probably hacked into the taxi firm's computers to find out which cabs had been pre-booked.

Jenny seemed satisfied with his explanation.

No doubt there would be more questions later, when it had all sunk in, but by then he would know what the result of today's events had been, and would be able to tailor his answers accordingly. But right now they were going home.

He was so glad she was unhurt.

They had hardly got through the door before Victor was on the phone again. Stressed. Desperate. The ambulance transporting Hinde hadn't arrived in Uppsala. The hospital was unable to contact the crew. Lövhaga was unable to contact the guards who had accompanied Hinde. Haraldsson had to come in.

He tried to get out of it, but Victor made it clear that this was a situation which required the presence of the governor. He told Jenny he had to go into work for a while. He really had no choice. Should he drive her over to one of her friends, if she didn't want to be alone? No, she wanted to stay with him. They walked back to the car together.

Jenny was quiet most of the way to Lövhaga. Probably going over the events of the day. That suited Haraldsson. He needed to think through possible scenarios, plan how to handle the situation that had arisen.

Time for some damage limitation.

Under no circumstances must anyone find out that he had had anything to do with all this.

For his sake. For Jenny's sake. For everyone's sake.

444

He started with Jenny. No one knew she had been missing. Oh yes, the girls at the office, but nobody else. What they knew would never come to the attention of the board at Lövhaga, so Jenny didn't constitute a risk. Even if she told anyone at the prison about her unpleasant experiences, no one would make the connection with Hinde's escape. Check!

Next question: should he attempt to retrieve the beetroot jar and the bottle from the chemist's?

It was risky. If they were found, the assumption would surely be that Ralph Svensson had smuggled them in to him. They wouldn't take fingerprints from something like that, would they? Not when they already had a suspect who had been in contact with Hinde for a long time. Of course everyone would think it was Ralph who had helped him. The best course of action would probably be to stay well away from Hinde's cell.

Or should he take a different approach?

He could demonstrate his initiative by searching the cell. 'Finding' those items. That would explain the presence of his fingerprints if there was an investigation at a later stage. But then Ralph's fingerprints wouldn't be on them anyway. Ah, but cleaners wore gloves, didn't they . . .

His thoughts were interrupted by his phone ringing. It was the chef, back at the house. Where were they? Haraldsson sighed; he had forgotten all about dinner. He explained that something of an emergency had arisen, and that they would have to miss the evening's culinary treat, unfortunately. The chef was understandably put out. Haraldsson would have to pay for the lot. The food, the wine, his travel expenses, his fee. Just so Haraldsson knew. Haraldsson didn't protest; he simply apologised and ended the call.

'Who was that?' Jenny wanted to know.

'It was a chef; he was coming to the house to cook dinner for us tonight.' Nice to be able to tell the truth for once without having to think and adapt.

'So you'd arranged it all?'

'Yes, but nothing's turned out the way I planned. I'm really sorry.'

'Well, it's not your fault.'

'No, but even so . . .'

'You're a star.'

She leaned against him and kissed him on the cheek. He smiled to himself, but in his head he was already thinking through the essentials again.

Yes, he could deal with the bottle and the jar, but what if someone searched the cell and found the photograph of Jenny? How would he explain that? He almost hoped that Hinde had taken it with him. But when they caught Hinde, if they caught Hinde, and found a photograph of the prison governor's wife on him . . . He would simply pretend to be astonished. Wonder how the hell Hinde had managed to get hold of it. It would remain a mystery . . .

★ ★ ★

Victor Bäckman was waiting for them in the car park when they arrived. He was surprised to see Jenny, but Haraldsson explained that it was their wedding anniversary and they wanted to be together. Victor swallowed the lie. He had more important things to worry about. They walked towards the building together.

'We've gone through his cell. We found an empty beetroot jar and an emetic bottle – ipecac. Also empty.'

'Where did he get those from?' Haraldsson asked as naturally as he could manage.

'Ralph must have given them to him.'

'I expect you're right.' Haraldsson nodded, mightily relieved.

'But that's not the worst thing.' Victor looked extremely troubled. 'We found a modem.'

'What does that mean?'

'He's had unlimited contact with the outside world. We're going through the computer now, trying to see if there's anything about the escape. But it's password-protected, so it might take a while.'

Haraldsson barely heard the last part. Contact with the outside world. That could definitely be used to explain a number of things if necessary. Victor's remit. Victor's mistake. Not his. It looked as if everything was going to be okay. He didn't dare ask about the photograph. Presumably they hadn't found it, or Victor would have mentioned it.

He suddenly realised that the head of security had stopped, and appeared to be waiting for some kind of response.

'What?'

'I said the hospital still hasn't managed to track down the ambulance. What do we do?'

'We contact the police and tell them we have a possible attempted escape.' Haraldsson was impressed by the authority in his voice, the way he had taken command of the situation. No more mistakes. Victor nodded, and together they went into the administrative block.

★ ★ ★

It wasn't long before vigilant journalists who were already interested in Lövhaga got wind of the fact that someone had escaped. The police force leaked like a colander sometimes. They also made the link with the missing ambulance, and the circus was underway. Haraldsson ducked and dived for a while, but realised that it would be best if he spoke to them so that he could control what was said. He issued an order that all media enquiries should be referred to him. It was like opening the floodgates.

The phone never stopped. Annika kept on putting them through, one after the other.

Different callers.

The same answers.

Yes, it was true that an ambulance which had picked up a patient from Lövhaga was now missing.

Yes, there were a number of points which suggested this might be an attempted escape, but it was too early to say anything definite.

No, he had no intention of telling them who was in the ambulance.

Every single one asked if it was Hinde.

He hung up. Oddly enough the phone didn't ring again. He got up and went over to Jenny, who was sitting in one of the armchairs. She had got herself a cup of coffee and a sandwich from the canteen, but had eaten barely half. What a wedding anniversary. Still, they could celebrate on another day.

The important thing was that they were together. He had never known an emotional rollercoaster like it. But he had managed the situation very well. He would continue to do so. The worst was over.

'How are you doing?' He crouched down in front of her and gently pushed a strand of hair off her face.

447

'I've been sitting here thinking.'

'I can understand that . . .' Haraldsson took her hand and squeezed it. 'Perhaps you need to talk to someone about what's happened. A professional.'

Jenny nodded, her expression slightly distant.

'Darling?'

'Yes?'

'How did you know where I was?'

Haraldsson stiffened.

Perhaps the worst wasn't over after all.

He had got home earlier than agreed. When he was in Östermalmstorg he had remembered that he had promised Ellinor he would do some shopping for dinner. It was probably the man ahead of him carrying two bags that reminded him. At first he was inclined to forget the whole thing; dinner with Ellinor and a neighbour he didn't even know struck him as utterly ridiculous. Like a piece of a jigsaw puzzle that just didn't fit anywhere. But the more he tried to push the thought aside, the more persistent it became.

There was something liberating about the simplicity of it all. A shopping list and a basket to put things in. Shopping alongside other people, just as if he was a normal, functioning individual. As if he had something to look forward to.

He went into the Saluhallen food hall and began to shop as he had never shopped before. Fillet steak, new potatoes, vegetables, fruit and a dozen or so dessert cheeses. He sampled Italian salami and prosciutto, and decided to buy both. Picked up basil and dill. Bought a French pâté which tasted divine. Top-of-the-range, freshly ground coffee. He didn't want to stop shopping. All these tastes opened up possibilities of something he had never experienced. At the bottle store he bought champagne, white wine, red wine, whisky and cognac. He thought about buying a vintage port, but he had run out of hands and plastic bags. He had to stop and put the bags down several times on the way home so that he wouldn't drop anything when his fingers went numb.

Ellinor rushed over and hugged him before he had even managed to put the shopping down. Her joy at seeing him was irresistible. He pressed closer. She smelled delicious. Her red hair was soft, her lips against his even softer. He held her tight. He just wanted to lose himself in her, in those lovely giggles. They stood

449

in the hallway for a long time. She let go first, but kept one hand resting on the back of his neck. Looked at the bags on the floor.

'How much have you actually bought?'

'Loads. I didn't bother with the list.'

She laughed. 'You're crazy.' She kissed him on the mouth again. 'I've missed you. All day.'

'I've missed you too.' At that moment he realised he wasn't lying. Perhaps he hadn't actually missed her. No, not her. But the direction in which she was taking him. That's what he had missed. For a long time. She took some of the bags into the kitchen. He watched her go. It was as if he had suddenly found himself in a siding heading in a different direction, and he never wanted to rejoin the main track. Never.

She came back, smiling at him. 'You've bought such lovely things.'

'Thanks.'

'Do you want to go to bed, or shall we have a glass of champagne first?'

'I don't drink.'

'Not even champagne?'

'No.'

'Boring!' She flashed him a flirtatious smile. 'In that case there's only one option.'

She pushed back her long hair and looked at him with that expression he found so difficult to resist. For a moment he was lost in the promise of intimacy, of closeness. But then he surprised himself.

'Shouldn't we do something about dinner first? I mean, you've invited our neighbour round.'

She looked at him with exaggerated disappointment. 'Like I said – boring!' She turned on her heel and went back into the kitchen. He followed her to help unpack the shopping.

He was surprised at his decision, to say the least.

Prioritising the neighbour over sex.

That was something new for him.

★ ★ ★

She decided on the menu. His culinary skills were limited, and he concentrated on washing and chopping the vegetables. She chatted away as she dealt with the meat: about her plans for the apartment,

450

the summer weather, the fact that she was worried about her plants. She was wondering whether to bring them over here. Sebastian simply listened for the most part – not necessarily to what she was actually saying, but to the sound of her. He didn't enter into any discussion. She was a bit like the glass of champagne beside her: sparkling and delicious, but best when you only took a sip.

'Do you mind if I put the radio on?' she asked.

He didn't even know he had a radio. Where was it?

'Of course not.'

'I love listening to music when I'm working like this. And when I'm working with you.' She switched on the little radio on top of the spice rack. He tried to remember how it had ended up in his apartment, but couldn't come up with an answer. The sound of lush strings playing a love song filled the room. He almost began to smile. She wasn't even ordinary champagne. She was pink champagne. Which he had always avoided in the past. Looked down on.

'It's Smooth Radio,' she said. 'It's my favourite station.'

'Mine too,' he said, even though he'd only just discovered that there was a radio station with such a stupid name.

Ellinor went off to the guest room for a few minutes while Sebastian piled salad leaves into a bowl. He wondered if he had any dressing. He certainly hadn't bought any. Typical. He had intended to buy that expensive balsamic vinegar, but had forgotten after his visit to the cheese counter. Ellinor came back.

'I was doing some cleaning and I found this. It looks as if it's full of important papers. Where shall I put them?' She was holding the carrier bag Trolle had given him. It looked as light as a feather in her hand. When he had brought it home it had been heavier.

Much heavier.

He suddenly saw Trolle in his mind's eye. That reassuring smile before he disappeared around the corner for the last time. Saw himself, standing there with the bag in his hand. A few metres away from Storskärsgatan and a vanishing Trolle. It was only a couple of days ago; it was a lifetime ago. The siding had suddenly rejoined the main track.

It had only taken a second.

That's how close they were, the two worlds. Moving along on parallel lines. All it took was a plastic bag full of guilt. He swallowed and stared down into the bowl of salad. He wanted to go back to the pink champagne.

'It's only rubbish; you can throw it away,' he said as nonchalantly as he could manage.

'Are you sure? I don't want to throw away something that might be important.'

'I'm absolutely certain.' He smiled at her to emphasise how totally unimportant the contents of the bag were to him.

She nodded and left the room again, singing along to the music as she went. He started slicing tomatoes. If it were up to him, the music on the radio and the woman singing in the room next door would never disappear. They would simply continue to build the illusion of a life. But it wasn't up to him.

That wasn't how it worked.

The tune came to an end and someone wanted to lend him money until payday. Then it was time for the news.

The illusion was shattered.

He was thundering along the main track once more.

At first he hadn't really heard what the woman on the radio was saying. Something about a missing ambulance. But then came the word that made him drop the knife. Lövhaga. He turned to face the radio. Listened as he had never listened before. An ambulance had disappeared after leaving Lövhaga. It was transferring a patient. At the moment the police had no further information. The newsreader went on to the next item, but by that time Sebastian was already in the hallway with his mobile in his hand. With trembling hands he searched for the number for Lövhaga. It was in the list of most recent calls. After Trolle's. He had called this morning when he was standing outside, trying to get in to speak to Vanja. Ellinor came into the hallway, wondering what was going on. She looked a little worried.

'Has something happened?'

'Shut the fuck up!'

She looked hurt, but he couldn't care less. He was no longer interested in her banal bubbling and babbling. Haraldsson's PA answered; he recognised her voice. She sounded tired. He didn't care about that either. He demanded to speak to Thomas Haraldsson. It was important. It was about the missing ambulance. There would be serious consequences if she didn't put him through immediately. She obliged. He heard Haraldsson's phone ringing. He barely looked at Ellinor, who turned around and went back into the kitchen. She wasn't pretending to be disappointed this time. Her head was drooping, as if her exaggerated behaviour might make him change his mind.

Haraldsson picked up after three rings. He sounded weary, completely lacking in energy, as if he had got stuck in the standard phrases he had repeated so many times.

'Thomas Haraldsson. How can I help you?'

'Sebastian Bergman. Riksmord. Who was in the missing ambulance?'

'We have decided not to release that information,' came the reply. 'It's a matter of protecting our . . .'

Sebastian interrupted him. 'I'll ask you just once more. Then I will destroy your life. As you are aware, I know the man who is in charge at Riksmord. Would you like me to tell you who else I know?'

Haraldsson didn't say anything.

Sebastian asked the question, even though he already knew the answer. 'It was Hinde, wasn't it?'

'Yes.'

'And when were you thinking of telling us this?' He ended the call without waiting for Haraldsson's response. He still didn't know exactly when the ambulance had disappeared and Hinde had gone missing, but it must have been a while ago, otherwise it wouldn't have been on the radio just now. Sebastian had a feeling it took quite a long time for news to reach Smooth Radio. Hinde had a head start.

And there was one thing Sebastian knew for sure: he would make the most of it.

He had to get hold of Vanja. Right now.

She loved to run. Winter and summer. Like most of her friends, she had tried out a wide range of exercise programmes and regimes, everything from spinning to yoga. But she always came back to running. It gave her the most energy, the most space to think. It was as if the rhythm of her feet and her breathing both cleansed the brain and reinvigorated it. Nor was she the kind of person who enjoyed exercising in a group. She preferred to challenge herself. This evening she was intending to go for a long run. Take the circular route she followed when she had plenty of time. She might even go round twice.

Tomorrow they would conduct the first interviews with Ralph Svensson. Torkel wanted her to sit in on all of them. They were just waiting for the preliminary DNA analysis. Torkel liked to have as many cards in his hand as possible before they started.

She ran across Lidingövägen and down towards Storängsbotten. Her goal was the forest, Lill-Jansskogen, and the well-lit tracks leading through it. For Vanja, there was nothing better than running in the forest. The stillness, the scents and smells of nature, made the experience more powerful, and the ground was softer, which meant less wear and tear on her joints. She was just increasing her speed when she felt her mobile vibrate in her pocket. She didn't always take it with her. Usually she wanted to be left in peace, but with everything that had happened she felt she ought to be available all the time. At first she considered ignoring it. She had just got her second wind, two short intakes of breath followed by one long exhalation, and would have preferred not to stop. But it might be Billy. Perhaps he had changed his mind about coming for a run with her. That would be the perfect end to the day. She stopped and dug out her mobile. Saw the name of the person who was calling. A mobile number she hadn't got round to deleting.

Sebastian Bergman.

She put the phone back in her pocket.

He could ring her as many times as he wanted.

She would never answer.

★ ★ ★

Sebastian called Vanja three times in a row. Twice she didn't answer, and the third time she rejected the call. Ellinor came back into the hallway with her glass of champagne, looking at him lovingly. Trying to make peace.

'Shall we carry on with dinner?'

His reply was to open the door and leave the apartment without so much as a glance. He slammed the door behind him, the sound echoing through the silent stairwell. Alone in the real world again. Where Edward Hinde was. At liberty.

He rang Torkel on the way downstairs. For once Torkel answered straight away, but his tone wasn't exactly friendly.

'Now what do you want?'

Sebastian stopped. 'Listen to me, Torkel. Hinde has escaped.'

'What the hell are you talking about?'

'You have to trust me. I think he's after Vanja.'

'Why would he be after Vanja? What makes you think he's escaped?'

Sebastian could feel his frustration growing with every passing second. Beneath it lay panic, just waiting to tear him to pieces, but he managed to hold it at bay. He needed to sound rational, not panic-stricken, or Torkel would never believe him. And Torkel had to believe him. Every minute could be important.

'I don't *think* he's escaped. I *know* he's escaped. I called Lövhaga. Have you got a television there?'

'Yes.'

'Check the text service. It should be there. There's an ambulance missing; it was transferring a patient from Lövhaga. That patient was Hinde.'

The seriousness in Sebastian's voice got through to Torkel. He switched on his television with the remote and selected SVT1. Text. The news item was at the top.

'It doesn't say it was Hinde.'

455

'Ring that fucking idiot Haraldsson if you don't believe me.'
Sebastian set off down the stairs again. He needed to feel as if he
was going somewhere. Doing something.

'I believe you, I believe you – but why would he be after Vanja?
I don't understand. The other murders were aimed at you. Why
would he be after her?'

Sebastian took a deep breath. They had reached the line he
never wanted to cross, but keeping this to himself was becoming
more and more impossible.

This thing he knew.

This thing that Hinde in all probability also knew.

The truth.

'You just have to believe me,' was all he could come up with.
'Please, Torkel, trust me. Call her. She won't take my calls.'

'Have you slept with her?'

'Oh, please! No, for God's sake! But I saw it in him when he
and Vanja met. She aroused something within him. I was there.
He could see that we were colleagues. That's enough for him.'

Torkel thought for a moment. Perhaps it didn't sound all that
crazy after all. Sebastian was right; she had been alone with him.

Perhaps the situation carried a greater risk than he had suspected.
A risk he definitely didn't want to take.

'I'll call her right away. See you at the station.'

The line went dead. Torkel had already gone. Sebastian stepped
outside, desperately looking for a taxi.

Vanja was running up the longest hill on the route. She shortened
her steps, pushed hard, maintaining her speed and her breathing.
Two short intakes of breath, one longer exhalation. The air deep
down in her diaphragm. It was going well. She felt strong. She
deliberately focused on her breathing as she reached the brow
of the hill. Checked her pulse monitor; eighty-eight per cent of
her estimated maximum heart rate. Her phone rang again. She
didn't even bother to get it out of her pocket this time. Carried
on running. The phone carried on ringing. Take the hint, she
thought as it finally stopped.

She lengthened her stride, maintaining her breathing as her legs
pumped. She pushed herself even more, up to ninety per cent of her

estimated maximum heart rate. Too early for a sprint. Over four kilometres still to go. She slowed down slightly. Two in, one out.

The route cut across a forest track. She glanced to the side and saw a car parked next to a pile of timber. A silver Toyota. The right-hand indicator was flashing. She had gone a few steps before she realised what she had seen. She slowed down and stopped. Bent over with her hands on her knees for a few seconds, then quickly straightened up. Too eager to wait. She put her hands on her hips and pushed out her chest instead. Got her breathing under control as she walked back. There it was. The engine wasn't running, as far as she could tell. Nobody around.

WTF 766.

It was the car that had been stolen in Brunna. She remembered the number, because she had heard Billy discussing with a colleague whether there could really be a car driving around Sweden with WTF on the registration plate. A discussion he would have had with her, if things had been normal. The colleague knew there were cars with LOL, so he thought there ought to be WTF as well. The vehicle licensing authority had no chance of keeping up with the fast-moving world of internet abbreviations.

Vanja walked along the track towards the car. She used her wristband to wipe off the sweat trickling down her forehead. Rubbed her cheek against her shoulder. Curious insects started buzzing around her, attracted by the perspiration and the heat she was giving off.

The car was empty. She shaded her eyes as she peered in through the window. Something dark had run down the seat and onto the floor. Blood, possibly. Tentatively she tried the door. She didn't have any gloves with her. Locked. She moved to the right and looked in the back. Nothing. She was just about to get out her phone and call in when she noticed it.

The smell. The stench. Unmistakeable.

Vanja moved behind the car to the boot. She didn't really need to open it. She knew what she would find. Not who, but what.

Musty. Sweet, yet acrid at the same time. Slightly metallic.

The smell of a dead body.

She tried the handle, hoping the boot would also be locked. It wasn't. It opened with a click, and Vanja quickly turned away, her hand to her mouth. Once she had her gag reflex under control, she turned back. Her breathing was shallow, through her mouth only.

It was a man. Elderly. Swollen. Bloated. Bluish-green. Thin, brownish-red fluid seeping from blisters which had burst. Decomposition fluid trickling from the mouth and nostrils. The whole impression was one of moisture, almost wetness. Vanja slammed the boot shut and moved back a few steps as she took out her phone.

The last call hadn't been from Sebastian, she noticed. It had been from Torkel.

She heard a snapping sound behind her. She spun around, on full alert. A huge man was standing six or seven metres away. Broken nose, hair in a ponytail, a red scar running from above his left eye and down over his cheek. Roland Johansson. He must have been behind the pile of timber. He had got close without her hearing him. Vanja slowly began to move backwards. Roland walked towards her. No sense of urgency. Keeping his distance. After just a few steps Vanja felt the car against the back of her thighs. She glanced down briefly, then back at Roland. The adrenaline was pumping. She could feel her heart pounding as she slid along the car until she couldn't feel it behind her any longer. One more step to the right. She was in the middle of the track now. Nothing behind her to get in the way.

Roland Johansson. Big. Strong.

She would never be able to defeat him in hand-to-hand combat. But she would be able to outrun him. He kept on coming. One step forward. Vanja took one step back. Calm. In control. Careful where she put her foot down. She mustn't stumble – that would be the end of it. Kept her distance. Ready to turn and run. Explode. He would never close the seven-metre gap between them. No chance. She could do this.

Roland stopped.

Now! Vanja turned and pushed off with her left foot as hard as she could. She was off . . .

. . . and immediately felt a burning pain in her chest, which spread through her entire body. Her right foot, which was supposed to move her forward, quivered helplessly, unable to gain any kind of purchase on the gravel. Her knees gave way. From far away she heard a scream, and as the ground rushed up towards her she realised that the scream was coming from her. The fall must have hurt, but she didn't register the pain at all. It couldn't compete with the initial agony that was still coursing through her body. Tiny stones pressed into her cheek as she lay there shaking. Through her tears she could see a figure approaching. She blinked. Hard. Couldn't say if the action was deliberate or not. Her body still refused to obey her. She was able to see clearly for a few seconds. Although it couldn't be true.

It was unthinkable. Impossible.

It was Edward Hinde.

With a Taser.

Sebastian yanked open the glass door and raced into the police station. Without a pass he only got as far as the woman on reception. She refused to let him in, however much he yelled. And Torkel hadn't arrived yet. He had called Sebastian a few minutes after their first conversation to say that Vanja wasn't taking his calls either. He had sounded significantly more worried this time, and said he was going to ring Billy to see if he knew where Vanja was. Torkel himself was on his way to the station.

That was ten minutes ago.

Sebastian ran back outside; as long as he was moving, things were less painful. He took out his phone and walked down towards Hantverkargatan as he waited for Torkel to answer. He spotted Torkel in his car a short distance away; he ended the call and ran towards the dark-coloured car, waving and shouting out Torkel's name. People on the street turned around, but he didn't care. Torkel must have seen him; the car braked and did a U-turn just past the traffic lights before speeding back towards him. It pulled up just in front of Sebastian and Torkel leapt out.

'Billy thinks she's gone for a run. That's what she told him she was going to do.'

'She usually runs behind the Royal Institute of Technology.'

'Are you sure?'

'Yes. I think she once mentioned it,' Sebastian added.

He knew exactly where she went running, of course. He had followed her several times. Not around the actual route, but to the point where she started and ended the circuit. She would probably go for the longer route; she usually did when she had time. If he had followed her, then perhaps Ralph had done the same. Shadowing the shadow. In which case Hinde might well know too.

Sebastian had been standing still for too long; the panic was

460

back. 'We have to find her!' he yelled. He tore open the passenger door as Torkel tried to calm him down.

'Billy's on his way. We're just waiting for him. He's been running with her a few times, so he might have more accurate information.'

Sebastian sighed; he really didn't want to wait. But Billy's knowledge of the circuit would make everything easier.

'So where is he then?'

'He'll be here any minute.' Torkel looked at him, his expression serious.

'Send a team in now.'

Torkel nodded and made a phone call. Sebastian just wanted to get moving. He was trembling, but was trying not to show it. As Torkel directed patrols to Lill-Jansskogen he pointed towards a figure cycling in their direction. Billy. He seemed to appreciate the urgency of the situation; he was pedalling furiously. Sebastian and Torkel went to meet him; Billy was breathing heavily.

'We need to move. You're driving, Billy.'

They ran back to the car. As they were getting in, one of their mobiles rang. The vibration told Sebastian it was his. He took it out and turned to the others. 'Hang on.'

He looked at the display. It was the number he had been longing to see. He let out a long breath. 'It's Vanja.'

He answered immediately. 'Where are you?'

The voice on the other end was not Vanja's.

'Sebastian.'

It was Edward Hinde.

Torkel and Billy watched as the colour drained from Sebastian's face.

'What do you want?'

The others suddenly realised who he was talking to. Nobody else would have provoked that reaction.

Hinde spoke with the easy assurance of the victor in his voice. 'I think you know that better than anyone. When were you thinking of telling her?'

Sebastian turned away from the others. He wanted to hide his feelings. He couldn't stand in the spotlight as his life fell apart.

'At first glance you two aren't particularly alike, but I shall be examining her more closely now I have the opportunity.'

461

'If you touch her I'll kill you!'

'Is that really the best you can do? You really are out of practice, Sebastian. It used to be a joy to listen to the way you put things. But I've come to realise that you're not quite so sharp these days.'

Sebastian could feel Hinde's pleasure through the telephone. This was what he had been waiting for all these years.

'Shut up. I'm tired of your games. You don't touch Vanja!'

'You stopped me after four murders, and I stopped Ralph after four murders. Doesn't that seem somehow poetic to you? We're just getting more and more alike, you and I.'

'I don't murder women.'

'No, you just fuck them. But your women are every bit as interchangeable as mine. They are all merely . . . objects. You just haven't had the courage to go all the way yet. You'd enjoy it . . .'

Sebastian almost passed out. The very thought of Vanja in the hands of the man on the other end of the phone was unbearable.

'You sick bastard . . .'

He couldn't reach Hinde that way. Sebastian could call him whatever he liked. Every single name in his vocabulary. It was of no significance; they were merely words. It was Hinde who held all the cards right now.

'Speaking of going all the way . . . Can you cope with losing another daughter?'

Sebastian had to make a real effort to hold on to the phone. He actually wanted to drop it, and to fall to the ground along with it. Two daughters. Both dead. What would he have to live for?

Then Hinde was gone, the connection broken. Sebastian stared at Billy and Torkel, who were almost as pale as he was.

'Hinde's got her. He wants me to find him.'

That was what it was all about.

It wasn't about taking his revenge through others.

It was genuine revenge he wanted. Hinde was after Sebastian's life.

Right now, at this particular moment, that was something Sebastian was prepared to accept. If he could just find him.

He looked at Torkel. 'I need to speak to Ralph.'

Torkel took Sebastian's pass out of his pocket and handed it over. 'Let's go.'

462

He remembered the brimstone butterflies from his childhood. They loved the meadow behind the house. When he was little he had managed to capture some of them. He would place them under an upturned glass and watch with interest as they tried to escape. Sometimes he let them die, trapped inside the glass. Sometimes he would rip off their wings and watch them crawl around in circles until they finished up motionless on their backs. It didn't really matter which method he chose. It was the struggle he wanted to observe. The struggle to survive, even though the outcome was already determined. It had been a constant throughout his life, finding the moment when the victim ceases to fight and simply accepts the inevitable. Few people achieved it.

He went on towards the house. It was a long time since anyone had been there. It felt good. The broken windows and the rotting wooden facade perfectly suited the scenario he had carried within him for so long.

Fantasised about.

Dreamed of.

Now, at last, it would become a reality. After this, it would be difficult to come up with a better fantasy to realise. Because she really was his daughter. There was no longer any doubt about that. Sebastian's reaction on the telephone had removed the last shred of doubt.

Roland had carried her into the house from the car. She was strong and had kept on fighting in spite of the sack over her head and the cable ties around her arms and legs. In the doorway she had tensed like a steel spring, and Edward could see that Roland was thinking of banging her head against the heavy doorframe to calm her down. He managed to stop him. He used the Taser again, pressing it against the back of her neck so that her entire body first went rigid, then slack in Roland's arms. He didn't want her damaged in transit. She must be as pure and lovely as possible. No grazes or bruising.

The two of them moved the old metal-framed bed into the large bedroom. He had been so pleased when Roland told him it was still there. The wallpaper was coming away from the walls, but he recognised the blue fleur-de-lis pattern that was still visible here and there. The room smelled musty and mouldy, but it would have to do. Nothing that a few scented candles couldn't fix. They arranged the thin mattress that Roland had brought over earlier. Tied her legs tightly to the bedstead and checked that she was secure. She was sweaty from the struggle, and Hinde caressed her warm skin reassuringly. Then they went out to fetch the rest of the things from the car.

Roland had parked the Toyota right by the gate. It was a warm evening, and they walked in silence through the grass which had begun to turn yellow with the lack of rain in recent weeks. He always felt so safe when he was walking along beside Roland's bulk. He had missed him, but now everything was fine again. When they reached the car Roland took out the large brown box which had been in the back seat all the way there. It seemed to be quite heavy. Edward looked at his friend.

'Did you bring everything?' he asked.

'Yes, but you'd better check to be on the safe side.'

Hinde shook his head. 'I trust you.'

He took the box and put it down. Turned to Roland, who was removing his jacket from the car and getting ready to go back to the house. Edward stopped him.

'This is where we part company. It's up to me now. Dump the car, will you? Leave the body in the boot.'

Roland nodded. Held out his hand, and they shook on it.

'You take care, Roland.'

'I will.'

He gave Roland a hug too. Between friends. Roland jumped into the silver car, put it in first gear and drove away. Hinde stood watching the car as it headed for the trees a short distance away. The early evening made the forest look dark, and soon the car had disappeared. The sound of the engine died away, and silence reigned.

There was no one here now except him and Vanja.

With a little bit of luck, Sebastian would soon be here too.

He picked up the heavy box and walked back to the dilapidated house. He had a lot to do.

The room was small. It smelled stuffy. Dust and sweat. The ventilation system was old, and the temperature was close to thirty degrees. Sebastian silently thanked the architect for the fact that it had no windows. If the sun had been shining in, it would have been unbearable. Torkel and Sebastian were sitting side by side, with Ralph Svensson opposite. Dressed in anonymous, regulation remand-centre clothing. Shoulders slumped. His gaze moved from one to the other, finally settling on Torkel.

'I'll talk to him. Nobody else.' Ralph nodded towards Sebastian.

'That's not your decision.'

'Fine.'

Ralph fell silent. Folded his hands over his stomach. Let his chin fall to his chest. Torkel sighed. He had no intention of letting protocol stand in the way of a possible result. Ralph was a link to Hinde, who had taken his colleague and friend. There was no time for anything but the approach that would lead to success in the shortest time. Torkel pushed back his chair and got to his feet. Placed a hand on Sebastian's shoulder before he left the room without a word.

As soon as the door closed behind him, Ralph raised his head and met Sebastian's gaze. He sat up straight, placed his forearms on the table, leaned forward. Sebastian sat in silence, waiting. Ralph looked at him searchingly. Something he had inherited from Hinde, but Sebastian doubted whether Ralph had all that much to back it up with. But he could play along for a while. It suited him very well, this silent game that was going on. It gave him time to gather his thoughts. Put his feelings to one side. Suppress his anxiety. Getting emotional wouldn't help Vanja. He needed to bring out the Sebastian who had once existed.

Ice-cold. Flexible. Analytical.

The man who could make a difference.

'Sebastian Bergman. I get to meet you at last.' Ralph broke the silence with a comment that revealed a certain fascination with his opponent. He was grateful for the meeting. This gave Sebastian a certain advantage. Svensson definitely wasn't in the same league as Hinde.

'How are you?' Sebastian asked, keeping his tone neutral, not responding to Ralph's opening remark with so much as a smile of acknowledgement.

'What do you mean?'

Sebastian shrugged. 'It's a simple question. How are you?'

'Why do you want to know that?'

Sebastian didn't want to know at all, but the years had taught him that it was an excellent question to start with. In all its simplicity it revealed more about the opponent than you might think. In this case the reluctance to answer might indicate that Ralph wasn't used to anyone asking about his feelings. He was uncomfortable. Or perhaps those who had asked didn't care about the answer, and therefore it was unnecessary to work out what to say on the subject. It might also indicate that Ralph had had bad experiences when it came to exposing himself emotionally, that too much openness had led to some kind of punishment. Sebastian didn't bother going into it. He quickly moved on and tried a different approach. Slightly provocative.

'How does it feel to be nothing more than a pawn in Edward's game?'

'It feels good. Better than just being Ralph.'

Sebastian digested this information.

Better than just being Ralph.

Weak personality. Inadequate. The idea that he had gone to Hinde and simply confessed was just nonsense, of course. Never in a million years would the man opposite him have come up with such an impressive idea. He would never do something like that. It would surprise Sebastian if he had succeeded at anything in his life. However, it was certainly true that he idolised Hinde. The newspaper cuttings they had found in Ralph's apartment told their own story.

Approval and acknowledgement.

Hinde had given him both, which would make it more difficult for Sebastian to get what he wanted. More difficult, but not impossible. All he had to do was drive a wedge between them.

'Do you know how we found you?'

'Yes.'

'You know who gave us your name?'

'Yes, they told me.'

'It must feel strange to be betrayed by someone you trust.'

'If the Master has a plan and this is a part of it, then . . .' Ralph spread his arms wide, palms up. If you didn't know that he had killed four women, you might almost think he was a pious soul. 'I am only a simple man, trying to follow in the footsteps of a great man,' he went on.

Sebastian got up and began to pace around the stuffy little room. Time was passing quickly. He had to make a real effort not to let the stress show. There were no short cuts. He knew that.

'I think you're more than that. That's why Edward made sure you ended up in here.'

'Are you flattering me?'

'Don't you deserve it?'

'I have the Master to thank for everything I am. So do you, in fact.'

'Oh? In what way?'

'Your books. Those are his words. His actions gave you your success. And mine. He is a great man.'

Sebastian listened closely. There was a slight hint of recitation. As if the words had been learned by heart. A mantra. True once upon a time, but maybe now there was a reason to question those words. Or was he just hearing what he wanted to hear?

'So you mean that both of us are just small fry? That's bloody annoying, if you ask me.'

'The difference between you and me is that you think you can measure up to him. I know I can't.' Ralph nodded to himself as if he had just gained an important insight. 'That is what he wants to show us. Our place in the hell we call our lives.'

Sebastian ignored the rhetoric and went to the heart of the matter. What do you want to do if you're right at the bottom of the pecking order? You want to climb.

'But you left your place.' Sebastian placed his hands on the table and leaned closer to Ralph. 'You evolved. You more than measure up to him.'

Approval and acknowledgement.

It seemed to work. Ralph tilted his head to one side. He wasn't just listening. He was listening and thinking. With a bit of luck he was also re-evaluating.

'Don't you think it's interesting that Edward gave us your name just when you were about to overtake him?' Sebastian went on.

'I don't see it like that . . .'

Perhaps he hadn't seen it like that until now, but the idea was definitely taking root. Sebastian carried on along the same path, feeling that it would lead somewhere.

Approval and acknowledgement.

'That's the way Edward sees it,' he said firmly. 'He gave you away for one reason and one reason only. He was afraid that you would become greater than him.'

Sebastian watched as Ralph sat up even straighter. Growing with every word. Every realisation.

'I don't think so.'

Oh, but you do, Sebastian thought. You might be a full-blooded psychopath, but you haven't got much control over your body language.

The wedge was in place, and now he must hammer it in. Not allow him time to think. Open up the chink in his armour.

'Ask me. Who was I afraid of, Edward or you? Who was on my mind all the time? Think about it.'

The words came pouring out of him. He didn't need to work out what to say, didn't need to consider the best way to put things. It was the truth, and it felt good to say it at long last. How afraid he had been. How bad he had felt. The only thing he had to remember was to keep the rage in check. Feed Ralph's ego.

He leaned even closer, almost whispering now. 'You were the one who hurt me. Gave me sleepless nights. Made me doubt myself. You were the star. You were the one who was living the life. Who were they writing about? Who was everyone in the entire city afraid of? Who was getting all the attention?'

'I still am.'

'Only for a little while longer. You're stuck in here, while Edward is out there, with the baton in his hand.'

Ralph looked up at him with an expression of total surprise. Sebastian had wondered if Ralph was aware of Edward's plans. Now he had the answer without even asking the question.

'What do you mean, out there? Has he escaped?'

'Yes.'

Sebastian watched as Ralph attempted to process the information. Make sense of it. He failed.

'Didn't you know about this? Didn't he tell you?'

Ralph didn't reply. He didn't have to. Disappointment was written all over his face.

'He obviously didn't want you to know,' Sebastian went on, ramming the point home to make sure Ralph didn't miss a single nuance of Hinde's betrayal, and to prevent him from coming up with an explanation for what had happened. 'He wanted to take away your power. I mean, who's afraid of you now?'

Ralph looked up at him in confusion. Sebastian felt he was ready to be won over.

'But you can hold on to your power,' he said, as calmly and reassuringly as he could manage. 'Take control over the person who has been controlling you. The disciple becomes the Master. Isn't that what you've always wanted? To be like Edward Hinde?'

'I am already better than Edward.'

'Edward', Sebastian noted with satisfaction. Not 'the Master' this time.

Ralph's mouth was set in a determined line. 'I took five.' Defiance in his voice.

Sebastian went cold. Five? Another woman? One they hadn't found? How could they have missed her? Who was it?

'There was that fat man,' Ralph explained when he saw that Sebastian didn't understand.

Trolle. Trolle was dead. He knew that already, deep down, but still the confirmation came as a blow. He closed his eyes. He had to maintain his focus. He was on his way in. He had already torn down several defences. Started to work his way through the armour. Mustn't get emotional now. Trolle was dead. That wasn't exactly news. Live with it. Win Ralph over.

'He doesn't count.'

'Why not?'

'That one wasn't planned.' Sebastian realised he was on thin ice here, but he hoped he knew enough about Ralph by this stage for the strategy to work. 'It's not difficult to kill somebody in the street,' he said. 'Any idiot can do that.'

'In the car,' Ralph said pensively.

'What?'

'I stabbed him in the car. But I understand what you mean. He wasn't part of the ritual.'

'And you're better than that.'

Ralph stared at Sebastian with warmth in his eyes. Edward had said they were alike, Ralph and Sebastian. He had been right. Both of them saw him. For what he was. For the person he was. He meant something. But Edward had deceived him. Gone behind his back.

Sebastian met Ralph's almost admiring gaze with a smile. A glow was spreading through his body. He was in. He had reached the insecure core that was crying out for approval. Now all he had to do was ladle it on.

'How are you feeling now? You've had a lot to take in.'

'Strangely enough, I feel strong.' Ralph paused, considered, then nodded to himself. Dignified.

'And you are. You're a worthy opponent. All you have to do is decide whose opponent you are. That's how you become a winner.'

'You mean I should take him on?'

'You're better than he is.' Sebastian took a deep breath. They had reached the tipping point. He could do no more groundwork at this stage. He had to get somewhere. Every minute could be critical for Vanja. 'I need your help.'

Ralph's expression was one of pure shock. 'You want me to help you?'

'It's the only way. Without me you can't go up against Hinde. You'll end up as no more than a footnote in the history books, while Edward lives on.'

'What do you want me to do?'

Sebastian had to make a real effort not to burst out laughing. He mustn't even smile. Bloody hell, he was good! It was nice to be back.

'Answer a question.'

471

'Okay.'

'If Edward can't go to a victim's home, where would he take them instead?'

'Do you know who it is?'

'Yes.'

'Has he already taken them?'

'Yes.'

'But you don't know where they are?'

'No.'

Ralph smiled and shook his head. He had regained control. Perhaps a little too much. Sebastian sensed that soon Ralph wouldn't choose one opponent, but would challenge them both. He had to speed things up while remaining suitably obsequious.

'You ought to read your book.'

'Which one?'

'The first one. Page one hundred and twelve.' Ralph was smiling again. Laughing quietly to himself.

'Am I missing something?' Sebastian wanted to know, even though he was already on his way out of the room.

'It's the emergency number: 112. The number you ring if you need rescuing. I like the symbolism, that's all.'

Sebastian didn't even bother to comment. He left the room, hoping he would never have a reason to come back.

'What did he say?'

Torkel met Sebastian outside the door and walked down the corridor with him.

'Have you got a copy of my books here?'

'What books?'

'The ones I wrote. Are they here?'

'In my office.'

Sebastian increased his pace, yanked open the door at the end of the corridor and set off up the stairs, two at a time. The lift would have been quicker, but he just had to move. Energy was surging through his body like a physical force, and Torkel struggled to keep up.

'Anything new on Vanja?' Sebastian called over his shoulder.

'No. We've searched the running track in Lill-Jansskogen. Nothing,' Torkel panted. 'We found the ambulance. Two dead, two injured. He definitely had help.'

'Roland Johansson.'

'Possibly. Probably.'

Sebastian continued up the stairs without slowing down.

'Why do you need your books? What did he say?'

Torkel was breathing heavily between sentences. Sebastian didn't reply. He just kept on going. Even he was slightly out of breath by now.

'Sebastian, answer me!'

Torkel's voice was almost at breaking point. Sebastian stopped. His former colleague was beside himself with worry. Of course. He deserved the few answers Sebastian was able to provide.

'He said it was in there, where Hinde is.'

'In your books?'

'In one of them, yes.'

473

'Well, you wrote it, don't you remember?'

Sebastian didn't bother answering this time. If he had remembered he wouldn't have been scurrying up the stairs. He would have told Torkel in the first place. The anxiety was preventing them from thinking clearly. He kept going, with Torkel close behind.

Once they reached Torkel's office, Sebastian went straight over to the bookshelf. He immediately recognised the brown spines with the yellow writing. He pulled out the first one. The title was *He Always Seemed So Nice*, with the subtitle *Edward Hinde – Serial Killer*. The quote was from a man who had worked with Edward for three years. Just like everyone else Sebastian had spoken to during the course of his research, his colleague hadn't suspected for a moment that there was anything dubious about Hinde. Hardly surprising. Edward Hinde was an extremely manipulative individual, adept at camouflaging his personality. Most people saw only what he wanted them to see.

'Do you know where to look?' Torkel asked eagerly.

'Yes. Just a minute.'

Sebastian quickly turned to the right page and began to read.

For a serial killer with Edward's need for structure, the choice of the location in which the murder takes place is extremely important. It is not chosen principally for its geographical situation. The distance from home, the ease of getting to and from the location and possible escape routes are all of less significance than the symbolic value . . .

He skipped further down the page.

The decision to strike in the victim's home environment is not first and foremost a matter of control; in every case the first occasion on which he was inside the house or apartment was when he committed the murder. The primary reason for the choice of crime scene is in fact the feeling of security. It may seem contradictory to state that he felt secure in a place he was visiting for the first time, but in a location where the woman does not expect to be attacked, the risk of resistance or escape is reduced . . .

Sebastian continued to skim the page.

'Here.'

If it is impossible to carry out the murder in the victim's home, the most likely scenario is that he will abort his mission. As a last resort Hinde

474

states that he could imagine trying to re-create, or even better to revisit, one of the places that has meant the most to him. For example, the place where his fantasies began, or where the series of murders began.

Sebastian closed the book.

'Where the series of murders began,' Torkel repeated. 'Where was the first murder?'

'I can't remember the exact address, but it was south of the city. Västberga or Midsommarkransen, somewhere like that.'

'Billy can look it up.'

Torkel left the room in search of Billy. Sebastian followed him.

'The fantasies must have started at home,' he said. 'After his mother's death. Where the abuse began.'

He met Torkel's gaze. The anticipation and tension were almost palpable.

'He grew up in Märsta.'

Edward's mother, Sofie Hinde, had lived in her parents' house until her death. It was an isolated farmhouse not far from Rickeby, north of Märsta. That was where Edward had grown up. Sebastian had visited the house twice while writing his first book at the end of the nineties. It was already unoccupied and abandoned back then.

He and Torkel were sitting in one of the special operations unit's lead cars, speeding north along the E4 with flashing blue lights. The rest of the squad were following in two large police vans. Torkel and the team leader were discussing tactics, a map in front of them. The local police in Märsta had already cordoned off the tracks leading to and from the property, but Torkel had decided the special ops team should be the ones to go into the house itself. They had the training and the equipment; the Märsta police would act as a reserve unit. It was a complicated operation. The house itself was quite isolated, which was a good thing, but with open fields all around, it would be difficult to get close without being spotted. The fact that the hostage was a police officer increased the pressure on them all. Not that occasions like this were ever free of tension, but it was somehow worse if things went wrong when a colleague's life was in danger.

Sebastian sat in silence for most of the journey. He had tried to provide as much information from memory as he could, but there wasn't a great deal. The house was large, he recalled. Two storeys. Rundown. What he remembered most clearly was the space under the stairs where Edward had been shut in as a child. He would never forget it. Cold and raw, with a single bulb hanging from the ceiling. A rough wooden floor and the stench of stale urine. The more he thought about that dark place, the more terrified he became. The mere idea of Vanja in Edward's former home was unbearable.

476

When they reached Upplands Väsby, Billy called. He had found the address of the house in Midsommarkransen in the archives, and was on his way over there with another team. He promised to report back as soon as he knew more.

So there were two teams now. With the same goal. To save Vanja. Torkel looked up from the map. 'Do you think she's in Märsta?'

Sebastian nodded. 'His parental home would be more important than the scene of the first murder. It would give rise to more fantasies.'

Sebastian fell silent and looked out of the window. For a second Torkel considered asking more questions, but then realised he didn't have the strength. He didn't want to know too much about the way Hinde thought. Not the details, at any rate. Sebastian could keep those to himself. All he cared about was finding Vanja.

The special ops team leader leaned towards him. 'We'll be there in twenty minutes. Max.'

Torkel nodded.

Soon it would begin.

Hinde was standing in the bedroom looking at her. He had undone the cable ties around her legs and removed her sweat pants. She had strong legs, and he had undone one tie at a time to be on the safe side, but she had remained motionless. He wasn't sure if she was conscious or not underneath the sack. He touched her warm, bare legs. Gazed at the black panties, just visible below the grey vest top. Enjoyed the moment.

Then he went over to the box, which he had placed in the middle of the room.

He opened it and reverently removed the nightdress lying at the top. It was made of soft cotton, and had never been worn before. It had almost the same pattern as the original. The one his mother used to wear was no longer made, and Ralph had searched shop after shop before he found this one, which Hinde himself had approved. The blue flowers were slightly smaller, but it gave him the same feeling as the ones he had used in the nineties.

He shook the nightdress a few times to air it, then draped it over the end of the bed. He went back to the box and took out the nylon stockings and the newly purchased carving knife. Spotted the food and drink underneath them. He would lay it all out in a little while. He wanted to get her ready first. He placed the nylon stockings next to the nightdress, then removed the knife from its packaging. Ran his thumb along the edge. It was very sharp, and felt well balanced in his hand. The blade was laminated with one hundred layers of alternating hard and soft steel, and could cut through most things.

She suddenly moved. Not much, but enough for him to conclude that she was conscious. It was time for the next step, which would involve a risk.

He wanted her to put on the nightdress herself. Perhaps not voluntarily, but he wanted to see her do it.

He began by securing her left foot with a new cable tie. There was some resistance, but he acted with firmness, and soon the job was done. He decided to use the nylon stockings later. That would be step two. He went and sat down beside her on the bed. The old springs protested, and it felt comfortable and soft with age. But that was of no significance. She wouldn't be sleeping in this bed.

Hinde reached for the knife and sliced through the rope holding in place the brown sack over her head and upper body. Grabbed hold of the bottom of the sack and pulled it off with one sharp movement. Now he could see Vanja's face and her blonde hair. She was conscious. He looked at her with interest. The silver tape fixed tightly across her mouth distorted the shape of her face a little, but she was beautiful. Her hair was tousled and her face was flushed from her struggles. But her eyes were blazing.

'Hello, Vanja,' he said. 'I told you we'd meet again.'

She made an angry sound in response, and he watched as she looked around in an attempt to work out where she was. He leaned forward and caressed her hair, trying gently to smooth it down. She tried to shake off his hand by throwing her head backwards and forwards. He grabbed hold of her hair to stop her from moving. Leaned even closer.

'This is what we're going to do.' He brought the knife up so that the sharp point was touching her throat. He pressed it hard against the soft area below her chin, just above the trachea. He saw her tense with anxiety.

'I am going to free your arms, but if you try anything I will use this. You know I am capable of doing so.'

She didn't respond.

'Nod if you understand.'

She didn't move a millimetre. She just stared at him.

He gave her a loving smile.

This was going to be a good battle.

He liked her more and more.

Sebastian could see the police officers moving through the forest ahead of him in a crouching position. The special operations unit had split into three teams. One was approaching from the forest to the east, with Sebastian and Torkel creeping along behind them. One would come from the lake to the north, and their main task was to cut off the escape route and act as backup. The team approaching from the west would actually enter the house. They would have to crawl through the tall grass to their starting point so that no one would spot them from the house, but the setting sun would be behind them, which meant they would be quite difficult to see in any case. The critical point would be the last twenty metres, when they would be most visible from the house; they would have to run towards the target in full view, but given the critical nature of the situation, there was no better option. The leader of the unit was with the western group, and was in radio contact with the others. He had agreed that Torkel and Sebastian would follow the eastern team as far as the ramshackle barn at the edge of the meadow and wait there. It would give them a good overview of the main building. The eastern team would then continue to the ditch in front of the barn, and would move in only when the first group had entered, armed with stun grenades which they would toss into the various rooms in order to throw Hinde off balance. The grenades themselves were actually harmless, but exploded with a blinding flash and a loud bang, which would shock and temporarily deafen anyone in the room. The hope was that this would buy them enough time to prevent Hinde from harming Vanja.

They were perhaps twenty metres away from the barn when Sebastian reached the top of a slope and saw the house at last. He stopped and crouched down. It looked worse than it had done the last time he was here. The garden was overgrown and the windows gaped emptily, the glass long gone. Part of the facade had disappeared, and it looked utterly desolate. He remembered that the local council had tried to sell it by auction, but obviously no one had been interested. It seemed that the house of a serial killer wasn't exactly a sought-after property.

Sebastian could see the northern group moving into position. He looked over to where the leading group ought to be, but couldn't see them. That was good. If he couldn't see them, then perhaps Hinde couldn't either. A part of him had wanted to be with them, but Torkel had been very clear. Sebastian would remain with him in the role of an observer. Nothing else. This was a job for professionals, not amateurs.

Vanja waited until Hinde had removed the cable ties from her wrists. She tried to surprise him with a sweeping blow, but he skilfully avoided her by quickly stepping backwards. She tried. He had expected nothing else. She struck out a few more times, but then Hinde stepped forward and hit her hard across the temple several times with the handle of the knife. She collapsed onto the bed again, the whole of the left-hand side of her head throbbing with pain. It felt hot, almost as if she was bleeding. She raised her arms to her face to protect herself against the pain.

'I can be gentle, I can be harsh,' Hinde said. 'It's your decision.'

No, it's your decision, she thought. She knew that Hinde would have no hesitation in killing her. But his eyes, full of excitement and anticipation, told her that he was enjoying himself. He wanted to go through every part of the ritual with her. The fact that he had asked to touch her hair at Lövhaga had been a part of what was happening now, she realised. Sebastian had been right all along. There had been a reason why Hinde had asked to see her alone. He had wanted to get close. Touch her. And she had let him do it. At the time she had thought it was a small price to pay for Ralph's name. She no longer thought so.

Finding herself at a future crime scene as the intended victim was a horrendous feeling. Knowing the significance of the details was terrible. Nothing escaped her attention. The nylon stockings by her feet. The nightdress draped over the end of the bed. The knife he was holding in his hand.

The other women had had the advantage of not knowing everything that was going to happen.

But she did.

She knew every step of the ritual.

At the same time, that gave her a small amount of hope. Time

482

was on her side, in a way. The longer she could stay alive, the longer those who were looking for her would have. Because they were looking. She knew that. They would be searching everywhere for Edward Hinde. He was no longer an unknown killer. He wasn't someone who could escape from Lövhaga without being a wanted man.

They were looking. They were looking.

That's what she had to tell herself, at least.

Hinde suddenly hauled her into a sitting position and tore off her vest top and sports bra. The attack had come from nowhere. He wanted to get started. She was wearing only her panties now. She hated the fact that her first instinct was to shield her breasts. That just made her weak. So she lowered her arms and allowed him to gaze at her. It was only her body, after all. It was her life she was fighting for. He threw the nightdress at her. It landed on her knee.

'Put this on.'

She looked down at it. So that was how it happened. The others had put the nightdress on voluntarily.

'Would you like to know something that everyone, including Sebastian, has missed? I have always wondered how that was possible. But I suppose it's because it is the most underrated of the five senses.'

She stared at him, her face expressionless.

'I didn't tell Ralph either. But soon you will know, Vanja. Soon we will have no secrets from one another.'

He walked across the room and took something out of a box in the middle of the floor. He came back holding a small, angular bottle in his hand. Smiled at her and squirted it several times over her naked body. She felt the mist of the perfume reach her throat.

'Mother's favourite.'

It was a strong smell.

She recognised it.

Chanel No. 5.

Radio traffic had increased over the last few minutes. First of all the northern team had confirmed that they were in position. After a while the team ahead of Torkel and Sebastian passed on the same message. The two men were standing by one of the shorter walls of the barn, from where they had the best view of the house; it looked every bit as desolate as before. The silence was almost deafening. Not even the flies were buzzing now. Sebastian's nerves were at breaking point. His entire body felt hot and sweaty. He was used to crime scenes, interrogating suspects, giving lectures. Not this.

He felt completely powerless. His whole life was at stake, but he was watching events from the gallery.

'They're going in,' Torkel said as Sebastian saw six black-clad figures appear out of the long grass a short distance away from the house. Only those critical twenty metres to go now. They ran as fast as they could without losing control. Their equipment was taped down so that the only sound to be heard from the group was the faint swish of the grass being flattened by their black boots.

Sebastian kept his eyes fixed on the house, feverishly searching each gaping window for any sign of movement. Nothing so far. He didn't know whether he found that reassuring or not.

The first members of the team reached the house and quickly pressed themselves against the wall by the front door. The others joined them. One by the big window on the ground floor. Two others took out their grenades and crept towards the door. Sebastian saw a helmet bobbing up and down in the ditch in front of them; the eastern team seemed equally restless and eager.

Once all those around the house had reached their designated locations, everything proceeded like a well-oiled machine. Sebastian watched as the first two pulled open the door and each lobbed a grenade inside. Those by the windows did the same thing. There

484

was a brief silence, followed by four almost simultaneous explosions. The windows were lit up by the flashes and the team rushed in. At the same time the men in the ditch leapt up and began to run, moving even faster if that were possible. Sebastian stepped out of the barn. He could hear more explosions from the house, and white smoke was pouring out through several of the broken windows. He realised that this was all going wrong.

He was the one who ought to be inside the house.

He was the one Hinde was waiting for.

He suddenly began to run as fast as he could. He could hear Torkel yelling after him: 'Sebastian, what the hell are you doing?'

He simply ran.

His legs sped across the grass. He stumbled at the ditch, but immediately regained his balance. Increased his speed even more, running as he had never run before. One of the officers from the second team saw him and gestured to him to stop.

Sebastian ignored him. He needed to find his daughter.

He reached the front door and dashed into the darkness of the house. There was a thick pall of smoke, and the smell of magnesium and other metals lay heavy in the air. He was so puffed he had difficulty breathing. He made himself move across to the storeroom under the stairs. It was the first place he thought of, but he stopped when he saw one of the police officers emerging from it.

'Was there anything in there?'

The man shook his head. 'No, it's empty. You're not supposed to be in here.'

'Was there any food in there?'

'What?'

He heard more explosions from the upper floor, and raced upstairs. The bedroom occupied by Hinde's mother was up there, and that was probably where they would be.

It was darker up here, and there was even more smoke. He found it difficult to get his bearings, and soon had absolutely no idea where he was. He began to cough because of the smoke, but tried to move in the direction where he thought the bedroom should be. There was rubbish on the floor, and he tripped over some loose planks. He grazed his hands, but quickly got back on his feet. He was losing time.

He was losing Vanja.

As he ran into the bedroom he bumped into a figure in the doorway. He jumped backwards, but it was the leader of the special operations unit.

'What the hell are you doing here?'

'Where is she?'

The other man shook his head. 'The place is empty. There's no one here.'

Sebastian stared at him. 'What?'

'There's no one here. No one at all.'

They were holding a short debrief outside the house. Torkel was standing with the special ops unit leader in front of the other officers. They had double- and triple-checked the house. Nothing. Sebastian had looked in the storeroom under the stairs himself. He had gone back there with some trepidation, and had borrowed a torch from one of the police officers so that he would at least have some light. It smelled the same as before. Worse, maybe. But it was empty apart from a few discarded beer cans on the floor. There was no food in the place where the young Edward Hinde used to arrange his secret supplies long ago. That was all the proof Sebastian needed. Hinde would never omit that particular detail. The hidden cache of food was the only security he knew. In many ways that was what gave him the courage to carry out his crimes. Sebastian was convinced that wherever Vanja might be, there would be food neatly arranged in a small, lockable room. It would remain there until the day they found her.

Probably dead.

Given the speed at which the search was proceeding at the moment.

Ralph had lied. This time Sebastian would forget the subtle games and make sure he got the right answer.

He looked over at Torkel and the other officers with growing frustration. He couldn't understand what was taking so long. They needed to get out of here.

At last they seemed to have finished. Torkel walked towards him, his mobile pressed to his ear. 'Billy,' he mouthed to Sebastian. After a few moments he looked up at Sebastian and shook his head. 'He didn't find anything.'

'Can I have a word with him?'

Torkel passed him the phone. Billy sounded stressed and exhausted. 'Like I said. There's a family living in the house in Midsommarkransen. They were having a big family get-together, grannies and granddads and the whole shebang. There's no way he could be there.'

'So what now?'

'I'm just on my way back to the office. I'm going to make a start on checking Ralph's computer. That's my strong point, after all.'

Billy ended the call without saying goodbye. Sebastian gave the phone back to Torkel and headed towards the car he had arrived in, but the special ops unit leader stopped him just as he was about to get in. After his behaviour during the operation, he could travel with the others. Sebastian didn't have the strength to argue; he merely shook his head wearily at their ridiculous idea of punishment and went to the car behind. These people seemed to get their priorities wrong all the time. He hated them. He got in the back seat. Nobody came to sit beside him. He didn't care. He didn't want to speak to anybody anyway.

After they had been driving for a few minutes and had reached the main road, his mobile suddenly vibrated; he still had it on silent from the operation. He took it out and discovered he had received a multimedia message. He had never had one of those before. The sender was a number he didn't recognise. He took a deep breath. Fear made his stomach contract, and his throat was suddenly dry. The message would be painful. He took another deep breath and opened it.

It was a picture accompanied by a brief message. The picture made any remaining colour drain from his face. A naked Vanja was sitting with a nightdress tossed on her knee. She was looking into the camera with a pleading expression on her face. He recognised the style from the photo wall in Ralph's apartment. Looking down on the subject, the naked skin, the fear. He looked out of the window to maintain his composure. Tried to wipe the image from his brain. When he felt he was back in control, he read the short message below the photograph.

'The first picture of my thirty-six. Where are you?'

He quickly clicked away from the picture and looked out of the window again. He felt sick, but managed not to let it show.

It was up to him now. Not those in uniform sitting all around him. That was the way Hinde wanted it.

That was the way it was going to be.

Ralph was lying motionless on the bunk in his dark cell staring up at the ceiling when he heard rapid footsteps out in the corridor. They stopped at his door and the security hatch flew open as a key was inserted in the lock.

'Are you trying to trick me?' Sebastian yelled. Straight to the point. No time for polite phrases. 'I thought you knew Edward, but I guess it was just talk.'

Ralph sat up quickly, brightening at the sight of Sebastian's face in the narrow opening. 'Wasn't he there?'

The door swung open and Sebastian pushed past the guard and into the cell. The look on his face was enough of an answer.

'Where did you go?' Ralph asked.

'Märsta.'

Ralph broke into a smile, shaking his head. 'That's not where it started.'

'Edward is like a mad dog. He might have decided it "started" anywhere he fucking likes.'

'But he didn't. I know exactly where he is.'

Just what Sebastian wanted to hear. He had hoped that admitting his failure would pay off, that it would give Ralph the chance to shine, but this had happened in record time. Now all he had to do was seal the deal.

'Where? Where is he?'

'I can show you.'

Sebastian frowned. There was something in Ralph's voice that made him realise Ralph wasn't talking about a map here.

'What do you mean, show me?'

'I'll come with you.'

'No.'

Harsh, perhaps. He saw Ralph's enthusiasm wane slightly, but

490

there was no point in charging straight for a dead end. The idea of taking Ralph anywhere was out of the question.

'You said I was like Edward,' Ralph said, getting up. His voice had acquired a hard edge that hadn't been there before. 'Better, in fact. He would never help you without getting something in return. I want to be there.'

'When we arrest him?'

Ralph pointed a slender finger at Sebastian. 'You can arrest him.' He pointed the finger at himself. 'I will get my fifth woman. I will be greater than Edward. The greatest.'

There was something dreamlike in his voice this time, and his gaze was fixed on some distant point. Sebastian could hardly believe his ears. This was beyond insanity. Did Ralph seriously believe he would be allowed to go with Sebastian and commit a murder?

Ralph fixed his eyes on Sebastian again. 'You're not the only one who will win.'

Evidently. It was as Sebastian had feared. Both he and Hinde were opponents now. Everyone was Ralph's opponent.

Sebastian's mobile pinged.

Another multimedia message.

The second picture.

Sebastian stared straight ahead. Deep breaths. Thought about the situation. Discovered surprisingly quickly that there wasn't all that much to think about, and called the custody officer who was waiting out in the corridor.

'He's coming with me.' Sebastian nodded in the direction of Ralph, who was now wearing an expectant smile, certain of victory. The officer entered the cell and Ralph turned around obediently, hands behind his back. He was handcuffed and led into the corridor, then the officer handed both Ralph and the keys over to Sebastian. Together they set off down the corridor.

Ralph was wrong.

Sebastian was the only one who was going to win.

At any price.

★ ★ ★

They went down in the lift. Neither of them spoke. Ralph was still looking smug as Sebastian bundled him out of the lift and opened a metal door. A long culvert opened out in front of them.

Pipes running along the ceiling, with green and yellow labels on them. Bare walls, apart from lights in the form of white hemispheres approximately every five metres on both sides. Sebastian pushed Ralph into the corridor. Their footsteps echoed on the bare concrete floor.

'Where are we going?' Ralph wanted to know.

'To the car park.'

After about twenty metres Sebastian stopped in front of a white door with two large lever handle locks, both angled up to the left. The words SAFE ROOM were stencilled in the middle of the door, with a notice underneath stating that a maximum of sixty people could be accommodated inside.

'Wait . . .'

Ralph stopped; Sebastian turned the handles to the right and opened the door, its hinges screeching. He groped around and found the light switches, then grabbed hold of Ralph's arm.

'What are you doing? Why are we going in here?'

Ralph resisted, but Sebastian more or less dragged him into the room and over to a radiator fixed to the wall opposite the door. He took out the key to the handcuffs, freed one of Ralph's hands, spun him around a quarter turn and fastened one of the handcuffs to the radiator instead.

'What are you doing?'

'Edward is good. But he's been stuck in Lövhaga for fourteen years because I put him there . . .'

Sebastian walked back to the door and left the safe room. Ralph looked around nervously. He could hear Sebastian's footsteps echoing along the corridor. The room was painted white. There were two benches fixed to one wall, but otherwise it was empty. Sebastian reappeared, carrying an old wooden chair.

'. . . which means I'm better,' he concluded his sentence.

He put the chair down just inside the door.

'You might be better than Edward, but you're handcuffed to a radiator . . .'

Sebastian turned and closed the door. The bare room amplified the sound as the heavy metal door slammed shut and Sebastian turned both locks. Ralph swallowed. They were locked in. He didn't like it.

'So I'm the best.'

Sebastian didn't appear to be in a hurry; he walked slowly over to Ralph. Came and stood very close. Ralph found it difficult to look him in the eye. This didn't feel good. This didn't feel good at all.

'But do you know what I'm not?' Sebastian didn't bother waiting for a reply. 'I'm not a police officer. Which means I can do this.'

Suddenly and with absolutely no warning he head-butted Ralph. His aim was perfect. His forehead hit Ralph smack bang in the middle of his nose. There was a crunching sound and blood began to pour from both nostrils. Ralph cried out and collapsed. Sebastian walked calmly back to the chair and sat down. He watched as Ralph raised his free hand to his nose and stared at the blood, as if he couldn't grasp that it was coming from him. Hitting Ralph gave Sebastian no pleasure whatsoever. However, it was a rapid and effective way of making him realise that Sebastian was capable of absolutely anything. It seemed to have worked. Ralph was still staring at the blood with a look of pure shock on his face and tears in his eyes. Sebastian leaned forward, resting his forearms on his knees and clasping his hands.

'I'm very good at forming an impression of a person by seeing how he lives. I've been to your apartment.'

Ralph sat there taking short breaths through his nose in an attempt to stop the flow of blood, which meant he had to swallow it instead. He was breathing heavily. Struggling. He really didn't want to lose. He had seized the power. He wasn't going to allow Sebastian to take it away from him. He would not permit that to happen. He was stronger than he had ever been.

'It's a question of finding the patterns,' Sebastian went on. 'In the little things. Seeing the connections. There were no blinds in your apartment. Not even in the bedroom. You had a torch in the bathroom. One by the bed. One in every room, in fact. A box full of fuses, batteries, spare bulbs.'

He paused for effect.

'I would say that you don't like the dark.'

The look he got from Ralph confirmed how right he was.

'What happens in the dark, Ralph? What comes to you in the dark? What are you so afraid of?'

'Nothing . . .' Barely a whisper.

'So it's okay if I turn off the lights?'

Sebastian straightened up and reached for the double switch on the wall. Ralph didn't answer. He swallowed hard, his eyes darting all over the room. Sebastian thought he could see beads of sweat appearing on his forehead. The room wasn't hot.

'Please, I know where he is,' Ralph begged.

'I believe you. But as I said to Edward, I'm tired of playing games with psychopaths.'

'I'm not playing games.'

'I can't take the risk.'

Sebastian flicked one of the switches. One row of lights went out. Ralph screamed.

'It will be so dark in here that you won't know if your eyes are closed or open,' Sebastian said quietly.

Just like back there, Ralph thought. Like it was in the cellar. With them.

He started shaking, tugging at the handcuff. Hyperventilating. Sebastian hesitated. Ralph's reaction was stronger than he could have imagined. He was obviously terrified. But Sebastian had to go on. He conjured up a mental picture of Annette Willén. If that wasn't enough, he had the pictures of Vanja on his phone.

It was enough.

He turned off the lights.

Ralph gasped and held his breath. He pressed himself against the wall and curled up into a ball, making himself as small as possible. He tried to keep quiet, but he could hear that every time he exhaled he was whimpering helplessly. Was that a strip of light, or a visual memory in his over-stressed brain? Was that the sound of the door opening? Yes, it was. They came creeping in. Naked. They had found him. The people in the animal masks. The animals in human form. They were breathing. Whispering.

'Switch the light on. Please . . . switch the light on.'

A thin beam of light was shining in his face. The torch on Sebastian's phone. Ralph turned towards it, trying to absorb as much of it as he could. The animal people were waiting in the shadows all around him. Swaying from side to side. Dancing with peculiar, padding footsteps. Waiting for the darkness to swallow him up again so that they could come close.

Around him.

On him.

Inside him.

'Where's Edward?' Sebastian asked, invisible behind the light. He turned off the torch.

'Off.'

The darkness. Swallowing him up.

'On.'

The light came back.

'Off.'

It was gone again.

'On. Which do you prefer?'

Ralph was incapable of answering. All he could do was pant.

'Off.'

Ralph was holding his breath. There was complete silence in the darkness. Apart from the whispering. The soft footsteps. The movement of the naked bodies. He was not alone. Never alone.

'Sebastian . . .'

No response. Something grabbed hold of his leg. Ralph let out a roar of anguish. He was transported straight back.

To the past.

To them.

It struck him with full force. More than a memory. He could smell it. Taste it. He could hear the sounds. They were here. Touching him. They were wild. It had been such a long time. It would never end. He tried to shake them off. Spun around, writhing and kicking. He felt a burning pain as the skin around his wrist was torn off. He banged his head on the radiator. Yanked at the handcuffs again, felt something snap inside his wrist. It didn't matter. He was incapable of screaming anymore.

The light went on. He was bathed in light. White, healing light from the ceiling. Sebastian came over to him. Ralph smiled gratefully.

'Where did it begin, Ralph? Where are they?'

He wanted to tell him. Wanted to yell it at the top of his voice. But all he could manage was a staccato mumble. Sebastian bent down.

'Åk–er–s–st . . .'

Sebastian leaned even closer. Ralph's hot breath against his ear. Only a whisper now. He listened and straightened up.

'Thank you.'

What could he say? This wasn't his proudest moment. But he had said so many times that he would do anything he could to get his daughter back. The same thing applied now: he would do anything to avoid losing another daughter.

He walked back to the door. Unlocked it and pushed it open. He turned and looked at Ralph, slumped on the floor. Blood on his face and trickling down his arms, his hair plastered to his forehead, eyes staring blankly.

Sebastian's mobile pinged.

The third picture.

He switched off the lights and left the room.

Nothing. Nothing. Nothing.

When they got back from Märsta, Torkel had sent cars out to the other three crime scenes from the nineties. Just to be on the safe side. Whatever happened, nobody would be able to say he hadn't done all he could – least of all himself. So he had also sent cars out to Bromma, Nynäshamn, Tumba and Liljeholmen, where the four most recent murders had taken place. He didn't really think Hinde would go there; they belonged to Ralph. However, Torkel would have sent patrol cars all around the world if he thought it might save Vanja. A female police officer kidnapped by an escaped serial killer suffering from a sexual neurotic disorder. Nobody expected him to treat this like a normal disappearance, and he was making no attempt to do so. He called in the resources he thought he needed, and in addition a number of off-duty colleagues had come in voluntarily to ask if there was anything they could do. The effort was immense, but so far it had led nowhere. All the cars he had sent out had now reported back.

Nothing. Nothing. Nothing.

Torkel wondered what to do next. The best and closest thing they had was still Ralph. It didn't matter what he wanted; he was going to speak to Torkel. If he knew anything, Torkel was going to get it out of him. He left the office and went over to the custody suite. Ralph's cell was empty. He went to find one of the guards.

'Where's Ralph Svensson?'

'Your colleague came and collected him about an hour ago.'

Torkel didn't even need to ask which colleague. He hadn't seen Sebastian since they got back from Märsta. He had leapt out of the car and disappeared the minute they arrived. About an hour ago. Torkel grabbed his mobile. Sebastian answered immediately.

'Yes?'

'Where the fuck is Ralph?'

'Calm down. He's in a safe room in the culvert. It might be an idea to go down there and switch on the lights for him.'

Torkel let out a long breath. He had been willing to go a long way to extract any information Ralph might have, but he knew that Sebastian was prepared to go further. Too far, probably. For a moment Torkel had pictured Sebastian removing a suspected serial killer from the building.

'Where are you?' he asked.

The brief silence that followed told him straight away that he wasn't going to like the answer.

'I can't tell you that right now.'

That could mean only one thing. He was about to go too fucking far, and then some.

'You know where Edward is,' Torkel stated flatly.

'Yes.'

'Give me an address. Stay where you are and wait for us.'

'No.'

'Sebastian, for fuck's sake! Do as I say!'

'Not this time.'

Not this time, Torkel thought. As if he had ever done what Torkel said. What anyone said. Taking orders wasn't one of Sebastian Bergman's strong points.

'You can't go there alone.' Torkel made one last attempt to reason with him. Find the right buttons to press. Get through to him. 'You might be suicidal, but think about Vanja.'

'That's exactly what I'm doing.'

Sebastian paused. Torkel didn't know what to do. Beg, plead, lose his temper? They would all be equally ineffective.

'I'm sorry, Torkel, but this is about Hinde and me now.'

Sebastian ended the call. The car headlights illuminated the sign for Åkers Styckebruk with an arrow pointing to the right. Sebastian indicated and turned off.

Whatever happened, it would soon be over.

★ ★ ★

Torkel had to restrain himself from hurling the phone to the floor. Fucking idiot. Sebastian, of course, but it applied to him too. He should have kicked him out. Shouldn't have brought him in. Not again. No way. Would he never learn?

Before he left he told the custody officer where to find Ralph Svensson. He told them to go and get him and put him in an interview room. He would be there in five minutes. First of all he was going to mobilise everyone available, with the aim of finding Sebastian. He must have taken a car; with a bit of luck they might be able to track him using the GPS. If not, they would find out whose car he had borrowed and put out a call right across the area, giving the make, model and registration number. The custody officer called back just as Torkel walked into his office. They had found Ralph Svensson, but he was in no condition to be questioned. He was virtually catatonic. No response when he was touched or spoken to. He had been hurt, or had hurt himself. Injuries to his face and head. Broken wrist. He was on his way to the hospital.

Torkel swore to himself. What the fuck had Sebastian done? Assaulted a suspect. He wasn't going to get away with this. Torkel would personally make sure he didn't.

'Torkel.' He heard Billy's voice from the doorway, and spun around.

'Now what?'

'I've found something. On Ralph's computer.'

Billy had been working flat out since he got back from the house in Midsommarkransen, partly because he really wanted to make a contribution, and partly because it helped him to push aside the thought of what would have happened if he had gone for a run with Vanja. Said yes. Been the friend he ought to be. Torkel had taken him aside and pointed out that if he had been with her in Lill-Jansskogen he probably wouldn't have survived – either that, or they would have had two kidnapped police officers to worry about. Billy had nodded, absolutely, that sounded more than likely, but it was also possible that he and Vanja would both be sitting here now if he hadn't turned her down. That they would have taken Hinde. He knew it was wrong to think like that, it was counter-productive, but he felt guilty. He simply had to do everything he possibly could to try to find Vanja before it was too late. Everyone working on the case knew that she was going to die, but nobody put it into words. The only question was how much time they had. In the worst-case scenario it was already too late, and those were the thoughts he had to suppress with work. They were utterly debilitating. So he had buried himself in the damaged hard drive from Ralph's computer, and his efforts had produced results.

Torkel went over to Billy's desk and bent down to look at the monitor.

'They've been communicating via this fygorh.se home page through a chat programme. I've managed to retrieve parts of their conversation.'

'Get to the point.' Torkel was impatient. He didn't care how Billy had got there, he just wanted to know what he had found.

Billy pointed at the screen. 'Here . . . Ralph is talking about a sports lodge out in the forest where he and his grandfather used to go. It's pretty incoherent, with a lot of stuff about people who look like animals and . . .'

'Okay, okay. And is that where they are?' Torkel demanded.

'No, but there's a reply from Edward, quite a long response about the importance of not forgetting. He talks about an uncle he and his mother used to stay with over the summer when he was a little boy. Apparently this uncle never touched Hinde, but his mother came off pretty badly. He links that to his own experiences, the fact that she was damaged. Look.' Billy pointed to a line lower down on the screen.

I think that was where it all started.

'Do we know where it is?'

'I ran a check on Hinde's mother and found her brother. He used to live in Åkers Styckebruk. He's dead now.'

'Have you got an address?'

'Of course.'

A post-it note with the address written on it would have done, Torkel thought, but he knew what Billy was trying to do. Compensate for the guilt he was feeling. Show that he had worked hard. Done all he could. Torkel completely understood how he felt. He patted his young colleague on the shoulder.

'Well done.'

Torkel had the special operations unit on the phone before he left the office.

At first she hadn't grasped what he was doing as he stood there with the mobile in his hand. It had happened so fast. But as he lowered the phone, smiled at her and told her to put on the nightdress, she realised he had used the camera. She should have known. She had missed it because it was a mobile and not a normal camera. She stared at him, her expression furious. He was going to have to put the nightdress on her himself. There was nothing he could do to make her put it on voluntarily. She knew the series of pictures of the victim were a part of his fantasy, and those she had seen in Ralph's apartment all began in exactly the same way. The woman naked and exposed, just as she was. The next would be a photograph of her wearing the nightdress.

It was going to take him a while to get that picture. She would make sure of it.

She shook her head and turned away from him. He forced her down on the bed, threatening her with both the knife and the Taser. She tried to fight back just enough, prolonging the struggle without making him feel he had to use one of the weapons. It was a difficult balancing act; she had to writhe and resist as much as possible, while still giving him the impression that he was on the way to achieving his goal, that he would be the victor in the end, so that he didn't decide to knock her out.

Anything to gain time.

Then she suddenly felt it. Something hard and sharp sticking up by the mattress on the right-hand side of the bed. It scratched her hand. He had started to push the nightdress over her face, and she had hurled herself as far to the right as possible, trying to get away from him. She tried to look at the sharp object, wanting to know what it was, but it was impossible from where she was lying; the angle was wrong, and the nightdress was almost covering her eyes. She tried to feel it with her hand instead. She couldn't find it; she could no longer reach the edge of the bed with her right hand. She decided to start struggling again, this time with the aim of getting her hand closer to the sharp object. She began with a silent roar, tensing her body so that it became as rigid as a plank of wood. It seemed to throw him off balance for a moment. She threw herself to the right so that her hand could reach further over; her fingers fumbled over the edge of the mattress, feverishly searching for the sharp object. She hoped it would be loose. Hinde was pushing her down again, trying to gain control. She let him have it, but held on tightly to the edge of the bed with her right hand. It worked. She allowed him to start putting on the nightdress as her fingers continued their quest. She heard the nightdress tear as he pulled it over her head, and she fought back with her left arm. Suddenly she found what she was searching for. It was something metallic, sharp and hard. She lost her grip on it in the struggle, but now she knew roughly where it was, and she soon managed to get hold of it again. It felt like a broken spring, and it was loose. She tugged at it with her thumb and index finger, but it wouldn't come out. So she changed tactics and started to bend it backwards and forwards in order to weaken it at the base. Backwards and forwards. As quickly as she could.

It came away and she concealed it in her hand with lightning speed.

She let him pull the nightdress over her head properly so that his focus would be on the task in hand. It worked. He was staring angrily at her as he picked up the knife again.

'I will use this,' he said.

She nodded. Allowed him to win. Gave in. She sat up and put on the nightdress, keeping the broken spring hidden in her clenched right hand. As she slid it over her body she dropped the spring between her legs, covering it with the fabric. She could feel it against her thigh like a tiny, slightly cold and sharp irritant.

It was anything but that.

It was hope.

Hinde took another picture of her. Then he came over and cut through the cable tie securing her left leg to the bed.

'Turn over.' Vanja knew what came next. He wanted her on her stomach. At first she thought about making it difficult for him, but then she realised she had a better chance of holding onto the spring if she did it herself. She placed her left leg over her right leg, pressing the spring between her thighs, then rolled her upper body. She cried out in pain as the cable tie around her right leg bit into her flesh, but she felt the spring move with her as she lay down on her stomach.

Hinde straddled her legs and began to tie her hands behind her back with a nylon stocking. He checked the knot carefully. It was as if he had slowed down now that she was lying there, ready for the next stage. He got up and stood at the end of the bed. Grabbed hold of her left foot and made sure her legs were spread wide apart before tying her ankle to the bed with another stocking. He did the same with her right ankle before cutting the cable tie. Satisfied with his work, he went back to the box. She watched him take out the various items in order. She recognised them. His supply of food and drink. He disappeared, presumably heading for a small, lockable storeroom.

She started to ease the nightdress up over her thighs so that she could get hold of the little spring.

She hoped he was going to be away for a while. She needed time.

The dirt track along which he was driving was overgrown and rarely used. It twisted and turned through the forest, which after a while was replaced by open fields on both sides. A short distance away he could see what appeared to be a house. The halogen headlights lit up the long grass in front of the car, and he felt as if he was driving through a sea of dry, yellow grass. The light was reflected back at him, making it difficult to see anything other than the dark outline of the house.

He soon reached a fence around a makeshift turning area. He stopped, switched off the engine, got out of the car and waited for his eyes to get used to the darkness. He stared at the house. It looked deserted; there didn't appear to be any lights on.

He carefully climbed over the fence. The building looming up against the night sky was much clearer now. It was perhaps a hundred metres away. It was large, but not in any way inviting. The moonlight cast a bluish sheen over the roof tiles and the facade, and after a while he was able to make out the dark holes where the windows had been. He started to walk. He thought he could see the faint, flickering glow of candlelight; it was as if the blackness inside suddenly acquired an orange tone from time to time, and faint, almost imperceptible shadows flitted over the windowsills and walls. Now he knew he was in the right place.

He kept on walking.

The tall grass rustled with every step he took towards his fate.

If he was lucky he would be able to trade his life for hers.

If he was unlucky, both he and Vanja would reach the end of their lives tonight.

★ ★ ★

Vanja had managed to pull up the nightdress and arch her back enough to push her bound hands between her thighs and get hold of the spring. It was now hidden in her right hand again. She could saw at the nylon stocking only when Hinde was out of the room. And that didn't happen often enough. He had gone out for a while to light candles, but otherwise he was there all the time. He seemed to be waiting for someone. It was as if the ritual, which had been so vital at the beginning, was now of secondary importance. He spent most of the time pacing back and forth, listening.

Vanja had the feeling she was no longer the main character. That she was lying there for a different reason. But it didn't matter to her. She was aware of the sharpness of the spring against her palm as she waited for him to disappear again so that she could carry on. So far her efforts had produced no perceptible results. Her hands were bound just as tightly; they were also beginning to feel cold and numb because of the restricted flow of blood. What worried her most was that her muscles were growing more and more tired. The question was how long she would be able to carry on.

If only he would leave the room.

But he was still standing there. Completely motionless.

★ ★ ★

Sebastian peered in through the broken window next to the front door and found himself looking into what must once have been the kitchen. It was dirty, with graffiti all over the walls. Someone

504

had ripped out the sink unit. An old wood-burning stove from the beginning of the last century was standing in the corner, illuminated by the moonlight. Sebastian was aware of the faint glow of candlelight, probably from the room next door. He listened intently, but heard nothing. He walked up to the door, which was ajar. Broken glass littered the ground in front of it. He straightened his back.

Time to announce his presence.

The door creaked loudly as he opened it and stepped into the dark, narrow hallway.

'Edward, I'm here,' he shouted, then stopped to wait for a reaction. Nothing. The house remained just as silent as before.

Obviously Hinde wasn't ready to show himself yet.

Sebastian turned left and found himself in the kitchen he had seen from outside. Half the floor had collapsed, and he had to walk around the black hole in the middle of the room. There was a stale, mouldy smell, and he headed for the flickering light from the room next door. It was large and impressive, and had probably been the dining room once upon a time. A large black mark on the pale wooden floor showed where a rug had once been, and the wallpaper had begun to sag and peel with age. It looked as if the wall had acquired arms and was reaching out to him. A single lighted candle sitting in its own wax was fixed to an old, ornate metal radiator. There were two doorways. Immediately in front of him lay another large room, forming a kind of suite with the one in which he was standing. To the right a corridor led further into the house. He could see another flickering light in that direction. Perhaps he was meant to follow the candles.

That was what he decided to do, at any rate.

★ ★ ★

She heard the voice. At first she couldn't place it. Or rather, she couldn't make sense of that voice in this context.

She turned to glance at Hinde and realised that her ears had not deceived her. His face was glowing with anticipation. This was the voice Hinde had been waiting for. For a long, long time.

He picked up the knife and slipped out of the room. She watched him go, forgetting for a second the sharp spring in her hand.

What was Sebastian doing here? Why had he called out to Hinde?

This couldn't be true. Sebastian never did anything for anyone except himself. That was how he worked. She knew that.

And yet he was here.

★ ★ ★

Sebastian had finished exploring downstairs. It was empty apart from a few more candles and some old rubbish. He went back to the stairs, looked up into the darkness and listened. Called out again. 'Hello there!'

Still no reply.

He set off up the stairs. When he was halfway he could see the glow of another candle. He was starting to tire of this game now. He called out again, even louder this time. 'Edward, I know you're here.'

He kept going. Some of the treads were rotten, and he had to step over them. When he reached the top he could see that he was at the beginning of a corridor. There were doors on either side, and one right at the end. They were all closed.

He opened the first door. The windows had been boarded up, so it was pitch-dark. He pushed the door all the way back to let in the small amount of light from the corridor, and walked in. It seemed to be empty, apart from an old desk in one corner. Nothing else.

He was about to leave the room when he heard a faint noise behind him in the darkness. He spun around, but it was too late. He felt Hinde's breath on his face, and the knife pressing against his throat. He tried to relax, and allowed Hinde to push him up against the damp, smelly wall.

'I've been waiting for this,' Edward hissed.

He was so close that Sebastian could feel his excitement. He tried to remain calm. The knife was sharp. If Hinde pressed just a little harder, it would pierce his skin.

'I've been waiting for you, but now it's time to begin.'

Sebastian met Hinde's gaze. His eyes were shining, in spite of the fact that there was so little light in the room.

She was alive. Vanja was still alive.

'Let her go,' he tried to say with as much conviction as possible. 'This is between you and me.'

Hinde smiled at him. The look on his face said it all. A shake of the head merely confirmed Sebastian's worst fears.

'No. I want you to watch. After all, you enjoy studying me. I thought it would be nice for you to have a front-row seat.'

Sebastian fought to maintain his composure. 'Let her go. Take me instead.'

'Instead? Never. Both of you, perhaps.'

He suddenly turned Sebastian so that he was standing behind him instead, still holding the knife to his throat. He pushed Sebastian out into the corridor.

'I'm in control now,' he said.

In order to emphasise the point he forced the knife upwards, making it difficult for Sebastian to breathe. Bundled him along towards the end of the corridor. Closer and closer to the door. Sebastian realised that was where they were going. The room beyond that door was their goal.

Even though he knew it was utterly pointless, Sebastian couldn't help himself.

He begged.

He couldn't lose her.

'Please, take me instead. Please.'

'Very noble of you. But no doubt you have your reasons,' came the reply.

They had reached the door. Hinde pushed it open with his free hand.

'Here we are,' he called out teasingly.

It took a second before Sebastian and Hinde realised the significance of what they were seeing.

The bed was empty. Torn nylon stockings lay in the spot where Vanja had been. Hinde was so surprised he loosened his grip on Sebastian, who reacted with lightning speed; he pushed the knife away and managed to break free.

He turned to Hinde, who was still lost for words.

'Things not going according to plan?'

Disappointed and enraged, Hinde lashed out at him with the knife. Sebastian moved backwards towards the bed. Even though he knew he was in a very dangerous situation, he couldn't help feeling a surge of joy. It looked as if Vanja had escaped. That was the important thing. He had been willing to give up his life for her when he walked into the house, and that was still the case.

Hinde made another sweeping movement with the knife, and Sebastian backed away towards the corner of the room. Soon he would have nowhere else to go. He searched frantically for something he could use to protect himself, but there was nothing. The longer he could hold out, the more of a head start Vanja would have. He tried to step over the bed, but stumbled and fell onto it. Hinde was there in a second, and although Sebastian kicked out at him, Hinde managed to stick the knife in his calf. The pain was agonising. Sebastian grabbed hold of the bedhead with both hands and tried to haul himself away from Hinde. He could see his own blood pouring from the wound in his leg.

Hinde stopped and quietly contemplated Sebastian, who was pulling himself into the corner with his leg dragging behind. He was suddenly happy to take his time.

'Perhaps things haven't quite gone according to plan. But at least I've got you.' He began to move slowly towards Sebastian. The icy composure was back as he looked down at the bleeding man in the corner. He raised the knife.

Sebastian looked up at him. He had nowhere to go, and prepared himself for the inevitable.

He saw the blade of the knife flash through the air. Felt a terrible pain in his midriff. Hinde pulled out the knife and raised it again. He was aiming higher this time.

'One stab for every year I've spent in Lövhaga, I think. Only twelve to go.'

Sebastian was beginning to lose consciousness, but fought to stay awake. He managed to spit out a response.

'Vanja is safe,' he said with a final smile. Hinde looked furious as he raised the knife again.

That was when Sebastian suddenly saw her. She flew across the room with something in her hand.

She was supposed to have run away. She wasn't supposed to be here.

No.

Hinde became aware of the movement behind him at the last minute, and spun around. He saw the Taser in her hand and just managed to duck before she fired at him. He turned the knife around and delivered a heavy blow to her head with the handle. Vanja dropped the Taser and fell to the floor. Hinde threw himself at her. She fought back, but he struck her again. Then he stopped and looked down at her limp body. He smiled at Sebastian.

'That's what I call love. She came back.'

Sebastian began to crawl towards them with the final reserves of his strength. His shirt and trousers were covered in blood. He was dragging his leg through blood.

'Don't do it. Don't.'

Hinde's expression was one of pure satisfaction. 'You must forgive me, but I'm going to move straight to the finale.' He looked down at Vanja, grabbed hold of her hair and pulled back her head, exposing her throat. 'Watch carefully, Sebastian. This is the last thing you will ever see.'

Sebastian could no longer feel the pain. He felt nothing. He crawled and crawled, but it seemed as if he was moving only a millimetre at a time.

It would all be over at any second.

As Hinde raised the knife, a voice suddenly came from the doorway.

Sebastian thought it looked as if Billy was standing there.

Billy. What was he doing here?

He heard a shot and saw Hinde fall backwards.

Then everything went black.

Sebastian didn't remember anything about the ambulance, his arrival at the hospital, or the operation. Not a thing. The first thing he became aware of, after seeing Hinde fall backwards, was opening his eyes as he came round. His wounds were extremely painful, and some overenthusiastic doctor was telling him how incredibly lucky he had been, before going into detail about the injuries he had actually sustained, and how much more serious the consequences could have been. Sebastian stopped listening.

He was alive and he was going to recover; that was all he needed to know.

They carried out the usual checks. Then Vanja and Torkel came in. Asked how he was feeling. Filled in the gaps between the stabbing and now.

'Have you had to put up with a lot of crap?' Sebastian asked Torkel, who looked exhausted. He probably hadn't slept at all.

'Not yet. But the day has only just begun.'

'Sorry.'

'I'll survive.' Torkel shrugged. 'Vanja is fine, we've got Ralph Svensson and Roland Johansson, and Hinde is dead. You know how things work in the police service. The way you get there doesn't really matter. It's the result that counts.'

'So you got Roland?'

'Yes, in another stolen car on his way back to Gothenburg.' Torkel paused; he seemed to be wondering whether to go on. 'And you remember Trolle Hermansson?' he said in a more subdued tone of voice.

Sebastian adjusted his position in the bed. He hadn't expected Trolle's name to come up. Not now. When it was all over. When he was safe. And Torkel sounded so serious.

'Yes?'

'We found his body. In the Toyota.'

'Fuck.'

Torkel shook his head wearily. 'He must have been working on some kind of private surveillance or something. He had no idea what he was getting into.'

Sebastian nodded feebly. That was true enough. Trolle had had no idea what he was getting into when he decided to help Sebastian.

'Poor bastard.'

'Yes . . .'

There wasn't much else to say. The case was closed. It was all they had had in common this time. It would probably be quite a while before they saw each other again. Both Sebastian and Torkel knew that.

'I need to go back to the office to finish things off,' Torkel said, waving vaguely in the direction of the door. He turned to Vanja. 'Would you like a lift?'

'I'm going to stay here for a while.'

'Okay. Take care, Sebastian. See you soon.'

A stock phrase.

Which meant nothing.

Torkel left the room, closing the door behind him. Vanja went and fetched a chair; Sebastian watched her with curiosity as she sat down by his bed.

'I wanted to thank you.'

'There's no need.'

'I heard you. On the landing. You offered to take my place.'

'Yes.'

'Why?'

Sebastian shrugged. It was painful. He winced. 'Because I enjoy charging in like a knight in shining armour.'

Vanja smiled and stood up. She leaned over and gave him a big hug. 'Thank you,' she whispered.

Sebastian couldn't answer. Didn't want to. He wanted to freeze this moment forever. This was what he had been yearning for. For months. Longer than that, to be honest. How long was it since anyone had shown him genuine affection? Ellinor, yes, but she was . . . Ellinor. He hugged Vanja back. For slightly too long, but she didn't seem to mind.

She was smiling at him again as she sat down.

Sebastian exhaled as slowly as he could. The hug had been very painful, but it had been well worth it.

'So what are you going to do now?' Vanja asked.

'Have you seen that slightly older nurse who . . .'

She gave him a push. That hurt too. He wondered if there was anything he could do that didn't hurt.

'I meant as far as work goes.'

'I don't know.'

Vanja nodded and glanced down at her hands, then she looked up at him, her eyes full of sincerity. 'I wouldn't mind working with you again.'

'Really?'

'Yes.'

'That means a lot to me.'

He held her gaze, hoping she could see that he really meant it.

Vanja's telephone rang. The moment, if there had been one, was gone. She fished her phone out of her pocket and looked at the display. 'I need to take this.'

She turned away from the bed for a moment as she answered. 'Hi, Dad . . . No, I'm at the hospital. Visiting Sebastian . . . Yes, that Sebastian.'

She flashed him a brief smile. He smiled back. At least, he hoped that was what he was doing. There were so many emotions.

Joy, sorrow, pride, pain.

'Yes, I was there,' Vanja went on. 'It's a long story. Can I call you later? . . . Okay. Love you too.'

She ended the call and put her phone away. 'That was Dad. He's seen the news about Hinde on the net.'

'He doesn't know what's happened?'

'No, and I'm not sure how much to tell him. He worries about me. I want to protect him. And Anna.'

It must run in the family, Sebastian thought. The desire to protect one's nearest and dearest from unpleasant truths. Like him.

'I'll let you get some rest,' Vanja said, getting to her feet. She picked up the chair and carried it back to its original spot.

'He's lucky to have you. Your dad,' Sebastian said to her back.

'I'm lucky to have him. He's the best.'

'I'm sure he is.'

512

Vanja headed for the door. She stopped, her hand resting on the handle. As if she was slightly reluctant to go. 'Okay, I'm off. Take care of yourself.'

'You too.'

He watched her go. Not in anger. Not after a heated exchange of words. Not after a fight. He made a decision. Whatever Trolle might have dug up about Valdemar, he was never going to use it. He wasn't even going to look at the papers to find out what Valdemar had done. As soon as he got home, he would burn the contents of the carrier bag. Valdemar's secret would die with Trolle.

He turned over. It hurt. Of course. He gazed out of the window. It was just after five o'clock. The sun had been up for about half an hour, and there was no heat in it yet. But it was going to be a beautiful day.

She had asked him what he was going to do.

He knew what he wasn't going to do.

He wasn't going to be her father. Ever. He was going to stop trying. If he played his cards right, he might get to be close to her. Be accepted. Not loved, but perhaps liked.

That was good enough.

He didn't have many things in his life that were good, so it would be stupid to throw this one away.

It would be all right.

He could feel it.

Everything would be all right.

Billy got to work early; he was the first one there. Maya had spent the night at her own place, so there was no real reason for him to stay in bed. He hadn't slept properly anyway.

He had shot a man.

Dead.

He had had no choice, nobody needed to tell him that, even though both Vanja and Torkel had said it immediately afterwards. Billy was absolutely certain that Hinde would have killed Vanja if he hadn't shot him. Had it been necessary to kill him? Impossible to say. Even an injured Hinde would have needed no more than a second to inflict serious injuries on Vanja. Fatal injuries. Billy just couldn't take the risk.

He and Vanja had talked briefly while she was waiting for the ambulance. The first one had taken Sebastian.

They had sorted things out.

A kidnapping and a fatal shooting had turned out to be very effective when it came to resolving conflict.

Suddenly everything else seemed fairly petty.

Unimportant, easily sorted.

He sat down at the computer and started up Ralph's damaged hard drive. Not that there was any real necessity. They had everything they needed on Ralph Svensson: fingerprints, DNA, traces of blood from the victims, the nylon stockings and the collection of press cuttings, not to mention a confession. Nobody would be looking for anything Billy might retrieve from Ralph's computer in order to secure a conviction.

He wasn't doing this for the case.

He was doing it for himself.

Just as it had been when he was worried about Vanja, work was the best way of suppressing those unwelcome thoughts. Thoughts

514

about the shooting. About the fact that he had taken a life. Besides, this was what he was good at. This was what he enjoyed doing. This was where the challenge lay. Where he got results. Maya could say whatever she liked, but it was these skills that had led them to Hinde. Saved Vanja.

Billy had reached the part of the conversation where Hinde told Ralph it was time to move from fantasy to execution. Hinde gave Ralph the names of his victims. One by one. Maria Lie. Jeanette Jansson Nyberg. Katharina Granlund. Gave him their names and addresses.

Meanwhile Ralph reported back on Sebastian's fresh conquests, including Annette Willén. On that occasion the reply from Hinde was almost immediate. She must die that same day. So that the link to Sebastian would become crystal clear. It was a strange feeling, reading the brief, precise lines and knowing that they had led to the deaths of four women.

He carried on reading.

There was a name he recognised.

Anna Eriksson.

Wasn't that . . . ?

In Västerås, Sebastian had asked Billy to help him find an address. For someone called Anna Eriksson. Same name. Admittedly it was fairly common, but it still seemed like a bit of a coincidence. Billy had found the address for Sebastian; now where was it?

He minimised the window from Ralph's hard drive and selected the 'Västerås' folder from the desktop. Opened it and selected the file that contained all the loose ends that he hadn't been able to link to anything in particular. Including that address.

Storskärsgatan 12.

He looked it up on Eniro. Discovered that Anna Eriksson lived there with Valdemar Lithner.

Lithner.

Hang on.

Vanja's mother was called Anna.

Was Sebastian's Anna Eriksson Vanja's mother?

All the pieces of the puzzle were laid out in front of him, but he couldn't see the whole picture. He approached the problem methodically. Started from the beginning.

Sebastian had been looking for someone called Anna Eriksson.

It turned out that she lived on Storskärsgatan.

Anna Eriksson was Vanja's mother.

Ralph reported Anna Eriksson at Storskärsgatan 12 as a possible victim.

Did that mean Sebastian had slept with her? It had to, surely. At some point, anyway.

Sebastian and Vanja's mother.

Was that why Vanja disliked Sebastian so much?

Billy leaned back, convinced there was more to all this. Why had Sebastian been searching for Anna when he was in Västerås? If he knew she was Vanja's mother, then surely he could simply have asked Vanja about her? But he didn't. What did that mean? He didn't know, or he didn't want to ask Vanja?

Instinctively Billy felt he ought to stop there. Perhaps he should even delete the information he had just discovered relating to Anna Eriksson. Nobody was going to need it, after all. He thought it over for a while. In the end his curiosity got the better of him. He copied the relevant pages onto his computer and deleted them from Ralph's hard drive.

Everything was on the internet – that was what people said. Billy knew it was true. And once the internal investigation started, he would have all the time in the world. Because he would be investigated. Not only had he drawn his gun and fired a shot, it had been a fatal shooting. His conduct would be examined, and he would be cleared of any wrongdoing. And while he was waiting, he would have his little project.

Ellinor woke just before six. Sebastian wasn't home. It looked as if he'd been out all night. His side of the bed was untouched. Ellinor stayed where she was. She didn't really need to get up; she had taken the whole week off work, and no one was waiting for her.

But she was waiting for someone.

She reached over to the bedside table and picked up her phone. Called Sebastian's mobile. He didn't answer. He hadn't answered yesterday evening either. The last time she tried it had been after one o'clock in the morning. Where was he? What was he doing? There was no way she would be able to go back to sleep, so she got up, pulled on one of his shirts and went into the kitchen. Filled the kettle and switched it on. Made herself two substantial sandwiches of cottage cheese and tomato while she waited for it to boil. Made herself a cup of tea and fetched the paper from the hallway before settling down with her breakfast. She glanced out of the window and found herself staring at the guttering on the building opposite. She hadn't known Sebastian very long, but he didn't seem to be the kind of man who worked all night. So where was he? Why hadn't he called, or picked up when she called him?

Was he with another woman?

He had spoken about someone called Hinde on the phone before he disappeared yesterday evening. Or spoken to someone called Hinde. Was it a surname? Was it a woman?

Perhaps it was someone who was in need of a friendly, explanatory chat about who belonged to whom, and how wrong it was to try to steal a person who belonged to someone else. Her ex-husband had been unfaithful. Left her.

He was dead now.

But when she thought back to the last couple of days, that didn't really add up. Sebastian had been very persistent; he had made a real effort to get her to be with him. Surely he wouldn't deceive her as soon as she had moved in, as soon as he had got what he wanted? So far he had been nothing but loving.

The perfect man.

She had judged him too quickly. She was slightly ashamed of herself. She would make it up to him when he got home. There could be other reasons for his sudden departure and overnight absence. There had to be other reasons. She thought back over the events of the previous evening as her untouched cup of tea grew cold. He had seemed stressed when he left, that was for sure. Perhaps there were problems, either at work or in his private life. Obviously she wished he would talk to her if there was something bothering him, but some men insisted on being stoical and coping on their own. They found it terribly difficult to ask for help. But he didn't need to ask Ellinor. She would help anyway, if only she knew how.

She began systematically going through everything they had done together yesterday. Was there a moment when he had acted differently? Tried to hide something?

She remembered the supermarket carrier bag she had found. She thought it contained important papers, but when she asked him about it he had gone quiet. In fact he had remained quiet for a while. He had seemed very pensive, and had looked a little bit sad. As if the contents of the bag were a burden to him, as if he was wondering whether to share it with her. Perhaps he had been asking himself whether he had any right to drag her into his problems, but had then decided against the idea. He had asked her to throw the bag away. In a casual tone of voice. As if it meant nothing to him. Nothing at all. Putting up a facade. Which she could now see right through. He wanted to protect her. They would have to talk about that when he got back. She didn't need protecting. She was far more capable than he thought. But she loved the fact that he had tried.

With a little smile on her lips she went into their bedroom and fetched the bag. She pushed her untouched breakfast to one side and started to empty the contents of the carrier bag onto the table.

Forty-five minutes later she had read every word.

Twice.

It was all to do with someone called Valdemar Lithner. He had done a number of foolish things. Illegal things, as far as she could make out. This made sense; Sebastian sometimes worked with the police. Was Lithner someone they were going to pick up? Someone they had been investigating, and now they had passed all the information on to Sebastian so that he could work on a psychological evaluation of the suspect? A 'profile'? Could well be.

But in that case, why had he asked her to throw away the contents of the bag?

Perhaps it just wouldn't stand up in court. Maybe it wasn't enough to take Valdemar Lithner into custody or arrest him or whatever it was they did.

But if that was the explanation, why had Sebastian seemed stressed about it all? Why hadn't he just told her the truth? Explained what it was and why there was no point in keeping it any longer?

No, it didn't make sense. Admittedly Ellinor had no legal training, but she was pretty sure that the papers she had in front of her would be enough to put Valdemar behind bars for quite some time.

So it must be something else.

Did this Lithner know that he was in trouble? Had he threatened Sebastian and the other police officers, forcing them to drop the case? She thought she had heard him say 'Hinde' on the phone yesterday, but it could just as easily have been 'Lithner'. The names sounded similar, and she hadn't been listening all that carefully. What if something had happened to Sebastian? Was that why he hadn't come home? She pulled herself up short. Ellinor Bergkvist wasn't a woman who allowed her imagination to run away with her. Among the documentation was a piece of paper with a name and a mobile number; presumably this was the man who had put it all together. She picked up her phone. It wouldn't do any harm to find out a bit more. Knowing the facts would reassure her.

A man answered almost immediately. 'Yes?'

'Good morning,' Ellinor said. 'I'd like to speak to Trolle Hermansson.'

'Who's calling?' the man wanted to know.

'My name is Ellinor. I work at the Åhléns department store. The items Trolle ordered have arrived.'

She couldn't help smiling. This was exciting! Sebastian would be proud of her. She was almost like a real police officer.

There was silence at the other end of the line.

'Hello? Who am I speaking to?' Ellinor asked.

'This is the police.'

'Is Trolle there?'

Silence. She had a feeling the man was hesitating. Trying to make a decision.

'He's dead.'

She hadn't expected that.

'I see . . . When did he die?'

'A few days ago. So I don't think anyone will be collecting whatever it was he ordered.'

'No, of course not. Thank you. My condolences,' she said, ending the call. She didn't feel in the least bit calmer. Quite the reverse. The man who had put together most of the material in front of her was dead. And Sebastian had told her to destroy it. It seemed that Valdemar Lithner would never be called to answer for his transgressions. Unless of course she helped Sebastian out.

If Valdemar Lithner was threatening her man, she had to act.

That was the least she could do.

Acknowledgements

Thanks to Norstedts. To Eva, Linda, Sara and everyone else who works with us and our books in various ways. We always feel so welcome and well taken care of. Particular thanks to Susanna Romanus and Peter Karlsson for your great support and constant encouragement.

Thank you also to Dr Anders Lindberg who happily listens to all our peculiar questions and not only answers them, but also comes up with suggestions and ideas. Everything that is medically accurate in the book is down to you; everything that isn't is our fault.

We would also like to extend special thanks to Rolf Lassgård for all the help and inspiration he has given us in the creation of Sebastian Bergman. You have been with us all the way, Rolf, and in every way.

And of course we must thank our families, who have had to put up with the fact that sometimes we have spent more time with Sebastian than with them.

Michael would like to thank Caesar, William, Vanessa and his beloved Astrid for all the love and for the words here and now. Thank you — you mean everything to me.

Hans would like to thank Lotta; I'm so lucky to have you. Sixten, Alice and Ebba, you make me proud and happy every single day. You're the best in every way, and I love you!